DAMON RUNYON (1884-1946) was born in Manhattan. . . Kansas; he was raised in Colorado. His father was a reporter who covered the Indian wars. Runyon himself was already writing for newspapers at the age of fourteen when he enlisted in the Spanish-American War, working afterwards as a professional journalist and achieving high recognition in this field. He became one of the best known sports writers of his time; his peers included such luminaries as Paul Gallico and Grantland Rice. Even today his name adorns a Manhattan (New York) watering hole, which is a hangout for many of today's sports reporters.

"Then suddenly," remembered his friend Walter Winchell, "like an old Dempsey left hook, he startled his best critics and severest friends with *magazine* stories. The sort that were not only read and enjoyed, but the sort that tilted circulations. From these delightfully comical stories about Broadway, the prize ring and the banditti—embroidered in a language rich with style—came a book called *Guys and Dolls*."

In all, Runyon produced only fifty or so short stories. However, twenty-six were filmed, some more than once. The classic Broadway musical *Guys and Dolls* was based on two of his short stories.

Yet Runyon was always first and foremost a newspaperman, and the re-publication of TRIALS AND OTHER TRIBULATIONS makes available again some of the best reportage by this multi-talented writer, whom the *New York Sun* called simply "a creative genius."

DAMON RUNYON

TRIALS AND TRIBULATIONS

INTERNATIONAL POLYGONICS, LTD.
NEW YORK CITY

TRIALS AND TRIBULATIONS

Library of Congress Card Catalog No. 91- 73844
ISBN 1-55882-106-6

Printed and manufactured in the United States of America.
First IPL printing September 1991
10 9 8 7 6 5 4 3 2 1

EDITORIAL NOTE

The compilation of this book, the last one to be planned by Mr. Runyon, had not been completed when he died. Consequently, introductory and transitional matter was not prepared by him personally. Otherwise, the book is wholly Runyon.

It seemed to us that any reader knowing Runyon only as a writer of fiction, knows only half of the man, and by no means the better half. For Runyon was first of all a great reporter; he continued to regard himself primarily as a reporter long after he had become known to most of the world as an author of short stories. He expressed more pride in his work as a reporter than in the accolades he won with his fiction. Contrary to what usually happens when a daily journalist achieves fame in some other field of endeavor, Runyon chose to remain a newspaperman, accepting assignments as they came—any kind, anywhere. In the course of his career he covered, and covered superbly, every type of news story: he went with fighting men to two war fronts to share their dangerous lives in the trenches; he painted brilliant word pictures of racing, prize fighting, polo, baseball, tennis; he wrote realistically of political conventions and reverently of a Eucharistic Congress; he did imperishable stories about the inauguration of President Roosevelt and his funeral; he recorded the saga of Lindbergh, the Lone Eagle; he made investigations of high finance understandable to average readers; he was a penetrating eye for the public at scores of notable trials.

It seemed to us that Runyon, the Master Reporter, was at his best in court rooms. It was an opinion with which he did not wholeheartedly agree, but he liked the idea of collecting some—though necessarily not all could be complete—of his better stories of trials and other tribulations in a book.

The dates appended to the stories are the dates of publication, usually the morning after the events recounted. The footnotes appearing in some pages are those of the editor of the book.

CONTENTS

The Hall-Mills Case   11

"Daddy" and "Peaches"   97

The Eternal Blonde   139

Arnold Rothstein's Final Payoff   206

Al Capone   226

Morgan the Mighty   252

Postscript   282

Trials and Other Tribulations

◆●◆●◆●◆●◆●◆●◆

THE HALL-MILLS CASE

Somerville, New Jersey, November 3, 1926

In this pleasant looking little town of Somerville, in the heart of old New Jersey, and in a pleasant looking little court house, all white and trim, the trial of the century starts this morning at ten o'clock.

It is legally titled The People *vs* Mrs. Frances Stevens Hall, William Stevens and Henry Stevens, sister and brothers, and the charge, as the reading population of the United States pretty generally knows, is the murder of Mrs. Hall's husband, the Reverend Edward Wheeler Hall, and Mrs. Eleanor Mills.

Four years ago the Stevens clan, and another member thereof, Henry de la Bruyere Carpender, a cousin, who is to be tried later and separately, are said to have shot to death the rector and her whom the gentlemen of the press call his love-mate, Mrs. Mills, on an old farm near New Brunswick, N. J.

The machinery of the law, functioning slowly and ponderously, as always, has just arrived at the production, in concrete form, of the evidence by which it expects to convince a Jersey jury of the truth of the allegations against the Stevenses.

Hundreds of thousands of words have been printed about the case since that day in September, 1922, when the bodies of the rector of the Episcopal Church of St. John the Evangelist, in New Brunswick, and the leader of his choir, Mrs. Mills, were found side by side under a crabapple tree, with bullet holes in them.

Love letters that had passed between them were scattered over the cold corpses. Hundreds of thousands of additional words will be printed in the next few days as the witnesses pass through the legal mill that will be grinding in the pleasant looking little court house.

The Hall-Mills murder case is now an old, old story to newspaper readers. It has probably been argued and debated at every breakfast table during the past few years. It can be recited to its smallest details by almost every resident of this part of New Jersey, the State that once made "Jersey justice" a byword.

But they are all eagerly awaiting the rehash of the tale that will begin tomorrow, expecting that it will produce some new and hitherto unpublished chapter that will answer definitely the questions that have been asked over and over and over again—Who killed 'em? Why?

The legal representatives of the people of the State of New Jersey think they have the answers in the proud woman and her brothers who will face the curious crowd tomorrow, and in the romance between the dead minister and the dead choir singer.

But they have it to prove to the satisfaction of the jury and a large number of citizens of New Jersey, for the Stevenses have their friends. The dead tell no tales.

It is on the stories of the living that the State relies—among them the testimony of the former circus rider, Mrs. Jane Gibson, called "the pig woman," who claims she saw the sinister little group beneath the crabapple tree the night of the murder while riding her mule in search of corn thieves.

She is one of the weirdest characters in all the weird cast that will assemble tomorrow to begin the mystery play. It includes the aristocracy of New Jersey and the skulkers of the back alleys of small town life. It is such a cast as David Belasco might revel in.

In the meantime, the thing has taken on some of the aspects of a big sports event. In fact, the telegraph switchboard used for the Dempsey-Tunney fight has been installed in the court house and forty-seven telegraph instruments have been hooked up. An enterprising radio outfit will unofficially broadcast the proceedings, play by play, so to speak. The little town of Somerville, which is the county seat of Somerset County, is all set to take care of a big crowd of visitors, and the indications are that the crowd will be here.

They would be better off if they remained at home, so far as any chance they have of morbid entertainment is concerned. The court house has a seating capacity of slightly over three hundred, and of this number one hundred will be representatives of the press and one hundred and eighteen will be witnesses. This will leave room for only about fifty-three casual spectators.

If speculators could have gotten hold of these extra seats, they would have cleaned up. They could command any price.

November 4, 1926

Whatever else may be said of it, "Jersey justice" moves like greased lightning once it gets started.

Within an hour from the time old John Bunn, court crier, lifted his sonorous voice in a thundering "Hear ye, hear ye," yesterday morning, they had a jury in the Hall-Mills murder case, and the trial of the century was on.

Twelve serious looking citizens, said to be good men and true, mainly beyond middle age, sat in the cramped space allotted to the jury and had been told what they were there for.

State Senator Alexander Simpson told them. He is chief of the prosecution, a small jockey-sized, fox terrier-like, little man with a wheedling voice with his fellow man. You can call it personality.

He dresses like a small town sport, fancy colored shirt, black leather spats and a dark suit with a pin stripe. His hair is gray and curly and oiled.

He stepped up to the jury and in quiet, almost confidential manner, as if telling them something on the strict Q.T., and using little, short words, he explained how Mrs. Frances Noel Stevens Hall and her two brothers, Henry Stevens and William Stevens, were there charged with the murder of Mrs. Eleanor Mills four years back.

The reader must understand that while Mrs. Mills and the Reverend Edward Wheeler Hall were murdered together the State of New Jersey has elected to try the defendants for the killing of Mrs. Mills first, just as it has elected to try Henry de la

Bruyere Carpender separately from the three now being tried.

Senator Simpson told his story briefly and well. He never raised his voice, yet he introduced several subtle touches of the dramatic when he explained to the jury the identity of the defendants. He said:

"You will have some difficulty in identifying them because they are all sitting together. This man who sits at the end is not a defendant. The man who sits next to him is a defendant, he is Henry Stevens. The man with the brown suit is not a defendant, I don't know who he is. The man sitting next to him is William Stevens, who is indicted, and the woman sitting next to him, behind Mr. McCarter, is Frances Hall."

The small attorney had a strangely detached and impersonal air as he indicated the different defendants who sat grouped together on the side of the room, which looks more like a small church chapel than what the popular imagination pictures a hall of justice.

It is on the second floor of the Somerset County Court House, a square-cut, white building of modern date, set in the center of a large grassy plot of ground in the heart of the little city of Somerville.

The court house seems to be a sort of hub of the city. The main street is on one side. The Cort Theatre is across the street from the court house, advertising Gene Tunney in *The Fighting Marine*. Big old trees stand around the court house, their limbs now bare. The leaves that draped the branches a few weeks ago are little brown eddies whirling over the court house lawn in a cool autumn breeze. A number of the town dogs were chasing one another through the gusts this morning as a crowd of townspeople began gathering in front of the court house.

Presently a ring of automobiles, mainly of the cheaper makes, surrounded the court house plot, standing nose to tail, so close together were they parked. You can duplicate the scene any court day in any county seat.

The sun was shining brightly, it poured through the windows of the chapel-like court room, which has a circular skylight overhead of stained glass.

High up in the court room on three sides are little galleries. One gallery, so narrow that there was room for only one row of people, was occupied by newspaper writers and photographers. The other two little galleries were filled with spectators, men and women, and some children.

An American flag hangs behind the judges' bench, covering another stained glass window. The judges are Frank L. Cleary, a youngish man with flattened-down black hair, and Charles W. Parker, who has no hair at all. Judge Parker is a gray man who wears glasses and takes many notes and decides all questions of law. They call this the Court of Oyer and Terminer, which corresponds to the Court of General Sessions of New York and to the district courts of the West. The judges sit side by side on a raised dais in big swivel chairs and both wear flowing robes of black silk.

During the morning session Mrs. Hall sat with her brother, "Willie," on her left and her faithful friend and relative, Mrs. Edwin Carpender, on her right. Mrs. Carpender lives across the street from Mrs. Hall in New Brunswick, and through all the widow's trouble has constantly attended her. Mrs. Carpender is a bright, chatty looking woman with a pleasant smile which shows many teeth. She smiled often and frequently whispered to Mrs. Hall.

Mrs. Carpender wore a black coat trimmed with gray squirrel and kept her gloves on all morning, like a casual visitor.

My mental picture of Mrs. Hall based on what I had read of her, was as a proud, cold, emotionless woman, of immense hauteur, and hard exterior. With that sort of picture in mind, I was scarcely prepared for the entrance of the real Mrs. Hall.

There was nothing dramatic in her appearance. She slipped in through a rear door with her brothers, a solid looking woman in a black hat and black cloth coat with a collar of gray squirrel. Under it she wore a black silk dress with a low collar edged with white. Her shoes were black. In her hat she had a bright silver ornament. She suggested what she is—a wealthy widow.

She carried a large flat black pocketbook and wore gray silk gloves. Her garb was probably expensive. It displayed what I would say is excellent taste. She has a motherly appearance, no less. She is one of the last persons in the world you would pick out as a potential criminal of any kind.

Her face is large, her expression set, almost graven in its seriousness. Her complexion is white to pastiness. Her skin is fairly smooth but there are folds under her chin. Her hair, such as showed around her temples, is sprinkled with gray. She looks more than the fifty-one years she admits. Willie is around fifty-two, Henry is fifty-eight.

Mrs. Hall looks older than the others. Her experiences have told heavily on her. She greatly dreads notoriety and here she is getting it by the newspaper page.

She sat very quietly, but greeted acquaintances with a smile that showed her teeth, but did not light up her blue eyes. She was all attention at all times, turning her eyes on every speaker and occasionally whispering to Willie or Mrs. Edwin Carpender or the bulldog looking Robert H. McCarter, chief of her defense, an oldish, ruddy man with a firm mouth.

Willie was quite the life of the party during the morning session. He shook hands with everyone around him, made frequent trips to the ante-room and was rarely still, but Mrs. Hall and Henry Stevens sat immobile. When the afternoon session opened the three moved closer to their counsel's table and Henry sat with his legs crossed, showing a pair of white sox.

Willie seemed more interested in the proceedings than did his sister or brother or anyone else in the court room for that matter.

They say Willie is not quite all there mentally. He loves to hang out in fire houses, and the clang of the engine bells is music to his ears. Still Henry L. Mencken was recently photographed in a fireman's helmet at New Orleans.

Willie is a heavy-set man with thick, bushy hair, which stands up on his head straight and stiff like quills upon a fretful porcupine that Mr. Shakespeare wrote about. It gives Willie a startled appearance, which is increased by a pair of thick, black, arched eyebrows and wide open, staring eyes.

He wears spectacles with heavy lenses. A heavy dark moustache, shaped like bicycle bars, sags over his mouth. He has no great amount of chin. He has a thick neck, heavily ridged in back. Take him all in all, Willie has rather a genial appearance. He somehow made me think of a successful delicatessen dealer.

He wore a wing collar with a four-in-hand tie, and a dark blue suit today. A gold watch chain was swung across his vest. He was as alert as a startled fox terrier as he sat listening to the proceedings, and frequently whispering to Edwin Carpender, a well-groomed, freshly shaven, Wall Street looking man. Willie constantly twiddled a pencil between his fingers, or tapped it against his knuckles.

Henry Stevens, who is said to be the man the State expects to prove fired the shots, leaned back in his chair, his face unchanging in expression. He has thick, flat iron-gray hair, and wears a moustache and spectacles. His complexion is ruddy. He looks like a doctor. He wore a dark suit and white linen today with rather a fancy four-in-hand tie. Willie frequently beamed and grinned, but Henry Stevens' face maintained a stern, implacable expression.

November 5, 1926

Always the spindle on the State's wheel of circumstantial evidence in the Hall-Mills murder case, whirling round and round the circle of the Stevens clan, stops dead at the pop-eyed Willie Stevens.

They splintered his alibi Wednesday. Yesterday fingerprint experts, including Joseph Faurot, of New York, with an outfit like a magician's kit of tricks spread before the jury, testified that Willie's fingerprint was on Dr. Hall's card that was stuck up in a tuft of grass at his feet when he was found murdered with his sweetheart, Mrs. Eleanor Mills.

The spectators in the little court room were still buzzing like a far-off swarm of bees over Faurot's testimony when Senator Alexander Simpson, chief of the prosecution, arose and informed the Court that the State's chief witness, Mrs. Jane Easton, as he called her, or Gibson, as she is better known—"The Pig Woman" —is dying in a Somerville hospital.

He asked that the Court, counsel and jury go to the hospital in a body and take her testimony.

The defense objected strongly, whereat Simpson said sarcastically:

"If she is seriously ill, no wonder the defense doesn't want to go down there."

His inference seemed to be that the defense would not be sorry if "the pig woman" passed permanently from the case, though her story, told before the Grand Jury, remains a matter of record.

Senator McCarter, head of the so-called million-dollar defense, arose looking grave and attacked "the pig woman's" character. He said:

"This woman is an absolutely unreliable witness, in our opinion. She has given, to our knowledge, at least six versions, all contradictory of what she says she saw.

"Naturally, we will subject her to a very rigorous and painstaking examination, and we most strenuously object to having the Court and jury and the defendants—and I question the Court's right to so order the latter's removal from incarceration—go to the hospital to see this woman."

It wound up with Justice Parker and Judge Cleary taking the matter into their own hands. They went to the hospital to determine the condition of "the pig woman" for themselves.

Simpson had expected to have Mrs. Gibson on the witness stand yesterday afternoon.

She was in court yesterday, but collapsed when she encountered her aged mother, Salome Cerrenner, brought here to testify for the defense.

Three doctors testified Mrs. Gibson had a fever of 104⅖, that she was verging on pneumonia and moreover was suffering from cancer.

It is "the pig woman" who insists she saw the little group gathered under the fatal crabapple tree the night of the murder and recognized Mrs. Hall and all the others.

After their visit to the hospital, and a discussion with the doctors, Justice Parker announced that Mrs. Gibson was too ill to be questioned or removed, that she was apparently resisting her illness, and that the Court would decide today whether the jury would be taken to her.

Joseph Faurot was still on the stand when Senator Simpson informed the Court of "the pig woman's" possibly fatal illness. He put in the better part of an hour delivering a sort of lecture to the jury on the subject of fingerprints in general, and Willie Stevens' fingerprints in particular.

One of the most interested listeners was this same Willie Stevens. He sat over on the other side of the room with Mrs. Hall and Henry Stevens, and his eyes seemed to be bulging right up against the thick lenses of his spectacles as he listened to Faurot tell the jury that there was no doubt the fingerprints on the mortuary marker at Hall's feet were Willie's.

However, Willie at times seemed amused.

He would whisper to those around him and grin.

His sister, Mrs. Hall, usually most grave, smiled often. Henry Stevens never changed expression, as the slow-moving, sedate Faurot, bald and moustached, told the tale of fingerprints.

No man ever entered a court room more completely equipped than Faurot. He had a load of photographs, and a big wooden box.

Simpson showed him Dr. Hall's card, which was sheathed in a glass case, and Faurot said he had examined the fingerprints found on this card, and compared them with the fingerprints of Willie Stevens. In his opinion the marks were made by one and the same digit, which was Willie's left index finger.

He explained all about the different styles in fingerprints among the human race, saying there are four, the arch, the whorl, the loop, the composite. Willie's type is the arch, he said and only about five per cent of the human race have it.

It was the State's round again today, all things considered. The fingerprint testimony seemed disturbing to the party gathered around the table on the defense's side of the room. There was much whispered consultation, and both Case and McCarter fought hard to keep out the fingerprints for the time being.

Ralph Gorsline and Miss Catharine L. Rastall, the couple that were in a parked car in De Russey's Lane on the night of the murders, were both on the stand today, but in the light of the fingerprint developments, and the announcement about "the pig woman's" condition, they do not rate high among the sensations of the day.

As a matter of fact they were not sensational at all.

Gorsline, married, a vestryman of Dr. Hall's church, had met Miss Rastall in the street in New Brunswick the night of the murder and invited her into his automobile, saying he would drive her home.

Instead of going immediately to her home, he drove to De Russey's Lane. He said he got there about 10:15, turned into a little lane off De Russey's and extinguished his lights.

Within a few minutes he heard a mumbling of human voices not far away.

Then came one shot, a woman's scream, then three shots in rapid succession.

Next he heard a moaning. He said he backed out of the lane in short order, and drove away, taking Miss Rastall home. The girl told about the same story.

Gorsline is a long, lean, lank man with a narrow face, and a narrow head, and a wide mouth with loose lips. Simpson mentioned him as a hostile witness in a comment to the Court.

Gorsline turned a pair of listless eyes on Simpson when the prosecutor asked him if he had not visited the Burns Detective Agency on October 1, 1922, and told a detective named William Garvin that his conscience troubled him and that he wished to tell the truth about that night in De Russey's Lane.

Simpson asked, "Didn't you tell Garvin that you saw Henry Stevens in the lane with a gun in his hand, and didn't you say he said to you, 'What the hell are you doing here? This is our affair —get out of here,' and fired three shots in the ground? And didn't you say you were taken to a lodge room and made to swear you wouldn't tell what you saw?"

Gorsline replied: "Absolutely not."

"Jimmy" Mills, husband of the murdered Mrs. Eleanor Mills, and a veritable little mouse of a man, who might have been the cartoonist Opper's original for the harassed Mr. Dubb of his cartoons, was the chief witness for the State today.

A shoemaker by trade, a church sexton and school janitor by occupation, he is middle-aged and has a peaked face, and sad eyes, and stooped shoulders. His voice is low—an apologetic voice. His manner is self-effacing.

He is such a man as you might imagine to be a hen-pecked husband at home, a man bullied by his children and by all the world, a man anybody could push out of their way without protest from him, a harmless, dull little fellow.

Yet, against this pathetic figure, shrinking on the witness stand, the bulldoggish old Robert H. McCarter was roaring questions before the day was over that showed that it is in the minds of the lawyers for the Stevens clan to prove this: That Jimmy Mills might have been the murderer of his wife and her sweetheart, the Reverend Edward Wheeler Hall.

Looking at the little man the idea seems almost preposterous, but for several hours the gruff old McCarter savaged him with harsh interrogation, obviously directed along the line of that theory.

He brought out the sinister suggestion that Jimmy Mills retained from his shoemaker's kit of years ago a shoemaker's knife.

He tried to make Jimmy admit that the night before the murder of the woman to whom he was married for seventeen years, Mills had found in her scarf some letters in her handwriting, unsigned and unaddressed, but presumably intended for the dead Dominie Hall and calling him "honey" and "dear" and that these were the letters found between the bodies of the murdered pair.

But Jimmy patiently said no.

He did not seem particularly flustered or nervous as he sat on the stand, just patient, long-suffering. Once when State Senator Alexander Simpson thrust before him a picture of his wife showing her as she was about a year before her murder, his eyes seemed to moisten.

McCarter made much of the fact that others have so often commented on: Jimmy Mills' failure to make any considerable inquiry for his wife from the night she disappeared until her body was found beside Dr. Hall's, which was the night she walked away from the house, replying to his mild query as to her destination:

"Follow me and find out."

The defense obviously would infer that Jimmy Mills did follow and did find out.

Just before the day's session adjourned, the State made a rather startling attack on Henry Stevens' alibi. He claims he was in Lavalette at the time of the murder, on a fishing trip.

Mrs. Mary Demarest, a large woman, with eyes that snap behind her glasses, took the stand and testified that she saw Henry Stevens in New Brunswick, on Friday, September 15, the day after the murder, and before the bodies were discovered.

Moreover, Mrs. Demarest, who is a cousin of Mrs. Minnie Clark, a member of Dr. Hall's choir, said that on two occasions she saw Dr. Hall and Mrs. Mills sitting on benches in a New Brunswick park with Mrs. Clark and Ralph V. Gorsline, the lean, lank vestryman, who testified the day before, obviously spying on them.

Mrs. Hall never turned her eyes on this particular witness, though she has watched most of the others. She sat today between Willie and Henry, the trio drawn closer today than usual behind their high-priced counsel.

Mrs. Hall has changed her attire but little since the first day of the trial, sticking to widow's black. She wore the same black hat and black coat with gray squirrel collar that she wore on the opening day, but had on a different black dress. A string of pearls almost hidden under the collar of her dress gave a small touch of white to her sombre garb.

She seems to be bearing up well. Her face remains absolutely colorless—pasty white. It would be difficult to read this woman's thoughts under any circumstances.

Henry sat grim, unchanging, at her left. He seemed to pay no attention whatever to Mrs. Demarest's identification of him. Willie, who is generally bolt upright, like a startled cockatoo, was apparently genuinely pleased when Mrs. Demarest said she knew him well, and thought at first that Henry was he.

Warden James Major, of the Somerville jail, a bald, heavy, bespectacled man, and Captain J. J. Lamb, of the New Jersey State Police, big. and sandy looking, testified as to the disposition of some fifteen packages of articles picked up on the scene of the murder. These relics of the four-year-old crime included a couple of handkerchiefs, and Simpson asked that they be marked for identification. Case protested, and the defense seemed somewhat uneasy over the proceeding.

Then came Mills. He spoke in a voice so low that McCarter said he couldn't hear, and both Simpson and the Court asked him to speak up. Simpson went after him very brusquely, and drew out the story of his drab existence as a small town church sexton and janitor, although he said he was only the temporary sexton of Dr. Hall's church. He had not really accepted the job, though he had discharged the duties for over a year.

Mills was neatly dressed. He wore a grayish suit with patch pockets, a rather nifty red tie under his white collar, and fancy sox. His thin dark hair was parted on the left side and smoothed down so tightly it had the appearance of a toupee. He was almost sporty, in fact. He sat with his hands on his lap and his fingers laced together. His answers at times displayed a very, very dull intellect.

He said he makes from $32 to $38 per week, and on that supported his wife and children. Simpson's voice got a little softer as he took Mills over his domestic life. Not once in the entire examination did Jimmy speak of his wife other than in rather an impersonal tone. He said nothing against her—nothing, and in speaking of her his tone was never resentful.

Simpson's voice became raspy again when Mills' recollection failed to jibe with his statement before the Grand Jury some years ago. Once there was a long pause in the examination, and Mills sat staring, dumbly staring into the faces of two jurors within touching distance of him. He was the picture of dejection.

He told of having seen Mrs. Hall in the church the day after his wife disappeared, and of her having asked: "Did you have any sickness in your home last night?"

He replied, "No; why?"

"Mr. Hall didn't come home all night."

"My wife didn't come home, neither. Do you think they eloped?"

Mrs. Hall answered—he said—"No, they're dead, or they would come home."

Simpson said: "Didn't you testify before the Grand Jury that she said, 'No, they're both dead—they've been together, and met the same fate?' "

Mills couldn't remember. He might have said it. He wasn't sure. He couldn't explain to McCarter later on why he thought there might have been an elopement. It just popped into his head —he wasn't sure why.

Poor Jimmy Mills has probably never been sure of anything in this life.

November 7, 1926

Henry L. Dickman, a prisoner from Uncle Sam's military bastile on Alcatraz Island, out in San Francisco Bay, furnished the sensation of the day.

He had been produced by the State to testify as to his activities in investigating the murder when he was a trooper of the New Jersey State Police.

At a moment when he had been made out a pretty disreputable character by the defense, a deserter from the Army and the Navy, and everybody was wondering why the prosecution had offered him, Senator Alexander Simpson, the pepper-pot of the prosecution, brought out from the witness that he had been given $2,500 by Azariah Beekman to leave New Jersey.

Azariah Beekman is now dead. He was the public prosecutor of Middlesex County, where the Hall-Mills murder was committed. He was one of those in charge of the investigation into the murder immediately after the finding of the bodies.

"He told me to get out of this case and stay out," Dickman said, after telling that Beekman had paid him the money. He said he left three months' pay at $100 a month behind him when he departed.

Dickman is a lean-flanked, rangy, raw-boned type of a man who walks with the spraddling gait of a cowboy. He suggests one of Frederic Remington's old cavalry types.

He said he was sentenced to Alcatraz for desertion. He was absent for forty-one days (without leave) on a drunk.

"That is one day longer than the flood," commented the gruff old McCarter.

He admitted to having served a term of 366 days for desertion from the Navy back in 1907. He first enlisted in the Army in 1913.

He was a member of the New Jersey State Police and was assigned to investigation of the Hall-Mills murder. He worked on the case until April, 1923, when he left the service.

He said he made a trip to Lavalette and talked with Henry Stevens, and that Stevens told him he was on a fishing trip with Henry W. Mellinger, of Philadelphia, at the time of the murder. He claimed he afterward saw Mellinger, and while Mellinger said he was on a fishing trip with Stevens at that time, he wouldn't swear to the exact date.

He asked Henry Stevens if he owned a .38-calibre gun, and Henry said he had at different times. The witness described Stevens as "nervous and evasive," but on cross-examination by Senator Case he did not seem to give a clear idea of what he meant

George V. Totten, a former Middlesex County detective in the original investigation was recalled to identify various articles found on the scene of the crime and there was a long wrangle between the lawyers as Simpson asked that they be admitted.

The Court granted his request and Totten identified the grisly exhibits one at a time. They included the articles found in Dr. Hall's pockets.

Now came a dramatic moment when one of Simpson's assistants hauled out a big, square, pasteboard box and the prosecutor began dragging therefrom the clothes taken from the dead bodies four years ago.

As Simpson was holding up the articles before Totten for identification a musty odor filled the room and Senator Case and

Timothy Pfeiffer, another of the attorneys for the defense, stepped in front of the defendants.

"Why don't you move out of the way—perhaps the defendants would like to see these things. You are obstructing their view."

"That is my purpose in standing here," replied Case, gravely.

Mrs. Hall sat with her gaze averted during this scene. Henry was as grim as ever. The frog-eyed Willie stared straight ahead, his moustache bulging.

A sadly crumpled blue dress with little red polka dots was held up by Simpson between his thumb and forefinger. It was Mrs. Mills' dress. A pair of bedraggled stockings. Then one after the other the clothes of the dead minister. As Simpson held up a coat and asked if it was Dr. Hall's coat, the detective shook his head.

"No, I think that's Mr. Willie Stevens'."

The dead clergyman's garment came out of the box later. All this stuff has been packed away haphazardly for four years, dragged out at intervals and piled back into the box unfolded. As a result it is in a sad state.

Totten told of being present at an interview between Prosecutor Beekman and Mrs. Hall soon after the murder, in which she detailed her movements on the night of September 14, 1922. Totten said he remarked to her that he had positive evidence that some woman had been seen entering the side door of her home at around 2:30 that morning and that she replied, "Yes, that was I."

She then told, he said, of going into the church with Willie about two o'clock that morning after her husband failed to come home, thinking he might have fallen asleep there. Not finding him she went to Mills' home. That was in darkness so she returned to her own home.

Judge Parker asked Senator Case how long the cross-examination would take and Case said it would be some time. The Court then said he would order a recess as all hands were worn out, but Simpson asked permission to examine one more witness who was John Toolan, former assistant prosecutor of Somerset County.

He read the minutes of the examination of Mrs. Hall in which she told of Dr. Hall leaving home about fifteen minutes after receiving a telephone call the night of the murder. She said she did not know who made the call. That afternoon Mrs. Mills had phoned and Mrs. Hall had talked to her. She asked if Dr. Hall was home, saying she wished to talk to him about a doctor bill.

Simpson's reason for having all this read into the record at this time was not exactly clear. It was merely repetition of a story that had been told over and over in the past four years. In it Mrs. Hall denied that she had ever seen anything wrong in the relations between Mrs. Mills and her husband or had ever heard any public gossip on the subject.

Court was adjourned to Monday morning, the jury remaining together in charge of the bailiffs. Judge Parker said he deemed it inadvisable that they go to any public or quasi-public church, which means that any church-going members will have to deny themselves their usual spiritual solace this Sunday.

While waiting for court to convene this morning, Mrs. Hall seemed quite animated. She chatted almost gaily with the irrepressible Willie Stevens and with members of her counsel. Her ordinarily grave demeanor was abandoned for the moment and she smiled frequently. She greeted McCarter with great cordiality and looked all around the court with interest.

It was a surprising change. She had on the same black hat and coat and gray gloves she has worn from the beginning. Both Mrs. Hall and the vivacious Mrs. Edwin Carpender, seemed particularly amused at what Willie Stevens had to say.

The frog-eyed fellow, who is described politely by the prosecution as erratic and whose hobby is chasing fire engines, gets more conversationalist attentions from his sister and the others around him than the grim looking Henry.

Mrs. Mary Demarest, the woman who testified Friday that she saw Henry Stevens in an automobile in New Brunswick the day after the murder when he claims to have been fifty miles away, resumed the stand this morning and Senator Case continued his cross-examination.

Mrs. Demarest was recently injured in an auto accident and had to be assisted to the witness chair, whence she glared with hostile eyes at the sparse attorney for the defense. They had not gone far in the cross-examination before the fiery Simpson and

Case were hooked up in a verbal tilt as Case tried to tangle up the witness. She answered no to one question so sharply that Senator Case asked: "Why do you say it that way?"

Senator Simpson objected on the ground that it made no difference whether a woman says no in C major or C flat, but Judge Parker told her to answer the question. She replied: "Because I am a loud talker and quick."

She insisted she had seen Henry Stevens on the day after the murder in an auto halted by the traffic as she got off a street car, and Case could not shake that statement.

He then took her back over her testimony that she saw her cousin, Mrs. Minnie Clark, and Ralph Gorsline apparently spying on the dead Dr. Hall and Mrs. Mills as they sat in a public park.

Case tried to bring out that Dr. Hall might have been holding a little service at the Parker House for Incurables that day as an explanation for the situation. Mrs. Demarest admitted that this was her first impression of the gathering and then she thought it was a trifle queer.

Case interrogated Mrs. Demarest with reference to her regard for her cousin, Mrs. Clark. He asked, sarcastically, "You love Minnie Clark, don't you?"

Mrs. Demarest said they had always been good friends, although she admitted she had testified in an inquiry in which attempt had been made to implicate Mrs. Clark as an accessory after the fact to the murder.

Anna K. Bearman, of New Brunswick, a well-dressed, gray-haired woman with a pince-nez on her nose, told of taking a brown coat and scarf from Mrs. Hall and sending them to a Philadelphia establishment to be cleaned, and dyed black. These are supposed to be the garments worn by Mrs. Hall on the night of the murder. Mrs. Bearman is a neighbor of Mrs. Hall's. She said that she personally volunteered to send the garments away.

On the cross-examination by McCarter, she said she had looked the garments over before sending them away and that there was not a spot on them. Mrs. Bearman's testimony seemed to help the defense.

November 8, 1926

"The Pig Woman," Mrs. Jane Gibson, strangest of all that strange cast of characters that is playing the weird production known as the Hall-Mills murder trial, was suddenly dragged into the center of the stage of events again yesterday.

Along toward eleven o'clock, when most of the good citizens of Somerville were in church, a white ambulance out of Jersey City rolled noiselessly up to the Somerset Hospital, where "the pig woman" has been lying supposedly very ill since her collapse in court on the opening day of the trial.

Senator Simpson hasn't believed that "the pig woman" was as ill as the doctors have made out since the day she keeled over in the court house after seeing her aged mother, who is said to be in Somerville prepared to testify that she was at "the pig woman's" home that night and that "the pig woman" never left the house.

Senator Simpson had an idea that the friends of the defense might be interested in keeping "the pig woman" out of court, because "the pig woman's" tale is very vital. If it is true, she was practically an eye witness to the murder. That is why the fiery prosecutor had the ambulance and officers suddenly swoop down on the Somerset Hospital today and remove "the pig woman" against the protests of Dr. A. Anderson Lawton. Said the doctor, "Senator Simpson, you are jeopardizing the life of this woman. I forbid her removal."

"You are no jailer. We are going to take her."

And take her they did.

November 9, 1926

"Hey, Gorsline, come down here where we can see you!"

Thus bellowed Senator Alexander Simpson, the buzz-saw of the prosecution, yesterday afternoon, as a tall, spidery-legged, pallid fellow stood up in the rear of the court room at the call of his name.

And Ralph V. Gorsline, the vestryman of the Church of St.

John the Evangelist, in New Brunswick, and a bit of a hand with the ladies, moved down the crowded aisle like a long shadow to what was probably the most trying moment in his forty-five years.

He had had many trying moments the last four years, at that. He is the chap that the State thinks could tell plenty about the murder of the parson and his sweetheart, the choir singer, if he would open his wide, loose-lipped mouth, still wider, and talk freely.

Mr. "Greasy Vest" William Garvin, a former manager of the New York office of the Burns Detective Agency, a stout man, with a bald head and glittering spectacles, was on the witness stand. He had kept his overcoat on. His coat beneath was buttoned closely to his vest from which he is said to derive his nickname.

The defense tried to get the nickname on the record, but the Court wouldn't permit it, although Mr. "Greasy Vest" Garvin smilingly said he had no objection. He watched the approach of the tall Gorsline with interest, because he had just been telling the jury a strange story.

It was about how a man had come to him a couple of months after the murder, and said that his conscience troubled him, and that he was in De Russey's gory lane the night of the murder and had seen Henry Stevens there with a gun in his hand.

"What the hell are you doing here?" Garvin's visitor related Stevens said. "This is not your affair. Get the hell out of here."

And fired two shots in the ground, the man said.

And the man "got" at once, he said.

The next night he was taken to a lodge room in New Brunswick, so Mr. "Greasy Vest" Garvin said his caller had stated, but to what lodge or by whom is not of record, and was there forced to swear that he would never tell what he had seen in De Russey's Lane that fatal night.

So Mr. "Greasy Vest" Garvin peered through his spectacles at Ralph V. Gorsline, as the skinny vestryman stood before him in the court room today, a dramatic moment, you may be sure.

Gorsline has a long face and chin like Fred Fulton, the old

plasterer-pugilist from Rochester, Minn., noted for his prodigious tumbles in the roped arena. The skin on Gorsline's face is drawn as tightly over the bones as the head of a drum.

The muscles of his thin face were twitching slightly as Garvin gazed. Gorsline's eyes met the glittering glare of "Greasy Vest" but briefly, then shifted away, Simpson demanded:

"Is this the man that came to your office and told you the story?"

Garvin replied positively, "That is the man."

"All right," said Simpson. "Go back, Gorsline. If you will stay here we will be much obliged to you."

Silent, and shadowy, the vestryman straddled back up the crowded aisle, avoiding the gaze of the witnesses and spectators who filled the chairs.

Gorsline is now manager of a bluing manufacturing concern in New Brunswick, the head of which is said to be a relative of Mrs. Hall. He is nobody's fool, for all he seems to have been something of a philanderer in search of romance. He did not seem to be flustered by his identification.

A milder sensation popped out at the morning session and another chapter in the amours of De Russey's romantic lane was written when a young fellow named Robert Ehrling was called to the stand by the State.

As near as I can judge everybody in New Brunswick who had a romance on hand carried it to De Russey's Lane, and everybody was busy that night of the murder. Robert Ehrling was there with a young woman in a parked automobile. He said he saw "the pig woman" in De Russey's Lane that night riding her mule, just as she has always insisted.

Her claim has been that she was out on her mule looking for corn thieves when she saw Mrs. Hall, Willie Stevens, and Henry de la Bruyere Carpender under the crabapple tree that night, although the defense intimates that it will prove by "the pig woman's" own mother and a boy that Mrs. Gibson did not leave her house that night.

Ehrling's testimony would seem to corroborate Mrs. Gibson. He is a slender young fellow. He carried a cap in his hand, and his hair was tousled. He identified himself as a wheelwright and truck driver, and said he knew "the pig woman" well, as he had often taken washing to one of her neighbors in De Russey's Lane.

He says as he and his girl friend sat in the automobile after driving around town most of the day, and having dinner at her house, "the pig woman" came up on her mule and paused by the auto a moment. Ehrling said he got a good look at her, then quickly looked away, as he didn't want "the pig woman" to recognize him. She went on down the lane on her mule.

The young man displayed a burst of chivalry when McCarter for the defense, asked him the name of his companion. He shuffled his feet and hitched around in his chair and mumbled he would rather not answer that one.

"Why?" said McCarter, fairly baying, like an old hound that had hit a new scent.

Ehrling, with some kindly aid from Simpson, finally explained that the young lady is now married and has a couple of children, and he did not wish to drag her into the case. McCarter appealed to the Court, and Ehrling stammered out the name of Jennie Lemford.

Ehrling also testified that two automobiles passed in the lane that night, one a sedan with a single occupant, the other a touring car. He thought the sedan was driven by a man with a moustache. Both Henry and Willie Stevens have such hirsute adornments.

The touring car had the curtains drawn.

The defense failed to shake the tale of the chivalrous Ehrling to any extent, and it paid no attention whatever to the testimony of one C. Russell Gildersleeve, a tall, darkish, well-groomed man who looks like Nick, the Greek, the plunger.

C. Russell was a lay reader in Dr. Hall's church for some years and he said he saw Dr. Hall and Mrs. Mills on Broadway, near Forty-ninth Street, in New York, about a year before the murder, this being the first touch of the "Roaring Forties" to the case.

Ah, yes, this Mrs. Frances Noel Stevens Hall is human after all, though she has been written of, spoken of, as if she were something less.

Human—and a woman!

She showed it yesterday afternoon.

The proud, stoical front she has been presenting to the world as she sits in the little chapel-like court room in Somerville, on trial for life, was shaken in a distinct shudder.

No tears—no handkerchief to the eyes, for her traditions of good form would perhaps forbid crying except in private—or public display of emotion, but there was a distinct sag in the black-gowned figure with the pallid countenance sitting between her two brothers.

It came when Senator Alexander Simpson fumbled around in a big pasteboard box on his table, and suddenly produced from many paper wrappings, a grisly exhibit in the form of a head and bust of a human figure.

He planted this dummy, or effigy, or manikin, or whatever it may be called, on the railing of the witness stand so that it faced the staring jury with ghastly, sightless eyes. It was for the purpose of giving Dr. Otto H. Schultze, medical assistant to the District Attorney of New York, a lay figure on which to illustrate the findings of an autopsy performed by him on the bodies of Dr. Edward Hall and Mrs. Eleanor Mills last month.

I was watching Mrs. Hall closely. I doubt that she was fully prepared for the production of the dummy, though she may have had some intimation of it from her counsel.

As the snorting little Simpson shook off the wrappings and the dummy came into view, Mrs. Hall started slightly.

So did every woman in the crowded court room.

You couldn't blame her. She would be all that has been said of her, and more, if she had been able to pass the incident over without some sign. The black hat on her head shook as if she had taken a swift breath, then dropped forward again, and she began fumbling with her big black pocketbook. She seemed to have difficulty opening it. She produced from it some sort of document and fumbled it with nervous fingers.

She kept her head down during the early stages of a sort of lecture by Dr. Schultze, then looked up at the ceiling. Not once did her eyes turn to the dummy, as her ears heard the doctor tell how the singing voice of the woman who stole her husband's love had been literally carved from her throat, tongue, windpipe, and larynx, that black night in De Russey's bloody lane when the State says Mrs. Hall was present.

Perhaps Mrs. Hall thought at first that the grisly figure was a likeness of the murdered choir singer. It was a likeness of no one in particular, just a medical dummy used for demonstrations of that part of the human anatomy.

It looked for a moment as if Mrs. Hall would collapse. You couldn't say if she turned color because there is no color in her face anyway. She would scarcely appeal as a sympathetic figure, but today I think everyone felt a little sorry for her.

Henry Stevens glanced at the dummy once, then averted his eyes and did not look toward it again. The eccentric Willie watched the dummy and listened to Dr. Schultze's lecture with apparent interest. But then, Willie is interested in everything, especially when old John Bunn, the court crier, bawls, "Hear ye, hear ye."

There were great red splotches that looked like blood on the plaster head, although of course it wasn't blood. The top part of the skull came off like a cigar humidor, and fitted into the hollow space of the skull was what was purported to be a representation of the human brain, though it looked like a gob of dried bread dough after it had been squeezed up in the hand.

Dr. Schultze is said to be the original of Arthur B. Reeve's detective character, Craig Kennedy. I believe Mr. Reeve admits it. Dr. Schultze is a bulky square-built man, who wears square-cut clothes. He had on a double-breasted suit of blue serge.

He has a big crop of iron-gray hair and is well jowled. He speaks in an incisive, professional tone, and was the best witness in the matter of self-assurance on the stand that has yet appeared.

He performed the autopsy on the bodies of Dr. Hall and Mrs.

Mills in a garage in North New Brunswick when they were dug up on October 28, 1926. They were originally buried for ten days without an autopsy, then exhumed and an autopsy performed, with which the State has never been satisfied. The hapless lovers have not been permitted to rest even after their death.

Dr. Schultze called the figure on the railing a manikin. It was in several pieces when Simpson first pulled it out of the box, and Dr. Schultze adjusted the brain and the skull. The eyes of several of the jury were fairly popping as they watched.

Then Simpson handed the doctor a sort of plaque with the model of a head thereon, which Schultze described as the cross-section of a head and the upper part of the neck. This exhibit was as grisly as the other.

The doctor testified that he had found three bullet wounds in Mrs. Mills' head, one in the forehead, about two inches above the level of the brow, one in the right cheek, and one on the right side of the face, all within an area of about four inches, and all made by .32-calibre bullets.

Mrs. Mills' throat had been cut, the slash severing all the muscles of the neck, the windpipe and the gullet down to the spinal column of the neck and cutting the large blood vessels. The upper part of the windpipe, the larynx and the tongue were missing.

Dr. Schultze gave it as his opinion that they had been cut out, not pulled out. He said he could not state positively whether the woman's throat had been cut after death, as has been frequently hinted. He said any of the bullet wounds would have caused death. He picked up a small ruler and demonstrated his remarks to the jury on the manikin.

The jurors all leaned far forward in their chairs and listened open-mouthed, displaying far more interest than in anything that has yet taken place during the trial.

Dr. Schultze said that the bullet that killed Dr. Hall passed through the frontal bone on the right side of the head and came out of the back of the skull. Simpson asked him if the dominie would have had to be in a stooping position to get that wound. He added, "Or else somebody would have had to be above him, or his head was tilted forward."

He said that Dr. Hall had a bruise on the knuckle of his right forefinger, and the defense on cross-examination said that Mrs. Mills had a wound on her lips—a small puncture, as he described it, but said it was superficial.

The interest of the defense in this wound was not apparent, but Case in one question asked the doctor if there were any bruises on her arm such as might have been made in a scuffle. He said no.

He said that he had found no powder marks around the wounds on either body, and in his opinion the gun that killed must have been held more than six inches away.

November 11, 1926

Barbara Tough, who pronounces it not "Tuff," but "Too," and who has an accent like Harry Lauder singing "The Safest of the Family," yesterday gave the jury a breath of the back stairs in the home of the dead minister.

Barbara told of coming upon a romantic little scene in the guild room of Dr. Hall's church four years before the preacher and his sweetheart were murdered. Mrs. Mills was perched on Dr. Hall's knee.

She jumped up as Barbara approached, the Scotch woman said, laughed hysterically and said, "It's only Barbara."

Barbara was a maid in the Hall home from February, 1918 to April, 1923. She had charge of the upstairs region. She is a spinster, short, determined looking, with eyes squinting at the world from behind big horn-rimmed spectacles. She said "haird" for "heard," and "Jairsey City" and she called Dr. Hall, "the Dominie."

She was a member of St. Mary's Guild of Dr. Hall's church, which she said was for the younger "gurrls," although Barbara Tough is no longer in that class.

She wore a brown coat and a black hat and a black and white patent-leather rosette ornament, the hat being perched high and primly on her dark brown hair, which was gathered at the back of her head in an old-fashioned knot.

No bobbed hair for Barbara Tough.

She spoke quickly and incisively as she described the home life of Dr. Hall and his wife, with a few sidelights touching on Willie, who lived in the house with them and who beamed at Barbara across the court room.

From Barbara Tough Senator Simpson brought out that it was common gossip in church circles that Dr. Hall and Eleanor Mills were very, very friendly. Barbara talked as if she had been on good terms with the dead woman. She always spoke of her as "Eleanor."

The sparse and unctuous Senator Case, of the defense, objected to the witness being permitted to relate gossip. In his remarks supporting his objections, he said that while the whole world might have gossiped about the relationship, yet it is entirely within human experience and human fallibility that Mrs. Hall knew nothing about it. "As she did, in fact, know nothing about it."

Simpson objected to Case stating as a fact that Mrs. Hall didn't know about it. He argued that the gossip was important, because the State contends that the motive for the murder was jealousy and hate. Wherefore he said, it became important to lay before the jury evidence of the notoriousness, the boldness, the openness of the illicit relations between Dr. Hall and Mrs. Mills.

The Court permitted Simpson to interrogate Barbara along that line, and she said she knew that Eleanor was "very fond of Dr. Hall, both as a minister and as a friend," and that it was easy to see that the dead woman was one of his favorites. In the two years before the murder, Barbara said it was general gossip in the church about the dominie and Mrs. Mills—among the church members, the guild and the choir.

At the morning session, which produced many gory details of the crime, what with doctors, who performed the various autopsies on the bodies, testifying, Senator Simpson had produced an old-fashioned black-handled razor.

Dr. Arthur L. Smith, of New Brunswick, had testified to being present at one autopsy and had said that Mrs. Mills had practically been decapitated by what he thought must have been a couple of slashes with some very sharp instrument.

Simpson showed him the razor and asked if it might have been done with that. Dr. Smith said it might, and, taking the glittering razor in a firm grip, he made a couple of passes at his own throat to illustrate how the throat-cutting might have been done with that weapon.

This was the first appearance in the case of the razor, and Case objected, but Simpson said he had some evidence bearing on it. When Barbara was on the stand he asked her if Willie Stevens had a razor. She said no: that Willie shaved downtown, but that Dr. Hall kept an old-fashioned blade in the bathroom. Simpson said: "When you say old-fashioned, you mean this kind?"

"Yes," Barbara replied, "but I think it was a bit smaller than that."

Simpson retorted: "I'm not asking you if it was this razor. That will be proved by someone else."

Willie Stevens' bulbous moustache shook with merriment at Barbara's reply, the defendant's lawyer laughed, and the court room roared.

Even Mrs. Hall smiled, while John Bunn bawled his inevitable "silence." It strikes me that there is a good deal of grinning and suppressed mirth around the table where the defendants' seven lawyers sit. They seem to have some difficulty concealing their mirth as the prosecution prods on slowly, trying to weave the chain of circumstantial evidence so firmly around Mrs. Hall and the Stevens brothers that the jury will find them guilty. Only Robert H. McCarter remains grim and unamused.

Barbara Tough said Willie had a small rifle in his room and had showed her a pistol. She didn't know what kind it was. She said Willie was up and around unusually early the Friday morning after the murder.

She got home herself the night of the murder at ten o'clock—"a sharp ten," as she described it, because she heard the clock strike. She slept in a room above Mrs. Hall's bedroom and heard Mrs. Hall up and moving around at two o'clock. The striking of the clock again. Barbara said Mrs. Hall seemed to be walking to her bathroom.

As to whether Mrs. Hall and Willie were at home when she

arrived at the house the night of the murder, Barbara Tough could not say. She didn't see Mrs. Hall until 9:30 the next morning, when Mrs. Hall said: "Oh, Barbara, Dr. Hall hasn't been home all night."

To which Barbara replied: "So the girls tell me!"

Evidently the family movements were no secret below stairs in that house.

Friday night Mrs. Hall telephoned the choir leader of the church that Dr. Hall was out of town. She heard Mrs. Hall answer the telephone on Saturday before Barbara knew the bodies had been discovered and heard her say, "No, Dr. Hall is out of town"; then, "Don't tell me anything on the telephone; don't tell me anything on the telephone."

Simpson asked her about some white silk sox that Mrs. Hall had her wash for "him," without saying who "him" was. This was before the bodies were discovered. He continued: "Did she say anything about their being used for burial purposes?"

Case interrupted, "I object to that as ghoulish."

Simpson replied, "Well, if it's as ghoulish as the murder it's pretty ghoulish."

It developed on cross-examination that washing out white silk sox was a usual chore for Barbara.

She told of the presence in the Hall home after the murder of Felix Di Martini, a detective, and of him examining her at length. The State will contend that it was an extraordinary situation for Mrs. Hall to have her own detective around digging up statements and evidence, if, in fact, she did not hire him to suppress evidence.

The testimony of the doctors at the morning session revealed a rather startling laxity of methods in the conduct of the early examinations of the bodies of Dr. Hall and Mrs. Mills. The body of the latter was buried with the bullets still in her head and Dr. George Hegeman, who performed the original autopsy on October 5, 1922, said he did not know that the tongue was missing because he didn't open the mouth.

Dr. E. I. Cronk, a cadaverous-looking man in a swallow-tail coat, testified that he happened to be in Hubbard's undertaking parlor one day when Senator Florence, then one of Mrs. Hall's attorneys, telephoned to Hubbard, and at Hubbard's request he— Dr. Cronk—examined Mrs. Mills' body. He said he examined the bullet wounds, and also opened the undertaker's sutures in the abdomen to see if she was to be a mother. He said he found no such evidence.

Dr. Smith testified to treating Mrs. Mills at the request of Dr. Hall in January, 1922. He operated on her for the removal of a kidney and said Dr. Hall agreed to pay him $200 at the rate of $10 per month, but all he got was $30. He saw Dr. Hall at the hospital frequently while Mrs. Mills was there, but Mrs. Hall knew of this incident. Dr. Hall was supposed to be paying for Mrs. Mills' treatment out of a church fund.

Charles J. Alpaugh, a stage driver, testified to seeing a Cadillac coupé and a Dodge sedan about twenty feet back of De Russey's Lane along toward midnight on the night of the murder, and to seeing two or three people coming down the bank to the cars as his own lights fell on them.

Furthermore, Alpaugh said, a Ford touring car, carrying two men, followed his bus out of the lane and finally cut in front of him. He seemed to think this incident most unusual and the State apparently attached some significance to it. Alpaugh said he could have identified the man in the Ford at the time but couldn't now.

The Court intended to sit today, but Senator Simpson said he had many protests from the American Legion against devoting Armistice Day to this purpose, and after the Court consulted the jury it was decided to take the day off.

November 13, 1926

Defiant, stagey, talky—what you might call "fresh"—but by no means hard to look at, as the saying is, Mrs. Louise Geist Riehl couldn't seem to remember yesterday all she related in November, 1922, to the Grand Jury that then was inquiring into the Hall-Mills murder.

She cocked her head on one side like a bird, and rolled her big circular eyes, with plenty of white around the pupils—the kind the boys describe as "goo-goo" eyes—up at the stained glass sky-light, and thought, and thought, and thought, as Senator Simpson tried to refresh her memory. It was about the telephone conversation between Dr. Hall and his sweetheart on the afternoon of the day of the murder, which the State contends Mrs. Hall listened in on, hearing the pair make the "date" that led them to De Russey's Lane that night and to their death.

Mrs. Louise Geist Riehl was then Louise Geist and a parlor maid in the Hall home. She afterward married one Arthur S. Riehl, a piano salesman, and when he filed suit for annulment of their marriage last August, he alleged that his wife knew more of the murder than she had told, bringing about a new investigation and this trial of Mrs. Hall and her brothers, that is daily unfolding its chapters, thrilling and otherwise.

Louise heard the telephone ring and picked up the receiver of the extension on the second floor, she testified yesterday. She recognized Mrs. Mills' voice, told her to wait a moment, and walked from the telephone to the top of the stairway near by and looked over the banisters, thinking Dr. Hall was downstairs.

She saw Mrs. Hall, who had apparently just walked into the house and had lifted the receiver of the downstairs telephone off the hook. Louise said:

"She had the receiver halfway to her ear, when I said, 'This is for Mr. Hall, Mrs. Hall—is he downstairs?' She said, 'No, Louise, isn't he upstairs?'

"Just then Mr. Hall called from his bathroom. I said, 'Oh, all right, he is up here.' Mrs. Hall placed back the receiver, turned around and walked out."

Senator Simpson seemed somewhat startled by this answer. He gazed steadily at the witness, and she stared back at him, defiantly. She seemed to sense his surprise. She is a tall young woman, of jaunty demeanor, rather mannish in general appearance, I would say. At least she does not strike me as particularly feminine. She might be described as handsome rather than pretty. She has brown hair, the rolling eyes aforesaid, a good complexion, and nice teeth, but she sometimes talks out of the corner of her mouth and she jerks her head to emphasize her remarks.

She knows how to dress. She wore a red hat, a dark coat, and tan gloves, and tan shoes and tan stockings, the effect on the human eye being of sartorial smartness.

"What did Mr. Hall say?" demanded Simpson.

"He said," replied Louise, after a moment given over to coquettish meditation, " 'Yes, yes, yes, that is too bad.' " She paused after each "yes," giving a good imitation of one side of a telephone conversation. " 'I was going down to the church a little later' "—this is Louise's statement of the dead dominie's talk.

" 'Can't we make arrangements for later, say about a quarter after eight?'

"I can't remember any more of the conversation," said Louise. "I suppose he hung up."

It was later on in the examination of the quite collected Louise that Senator Simpson said:

"I am surprised at this witness' attitude on the stand when she says she saw Mrs. Hall put back the receiver, because at no time in her statement before the Grand Jury or to the prosecutor has she so sworn.

"I want to show that this witness swore on numerous occasions that all she saw was Mrs. Hall take the receiver off the hook and that she [Louise] walked away. I am distinctly surprised at her attitude because I sent her original statement out to read and she read it and my messenger, Cleluch, tells me she was charmed to have a chance to refresh her memory, but it didn't refresh her much."

"Did Cleluch say I was very glad to read that testimony?" demanded Louise, truculently, leaning over the rail of the witness stand.

"Never mind that!" interjected Judge Parker, sharply.

"Did you not so answer in Middlesex?" insisted Simpson.

"I presume I did," replied Louise, not quite as airily as before, "but the question was put to me altogether different."

She said that the morning after the murder she was awakened by a rattling of the shutters, which was usually Dr. Hall's signal when he was going to New York and wanted an early breakfast. She went downstairs and found Willie Stevens. When she asked him what he was doing up so early he said, "There was something terrible happened last night and Frances and I have been up most of the night."

She said he seemed a little nervous, but she "didn't look at him very good." When Senator Simpson asked her if she had not described his condition to the Grand Jury as "looking as if he had a katzenjammer," Louise said she didn't really think she had ever used that word. She said it with almost an injured air.

She described Mrs. Hall's condition as rather tearful the morning after the murder, but she did not seem to be any too satisfactory to Simpson as a witness. It would appear that a number of witnesses have failed to relate what the prosecutor expected.

He scored rather heavily with the testimony of Mrs. Nellie L. Opie, a stout matron, who was next door neighbor of the Mills family and said she had known Eleanor Mills for twenty years. She told how Dr. Hall called almost every day at the Mills' home when the father and two children would be at the school where Jimmy Mills was the janitor and the children, pupils.

The neighbors gossiped about it freely, Mrs. Opie said, and when Senator Case insisted she mentioned several, one of them a Mrs. Latham, a parishioner of Dr. Hall's.

"What did she say?" demanded Case.

"She said if Dr. Hall could call on one of his parishioners eight or nine times a week and not call on her once a year she was going to another church," replied the witness, and the spectators whooped so loudly that Judge Parker threatened to clear the court room.

It was Mrs. Opie who got the message from Dr. Hall over her telephone the day of the murder. The dominie had been sending his messages to his sweetheart via that route a couple of times a week for years. On this particular day Mrs. Mills did not respond to her call from the window and the preacher merely told Mrs. Opie to tell Mrs. Mills he had telephoned.

Mrs. Opie saw Mrs. Mills shortly after seven o'clock that evening, one of the last to see the murdered woman alive. Senator Simpson again produced his pasteboard box containing the clothes of the murdered pair, and Mrs. Opie identified a blue dress with red polka dots as the garment Mrs. Mills wore.

After the murder, she said, Mrs. Minnie Clark and Edward Carpender called at the Mills home. They came in an automobile, and in this automobile Mrs. Opie said she saw a lot of papers in boxes, or little drawers.

Answering an objection by Senator Case, Simpson said he will show that papers were removed from Dr. Hall's house on the Saturday following the murder and that the State claims these papers were the same papers in Carpender's car. Edward Carpender was in the court room, and at the call of his name stood up and was identified as the man who visited the Mills' home.

The strange manner in which the bodies were hurried to the grave was brought out by Simpson through John B. Hubbard, an undertaker of New Brunswick, who said he was the coroner of Middlesex County at the time of the murder. He admitted, rather reluctantly, that the bodies were buried without an autopsy, the body of Dr. Hall being taken to the Stevens' family vault in Greenwood Cemetery in Brooklyn within forty hours of the discovery of the murder.

He said he made no efforts as coroner to have an autopsy and that he thought the bodies ought to be buried at once because of their condition. They were disinterred ten days later for an autopsy.

November 14, 1926

Out of the grave came the heart of the dead dominie today in the form of musty letters that fairly smoked with his love for the little choir singer.

A bad, bad love, the world and convention says, but the dead preacher told it hotly, feverishly on paper, and the woman he didn't love—his wife—heard it all recited over and over and over again in the little court house at Somerville where she is on trial for her life.

She heard her dead husband calling another woman "dear heart of mine," and "dear wonder-heart" and telling that other woman what an inspiration she was to him and how he loved her—burning words and fierce phrases that belonged by rights to the listening woman.

But not by one change of muscle in the pallid mask that is her face, not by one gesture or change of attitude did Frances Noel Stevens Hall indicate she heard the words other than some recital of ordinary phraseology.

She seemed strangely detached from the scene as State Senator Simpson read the letters in a dull, matter-of-fact tone to the stolidly listening jury. The lawyer might have been reading about someone she never heard of in her life.

The letters were four years old and they have been much handled and much thumbed since the bodies of the preacher and his sweetheart were found side by side in De Russey's Lane, but time has not dimmed the flaming terms in which Dr. Hall poured out his passion for the dead woman.

Mrs. Hall lowered her eyes as Simpson began reading, but not in confusion and emotion. Presently these eyes were roaming over the court room again, hard and cold, as the voice of Simpson went on reading, rapidly, distinctly. He started out with one dated Christmas, 1921, a year before the dominie himself came to collect the wage that he always taught his flock was the wage of sin. This card said:

Dear Heart of Mine: This red, red rose, my Christmas gift to you, is but a symbol of love, devoted, faithful, true. For love is like a rose, dear heart, fresh as the early morn. God took the beauty of the skies, the glory of the dawn, the fire of passion, the calm of eve. The golden glow and with the mystery of the stars, he made the love we know. So in this rose you find me, dear, the love it can impart; love, loyal, true and absolute, the offering of my heart. E.W.H. DD.L.

Christmas Day, 1921.

While Simpson was reading the letters from typewritten copies the pallid Timothy Pfeiffer of counsel for the defense sat on the edge of a table holding the original copies and often interjecting a correction. Pfeiffer was once a Princeton quarterback and is a tall, well-dressed, rather aristocratic looking fellow, who has been very active in Mrs. Hall's behalf since after the murder. Simpson's copies seemed full of errors and Pfeiffer was quick to interrupt even when the word or phrase was more eloquent than as read by Simpson.

The twelve men in the jury box listened as the fiery little chief of the prosecution read letter after letter in a dry conversational tone without a vocal attempt to bring out high spots. Simpson finally let Francis Bergen, the prosecutor of Somerset County, relieve him in the reading and Bergen put a little more emphasis to such terms as "burning kisses" and the like.

One of the jurors yawned behind his hand. Another toyed with his moustache. None of them seemed startled by the letters. Perhaps they are not of the type that can understand a man using such endearments to a woman as "My Anchor" and "My Rock." That language probably seems a little high flown in love-making in Central New Jersey.

Willie Stevens listened with his head up. Willie misses very little that goes on in the court, but his interest is that of a child. I am not so sure that Willie comprehends the gravity of this matter. His demeanor in court would indicate no great sense of responsibility.

You really have to feel sorry for Willie for all he has been depicted as a humorous figure. You would not laugh or joke at him if he were crippled in body, but some people seem to think he is funny because he is somewhat mentally deformed.

To me the strangest figure of the trio now on trial is Henry Stevens. Those who know him say he is a nice fellow, fond of fishing and hunting, and a companionable sort on such expeditions when companionship is something of an essential. But he has sat in court for nine days scarcely changing expression, apparently a grim, dour man, though this conception of him scarcely jibes with the stories of his friends. His wife is always close to his side. She has been wearing a bright green hat the past two days and her manner is less buoyant than at first.

She has been described as the brains of the defense, but she sits very quietly just behind her husband, and only occasionally joins in the whispered colloquies. Neither Henry Stevens nor his wife gave any sign that they heard the love letters that were read today.

November 15, 1926

Herbert Mayer, a reporter on the New York *Mirror*, was the first witness at the morning session, McCarter completing the cross-examination begun late Friday. Mayer's testimony was mainly concerned with his connection with the calling-card found at the feet of the dead preacher and said to bear Willie Stevens' fingerprints.

Mayer worked on the case for nearly a year digging up and running down information for his paper. Then Senator Simpson offered for identification what he said was the diary of Dr. Hall found in Mrs. Mills' home and her scarf.

McCarter objected and Simpson said it is part of the State's case to show the relationship of Dr. Hall and Mrs. Mills.

It was a big brown notebook of the kind carried by school children.

It is said that Jimmy Mills sold the diary and some letters to a newspaper for $500. The judges examined the notebook and conferred together, and Judge Parker said they thought it ought to go before the jury.

Simpson also offered a bunch of letters found in Mrs. Mills' home and they were admitted over the objection of the defense. There was quite a packet of the letters and a bundle of loose sheets from the diary.

Harry A. Kolb, a milk-wagon driver of New Brunswick, who delivered milk to the Hall home, told of finding a door open at the back of the house on the morning of September 15, 1922, when he deposited his lacteal offering at five o'clock. He had never seen that door opened before. The condition of the door of the Hall home on that morning is considered important by the State.

A fresh-cheeked youth of eighteen with a clear voice, named

William J. Grealis, delivered a new suit of clothes to the Hall home on the Saturday the bodies were found and Willie Stevens gave him an old suit to take back to the store where Grealis was employed, to be cleaned and scoured. He said Willie seemed very nervous and insisted that Grealis go out the side door instead of the front door, saying they had trouble in the house. The young man said he saw the old suit when it was unwrapped at the store and the trousers had dark spots around the waistband.

This testimony did not seem startling. The young witness was only fourteen at the time of the incident related.

Peter Tumulty, bald and gray, who used to work for Mrs. Hall but who is now a gardener for Henry Carpender, was the next witness. Peter was questioned by Simpson as to washing the Dodge sedan belonging to Mrs. Hall on Friday after the murder. Peter said he didn't see the Dodge that day. He had a very poor memory which Simpson tried to refresh by reading from previous statements when Peter said the Dodge was out Friday. The gardener then admitted he might have so stated.

Peter said he afterward bought the Dodge sedan from Mrs. Hall when she went to Europe. Simpson tried to find out if the Dodge had a damaged mudguard after the murder, but Peter hadn't noticed it if it did. Case's cross-examination was very brief.

Simpson shouted for a couple of witnesses who failed to appear, then he called Mrs. Agnes W. Storer, the organist at Dr. Hall's church since 1904. She is a pleasant looking woman with gray hair. She said Mrs. Mills sang soprano in the choir and was very regular in her attendance. She said she got a message from Mrs. Hall on Friday, the day after the murder, saying that the preacher was out of town and would not be present at the choir rehearsal that night. Mrs. Storer admitted that she never asked Mrs. Hall why she had sent that message after hearing of the murder.

The organist admitted that she had taken a trip to Italy with Mrs. Hall after the murder and Mrs. Hall paid her expenses. She said that at no time during the trip did it occur to her to ask Mrs. Hall why she telephoned her about Dr. Hall's absence, although this was before the bodies were discovered. During a pause in Simpson's questioning Mrs. Storer looked at Mrs. Hall and seemed to smile ever so faintly.

November 16, 1926

"And did Mr. Elisha K. Soper say in that conversation with you a week after the finding of the bodies of Dr. Hall and Mrs. Mills, that he was in the vicinity of De Russey's Lane the night of the murder, that he saw an automobile with lights so bright that the man driving the car had to slow down"—

The voice of State Senator Alexander Simpson droned through the drowsy air of the nodding court room today, then suddenly rose shrilly, like a whistle:

"AND THAT HE RECOGNIZED THE PEOPLE IN THE CAR, A WOMAN AND TWO MEN, AS MRS. HALL AND HER BROTHERS?"

Everybody sat up straight.

The witness to whom the question was directed was Ira D. Nixon, a sandy-complexioned, prosaic looking oil salesman, with pale eyes and an earnest manner, who had been prodded into the court room by his conscience, as he gravely explained, after a silence of four years.

"He did!" he answered firmly to Simpson's question.

But before he answered, State Senator Clarence Case, of counsel for Mrs. Hall and her two brothers, the persons, perhaps, vitally affected by the matter, was on his feet, much startled and a little groggy, it seemed, fumbling for words in which to frame his objections.

Behind him, gathered about a long table, gruff old McCarter, the pallid Pfeiffer, and three or four other members of the so-called million-dollar-defense, gazed at the witness with wide eyes.

On behind them, the sombre-garbed Mrs. Hall and the bulbous-eyed Willie, and the grim Henry, sitting in a row with several of their relatives around them, stared, scarcely moving.

No one had expected this witness, Ira D. Nixon, who said he

is forty-two years old and has lived in New Jersey all his life. He is now located at Newark, where he has his own company, selling lubricating oil.

He was called to the stand by Simpson immediately after Elisha K. Soper, a chunky-built, gray looking man, had testified that he had seen an automobile in De Russey's Lane on the night of the murder carrying a woman and two men, as he was returning from a lodge meeting in Somerville, but who stated positively that he didn't recognize the passengers.

Soper and Nixon worked for the same concern, the National Oil and Supply Company of Newark, in 1922. On Saturday, September 23, 1922, a week after the murder, they met in the office as they were drawing their pay, and it was then, Nixon said, that Soper told him about recognizing Mrs. Hall and her brothers in the automobile.

"Now why are you here today?" demanded Senator Case when he took the witness over for cross-examination.

"For the simple reason that for the last four years I have had the information that I am giving to the State of New Jersey today, and I thought I owed it to the State of New Jersey to come back and tell it," replied Nixon.

"You came here expecting that Mr. Soper would not testify that way?" demanded Senator Case.

"I had no knowledge as to how Mr. Soper would testify," said Nixon, "but I really anticipated that he would corroborate me."

He had come, he said, without being subpoenaed—as a volunteer. Not until last Saturday evening did he communicate with the authorities in Jersey City and tell them what he knew, and they asked him to appear today.

He had first talked it over with his father and several friends, and they advised him to tell the jury what Soper had told him. Later Soper was recalled to the stand by Simpson, and Case got another denial out of him that he had made any such statement to Nixon.

And there the matter stands as a question of veracity between Soper and Nixon, but the lubricating oil man was certainly dynamite for a moment to the defense.

They dragged the shame of the dead Mrs. Eleanor Mills around the court room today through the medium of the letters she wrote to her dominie sweetheart, and which were strewn over the lifeless bodies under the old crabapple tree.

She had a vast passion for the philandering pastor, no doubt of that. She breathed it in white-hot language that seemed a little hoity-toity for the wife of a church sexton and school janitor. The lady must have read some warm literature to get some of the phrases.

Francis Bergen, the prosecutor of Somerset County, who is aiding Simpson in the conduct of the case for the State, read the letters in a sing-song voice. He was inclined to soft-pedal such sizzling segments as "Never will I say you want my body rather than me—what I really am. I know that if you love me you will long and ache for my body."

When he came to her saying she yearned "to pour kisses on my babykin's face and head," the prosecutor fairly blushed. He is a big man and probably felt very, very foolish as he read the endearing lines.

The usually beaming Willie Stevens lifted his protruding moustache in a snarl that showed his white teeth several times during the reading. Willie seemed greatly annoyed. Mrs. Hall went through this ordeal even more stoically than she did the reading of her dead husband's letters Saturday.

She lowered her eyes once, then lifted them and kept them roaming over the court room. She did not seem to be listening. Henry sat "reared" back in his chair, scarcely stirring.

But if Mrs. Hall displayed no sign that she heard the reading of the letters, she was obviously quite conscious of the testimony of Mrs. Elsie Barnhardt, a sister of Eleanor Mills, who testified to Eleanor's love for the dead dominie and said the pair planned to elope to Japan.

Mrs. Barnhardt is so ample that you have to call her fat, but she has a pleasant, good-looking face and a soft, low voice. As she left the witness stand she passed Mrs. Hall, and the woman accused of the murder of her sister let her cold eyes travel over Mrs. Barnhardt's wide figure from head to foot.

It was a look of bitter contempt. Never before has Mrs. Hall deigned to give a witness such a scrutiny.

Mrs. Barnhardt wore a black coat with an ermine collar, with an imitation rose, green-colored, on the lapel. She said she saw her sister and Dr. Hall together many times and "knew that they liked each other very well." They were going to Japan as soon as Charlotte, Mrs. Mills' daughter, finished school.

She said she once cautioned Mrs. Mills about being so open in her relations with the preacher, and Mrs. Mills said she wasn't going to hide it from anyone, and didn't care who knew it. That was seven or eight months before the murder. One night Mrs. Mills stayed at Mrs. Barnhardt's house over night and went to New York the next day to meet Dr. Hall.

They were going to a show Mrs. Barnhardt said, she thought it was *Shuffle Along,* the Negro musical opus that had a long run on Broadway.

She said she had seen Mrs. Mills and Mrs. Hall together, but that Mrs. Hall seemed hostile toward her dead sister, notably at a Hallowe'en party at the church when the preacher danced twice with Mrs. Barnhardt and the rest of the evening with Mrs. Mills, and again on a trip to Bound Brook, when Mrs. Hall would not ride in the same car with Mrs. Mills.

Mrs. Barnhardt said her sister told her that Mrs. Minnie Clark liked Dr. Hall and was jealous of Eleanor. They had been good friends until their mutual regard for the pastor came between them.

She said Mrs. Mills always made her own clothes and identified a pair of sadly crumpled cheap cotton stockings taken from the dead woman that Simpson held out to her.

Under cross-examination by McCarter, of the defense, she admitted being present at the Mills home one night when Mills criticized his wife for her church activity.

"I care more for the little finger of Dr. Hall than I do for your whole body," the witness said her sister declared in the presence of her children, Charlotte and Danny.

Always there seems to be sneaking silently along the twisting trail of circumstantial evidence by which the prosecution is trying to lead the jury to the doors of Mrs. Hall and her brothers, the figure of one Felix Di Martini.

Always the figure is vague, unseen, but at frequent intervals in the testimony, a listener senses the presence in the weird mystery of Felix Di Martini, as they might sense a shadowy skulker in the house.

He is a private detective by occupation and was employed by Mrs. Hall, after the murder of her husband, four years ago.

The prosecution infers that Felix Di Martini was, in truth, employed by Mrs. Hall, to suppress evidence, and yesterday it produced a woman witness who swore Felix Di Martini offered to take up a $2,500 mortgage on her house, and give her something more if she would forget that she saw Henry Stevens in New Brunswick the day after the murder, when he claims he was at his home in Lavalette.

The witness was the buxom Mrs. Mary Demarest, cousin of Mrs. Minnie Clark, who is said to have been Mrs. Eleanor Mills' rival for the regard of Dr. Hall, and who afterward, the prosecution would have the jury believe, became a spy on Mrs. Mills and the rector for Mrs. Hall.

The stout Mrs. Demarest, her eyes snapping from behind her nose glasses, told of a visit to her by the ubiquitous Felix Di Martini who questioned her about her story that she had seen Henry Stevens on Friday, the day following the murder.

" 'I'm working on this case,' " Mrs. Demarest said Felix Di Martini told her. " 'Do you know you are hurting your cousin?' I told him I didn't think I was doing her any harm if she was not doing any wrong," said Mrs. Demarest. "Then he said, 'Listen you haven't seen Henry Stevens in New Brunswick.'

"Oh, but yes I have," the witness said she replied.

"Oh, no, but you didn't," said Felix Di Martini.

"Now," he said, "you know you are hurting Henry Stevens, too. You've just taken over this house, haven't you?"

"I said, 'Yes,' " the witness related, "then he said, 'You've got a mortgage on this place for $2,500.'

"I asked him how he knew, because I never told anyone, and he said, 'I found it out. How would you like to have that $2,500 and a little more to keep your mouth shut?' "

The witness paused and there was a stir in the court room.

"What else, if anything, was said?" inquired State Senator Alexander Simpson, of the prosecution.

"I said, 'No thank you,' " the witness answered quickly. "I said, 'if I wanted to clear the mortgage off on this house I would rather go to work in a factory in preference to taking Dr. Hall's blood money to keep my mouth shut!' "

Then she added warmly:

"I saw Henry Stevens, and I spoke to my cousin about it, and she said she saw him the night before."

The suave State Senator Case could not shake Mrs. Demarest on cross-examination.

The fiery Simpson gathered in all the loose ends of the State's case yesterday and said that he will conclude Thursday with "the pig woman," Mrs. Jane Gibson.

Simpson, a born showman, came bouncing into court in a shirt and collar with astonishing stripes. Not even Flo Ziegfeld would have dared such a garment, and Mr. Ziegfeld is the author of colored shirts in this country. The jury looked slightly dazed as it gazed upon Senator Simpson.

He promptly began setting the stage for one of his most dramatic scenes in the form of a picture show depicting the terrain of the celebrated De Russey's Lane. He had a stereopticon set up on one side of the court room, and during the noon recess the attorneys for the defense were given an opportunity of a sort of pre-view that they might judge just what he intended to do.

Then they interposed objections and the show was off. The defense has interposed many an objection during the trial. The smooth Senator Case, or the human snapping-turtle, Robert M. McCarter, are generally on their feet objecting to the maneuvers of Simpson. Willie Stevens looked a trifle disappointed when the stereopticon apparatus was removed from the show room. He had probably been anticipating a little entertainment.

Peter Summers, a slight dark man, wearing spectacles, testified that he worked for the mysterious Felix Di Martini as a private detective on the Hall-Mills case back in 1922, when Di Martini was stopping at the Hall home, and that his instructions were to go around cigar stores and pool rooms in New Brunswick, listen to what people were saying about Mrs. Hall and to get the names and addresses of any persons who might say anything offensive about her.

Summers also said he was instructed by Di Martini to go to the Max Motor Company in New Brunswick and report to a man named Mathews who put him to work. He said he was placed close to Freddy Reinhardt, a brother of the dead Mrs. Mills, and a man named Gibson, husband of "the pig woman," and told to find out what they knew.

Simpson has undoubtedly made greater headway toward making out a case against Mrs. Hall and her brothers than any time since the trial began. The testimony of the volunteer witness, Ira D. Nixon, that E. K. Soper told him he recognized Mrs. Hall and her brothers in De Russey's Lane the night of the murder would seem to be particularly damaging.

But the State's case depends largely upon the woman who will appear Thursday, Mrs. Jane Gibson.

November 19, 1926

"The Pig Woman" told her story yesterday—told it while stretched out, corpse-like and waxy, on an iron bed in front of the staring jury with a nervous doctor and nurse at her side, and a hospital odor filling the air of the jammed court room.

It was an unreal, creepy sort of business. Perhaps you can imagine attending a wake, and having the dead suddenly begin talking in and out-of-the-grave sort of voice. That is the way the sick "pig woman," officially Mrs. Jane Gibson, or Easton, talked.

She had finished. Court had taken a recess, and the jury had sidled out a rear door. The doctor and nurse and several big policemen were bundling "the pig woman" up in blankets and making ready to lift her back on the stretcher to carry her out to the ambulance that brought her from Jersey City.

From under the bed covers came a white hand, pointing at Mrs. Frances Noel Stevens Hall, who had been identified by "the pig woman" as a member of the slaughter squad she saw under the old crabapple tree in De Russey's Lane.

"So help me God, I told the truth!" cried "the pig woman."

"You know I told the truth," she said still pointing at Mrs. Hall.

The blood rushed into the pallid countenance of the woman who is accused of being a party to the murder of her husband and the choir singer. She was surrounded by relatives, the group including not only her brothers, but a number of the women members of the rich Stevens-Carpender family. One of the women laughed a light, tinkling laugh.

The doctors and the nurse and the big policemen kept on bundling up "the pig woman" and suddenly she dissolved into tears, weeping silently. Her chalky cheeks were wet, and her body shook under the blankets. The nurse drew a blanket up over her head, and "the pig woman" was borne from the room.

It was the first time she openly cried in years, this strange woman who farmed a lonely patch of ground and raised her pigs and chickens outside the little city of New Brunswick, friendless but unafraid. She has been a drifter along the rocky shores of life in her time, no doubt of that. She has seen much, and some of the things she has seen she wants to forget.

But there is one thing she apparently cannot forget, and that is the thing she saw under the crabapple tree in De Russey's Lane, fighting and shooting, and lights and faces, while a ghostly voice seems to forever ring in her ears—the voice of a woman, "screaming, screaming, screaming, screaming," as she babbled today in her testimony.

One of the faces she saw, "the pig woman" said, was the face of Mrs. Hall, as she knelt down, fixing something on the ground. Mrs. Hall wore no hat, she said.

The nurse and doctor raised "the pig woman" up in her bed so that she faced Mrs. Hall sitting with her relatives.

"Do you mind removing your hat, madam," asked Senator Simpson.

With a disdainful gesture, Mrs. Hall lifted her black hat from her head, disclosing a wealth of iron-gray hair very carefully groomed, as if she might have been expecting such a request. Mrs. Hall's eyes did not meet the eyes of the staring "pig woman."

"Is that the woman?" asked Senator Simpson.

"Yes," said "the pig woman," and her attendants lowered her down in the bed again.

You could see just her face and shoulders as she lay in bed. She looked ill enough, in all conscience.

She wanted to come, no doubt of that. She showed that by the eager manner in which she began talking from Simpson's first question. It was after eleven o'clock before the ambulance carrying her by slow stages got in from Jersey City, and there was a big crowd inside and outside the court room.

"The pig woman" is around fifty-three years old, and they say that in her prime she could toss a hundred-pound sack of oats around as if it were an apple. She was obviously quite weak today, and the doctor kept taking her temperature and feeling her pulse. Occasionally the nurse gave her a sip of water through a tube.

Her face was quite white. Her brown hair, showing little gray, hung in wisps around her face. "The pig woman" wears it bobbed.

She has a nervous affection which keeps her batting her blue eyes, and while she talked she continually rolled her head from side to side. Her hands are small, and look too frail today to have done the manual labor incidental to farm work.

She wore a white nightgown with a bathrobe of Turkish toweling over it. She often closed her eyes, but when they were open they showed wide and restless. She hesitated very little in answering questions. She has a square-cut chin, and a wide slit of a mouth. It is a hard-looking mouth. And yet "the pig woman" was probably handsome in her day and way.

For the first time since the trial started, Henry de la Bruyere Carpender, a cousin of Mrs. Hall, was in court. He is a prisoner in the county jail, charged with the murder of Dr. Hall. It is specifically for the murder of Mrs. Mills that Mrs. Hall and her brothers are being tried.

Henry de la Bruyere Carpender is a tall, bald man, well groomed, a Wall Street broker, and distinctly of that type. You couldn't miss him the first guess.

"The pig woman" said she saw Henry de la Bruyere under the crabapple tree and he was asked to step to her bedside. He advanced with no little poise and stood staring down into the eyes of "the pig woman."

"That's the man," she said faintly.

Henry de la Bruyere Carpender returned to his seat, still well poised. Her definite identifications of the persons she saw on the scene of the murder were Mrs. Hall, Henry Stevens and Carpender. She said she saw Mrs. Hall prior to the drama under the tree with a man she thought was a colored man, and this man the State claims, was the frog-eyed Willie Stevens.

"The pig woman" had been robbed of some corn, and she had tied her dog to a tree outside the house and she was sitting listening for marauders. She heard the dog bark, then she heard a rickety old wagon.

"It rattled, and rattled and rattled," she murmured.

She went toward her corn field, and she saddled up Jenny, her mule, and started out on the road to follow the wagon. She passed an automobile in De Russey's Lane in which she saw Mrs. Hall and the man she thought was a colored man.

Jenny, the mule, brayed, and fearing it would give warning to the corn thieves, she tied the mule to a tree and proceeded on foot.

"I heard voices, mumbling voices, men's voices and women's voices. I stood still. The men were talking, and a woman said very quick, 'Explain these letters.' The men were saying 'G—— d—— it,' and everything else. (She would not speak the oaths.) Somebody was hitting, hitting, hitting. I could hear somebody's wind go out and somebody said, 'Ugh.'

"Then somebody said, 'G—— d—— it, let go.' A man hollered. Then somebody threw a flashlight toward where they were hollering. Yes, and I see something glitter, and I see a man, and I see another man, like they were wrestling together. The light went out and I heard a shot. Then I heard something fall very heavy, and I run for the mule.

"I heard a woman's voice say after the first shot, 'Oh Henry,' easy, very easy, and the other began to scream, scream, scream so loud, 'Oh my, oh, my, oh, my,' so terrible loud. That woman was screaming, screaming, screaming, trying to get away or something, screaming, screaming, screaming, and I just about got my foot in the stirrup when 'Bang, bang, bang,' three quick shots."

Thus her story. The court room was very silent as she prattled from her bed.

When she got home and put her mule in the stable she got her foot wet and discovered she had lost her moccasin, and she started back looking for it. The moon was out by now, and going back to the spot where she thought she might have lost the moccasin she heard a screeching, like a screech owl.

She heard the voice of a man, then "it seems kind of like a woman hollered," and by the light of the moon she saw a big, white-haired woman kneeling down.

On cross-examination she said she thought at first that a white woman had been assaulted by a colored man, but she didn't go forward to interfere because she felt it was none of her business. She had trouble enough of her own. It served the woman right for being out with a colored man, "the pig woman" said.

Senator Case cross-examined her rather gently, but insistently, with the other members of the counsel for the defense frequently whispering suggestions to him. Case was obviously conscious of the dramatic effect of the scene. He spent some time dealing with her past, asking her about various men and her relations with them, but she denied them all.

Case asked her if she hadn't been known as Anna King, and if she wasn't a singer. She said no. Then he showed her a photo of two girls and wanted to know if that wasn't herself and her sister.

"Does it look like me?" demanded "the pig woman" rather tartly.

And finally she was taken away.

The doctor and the nurse watched her closely, often stopping the examination to give her a rest. Once they asked her if she didn't want the examination to go over another day, but she said no.

"It's the last time, and I want to get through with it," she said.

And she did, leaving behind wonderment that if she hadn't told the truth, and nothing but the truth, what motive could have possibly prompted her to risk her life to relate a story that may send four people to prison, if not to the electric chair.

November 21, 1926

By ugly inference today Alexander Simpson rattled what rumor has long been whispering is an old skeleton in the family closet of the proud Stevens-Carpender clan—that there is Negro blood in the veins of Willie Stevens.

Simpson mentioned the "bar sinister" in almost the first question he popped at Henry Stevens, first of the three defendants to take the witness stand.

Henry Stevens, flushing deeply, denied the inference, as he denied that he was anywhere near De Russey's Lane the night of the murder, or that he knew anything about it.

When the afternoon session began, Simpson continued the cross-examination of the defendant, the fiery little attorney growing more and more aggressive with each question.

He finally whipped out the grisly-looking surgeon's manikin, or dummy, that was used by the medical experts early in the case to demonstrate the wounds that killed Dr. Hall and Mrs. Mills, and planted it on the railing of the witness stand.

He faced it so the bulging, sightless eyes of the red and white plaster thing stared at the somewhat startled Henry. Simpson wanted the defendant to show him on the dummy just how he cut the throat of a bluefish. Case objected, then Simpson asked Henry to show the operation by motions in the air. Henry contented himself with a verbal explanation of the business.

"How old are you?" asked Senator Case as Henry Stevens took the stand in the morning.

"Fifty-seven," replied the witness, with a smile. "It happens to be my birthday today."

He doesn't look it. His heavy dark hair is well sprinkled with gray and so is his bristling moustache, but he carries himself well.

He has given the impression, in repose, of a grim fellow but his voice and manner belied his appearance when he began' testifying. He was pleasant, affable. He often smiled. His voice is firm, but has a kindly tone. He answered questions without hesitation, and clearly.

He always looks well-groomed. He wore a white linen shirt and a white starched turned-down collar. His tie was black with a blue stripe, a nifty bit of haberdashery. He wears spectacles without rims. He had on a dark, well-cut, neatly pressed suit of clothes. He had discarded the white sox he usually wears for gray silk. His shoes were black and high.

He sat with his shoulders squared back facing Case, his fingers laced together across his vest front. He had been freshly shaven and looked like a well-to-do business man.

He is of medium height and weighs around 175 pounds.

He strikes one as a man who keeps himself in rare physical condition at all times. The jurors watched him with more interest than they have yet given any witness, even "the pig woman."

Henry Stevens' wife kept the same seat she has occupied throughout the trial. She watched her husband from behind Augustus Snyder, Jr., and Russell Watson, members of the counsel for the defense, both young and both bald. A great many persons connected with this case seem to be bald-headed.

Mrs. Stevens has been wearing a hat of vivid green and atrocious design the past few days. She had on a gray coat with a big fur collar today. It is noticeable that Mrs. Hall and Mrs. Stevens have rarely conversed since the trial started. They scarcely look at each other, in fact.

It is said Mrs. Hall never approved of her brother Henry's wife and Mrs. Hall is probably not one who changes her mind.

Senator Case stood leaning against the press bench facing the witness as he interrogated Stevens. Senator Simpson sat listening with his chin in his hand and the light glinting on his oily locks. He occasionally interrupted the testimony by grumbling an objection. Sometimes he took notes.

Henry Stevens' story under ordinary circumstances would have been a deadly dull recital of a couple of dull days in a prosaic existence. But it has transpired that his smallest movement on Thursday, September 14, 1922, and the day following have become of the gravest importance to him. His very life may depend on the events of these days.

"You're a little deaf?" asked Case as Henry asked him to repeat a question.

"A little," replied the witness, and Case raised his voice.

There was much of fishing in Henry's tale, and of fish, too. He seemed to be always fishing at his seaside home at Lavalette, fifty miles from De Russey's Lane. He seemed to like to dwell on the size of the bluefish he caught at Lavalette. He lived there in the summer and in New York in the winter.

Several of the jurymen brightened up and gazed at Henry understandingly as he spoke of his fishing. They knew about fishing in New Jersey. Yet Henry does not strike one as the typical fishing type. The trap shooting that he followed as an expert for the Du Pont company for years, would seem to fit him to a T however. He conducted a sort of demonstration school for the Du Ponts on Young's Million-Dollar Pier at Atlantic City, as a sort of advertising stunt to get the public interested in trap shooting.

It has been said that a dead-shot must have held the pistol with which Dr. Hall and his sweetheart were killed. One bullet in the head finished the dominie and three bullets in the head, placed close together, did for Mrs. Mills. The State has intimated that Henry Stevens, an expert with firearms, fired the shots, but

Henry said today he had confined himself to shotguns. He said he had not owned a pistol since 1915, although he bought a .38-calibre automatic for Mrs. Stevens a couple of years ago.

He fished on the beach at Lavalette part of the day of the murder, he said. This Lavalette is a little place on a strip of beach between Barnegat Bay and the ocean, eight or nine miles south of Point Pleasant. His wife was in New York. He had supper at six o'clock prepared by Mrs. Evanson, a woman of Lavalette, who helped Mrs. Stevens with her housework. He went out fishing again and remained on the beach until after nine o'clock. The fishing at Lavalette is mainly surf casting.

He went to bed about 10:30 and was up before sunrise the following morning to catch mullet for bait. He explained about mullet to Senator Case. You have to catch 'em before it gets light. A mullet is a small fish esteemed most appetizing by larger fish.

Henry Stevens fixed his presence on the beach at Lavalette by a number of small incidents such as weighing a bluefish for a neighbor. He recalled that it was a pretty fair-size bluefish, at that. He detailed his movements on Friday minutely, apparently filling in every little gap with some prosaic incident.

He said he did not go to New Brunswick until he got a telegram from one of the Carpenders that Dr. Hall was dead and did not know what happened until he bought a newspaper en route.

"Did you have anything to do with the murder of Dr. Edward Wheeler Hall and Mrs. Eleanor Mills?" asked Case finally.

"No," said the witness, simply.

He paled perceptibly as he turned to face Senator Simpson for his cross-examination. He seemed to sense what was coming.

The State's attorney did not get out of his chair as he asked the first question, but presently he was on his feet, close to Henry Stevens and shouting.

"You say Mr. Willie Stevens is your brother?" asked Simpson.

"Yes," said the witness.

"Is he your full brother?"

"Yes."

"Where was he born?"

"At Aiken, South Carolina."

"You know there is no birth record of him in the church in South Carolina where there is a birth record of yourself and sister, do you not?" demanded Simpson.

"No," said the witness.

"Have you any knowledge on the subject?" persisted Simpson.

"No."

Henry said he was about two years older than Willie.

"Is he by the same father and mother?" asked Simpson.

"Yes."

"He is not by a mulatto?" asked the State's attorney, unfeelingly.

The witness turned as white as his collar but he said no, without apparent heat. Willie looked at Simpson a little startled but Mrs. Hall gave no sign she heard and it is likely they all expected the question.

"Can you explain the differences in your faces?" demanded Simpson.

"I cannot," said Henry.

Henry Stevens clasped one knee in his hand, as if to steady himself as Simpson popped questions at him about his knowledge of small-arms. He insisted he had no knowledge of any guns but shotguns despite a statement made by him in 1922 and read by Simpson which indicated quite a familiarity with pistols.

"It would take a pretty good man with an automatic to put three shots within a space of four inches in a woman's head, wouldn't it?" asked Simpson.

"It depends on how close he was," replied Henry.

"Suppose he was six feet away and it was dark and he could only tell by the direction of the voice, it would take pretty good marksmanship?" asked Simpson.

"I don't think it would take marksmanship at all," said Henry.

Simpson cross-examined him very briskly on discrepancies in different statements. He stepped up to the rail of the witness stand within two feet of the witness, Henry staring at him defiantly.

He said his relations with Dr. Hall had always been cordial although he had not approved of his sister's marriage to the dominie. He was not present at the time. It was a shock to him, he said, when he heard of Dr. Hall's murder, but he admitted he didn't go to see the body.

He couldn't seem to explain just why he hadn't hastened to see his sister and brother Willie after they were arrested for the murder.

"You didn't go to see them because you were afraid someone would identify you?" shouted Simpson.

"No," said Henry.

November 23, 1926

Mr. Arthur Applegate's "big blue" waggled ghostly fins through the proceedings in the Hall-Mills murder trial the greater part of yesterday.

That was some fish. It will probably always remain the most historic fish ever captured in the vicinity of the little town of Lavalette, where "big blues" are by no means uncommon.

By Mr. Arthur Applegate's "blue," many of the leading citizens identify the night that Henry Stevens is alleged to have been lending a helping hand in the murder of Reverend Hall and Mrs. Mills, as the very same night that Mr. Applegate snatched that "big blue" out of the surf at Lavalette.

They came to the court house in Somerville in a small drove today to explain this to the jury. Some of them couldn't remember anything else in particular, but they all remembered Mr. Applegate's "blue," and Henry Stevens' weighing of the piscatorial trophy for Mr. Applegate four years ago.

Most of them quit the witness stand glowering at State Senator Simpson, who seemed to be strangely avid for details concerning Mr. Applegate's "blue" and the circumstances ante- and postdating that famous subject for a broiler. If looks could kill, Senator Simpson would undoubtedly be quite as dead as Dr. Hall or Mrs. Mills, or even Mr. Applegate's "blue" at this writing.

He was very personal, and pertinent, with the citizens of Lavalette, and they didn't like him a little bit. But by the time the witnesses—eleven of them—male and female—got through, they had Henry Stevens pretty well established on the beach at Lavalette weighing Mr. Applegate's "blue," fifty-odd miles from De Russey's loving lane at about the hour when somebody was pumping bullets into the heads of the Reverend Hall and Mrs. Mills under the crabapple tree, and cutting Mrs. Mills' throat.

At least they had him there to their own, and apparently to the satisfaction of the numerous lawyers for the defense, because they began building up an alibi for Willie Stevens, who may take the stand in his own behalf tomorrow.

Willie's eyes, which bulge like a Pekingese's, were beaming this afternoon with pleasure as he heard his family physician, Dr. Lawrence Runyon—no relation to the affiant—of New Brunswick, relate that he is above the average in intelligence and reads books that would make fools of "a lot of us." Perhaps the doctor meant only the Runyons.

But Willie, too, joined in the general glowering at Senator Simpson when the State's attorney began cross-examining Dr. Runyon on the subject of epilepsy and asked questions that were designed to show Willie as a bit of a "nut."

Willie's bushy hair seemed to get more rigid as he listened to Senator Simpson, but the doctor's friendly replies appeared to reassure him.

Mr. Arthur Applegate was really more glowersome at Senator Simpson than any of the others. The delegation from Lavalette somehow couldn't satisfy the Senator that Henry Stevens was weighing that "big blue" the night of the murder.

He kept finding little discrepancies in what some of them said today bearing upon Mr. Applegate's "blue" and what they had previously said. The Senator was almost querulous about the matter, especially with Mr. Applegate.

Mr. Applegate is a big, husky gentleman, who looks like an old-time Iowa tackle of the days when they didn't use anything but the flying wedge, but his voice was mild, and slightly sibilant, due to the absence of certain of his teeth, and his manner was deprecating.

He has iron-gray hair and a friendly aspect, and he wore a sweater under his coat. He followed to the stand a Mrs. Maizie

Applegate, a ruddy-cheeked, healthy looking lady, in a black caracul coat. She has a square chin, a slightly strident voice and a determined manner. She told just a trifle shrilly how she saw Henry Stevens on the beach around ten o'clock the night of September 14, 1922, when Mr. Applegate caught the "big blue" and Henry weighed it.

"You are the husband of the last witness?" Mr. Simpson asked Mr. Applegate, curiously.

"Yes," said Mr. Applegate, softly, and in a most resigned tone.

He had told Senator Case on direct examination that he had quite some trouble that evening catching fish.

"I had several bites, and I kind of had a little complaint in regard to the hook being too large," he said. "The fish were running small, at least I thought they were, because I saw a couple caught which weighed a pound practically or maybe a pound and a half, and Mr. Stevens gave me a hook that I caught the blue on."

"Quite a sizable fish, was it?" asked Senator Case with interest, while the Jersey jurors leaned forward apparently in keen sympathy with this chatter.

"Fairly good-sized, yes," said Mr. Applegate, crossing his legs with the air of a raconteur.

"Excited some interest on the part of those around you?"

"It excited me more than anybody else, I guess," said Mr. Applegate contentedly.

"Did you on the third of September, while being examined under oath at Tom's River, say you thought the day this blue fish was caught was Friday," demanded Senator Simpson when he seized upon Mr. Applegate for cross-examination.

"No, not on the third," replied Mr. Applegate, uncrossing his long legs.

The State's attorney handed him a document, and asked:

"Is this your signature?"

Mr. Applegate held his tongue.

"Don't you know your signature?"

"I practically do," said Mr. Applegate, when Senator Simpson persisted in the question.

"Is this your signature?" worried the attorney.

"Well, I wouldn't swear to it," said Mr. Applegate. "It looks some like it."

In this document is said to be a statement by the captor of the celebrated "big blue" that he could not tell what night the fish was weighed.

"You have a peculiar memory," suggested Senator Simpson.

Thereupon the harassed Mr. Applegate turned, even as the well-known worm:

"I think I am about as peculiar as you are," he snorted.

"In memory?" queried the surprised Simpson.

"In all ways," replied Mr. Applegate.

Later on, when the State's attorney asked him if he is still a carpenter he said:

"I have not changed my occupation, and I have not changed my truth. I have a little sympathy in my heart, and that is more than you have, Mr. Simpson."

But of this crack Senator Simpson, for a wonder, took no notice.

Mr. Applegate said that at the examination mentioned by Simpson he had been called a d—— liar and a perjurer by Inspector Underwood, of the Jersey City Police.

"But was Sheriff Grant, of your county, there, and isn't he a good friend of yours?" inquired Simpson.

"It don't seem so," said Mr. Applegate, mournfully.

Mrs. Agnes Storer, organist of Dominie Hall's church, was recalled by the defense, and testified by her record of choir attendance that Ralph V. Gorsline was present at the morning and evening services on October 1, singing away with the choir when he was supposed to be in New York telling Mr. "Greasy Vest" Garvin, the private detective, of certain incidents in De Russey's Lane the night of the murder.

"The testimony was that he was in New York the week of October 1, not any specific day," said Senator Simpson, and Judge Parker, admitted Mrs. Storer's statement until the detective's testimony can be looked up.

"What did Mr. Gorsline sing?" demanded Simpson, on cross-examination.

"Baritone," said the lady. "He often sang solos."

"What was his favorite hymn?" asked Simpson.

" 'If You Love Me Keep My Commandments,' " said Mrs. Storer, and even the reporters, with a memory before them of the lank vestryman who kept his trysts in De Russey's Lane in a parked automobile with the lights out, almost collapsed under the strain.

Dr. Runyon, bald and a bit belligerent, and not entirely up to the Runyon type in pulchritude, described Willie as not as far advanced as some of us in school, perhaps not absolutely normal mentally but able to take care of himself.

The doctor said he hadn't come as a mental expert, merely as Willie's physician. He said Willie's personal habits were all right, and that he was never sick enough to be in bed.

"Do you know anything about him starting a fire in the yard and putting on a fireman's hat and coming out with a bucket of water to extinguish it?" asked Simpson.

The doctor said no. He said the only time he ever saw Willie worked up was when he came home from his examination in connection with the murder in Somerville four years ago. Simpson tried to draw something from him on epilepsy, but the doctor declined to qualify as an expert.

"Isn't it a matter of common gossip that Napoleon and Julius Caesar were epileptics?" asked Senator Case, but the Court wouldn't let them go into that.

James P. Major, warden of the Somerset County Jail, said Willie had always been tranquil under his charge, and John J. Kline, a New Brunswick fireman, testified that he never saw Willie in a derby hat or heard him stutter, which testimony is designed to offset the early story of the couple who placed a disheveled and excited Willie hunting the Parker home on the night of the murder, stuttering and wearing a derby. Willie hung out around the firehouse, playing cards and ran errands for the firemen, Kline said.

"Do you mean to say that this gentleman who did no work and

lived at the home of his sister, a lady of position, ran errands for firemen?" demanded Simpson, as if vastly surprised. "Well, did you ever hear him say one day as he saw Mrs. Mills pass the firehouse. 'I'll get that b——h yet. She's made more trouble for my sister than anyone living?' "

"No," said Kline.

And Willie smiled at him from across the room as an old acquaintance.

November 25, 1926

"Crazy Willie" was well satisfied with himself, and so were all his relatives, as he stepped down from the witness stand to make way for a long parade of witnesses for the defense that included ecclesiastics of the Episcopal church, in vestments; well-dressed, haughty women, and surreptitious customers of De Russey's loving lane, and finally Harry de la Bruyere Carpender.

Promptly the chief of the prosecution objected to the question concerning Harry de la Bruyere Carpender's presence under the crabapple tree, on the ground that the State is not trying Carpender at this time, but the witness' answer came ahead of the objection, and "No, I was not," will undoubtedly always be Harry de la Bruyere Carpender's reply to the same question.

Senator Simpson completed his cross-examination of Willie Stevens this morning in short order, and never did he drop the strangely confidential manner that he adopted with the witness when Willie took the stand Tuesday.

He did not attempt to harass or excite Willie, and while some said it was a weak cross-examination I thought it amazingly skillful. Simpson undoubtedly realized, from the beginning, that great sympathetic appeal to the jury, and he took care not to appear in the light of bully-ragging the grown-up man who remains in many ways a mental child.

Willie was as bland and naive as ever, but he seems to have grown more tolerant of the friendly Simpson. He said he had never been to Mrs. Mills' house but twice, once when he took her a Christmas present from Mrs. Hall.

Simpson pressed him closely, but politely on his exact movements the night of the murder, and finally asked:

"Now about this epilepsy. You say you have never suffered with epilepsy; would you object if I had a physician not now, but during the trial—would you object to his talking to you about this epilepsy?"

"I would rather consult my lawyer," said Willie, with surprising swiftness. "Is that permissible?" he added, as if anxious not to overstep the rules.

"Certainly—you show good judgment," said Simpson, and Willie beamed.

He was commencing to half like this affable little man. He was commencing to enjoy himself. He turned and smiled at Judge Parker and asked if he spoke distinctly enough.

"And you never on the night of the murder inquired for the Parker house, near the lane of Mr. and Mrs. Dixon, whom you saw on the stand?" asked Simpson.

"I never did any such thing," replied Willie, with heat.

When the State's attorney said, "That's all," Willie gave him a bright thank you. He may have been extremely well drilled in his story, as the prosecution suspects, but he has a remarkable memory, and made a strong witness for the defense.

There followed a long line of witnesses beginning with the Reverend J. Marvin Pettit, who looks just that way—I mean just like a man named Reverend J. Marvin Pettit, and who succeeded the dead Dominie Hall in the Church of St. John the Evangelist. It came out, by the way, during the day, that the Reverend Hall was buried in his vestments.

The Reverend Pettit, big and bland, produced the church records on Willie's birth.

Professor Raymond Smith Dugan, which John Bunn, the court crier, pronounced "Doogan," a distinct affront to the Philadelphia Dugans, gave testimony that the moon rose over De Russey's Lane the night of the murder at 11:30 Eastern Standard Time. He is a professor of astronomy at Princeton, bald and a bit skinny, but most astronomical looking.

Mrs. Mabel Clickener, in a long brown coat, young, and thin-faced, a daughter of Mrs. Demarest, the woman who put Henry Stevens in New Brunswick the day after the murder and also placed the Reverend Hall and Mrs. Mills in a New Brunswick park with Ralph V. Gorsline and Mrs. Minnie Clark spying on them, denied her mother's tale so far as it referred to the park.

"You work for Johnson and Johnson, don't you?" asked Simpson, bringing, for the first time in the case, the names of those big porous-plaster boys of New Brunswick, with whom one of the Carpenders is related by marriage.

The witness said she did.

George Hubener, a park officer, never saw Reverend Hall and Mrs. Mills in the park. He was long, and thin, and not very talky.

John Chambers, in spats, the first to appear in court, a huge wrist-watch, a fancy kerchief sticking out of his breast pocket, and a rather dandified appearance generally, for one of his years, testified about Mrs. Hall sending her garments out to be dyed black.

Mrs. Moncure Carpender, the first of the Carpender crowd to appear, wore a brown coat trimmed in sable and was very reticent. She testified she had seen no spots on the garments. Mrs. Anna Bearman, who is a cousin of Mrs. Hall, and whose husband is head of the big bluing manufactory in New Brunswick, denied being in an automobile in front of the Hall home on Saturday, September 16, 1922, as some witnesses have said.

Canon Wells, who is bald, wears horn glasses, and has a most ecclesiastical appearance, said he was at the Hall home the day of the funeral and saw no scratches on Mrs. Hall's face. Reverend Edward Vickers Stevenson, a Mrs. Bennett, and others testified to the same thing.

Mrs. Jennie Wahler, denied that she was in De Russey's Lane with Robert Ehrling, who said "the pig woman" passed them there the night of the murder, and Willard Staub, a gallus-looking youth, testified that Ehrling had told him he could get some money by saying he was there that night.

Ferd David, a county detective of Middlesex County, was on the stand again—big, bald and bullet-headed, and testified that "the pig woman" had never identified Henry and Willie Stevens in the office of the prosecutor, and that Mrs. Gibson told him she never got off her mule in De Russey's Lane that night, but under cross-examination he admitted that he did testify before the Grand Jury that "the pig woman" had identified the pair.

It was a mixed-up day with a lot of testimony getting in.

November 27, 1926

"Felix Di Martini," bawled old John Bunn, the sonorous crier in the court of Oyer and Terminer in Somerville, just before noon yesterday, and the spectators went "buzz-zz-zz-zz," and everybody felt a little bit shivery and excited.

The jurors haunched themselves over to the edge of their chairs, the newspaper reporters seized fresh wads of copy paper, the photographers backed against the western wall of the witness stand.

Then everybody fell back again as they got a good look at him. It was plain to be seen that the general thought in terms of disappointment was: "So that's Felix Di Martini, is it?"

It wasn't to be expected that he would come to court with horns and a tail, but he had a right to look sinister, at least.

We had been hearing of him as Mrs. Hall's private detective going pad-padding around after the murder, listening, watching —now snooping under windows of terrified females, now fastening "piercing black eyes" on lone, lorn women, now offering bribes, and now making dire threats in what the State conceives to be an effort on the part of Mrs. Hall to choke off any evidence damaging to her and her brothers in connection with the massacre of the parson and his sweetheart.

All of which Felix Di Martini may have done, only he didn't look the part as he stepped out of the shadow of the case today, called by the defense, with horn-rimmed spectacles riding his nose, a lead pencil sticking out of one vest pocket, and a cigar out of another, to spend a bad half hour with State Senator Alexander Simpson, the chief of the prosecution.

And when Felix Di Martini finally moved off the stand this afternoon, Captain Harry Walsh, a nimble-looking member of the Jersey City Police Department, tugged at his coat sleeve with one hand, and gave him a warrant with the other, charging Felix Di Martini with being an accessory after the fact to the murder of Preacher Hall and Mrs. Mills.

All of which comes out of what the prosecution regards as Felix Di Martini's pernicious activities in Mrs. Hall's behalf some four years ago. The representatives of the State probably were not looking for Di Martini's appearance. He gum-shoed into town from New York last night with his attorney, State Senator J. H. Harrison, former prosecutor of Essex County. There are almost enough State senators in the Halls-Mills case to constitute a Senate, quorum.

Di Martini remained hidden until yesterday morning, entering the court room shortly before noon, and disappearing into an ante-room. The luncheon recess was about to be announced at 12:30 when Senator Case called for him and Di Martini came out of the ante-room and advanced to the stand.

"Get him now," barked Simpson, to Captain Walsh, and big Inspector Underwood, also of the Jersey City Police.

The officers moved on the uneasy Di Martini, but Senator Case bustled up the bench and said to Judge Parker:

"Your Honor, I want this man sworn now before recess in order that he may not be arrested until he has testified, and that he be kept in the custody of the Court."

Which was done.

He was released on $3,000 bail by Judge Cleary following the afternoon session, at which he did not exactly shine as a witness for the defense. In fact, Willie Stevens eyed him in plumb disgust as Di Martini floundered under Simpson's questions. Willie is now by way of an expert on the gentle art of witnesses.

Let us have another look at Felix Di Martini as he sits on the stand assuring Senator Simpson that he had desired to solve the Hall-Mills murder no matter whom it hurt, yet admitting that with all his seventeen years of police experience behind him he hadn't thought it necessary to see the only reputed eye-witness, "the pig woman" and learn her story because he didn't believe it in the first place, and in the second place was "working on another angle."

That angle, he said, was an investigation of the drab Jimmy Mills, at whom the defense, by inference, early in the case pointed the old finger of suspicion.

His manner was conciliatory. The black eyes that "the pig woman" described as "piercing," carried a hunted expression today. Once or twice he glared with great fury at Senator Simpson, only to lapse back into conciliation. He frequently mistered the Senator. Once he looked as if he was about to leap out of his chair at Simpson, but quickly relaxed again.

He is a chunky-built fellow of medium height, with a shock of curly black hair slightly streaked with gray, and a Roman nose with large nostrils. He has bad teeth. His complexion is dark, his eyebrows black and thick, and his jowls were black with stubble today. An Italian, as you perhaps gather from his name.

He is around forty.

He wore a dark suit, with white linen and a black tie, and brown shoes. He had a good record in the New York Police Department for years before he became a private detective.

For a man of his experience, he did not seem quite logical as a witness, to say the least. He presented bills indicating that he cost Mrs. Hall a matter of $5,090 for working on the case about 121 days.

He not only denied that he had ever seen Mrs. Jane Gibson, but he also denied about everything else that has been said about him in the case. He was particularly emphatic in denying that he offered Mrs. Mary Demarest $2,500 to take up the mortgage on her home, if she would forget that she thought she had seen Henry Stevens in New Brunswick the day following the murder.

"Didn't you speak to Mrs. Demarest and call her by her first name in an elevator in Brooklyn the day you were arrested?" demanded Simpson.

"I did not," said Di Martini.

He stood out as the best denier that has yet taken the stand for either side.

Di Martini was troubled with a little cough as he testified. Sometimes he took a couple of coughs between answers as Simpson plunged at him with something of the old Simpsonesque manner that has been missing the last couple of days.

He denied that he ever even knew of the existence of a Mrs. Demarest, denied that he was employed before the murder to shadow the Reverend Hall and Mrs. Mills, a new inference by Simpson, denied that he ever visited Jimmy Mills, and tried to make him admit that he owned a butcher-knife.

He denied that he tried to "frame" Jimmy in any way; denied threatening William Phillips, a watchman; denied threatening one of his former operatives on this case, Peter Summers, when he heard Peter intended testifying for the State.

He spoke up right pertly in his answers, and occasionally gave Simpson a slight argument. Once he pointed out that Simpson asked him two questions in one. When Simpson tried to go into his activities in the Hall home, where he lived for some time, the defense objected, and Simpson very briefly stated the whole idea of the prosecution with reference to Di Martini when he said: "We claim the way the defendants acted in putting detectives in the house was not the action of innocent persons."

November 28, 1926

For one fleeting moment late this afternoon it looked as if the chilled-steel nerve of Mrs. Hall was giving way as she sat white-lipped, and gray of face, on the witness stand with Alexander Simpson wolfing questions at her.

Out of a conversational calm of cross-examination that had all the aspects of a social tête-à-tête, the little New Jersey State Senator suddenly began belting away at her with fury.

"You did not suspect your husband with Mrs. Mills, did you?" he asked, quietly enough.

"No," said Mrs. Hall, gazing at him with the same cool, level look she had been giving since he started his cross-examination a few minutes previously. The fingers of her ungloved right hand were picking at the tips of the gray silk glove on her left hand, the only sign of nervousness she had betrayed all afternoon.

"You did not know anything about Mrs. Mills' movements, did you? You did not know whether she had lovers or not?" said Simpson, still keeping his low pianissimo.

"No," said Mrs. Hall, gently.

"You had no reason to suspect anything between her and your husband?"

"None whatever."

Now Simpson moved closer to the black-robed, wintry gray woman fenced off from him by the railing of the witness stand. His voice rose.

"And yet you went to Mills, the morning after, and murdered him—put your husband with Mrs. Mills, and murdered him. You said, 'They have met with foul play, they are together, they are dead.' Didn't you say that in the morning when you went to Mr. Mills?"

A startled expression came into Mrs. Hall's eyes. The nature of the question, or rather the manner in which it was couched, which was in the strange metaphor of the law, was enough to startle anybody perhaps.

"I don't think I said so—no," she said, hesitatingly.

Robert H. McCarter hastened to her aid.

"It doesn't appear that she said any such thing," he interposed.

"It does," replied Simpson, "Mr. Toolan (an earlier witness) has sworn that she said it."

"Suppose you ask her first whether she said it," suggested Judge Parker.

"Did you say to Mr. Toolan that on that morning after the murder you went to Mr. Mills and he said, 'My wife has been away all night,' and you said, 'They have been away together, they have met foul play, they are dead?'"

"I don't think I said that," replied Mrs. Hall, her voice almost faltering.

"You don't know whether you said it?" demanded Simpson loudly.

"No, I don't think I said that," she answered, without confidence.

"Say you did not say it," insisted Simpson.

"I say I don't think I said it," she answered.

"Why can't you make a direct answer that you did say it, or did not say it?" demanded Simpson.

"If you have it down there I must have said it," the woman they called "The Iron Widow," answered. "But I don't think I did say that."

"Oh," said Simpson, "you know whether you said it, yes or no."

"I don't think I said that," contended Mrs. Hall, her voice very low.

"Did you say it, or didn't you?" cried Simpson, and the court room was very quiet as the spectators watched Mrs. Hall, who up to that time had been as composed as if she were chatting in her own drawing room. Her fingers kept plucking at her glove tips.

"Did you say it, or didn't you?" Simpson shouted.

"I said I don't think I said that."

"Why can't you make a direct denial?" he asked.

"If you have it down there I must have said it, but I am quite sure that I did not say that," she answered wearily. Then, suddenly, Judge Parker glanced at the big clock over the door and announced an adjournment of court until Monday morning.

It was almost as if a chap in the prize ring had been reeling around, a bit groggy under a punch, only to be saved by the bell.

Mrs. Hall quickly left the stand and was as quickly surrounded by a cordon of her relatives, and soon disappeared from the court room.

Up to the last few moments of the cross-examination she had impressed all listeners as a remarkable witness, quite as good as Willie, whom she admitted needed the care of others "in some respects," and better than Brother Henry, whose tears on the witness stand were spoken of by the biting Simpson as he pressed

Mrs. Hall for her reason why she hadn't notified Henry of her husband's disappearance.

"The affection in your family is notable," he said. "You noticed it when your brother cried on the stand when his mother's name was mentioned. It has been a subject of remark among your friends how close you, Mr. William and Mr. Henry have been in trouble. But you never communicated all day Friday with your brother Henry, but you let the day drag along and you went to bed yourself without indicating to Mr. Henry in any way that you were in trouble?"

"I thought it was more natural to notify Mr. Hall's sister, Mrs. Bonner," she said.

In her examination at the hands of her own attorney, she had protested her love for her husband, the dead dominie, and her faith in his fidelity and devotion, and of her ignorance of his relations with the choir singer.

"During all the time that Dr. Hall was writing the love letters you have heard here, did you not see any change in his demeanor?" demanded Simpson.

"Absolutely not," she said, firmly.

"He was just as affectionate and just as devoted and just as loyal all during the time that he was writing that his heart was full of love for Eleanor Mills, that he loved to hear her dear voice come in through the window singing the hymns, that he did not know how he could do without her, that his whole heart was filled with her, all during that time you, as a well-educated woman of the world, never noticed any difference in him?"

The vaguest shadow of a smile flitted over her face, perhaps at the grandiloquent manner in which Simpson spoke of love, but her voice was still firm as she replied:

"Absolutely not."

Nor did she flinch when her own counsel, McCarter, asked her if she had murdered her husband and the choir singer in De Russey's Lane four years ago, or had anything to do with the crime.

Her voice lifted ever so little as she said no.

December 2, 1926

Old Robert H. McCarter, a man of great forensic violence, boomed at the jury all afternoon yesterday in the first summing up for the defense, but before he started off, the prosecution tossed in the towel.

That is to say, it conceded that it is licked.

"You might just as well try this case before twelve trees," firecrackered the obviously much irritated State Senator Simpson, while arguing a motion for a mistrial on the ground of misconduct by the jury, which motion was later denied him.

"Perhaps with more satisfaction," he added bitterly. "Because the trees in the course of time will bud, and blossom, and these jurors never will."

After the session of court, and with the little chapel-like court room still echoing with Mr. McCarter's vocal thunders and lightnings against all and sundry who had testified for the State against Mrs. Frances Noel Stevens Hall and her brothers, Willie and Henry Stevens, the special prosecutor admitted he has no hope of getting a verdict of conviction from the twelve good men and true of Somerset County, who have been listening to the case for twenty-two days.

But he intimated that Mr. McCarter might need some of his oratory later on. Senator Simpson said that he is going into the Supreme Court immediately at the conclusion of the trial and ask for a "foreign" jury to try these same defendants or Harry de la Bruyere Carpender on the indictments that will still be pending.

You see Mrs. Hall and Willie and Henry Stevens are being tried only for the alleged murder of Mrs. Mills. You can get 100 to 1 that they will walk out of the court house free of that charge within the next few days. The price was never shorter than 2 to 1 and has steadily gone up.

But there still remains the charge that they murdered the preacher of philandering proclivities, and the suave and polished Wall Street broker, Harry de la Bruyere Carpender, is in the county jail on that same charge.

Senator Simpson presented a batch of affidavits yesterday be-

fore Mr. McCarter began roaring "rascals" and other pleasantries
at the witnesses for the State, to the effect that some of the jurors
have been gabbing loquaciously about the case outside of the
court room and slumbering in their chairs inside the room, that
they have been unguarded and have been calling him—Simpson—
the most unlovely names.

"I say these affidavits demonstrate there can be no fair verdict
in the case," he said. "They demonstrate the bias and the prejudice
of these jurors, and that on the second day of the trial before the
evidence was clearly under way some of them practically said
they would not convict if the murder was committed before their
faces."

He made his motion just as court convened this morning, and
the jurors were excluded during the hearing, although old Mr.
McCarter and Senator Case wanted the twelve good men and true
to hear what Simpson was saying about them.

It is quite likely they had a fair idea at that.

They looked somewhat sheepish as they were herded out a side
door by the constables. They are not supposed to read the newspapers during the trial, but probably rumors had come to their
ears of the to-do over them.

Senator Simpson practically slammed the door on the last
juror and while advancing his argument he suddenly turned on
the defendants and said in a rasping voice:

"Never was such a situation in the administration of justice or
the trial of a homicide case. Here is a social tea every day, port
wine drunk; and these defendants surrounded by their relatives,
and snickering sneering counsel.

"Never was a homicide case tried in such an atmosphere as
this."

Among the affidavits he presented was one from Gilbert E. Van
Doran, the aged proprietor of the Colonial Hotel, where the jury
is housed, and which told of overhearing conversation among the
jurymen, in which some of the jurors denounced Simpson, and
"the pig woman," and said they would show Hudson County it
couldn't come into Somerset County and run things.

He specifically named Jurors Roache and Pope, and said that

the day "the pig woman" testified, they were joking about the good meals and good times the jurors were having, and he said to them:

"Wait until you get locked up in the jury room. Your good times will stop. You will have to pay for your own feed."

To which either Juror Pope or John Young replied, Van Doran swore: "Oh, h—l, we won't be in there twenty minutes."

The venerable Van Doran, who is far up in the seventies, was waiting outside in case they wanted him on the witness stand. He is not well, and a doctor was called for him while he waited.

Another affidavit was from Mrs. Emma Simpson, the housekeeper at the Colonial, who said the jurors often used the telephone without being under guard, while the other affidavit related to them holding conversations in the street with friends, and to some of them apparently sleeping in the court room.

Charlotte Mills, the daughter of the dead woman, was one of the affidavit makers. She said she saw Juror Tillman, unescorted by constables, talking with Mr. McCarter and Attorney Studor, of the defense, in the court room although the lawyer's explanation of this is that they were condoling with Tillman on the death of his brother, which occurred during the trial.

Senator Case, who lives in Somerville, waved his hands in the most deprecating manner as he spoke of the aged Van Doran. The Senator said everyone knew Van Doran is as cross-grained as a knot. Later, in some horror, he speedily denied Senator Simpson's statement that he had mentioned Van Doran as a cross-grained nut. There is vast difference in Somerset County between a knot and a nut.

Judge Parker finally announced that he would take Senator Simpson's application for a mistrial under advisement, then both sides added to the over a million words of testimony already produced by the case, by putting on witnesses to clear up certain points in the testimony that had gone before. The State's rebuttal rested at 11:10, then the defense put on a couple of other witnesses.

Mr. McCarter, in reply to a query from Judge Parker, said

he wanted all afternoon to do his talking and Senator Case said
he would require at least a couple of hours.

As soon as court convened for the afternoon session, Judge
Parker announced that Senator Simpson's motion was denied,
whereupon Mr. McCarter advanced, clearing his throat, and
rattling a wad of yellowish note paper, on which he had scrib-
bled many notes. He took a position just in front of the jury, and
presently his voice was jarring the window panes.

He is a bulldoggish looking man, with an underlip that pro-
trudes like a red dashboard. Of about medium height, he is bull-
doggy-built, chunky, red of jowl and bald of bean. He is always
very well groomed. He wears half section eye-glasses about mid-
way of his nose, so they seem to be riding most precariously, and
his eyes peer out over the rims as often as they look through the
glasses.

He is one of those old-fashioned spellbinders. He is a former
attorney-general of the State of New Jersey, and argument before
a jury is obviously his long suit. He makes many facial grimaces,
and stamps his foot, and even becomes a bit tearful as he talks.
At least, he did yesterday afternoon, especially when he spoke
most feelingly of "Willie Stevens—God bless him."

Willie sat right up in his chair, and beamed behind his glasses.
He regarded Mr. McCarter with vast interest thereafter, as obviously a man who appreciated him. Mrs. Hall, in her usual black
dress and hat, and banked in by her relatives, listened intently
and often smiled, too, while Henry Stevens seemed greatly entertained. Mr. McCarter was speaking specifically for Mrs. Hall and
Willie, but he paid some attention to Henry's alibi, too.

He was still booming away as court adjourned at four o'clock
with two hours and a half of oratory behind him, and he had not
yet touched on "the pig woman" that Senator Simpson surmised
would take Mr. McCarter another hour. Occasionally Mr. McCarter took a shot at Senator Simpson, who sat with his chair tilted
against the press stand, listening, and Simpson would come right
back at him.

Mr. McCarter was disappointed, he said, that Edward H.
Schwartz, of the Newark police, one of the fingerprint experts

for the defense, wasn't present. He said Schwartz was a rascal, and that he would tell him so the first time they met in the street.

He said that the calling-card that the State alleges is the card that was found stuck up at the feet of the dead dominie is not the same card at all, and that the fingerprints on the famous exhibit S-17 presented by the State are a complete fraud.

He was also regretful, he roared, that Phil Payne, the editor of the *Daily Mirror*, the New York paper that dug up the case after it had been interred four years, was not present. He referred to Mr. Payne as "Mephistopheles," a characterization that would undoubtedly have astonished the mild-mannered editor.

Then there was Mrs. Mary Demarest, the lady who said she saw Henry Stevens in New Brunswick the day after the murder. Mr. McCarter said some harsh things about Mrs. Demarest. He said he was glad he didn't have that kind of a wife. Mrs. Demarest was in the court room, and of course she did not have the opportunity of saying what she thought of Mr. McCarter, but she was observed in a thinking attitude just the same.

He attacked the story of Mr. and Mrs. Dixon, who said they saw Willie Stevens at North Plainfield the night of the murder; he attacked the tale of Mrs. Anna Hoag, who claimed Henry Stevens came to her house near De Russey's Lane a couple of years after the murder. He attacked each and every story put forward as a link in the State's chain of circumstantial evidence, and was still saving up for "the pig woman."

He quoted Shakespeare. He misquoted *"Silas Marriner."* He aimed many a finger here and there, like a revolver barrel, as he talked, and he beat a heavy fist against a palm at proper intervals. Mr. McCarter is no amateur in the matter of mannerisms when it comes to addressing a jury.

This particular jury, gradually emerging from the depression that seemed to weigh upon it while it was an object of criticism, listened intently to him, and often smiled at McCarter's rather weighty witticisms.

The jurors seemed "human," as Senator Case said they were in his argument against the motion for a mistrial, to which a review of this witness' notes indicates that Senator Simpson barked:

"Well, I'd like to have affidavits on that point about a couple of them."

December 3, 1926

"The pig woman" and Jimmy Mills were presented yesterday by the attorneys for the defense in the Hall-Mills murder trial as the possible killers of Preacher Hall and his sweetheart.

Old Mr. McCarter seemed to favor Jimmy Mills. The more youthful Senator Case leaned toward "the pig woman" as he harangued the jury for over three hours in the final summing up for the defense.

As he drew near his forensic finish Senator Case's eyes bubbled tears. He seized the big family Bible of the Hall-Stevens family, which was brought in during the trial to show the birth records of the defendants after the State's ugly insinuations of Negro blood in Willie.

He flourished the Bible with dramatic gesture before the eyes of the jurors whom Senator Simpson, chief of prosecution, likened to "twelve trees" in his application for a mistrial Wednesday.

His thin features were wrinkled in seeming mental agony as he shouted:

"It is the evil in society that is on trial against the good, and by no act of yourself let decent lives be condemned by those who are themselves condemned by God in this Book, which contains the lineage that that man tried to blacken. This Book, that was close to the mother that bore him, and this Book that this little woman here (Mrs. Hall) treasures.

"This woman, who shielded the life of a man who was minister of the church, as his helper, and in the affection of which she believes, and gentlemen, let her and let them go on believing in this and living the best they can the lives this tells us we should live."

One of those old-time "tear jerkers" the sophisticated and the blasé will say. Perhaps it was. In any event, it jerked the tears.

Henry Stevens wept silently, though Henry seemed to be somewhat lachrymose anyway, for such a grim-looking man. Three jurors had distinctly damp eyes. There was snuffling throughout the packed court room.

Mrs. Hall sat stiff and proud, apparently unmoved. I believe her calm is commonly referred to as stoicism. It strikes me as determined repression. Her pale face did not change expression even when the lean Senator Case went to her, picked up one of her gloved hands, the right, and shouted: holding the limp unresisting hand up so the jury could see:

"As in the beginning, perhaps also at the end it may not be improper to say prisoner, look upon the juror; juror, look upon the prisoner. Are you content that this hand shot the gun that killed those people and that this is the hand that pulled the knife that severed the head from Mrs. Mills' body. Are you content to say that?"

Mrs. Hall probably did not expect this dramatic touch any more than she earlier expected Senator Case to have her stand up beside him so that the jury could see she isn't "a big, white-haired woman."

If her pride revolted inwardly against this singular exhibition, her face gave no sign. She is either a dead-game woman, or an amazingly unfeeling one, and I am inclined to the former.

Willie Stevens' froggy eyes were beaming with pleasure all day at the many complimentary references to him by his counsel, though he may not be so pleased with State Senator Alexander Simpson's remarks tomorrow. Senator Simpson will take about two hours for what will probably be a perfunctory verbal gesture, in view of the fact that he is quite convinced that he cannot hope to secure a conviction from this jury.

However, there is a possibility of a disagreement.

Old Mr. McCarter was not quite as direct in his suggestion that Jimmy Mills might have committed the murder, as Senator Case was in depicting "the pig woman" as the gun-and-knife handler of four years ago.

Besides visualizing "the pig woman" as the possible killer, Senator Case could also seem to see quite vividly in his mind's eye, one Raymond Schneider bending over the body of the Reverend Hall sometime after the murder and rifling the dead dominie's pockets of money and watch, and maybe dropping at the feet of the dead man the calling card that the State claims bore the fingerprint of Willie Stevens. The defense says this print is forgery.

Raymond Schneider is the young fellow who came upon the dead bodies under the crabapple tree when he was taking a stroll with Pearl Bahmer, his sweetheart. He afterward was sent to prison for perjury for saying that one Clifford Hayes had confessed to him of the murder. The crabapple tree tragedy also disclosed that Pearl Bahmer's father, Mike, who died the other day, was a bad character, and he was jailed for his improper guardianship of her.

Raymond Schneider is now working in New Brunswick. Senator Case did not say he had anything to do with the murder, but he said the State was afraid to produce him as a witness because it was afraid the defense would prove the rifling of the bodies. Senator Simpson will undoubtedly contend that the mention of Mrs. Gibson, Jimmy Mills and Schneider is for the purpose of drawing what he calls "a red herring" across the trial.

We heard almost as much New Jersey County politics in the arguments yesterday as of the crime under the old crabapple tree, the attorneys for the defense pointing out time and time again to the Somersetians sitting on the jury, that this case was largely the product of Hudson County officials. There is keen rivalry between Hudson and Somerset Counties.

Mr. McCarter, a little hoarse from his vocal violence of the day before, resumed croaking at the jurors as soon as court convened. He had donned a new suit of a pleasant brown. Mr. McCarter is a dressy old gentleman.

Mr. McCarter paid some attention to the insinuation against the late Azariah Beekman, prosecutor of Somerset County, alleged by the State to have been active in suppressing evidence in the early stages of the case. Mr. McCarter deplored those insinuations no little. All the jurors knew Mr. Beekman, it is said. He was a much-loved man in Somerset County. A lot of Somerset County folks think that it is Beekman's reputation that is on trial, not the Hall-Stevens clan, so naturally Mr. McCarter made much of that.

He did not boom about "the pig woman," as was expected. He said he would leave that to Senator Case. He merely hoped that the jurors would not be deceived by the drama which attended the production of "the pig woman."

Then, assuming a posture against the witness stand, old Mr. McCarter aimed a stubby finger of suspicion at poor little Jimmy Mills, the drabbest figure in all the sordid show. Jimmy is back at his janitoring in New Brunswick. Another victim of the tragedy, Charlotte Mills, his daughter, was taken ill in court Wednesday.

"I am not here to vindicate or to scold that dead couple," bellowed Mr. McCarter. "They have their account to make with their Creator, but I am here as a man with red blood in his veins, to question the innocence of a husband who placidly admits his wife to be absent for forty hours without raising a finger to find out where she is or what has happened to her, except to say to Mrs. Hall, 'Perhaps they have eloped.'

"And then, after the news—is it news?—is brought to him, he calmly sells to a newspaper the incriminating letters showing that she is an adulteress, and finally—and finally—we lawyers have a proverb, 'You know a person by his associates'—it is brought out, as you heard earlier in this case, that on an evening within the first week after this tragedy was discovered, this Jane Gibson, alias Jane Easton, alias Jane, 'the pig woman,' visited the Mills' house, and spent an evening there and then she becomes a witness. Then she hears all these things and sees all these things. And then the chorus is formed to fasten this crime on the Hall family, and 'the pig woman' looms on the scene."

He painted a picture of the "capture of Somerville" by Simpson and his assistants and their daily march through the streets during the trial. He said it reminded him of a hymn that was popular in his days at Princeton which ran: "See the mighty hosts advancing, Satan leading on."

The populace gathered in the court room, laughed until Justice Parker hammered with his gavel. Simpson, who had his chair tilted against the press stand, grinned cheerfully at Mr. McCarter, who seemed to be growing apoplectic. His face got red and redder.

He said he had been taunted about being an old gentleman, but he hoped he preserved all the traditions of the old New Jersey bar.

McCarter really sounded very sad as he mentioned this fact. Mr. McCarter may never have heard about "kind applause," but he knows how to get it as well as any aged actor you ever saw.

"Ah, Mr. Simpson, you may try those tactics in damage suits, against big corporations," said Mr. McCarter, very sadly, speaking of Senator Simpson's handling of Mrs. Hall when she was on the witness stand. "But you ought not to do it. You ought not to do it."

Senator Simpson looked most contrite.

"I am not here to exculpate either Mr. Hall or Mrs. Mills," said Mr. McCarter in a trembling voice. "As I have said before that is for them to account to their Maker for, but I do say that I admire the woman, who, until the actual facts are brought to her attention, proudly preserves her belief and respect for the man whom she had married eleven years before, and who, as far as she knew, was a faithful minister of the Gospel. But since, and just before this trial commenced, she was permitted to see that correspondence and, like Ophelia in Shakespeare's great play*:

" 'Be not like some injudicious pastors
    Who teach me the stoney and thorny way to heaven
    Whilst like a puffed and ragged libertine,
    Himself the primrose path of dalliance treads
    And recks not his own rede.' "

The jurors, whom Senator Simpson likened to twelve trees, only giving the trees a little the best of it, stared at Mr. McCarter entranced. They evidently felt he was a good show.

The old gentleman wound up in a blast of oratory that shook

* The lawyer's quotation was not precise.

him all over and almost shook the building as he made reference to that "motley crowd," who, under the guise of ferreting out crime, are seeking wealth and hoping to gain political ascendency. Mr. McCarter spoke a little less than an hour, then Senator Case got up. The senator looks like a schoolmaster and talks like one, and he heightened the pedagogical suggestion by pushing a little desk in front of him, with a glass of water and a pile of books and papers on it.

He is a spare-built man, resembling the late Woodrow Wilson. He holds himself tightly—squeezed up so to speak. He thawed out as he got heated with his own oratory and was presently swinging his arms until his coattails flapped, his face got red and the frat key on his watch chain waggled furiously.

Senator Case lives in Somerset County. He is some pumpkins politically in this bailiwick. The jurors are his fellow citizens. He spoke of them as his friends as he started. Case and Simpson are political rivals on the floor of the New Jersey State Senate. It is said Case wouldn't mind being Governor, and Simpson doesn't care if an admiring constituency sends him to the United States Senate.

Senator Case devoted the earlier part of his address to an eulogy of Mr. McCarter, deploring the jabs at him by Senator Simpson on account of his age. Now neither Simpson nor Case are spring chickens when it comes to that, but to hear Senator Case talk you might have thought Simpson had committed assault and battery on Mr. McCarter's gray hair. Some of the jurors are old.

Senator Case said Senator Simpson had been "nos-tee." He meant "nasty," of course, but he shirred over the word as if it were a dirty crack.

I gather that Senator Case is the kind of man who would consider "nasty" a very bad word. He said a lot of other things in this case had been "nos-tee" but he was particularly sorry about Senator Simpson. After he got well warmed up Senator Case said he could explain how that card S-17, got at the feet of the dead Dominie Hall, which the State says bore the fingerprints of Willie Stevens. He said in his opinion it was placed there by Raymond

Schneider, the young fellow who discovered the bodies of Reverend Hall and Mrs. Mills.

He said the reason the State had not produced Schneider as a witness was because the defense would have proved that Schneider rifled the body of the preacher. He did not infer that Schneider committed the murder. He said the rifling was done sometime after the murder.

Senator Case charged unfairness to the prosecution and placed some stress on the fact that Jersey City officials were so active in Somerset County affairs. The senator made plenty of that Somerset-Hudson-County phase of the situation. There is no love lost between the counties. Senator Case, who carried Somerset by about 6,000, kept referring again and again to Hudson County's interest in the affair.

He, too, dwelt feelingly on the attack on the dead Azariah Beekman's character. He charged the prosecution with vindictiveness in its conduct of the case in bringing in the question of Negro blood in Willie Stevens' veins, in its production of ghastly exhibits.

He went into the story of "the pig woman" in detail and said she lied. When he came to reviewing that part of "the pig woman's" testimony where she said she saw by the light of the moon "a big, gray-haired woman" in De Russey's Lane the night of the murder, Senator Case walked over to Mrs. Hall.

He asked her to stand, and as she rose he placed his hand lightly on her shoulder. The top of her hat just reached to the level of his bald head.

"A big, white-haired woman," he said; "is this a big woman? And her hair is just commencing to turn gray now. Four years ago she was still young."

Mrs. Hall had evidently not expected this demonstration. She looked surprised as her ally approached her. She is a short woman with a large head and face that suggests considerable size when she is seated.

Senator Case had not finished when the noon recess came and picked up where he left off at the afternoon session. He began to get a little hoarse as he went on picking holes in "the pig woman's" story. He kept waving the banner of loyalty to the old home county before the jury as he spoke of the local witnesses for the defense. Also he gave a demonstration of how the crime occurred, using the pale Timothy Pfeiffer as a sort of lay figure.

He thought the couple were shot as they sat side by side, the preacher's arm around Mrs. Mills' waist, that there had been no quarrel, or struggle. The dominie was probably shot first, he said and Mrs. Mills throat was probably cut to stop her moaning, all of which he said further disproved the tale of "the pig woman" about seeing a struggle.

He didn't know why she told such a story, although he suggested, among other things, the use of drugs, a guilty conscience of her own, a disordered mind, pure prevarication or self-hypnotism. Then he got going on his suggestion that she might be considered as the possible killer.

A little man with oily gray hair and a very blade of a voice stood before the bar of "Jersey justice" yesterday and made it listen to him.

Made it listen, I say, and wait. And think. For five hours.

A little man, as bold as a lion, and as brazen as brass, to use some good old similes. Insolent. Insulting.

But a man with something to say. His name? Alexander Simpson, State Senator from Hudson County, N. J., and special prosecutor in the Hall-Mills case.

The case went to the jury at 1:50 yesterday afternoon. They did not return until 6:49 P.M. For the bold and brazen little man, Alexander Simpson threw at the jurors—farmers, working men, and business men of Somerset County in central New Jersey, a challenge that they could not lightly regard in spite of their final verdict.

Mrs. Hall's thoughts on Simpson must have been interesting. Those close to her say she has always viewed him with contempt. They also say the real reason for her apparent stoicism is a proud resolve not to let him see she is affected by him.

When Simpson referred to the Hall-Stevens-Carpender clan as the reigning family of the Johnson and Johnson aristocracy of

New Brunswick, whose crest is a mustard plaster, and the court room tittered, she did not change expression, though this was perhaps a deeper stab to her pride than all his gory references to the murder.

Simpson at no time attempted to spare her feelings. This seemed strange, in view of the fact that he said frankly she did not actually commit the crime. His claim was that she was merely there. She rarely glanced at him while he was talking.

The day before, when he was tilted back in his chair listening to the arguments of her counsel, she often looked at him as if carefully considering him.

The morning session was given over to the summing up of Senator Simpson for the State—probably one of the most remarkable addresses ever delivered in a court room, if only because of his tone toward the jurors.

"The defense thinks it very stupid of me to antagonize you," he said with scorn. "Well, of course, if I were trying an automobile accident case I would pat you on the back and tell you what fine men you were, what a splendid county you came from, how intelligently you followed the evidence.

"But I am not trying to get in your good graces. I am not trying to win a case. I am speaking for the great State of New Jersey in this abominable murder. The challenge to you on your oath is, What do you say of the evidence? That is the challenge to you —the big challenge.

"We are not pleading for a verdict. We are not smooching for a verdict. We are not trying to win a case at the expense of human blood, but we are talking to you just as if you did not know Senator Case, just as if you were under no obligation to Senator Case, just as if you were going to take this evidence and decide it right on the evidence."

He moved very close to the jury and stood with his hands in his trouser pockets and spoke in an ordinary conversational tone. His voice was very distinct, though he did not raise it at first. He lounged against the witness stand until he got warmed up, then he would walk so close to the jurors that he almost stepped on the toes of the men in the first row.

He did not wax flowery. He talked more as one man to another, but, underlying his remarks was a castigation of those of the jury who were involved in the charges in the affidavit that Simpson filed with his application for a mistrial. The faces of the jurors were a great study as the little man buzzed at them waspishly.

He addressed some of them by name, moving close to each man he addressed. At times he seemed almost insolent. He has a trick of shortening up nearly all his sentences and using little words.

Let me see if I can show you how this little man worked, without verbal fireworks or flourish, or oratorical effect, yet a consummate showman.

"Now who was the woman who was murdered?" he asked quietly, stepping to his pile of exhibits. "There she is," he answered himself, stepping back with a big photograph of the murdered woman, Mrs. Mills, and holding it up before the eyes of the jury.

No flourish to the action, but amazingly effective.

"Just as much a human being as your wife or your daughter," he said. "A nice looking woman, the mother of two children.

"The husband was not particularly inspirational, as I judged from his testimony on the stand. A good woman, working in the church," he went on.

"Here is the church," he said, stepping to the table again, getting another photograph which he held up. "She sang in the choir, Episcopal Church. There was the cross."

He indicated with his finger.

"A man preached in front of the cross. She sang here. And the man that preached was this man."

He held up a photo of the dead dominie in his vestments.

"A fine looking man," said Simpson. "A splendid looking man, just the kind of a man who would attract a woman whose heart was empty and hungry. She heard him preach his sermons. She heard him read that wonderful service of the Episcopal Church, 'I am the bread of life.'

"That wonderful sonorous language," said Simpson. "Heard him read the Bible, a wonderful English. Heard him read the Psalms out of the Episcopal Psalter. Tyndale's translation, the most wonderful translation of all. Was it any wonder that this woman should come under the spell of this man?"

Now the little man suddenly reached over and took from Captain Walsh, one of his assistants, a battered pair of brown shoes and a pair of black cotton stockings.

"Here are her stockings," he said, simply, holding them up. "Here is the pair of little brown shoes, all worn down with rubber heels. That is funny attire for a harlot. A harlot usually has much better stuff than that."

As Simpson vizualized the crime, Henry Stevens fired the shots that killed the parson and his sweetheart. Mrs. Hall and Willie were there he thought. But they had not gone there to commit murder. They had gone because Mrs. Hall, consumed by jealousy, wanted to confront them with their letters.

A quarrel followed—then the shooting. Simpson did not say who cut Mrs. Mills' throat—but he did say that Mrs. Hall knew. He glided over Willie, briefly, as a childish fellow, who had been taught his story by rule and rote, and did not attack Henry with any particular verbal violence.

It was against Mrs. Hall that he was vitriolic. She sat unmoved, listening, a woman of stone, as he referred to her, sarcastically, as "this Christian lady."

He said she was proud, and stern and cruel.

"Look at her eyes," he said, "if you want to know about the truth of this thing. This woman who is so cold-blooded that, when she is on trial for murder involving the murder of her husband, claiming that she is telling you twelve men the truth, she stopped, pointed out a photographer who was taking her picture and asked the judge to stop him. As cold-blooded as that."

He paid his chief witness, Mrs. Jane Gibson, "the pig woman," high compliment. He said he thought she was a big character in coming forward to tell the truth, though it had resulted in persecution that had almost ruined her.

He said he had received many anonymous letters showing that others knew of the murder, but were afraid to come forward because of what had happened to "the pig woman." He sneered at defense's attempt to direct suspicion to "the pig woman" and said they might just as easily try to prove that the murders were committed by Jenny, the mule.

"You may kick this case out in twenty minutes," he said, looking directly at Juror Young, who was alleged, in one of the affidavits, to have made that remark, "but if you do you may kick yourselves out."

No man ever faced a jury with less regard for what it thought than Simpson, yet he made a clear summation of the State's case.

　　·　　　·　　　·　　　·　　　·

The jury was out for five hours and four minutes.

When it came in, at 6:49 P.M., December 3, 1926, it brought a verdict that freed Mrs. Hall and her brothers, Henry and Willie, of the charge of murdering Mrs. Mills.

Next day, the prosecuting attorney of Somerset County noll prossed the indictment of Mrs. Hall and the Stevenses for the murder of Reverend Hall. The indictments of Henry Carpender in both cases were quashed.

That was the end of it.

"DADDY" AND "PEACHES"

Carmel, New York, January 23, 1927

That gallus old codger, "Daddy" Browning, and his flapper wife, the celebrated "Peaches," go to bat with their matrimonial pains and aches here tomorrow morning.

The veterans of the press benches of Somerville are massed behind their typewriters and telegraph keys nearly a hundred strong in this pastoral little town, and a pleasant time is anticipated by one and all when Daddy and Peaches start telling the low-down on each other.

Some say it will be very low-down.

The populace expects to hear more or less "dirt." It would be a terrible blow to the nation if this should turn out to be a dull narration of conjugal incompatibility without any paprika in it. You can hear those kickless stories anywhere.

If you have followed the public prints to any extent the past year, you know that Daddy Browning is Edward W. Browning, a New York real estate man of reputed wealth, and of at least fifty-one years of age, giving him plenty the best of it, who likes his girl friends young.

He is what you might call a "chick chaser." That, I believe, is the term for old guys who choose 'em very youthful. Old girls who like young men are called "veal hunters." Thus the English language is enriched every day.

When it comes to the dolls, old Daddy Browning seems to be of the genus sap. Moreover, he appears to have a strong yen for publicity, and who shall say he has not had plenty of it since he

97

married Frances Heenan Browning, the "Peaches" aforesaid, at the glowing, mature age of fifteen?

Now he is endeavoring to shake Peaches off the Browning family tree, and the matter comes up at this time in the form of a plea by Daddy for separation. Peaches has filed a countersuit against Daddy that will come up later. Daddy, dear old Daddy, was more like a stepfather to her, she says.

Sometimes Daddy is called "Bunny," so I understand. He is also called other things less endearing by coarse persons who do not comprehend the influence of sweet love on a gent's heart and blood pressure.

Daddy Browning is a dressy old boy. They tell me he has more neckties than Sulka's, with pants to match. Much of his publicity after his marriage to the fifteen-year-old Peaches came from the way he threw his bankroll around in her behalf, though Peaches now says he always had a rope tied to it. She says he wears fish-hooks in his pockets so that when he gets his hand in 'em he can't get it out.

Prior to the advent of Peaches, the old boy broke into print through an advertisement for a girl companion for Dorothy "Sunshine" Browning, a child now ten years old, whom he adopted when she was about six. Many young women were almost trampled to death in the ensuing crush of applicants for the job, and Daddy finally nominated Miss Mary Spas and adopted her, also.

A condition of the advertisement was that the girl must be under sixteen. Captious observers of Mary said they would hate to be hanging since she was sixteen, and finally it came out that she had omitted the winters in calculating her summers. Daddy gave her the air, but Mary now has suits pending against Daddy for something like half a million, and mentions an attempted assault at the Kew Gardens Inn among other things.

You can readily see that Daddy is having his troubles with those kids, but not half as much trouble as he might have had if he had gone pestering around fifteen-year-old children out in— well, let me say out in Trinidad, Colorado. You see, I know Trinidad, Colorado.

But the effete East seems more blasé about these things, and thus we have the great moral spectacle in this modern civilization of a legal hearing involving a gray-haired old wowser and a child-wife attracting more attention than the League of Nations. Such is life in the snow-clad hills of Putnam County, New York.

I say snow-clad because it has been snowing all day, and the chances are Daddy and Peaches will have to travel to the old, picturesque colonial court house tomorrow morning on skis. Carmel has a population of about five hundred, and it squats on the shore of Lake Glendida, which is part of the reservoir system of New York City.

The lake is frozen tighter than Daddy Browning's pocketbook as described by Peaches, and skating would be fine if anybody had any skates, or the desire to skate. The natives and the visiting firemen spent the day hived up in the tepees of Carmel, speculating on the outcome of the trial and its effect on business in Carmel.

There have been a few mild squawks among the visiting firemen because the price of bed and board has been jacked up to some extent in Carmel, but one can scarcely blame the citizenry. They do not get a crack at outsiders as often as other communities. They may never get another Browning trial.

There is some chatter that the hearing may be moved to White Plains, or possibly to Poughkeepsie. I hope and trust that in the latter case it will not produce at dear old Vassar the drastic steps taken by the head of a local seminary for young ladies. I am informed that they have been instructed to keep away from public places during the hearing.

I am wondering if this order is by any chance a reflection upon any of the visiting Apollos and Adonises of the New York press, or merely a wise precaution against Daddy Browning.

The hearing is before Supreme Court Justice Albert H. S. Seeger. There will be no jury. One of Daddy's attorneys is John E. Mack, of Poughkeepsie, who was appointed guardian ad litem for baby Stillman in the Stillman divorce squabble, another of our historical moral episodes of this century. His attorney of record is

Francis C. Dale, an able barrister of Cold Springs and New York City.

It was at Cold Springs that Daddy married Peaches last April. He had met her at a dance after the episode with Mary Spas, during which Daddy became known as "the Cinderella man." This was because he loaded Mary up with clothes and what not, and drove her around in a Rolls-Royce. It is said now that this Rolls-Royce was hired, but a hired Rolls-Royce is none the less a Rolls-Royce.

Henry Epstein is Peaches' attorney. Peaches was married to Daddy with the consent of her mother, Mrs. Catherine Heenan, and it is said that Mother Heenan's ears feel like they are all afire just from what Daddy is thinking about her. Mother Heenan is expected to figure in this hearing tomorrow no little.

There was a mysterious incident in the romance of Daddy and Peaches that may be cleared up during the hearing. Someone threw a lot of acid in Peaches' face, and she still wears the scars. Some say this and some say that about the acid-throwing. Now it can be told, as Sir Philip Gibbs said of the war.

Mary Spas tossed off a hooker of iodine after her jam with Daddy Browning at the Kew Gardens Inn, so it is related, but nothing came of it. However, it was considered another quite thrilling chapter in the life, and so forth, of Daddy. He was a divorcé. Some say his income is around $300,000 per year. If it was about $1,200 you would never have heard a whisper of him.

Organizations devoted to the welfare of children have made various motions toward getting Dorothy Sunshine Browning away from Daddy at different times, alleging that he is an unfit guardian, but she is still with him, and, moreover, is very fond of him. I do not know Daddy's exact pose in life, but some say he regards himself as a philanthropist. It may be so.

Anyway, Carmel is all agog—in fact, I might say it is all agoggogga—over the events of tomorrow. The court house is in apple pie order, the telegraph wires are tuned in to the Queen's taste, and your correspondent's typewriter is well oiled.

I regret to report that the opening scene of the great moral opus, entitled "The Saps of 1927," and featuring the inimitable Daddy and Peaches Browning, fell a little flat today.

It was not the fault of the principals. It was their material. There was no "dirt" whatever. Nothing came out that you couldn't mention freely in any modern drawing room or speakeasy.

The upshot of the whole business today was this:

A couple of witnesses, telling pallid, colorless tales, were examined in Daddy's suit for separation against Peaches, that buxom matron of sixteen, who sat encased in a mink coat and in a rather blubbery state of mind and emotion during the hearing.

Daddy charged that Peaches abandoned him, and wouldn't come back. The testimony of the witnesses was designed to prove this to Supreme Court Justice Seeger.

Then Henry Epstein, Peaches' attorney, made a brace of motions, one that the suit be dismissed as to the abandonment on the ground that no proof had been presented, the other to dismiss the suit as to Peaches' refusal to return on the same ground —no proof.

Judge Seeger denied the second motion and withheld decision on the first, but sustained a motion by Epstein to hold the hearing at White Plains beginning tomorrow morning.

And that was that.

The good citizens of Putnam County, who packed the little low-ceilinged court room, noisily stamping the snow from their galoshes, and removing their mufflers and ear-tippets as they entered, seemed somewhat disappointed.

Some were almost indignant, especially when it was decided to take the show over to White Plains tomorrow afternoon. The taxpayers of Putman County didn't get as much as one bedtime story for their money. It may be made an issue in the next election. True they got $1.50 per pair of mutton chops, but I doubt if that makes up for their loss of what they expected.

They came with their wives, grandmothers, maiden aunts, and

one little baby in arms. Some of the ladies brought their tatting, anticipating startlement that might cause them to drop a few stitches. The baby howled at intervals, then stopped so suddenly that everybody looked around, thinking perhaps a heartless mother had stuffed a galosh in its maw.

But it seems that the mother had merely whispered to the baby that Daddy Browning was entering the room. It was a girl baby.

Daddy Browning—the old boy himself—rolled up to the vintage court house in a blue Rolls-Royce, and faced the cameras like a man. In fact, like several men. He had more law attending him than a rich bootlegger, as he stalked into court.

Daddy wore a blue sack coat, with thin white penciling, and the coat was a tight fit. He had the bottom button fastened so that his chest protruded in front like a platter, and his pistol pocket stuck out so far behind that several of his lawyers following in his rear couldn't get through the doorway until he was well in the clear.

A rattle of applause broke out among the spectators as Daddy Browning came down an aisle, walking first on one foot, and then on the other. Judge Seeger hammered his desk, and said he would clear the court room if there were any more such demonstrations. The judge is an iron-gray man in a pepper-and-salt suit, and an air of determination.

When the applause started, Daddy looked around as if he had some idea of taking a bow. Some say he probably brought his own claque with him, but I am inclined to scout this theory, as I saw my sorrel secretary, The Bull, in the background leading the applause.

The Bull is one of the lads from the neighborhood of Sixty-ninth Street and West End Avenue and he jockeyed your correspondent over the snowy roads from New York to this spot in a roadster. Feeling certain that The Bull knows nothing of the merits of the case, I asked him why he had applauded Daddy, and he said:

"Well, I thought he was Leon Errol coming in to do some funny falls for us."

You see how much a man may be mistaken.

Daddy is of medium height, and his figure is probably not what it used to be. Only the last button on the coat gives him a waistline. He has a florid complexion and gray hair, that has been worn off the top of his head like the nap on a wool coat.

He has dark eyes that are constantly shifting their gaze. Daddy's eyes remind me of the orbs of Mr. Harry K. Thaw, that other celebrated connoisseur of feminine youth. I say this with all due respect to both Daddy and Mr. Harry K. Thaw.

Peaches was already in the court room when Daddy arrived. In the shuffle and scuffle of the entrance, and being propelled forward by the solid movement of his attorneys behind him, Daddy was shunted so close to her chair that he could have reached out and touched her. He gave her one swift peek, and sharply turned away.

Peaches immediately opened a handbag about the size of a laundry sack, fumbled therein and extracted a handkerchief, which she applied to her eyes. Her mother, Mrs. Catherine Heenan, who sat beside her, leaned forward and whispered in her ear, but Peaches continued somewhat lachrymose throughout the hearing.

One of my sage ancestors once told me that whenever I contemplated matrimony I should go around and take a look at the girl's old lady, meaning her mother, and see what twenty years had done for the parent. I should say that a decade hence Peaches will be the present Mrs. Heenan to the life. She is the image of her Maw.

Peaches is large and blonde. Her hair is a straw color. She is one of those expansive, patient looking blondes, who are sometimes very impatient. She has blue eyes which contain an expression of resignation. She has stout legs. I hesitate to expatiate on so delicate a matter, but they are what the boys call "piano legs." Her feet are small. She had them encased in neat brown ties.

Under her mink coat, which probably cost a couple of thousand dollars, she wore a blue dress, blue being a color that matches her complexion well. Her hat was blue, and fitted close over her hair. There were wisps of brown feathers on either side of the hat. She wore a big diamond pin on her breast and a diamond pendant around her neck.

Take her by and large, she was gotten up very expensively, and if you care for the large type in blondes she is reasonably pulchritudinous. I mean to say she is what you would call good looking—if you like 'em in her style. They say she was fifteen when she married Daddy. She could pass for twenty, and nobody would bat an eye.

Her mother was dressed in black, with a black fur coat around her, black hat, and black shoes and stockings of a color that I believe the girls call "nude." Mrs. Heenan, too, suggested that she had spent some money on her appearance. She sat close to her chick and child, and she took a couple of offhand glares at Daddy that would have done him no good if glances were lethal weapons.

Peaches' mouth droops in an adenoidal manner. She smiled wanly at a couple of acquaintances in the press seats, crossed her stout legs, and tried to compose herself as the proceedings opened. She had a spray of orchids pinned to her mink coat, but she was scarcely the picture of a forlorn little child-wife that I had expected. It is very difficult for any one to look forlorn in a mink coat.

There was an informal, jovial aspect to the brief hearing. The bench and bar made humorous sallies, especially Mr. John E. Mack, who did the talking for Daddy's side, and who has a Texas hair cut and looks like a Missouri statesman of the period of Bill Bryan. He is of Poughkeepsie, I believe.

It developed at once that both Daddy and Peaches have suddenly been overtaken by a yearning for privacy in the discussion of their matrimonial caterwauling. They want it behind closed doors. Up to this time neither Daddy nor Peaches has been a shrinking violet in the matter of publicity, especially Daddy, who has eagerly held his jowly countenance up to every camera in New York City, while Peaches has told her story almost from the housetops.

But Henry Epstein, a small, neat-looking man, with a close-clipped black moustache, and a low, confiding voice, asked Judge

Seeger for a hearing in chambers as soon as the session opened this morning. He requested that the press and public be excluded, intimating that the testimony might be such as to be inimical to public morals, something Daddy, at least, hasn't apparently given much thought to in the past.

Epstein is said to be related to Max Steuer, the great trial lawyer of Manhattan Island. His request was not altogether unexpected. Mack supported it, saying that while Daddy himself wished a public hearing he disagreed with his client on that point and thought that public decency should be considered.

Judge Seeger said he would rule on the point later, but he suggested that the parties to the matter hadn't manifested any desire for secrecy in the past. He added that he had received a letter from a women's organization in Carmel asking that the hearing be private. Carmel, at least, will not be further troubled by the publicity of the case.

It is doubtful that Judge Seeger will grant the request for a private hearing, perhaps on the ground that publicity may serve as a deterrent to other cases of a similar nature. A private hearing would compel the newspaper men and women who were banked in the jury box and the spectators' seats in the court room today to get their information as to the progress of the case outside the court room, perhaps from Daddy or Peaches themselves.

The first witness called by Mr. Mack for Daddy's side was Edward P. Kearney, a chauffeur in the employ of one John J. Goishow, of New York. He drove the Rolls-Royce that was Peaches' envied chariot in the early days of her married bliss or what-have-you. It was supposed to be Daddy's own car, but it later developed that he merely rented it.

Anyway, Kearney, a solid, chauffeurish looking gent, told of taking Peaches and her Maw and her trunks from Daddy's apartment in the Kew Gardens Inn to Mrs. Heenan's home in One Hundred and Seventy-fifth Street and of hearing Peaches say: "Money isn't everything after all."

An astonishing discovery, as the reader must admit. This was the occasion when Peaches is supposed to have quit Daddy's home—when she gave him what is technically known as "the air."

Epstein cross-examined him, but briefly—so briefly that you might think he had little interest in the testimony of the mahout of the Rolls-Royce. He denied that he worked for Browning. He said Goishow, a name that led to quaint repartee between Mr. Mack and the bench, was his employer.

John P. Gorman, a bald man, who said he is Daddy's secretary, testified to listening in at Daddy's request to a telephone conversation between Daddy and Peaches' mother after Peaches had quit Daddy.

Gorman said he often listened to conversations between Daddy and other persons, at Daddy's request via an extension phone.

He said Daddy asked Mrs. Heenan to let him talk with Peaches, and that Mrs. Heenan said: "Peaches is through with you, Mr. Browning."

Kearney's testimony was designed to show the court that Peaches had abandoned Daddy, and Gorman's testimony to prove that she wouldn't come back to Daddy. As Gorman concluded, Mack said his side rested.

Epstein was as brief with Gorman as with the other witnesses. He asked Gorman how much money he got from Daddy, and Gorman said his salary is $3,000 per year. Epstein demanded: "Didn't you thank Mrs. Browning for getting you a raise?"

The witness said no. And that's all there was to the hearing, save that Epstein presented his application for a transfer of the case to White Plains, and it was granted. It seems that the attorneys on both sides had agreed to such a transfer beforehand.

There was some applause as the first witness left the stand, and again Judge Seeger admonished the spectators. I looked around hastily, and did not see The Bull slapping his hands together. He was, in fact, asleep. One might infer from the applause that Daddy's side is the favorite side in this community, but they might have applauded just as hard had Peaches had an inning. Applause often goes with the fellow in front at the moment.

As Daddy and Peaches left the court room to take their respective cars, Daddy his Rolls-Royce, and Peaches a less pretentious buggy, they were surrounded by the crowd. Both stood for more photos, but not together. It is not of record that they were asked for a group-posing, and it is no cinch it couldn't have been had.

The typewriters were hastily folded up tonight and the procession moves on to White Plains. But I must warn Daddy and Peaches that the great American public will not tolerate many more pale performances such as they gave this morning. If they haven't got any scandal to offer, they might as well send for Mr. Cain, the theatrical warehouse man, and put their show in storage. He has a lot better shows as it is.

White Plains, New York, January 25, 1927

Your correspondent's manly cheeks are still suffused with blushes as he sits down to write of a few peeks into the bridal chamber of dear old Daddy Browning and his Peaches.

He is almost sorry now that Judge Seeger did not grant the application of Peaches' attorney for a private hearing. Your correspondent would have been spared the embarrassment of listening to Peaches' narrative of the strange didoes of Daddy.

But the thing being public, your correspondent, in common with the rest of the world, risked one eye at the keyhole, as you might say, and heard the buxom and at times blubbery Peaches tell about Daddy on the nuptial night—and on many other nights, too.

How that old boy did carry on, hear Peaches tell it! Hey, hey! Not a word to the major, as the girls say.

The gods on Mount Olympus, or wherever it is the gods assemble, must have held their sides with laughter today—and probably their noses, too—as they looked down and watched the earthworms wriggling in the muck heap of a modern-day matrimonial squabble.

They must have guffawed, these gods, as they saw a court room jammed with men and women and young girls, with their ears distended, and a street packed with people almost rioting in their desire to get a peep at the principals in a duel of defamation.

The gods must scent familiar odors rising from this particular spot on the globe and perhaps wonder if somebody didn't bury a load of limburger cheese hereabouts and go away and forget it, for it was in the court house in White Plains that the Rhinelander case of unfragrant memory almost asphyxiated the populace.

It was in another court room, however, than the one in which Peaches sat prattling away this afternoon when a recess was taken until tomorrow morning, and Daddy Browning went bouncing down the court house steps to the cheers of the assembled citizens.

In this instance I think the cheers were inspired, largely by a crafty newspaper photographer who desired to get some good action pictures of the multitude, and who bawled, "Three cheers for Daddy."

I think few citizens resist an impulse to cheer when properly approached. Thus the White Plains welkin rang with a couple of strong yip-yips. The third was not so strong. Somebody said, "Tiger," and I distinctly heard the unmistakable noise that you make when the tongue flutters between the teeth.

But Daddy bowed in all directions. He was a little bit flustered on emerging from the court house after hearing Peaches tell those tales out of school about his alleged abnormalities and one thing and another.

I would not think of disclosing some of the allegations in a family newspaper. Your Uncle Samuel would bar it from his mails. They are the things that are only put in plays nowadays—the kind of plays that Mayor Jimmy Walker often speaks of censoring.

They were pretty raw. Peaches herself did not want to blurt them out before the crowded court room, and she looked appealingly at Judge Seeger when Mr. Henry Epstein, her attorney, pressed her for answers to certain questions. She asked, "Must I tell all these people?"

Judge Seeger said softly, "Yes."

Peaches cried into her handkerchief, and told.

At one point she broke down and sobbed so lustily that Mr.

Epstein asked for a brief recess. Peaches' mother was sitting back among the witnesses today, and hurried to her daughter's comfort when Peaches was taken into an ante-room.

I thought that perhaps the testimony might cause some of the female spectators to step outside for a breath of air, but not one stirred.

I think that possibly, next to your correspondent, Mr. Henry Epstein was perhaps the most embarrassed person in Westchester County as he questioned his client. He had asked to have the hearing in private, but when Judge Seeger denied the motion at the opening of the hearing, Mr. Epstein set his teeth and plunged on in, like a man hopping into a cold tub.

When he got to the point where he wanted Peaches to tell the Court those things that I cannot tell you, he again asked that the room be cleared, but the Court said no.

Mr. Epstein turned quite pale, wiped his close-clipped little black moustache with a neat handkerchief, took a big swig of water, fumbled with a pencil, and questioned Peaches in a low, soft voice. Embarrassment leaked out all over him.

Peaches left her expensive looking fur coat in her chair when she took the stand. Some say this is a sable coat that cost $20,000. I believe Daddy himself claims he paid $5,500 for it. I classed it as a mink, but these girls are wearing so many different animal skins nowadays that one is apt to get confused.

It probably cost even less than Daddy himself says, if Peaches' tales of his economy in other respects are true.

She wore the same blue dress and the same blue hat that she wore at Carmel yesterday when the hearing was transferred to White Plains.

A close-up of Peaches takes away none of the buxomness of a distant view, but it removes some of the expensiveness of her get-up of a first impression. She had a little round watch suspended from a chain around her neck, an article of jewelry that cost not over $30, and she wore her monogram in near-diamonds on her breast.

A huge but not expensive slave-bracelet was around one arm. The best piece of jewelry that she displayed today was her wedding ring, a diamond circlet that she said cost Daddy $200.

However, under cross-examination she admitted that he had given her one ring that cost $3,500 and a bracelet that stood him $2,500. She said she got $50 per week for pin money, and Daddy paid all her living expenses. Moreover, her mother got an allowance from him.

She weighed 140 pounds when she was married in April and had shot up to 160 pounds when she quit him six months later. She is certainly a bit to the hefty side, although she is only sixteen. Her chin and neck are sadly disfigured by the mysterious acid burns that she got one morning while asleep shortly before her marriage to Daddy.

These acid burns came in for some investigation by John Mack, who is a peremptory sort of man in handling a witness, but given to joviality. She said she had no idea at the time she received the burns who could have thrown the acid on her, but today on cross-examination she said she thought Daddy might have had something to do with them.

At least she expressed the opinion that she wouldn't have been burned if she had never met Daddy. She was a bit hazy as to just how she arrived at this conclusion.

She struck me at times as a little bit more sophisticated than her years would suggest when Mr. Mack was cross-examining her. She used very precise language, but now and then she would grow a bit tempery, and would say "sure," and "positively." She called a bell-boy, a "bell hop," which I believe is accepted English in some circles, but not always in the best. She invariably said "gittin'." Her voice and manner are quite mature.

Daddy listened to her with interest. He frowned when she spoke of some of his antics, and laughed at her recital of others. There was a matter of a goose, described by Peaches as an African honking goose, which was brought home by Daddy in jocular mood one evening, and which caused Peaches much pain and mental anguish, she said.

It seems that the goose was a live goose, and it caused disorder in the apartment that tickled Daddy no end. Then he put it in a cage on the back of his car and journeyed to Long Beach with the goose honking all the way. Mack suggested jovially, "You didn't think you had married a goose?"

Peaches answered with an attempt at severity, "No."

She admitted a photograph taken of her and the goose at Long Beach, however, but said that was Daddy's doings.

January 26, 1927

Our legal pulling and hauling here in the interests of the moral uplift of the nation came to a halt today until Monday.

The pause is not, as you might suspect, to give the sanitary authorities of this pleasant Westchester County town a chance to fumigate the premises. It is to give Daddy Browning's attorneys time to marshal testimony to refute the many, many things that Peaches said about that great big gander man.

Also what some of Peaches witnesses said about him today, which was plenty. There was one witness, for instance, who came along at the afternoon session, a Miss Marion Tussey, of New York, one of Peaches' friends, who testified that as late as last Saturday Daddy came snooping around her house asking her if she hadn't taken Peaches on nude parties, and hadn't she chaperoned Peaches to a doctor for an illegal operation?

All this before Peaches' marriage to Daddy, you understand. Miss Tussey said she told Daddy she hadn't done anything of the sort, wherefore, so she testified, Daddy remarked that it would be worth her while if she could think up something to that effect, and would get her a lot of publicity. It probably would.

Miss Tussey is a young woman who is a bit on the fleshy side. I mean to say she is plumpish. She was one of a quartette of ladies who came in together today, and who all appeared on the stand, the party including Peaches herself, Peaches' mother, a Mrs. Catherine Mayer, and Miss Tussey.

Put 'em all together, they spelt hefty.

But by Monday morning Daddy expects to have enough evidence assembled in White Plains to prove that everything Peaches and her witnesses said is all dead wrong, and that he is the nicest, whitest, kindliest, and possibly the happiest fifty-two-year-oldster that ever joined hands in wedlock with a fifteen-year-old flapper.

Barring certain alleged abnormalities, Peaches has so far merely made Browning out a little bit dizzy for a gent of his years. The most serious charge she made against him was an innuendo in reference to ten-year-old Dorothy Sunshine Browning, his adopted daughter.

I gathered from a statement made this morning by John E. Mack that he expects to produce some snappy testimony on behalf of his client. The folks can hardly wait to hear it. The folks have been somewhat disappointed so far. The testimony has been putrid in spots, but it might have been worse.

Peaches confessed to a little fib at the morning session through her attorney, the abashed Henry Epstein. He got up and told Judge Seeger, in a soft, low voice, that last evening after leaving the court house, Peaches had sent for him and told him that the red-backed diary she produced in court yesterday as a diary she had kept before her marriage was not the original manuscript.

Mr. Epstein seemed pained as he mentioned this circumstance. He said he asked her if she had the original diary, and she admitted she had. Then he told Peaches to produce it in court today. Mr. Epstein said gently:

"I consider that my duty as an officer of this court and as attorney for my client requires that the truth and all of the truth should be known."

Mr. Mack took hold of that with avidity. Peaches was on the stand, still under cross-examination at the time, and he asked for the original diary. She pointed to her handbag, on her attorney's table, and another red-backed book, somewhat similar to the one she displayed yesterday, was produced.

Peaches said she had kept the diary until the day she was married. It seems that she made record of the little episodes of her girlhood such as casual "neckings" with the flaming youth of her acquaintance. I believe they call it "necking" now, but when your correspondent was a "necker" of no mean standing back in the dim and misty past, they called it "lally-gagging." Times have changed. The girls didn't keep diaries then, thank heaven.

Well, Peaches had set down the names of the "neckers" or

"neckees," as the case might be, so she said, but she had great respect for the boys she went out with, they were all very nice to her, and she wished to keep them out of the court record. The diary she had produced yesterday was one she had written at the suggestion of a young man, Joseph Morris, she said. Joseph is in the court record, anyway. Mr. Mack inquired:

"Were the boys mentioned in the original diary, boys that you had made love to, and that had made love to you?"

Peaches answered, "They were."

The world do move, my friends. Talk of "love" at fifteen and less. The world do move.

In her copy she had omitted all names.

Some of the pages had been torn out of the original diary, and Mr. Mack inquired about them. Peaches said there had been nothing on those pages. She admitted, as Mr. Mack read from her testimony of yesterday, that she had fibbed about the diary. Her cheeks were scarlet against the blue of her hat as she confessed the little lie.

Mr. Mack wanted to put both diaries in evidence, and Mr. Epstein objected on the ground that they pertained to events before Peaches' marriage and therefore could have nothing to do with the present hearing. Mr. Mack said:

"Your Honor will find in the diaries, unless I am mistaken, and I am satisfied that I am not, the writings of this young lady to show that she was a woman of the world, even though young. They are extremely important as bearing upon her story that she was an innocent girl at the time of her marriage, and knew nothing of the usual marriage relations."

Peaches answered sharply, "I was a good girl when I married."

Mr. Mack went on:

"They are part of the res gestae, and with the letters which I intend to offer will give Your Honor a picture of this marriage of December and May and bring into Your Honor's mind, in my opinion, the conviction that the story which this lady told on the stand is, under all circumstances and all the evidence, unbelievable."

But Judge Seeger sided with Mr. Epstein and would not admit

the diaries, though he said Mr. Mack might file briefs to support another similar motion.

Peaches was finally excused after she had identified a mass of letters shown her by Mr. Mack as her handwriting, and a number of copies of a newspaper containing the tale of her marital woes with the elderly Daddy.

Daddy dug these letters and papers out of a huge, black valise, of the "telescope" variety. Both Peaches and Daddy seem to be disregarding this royal opportunity for sartorial display, as she has worn the same dress and hat since the trial started, and though Daddy is said to be the owner in fee simple of a thousand neckties, he has worn the same one, of a scrambled-egg pattern, from the beginning, and the same suit.

Peaches said she got $15 per week in the auditing department of Bedell's before her marriage and attended Textile High. Large round tears welled up in her eyes a couple of times, but she did not break down, though her mother, Mrs. Catherine Heenan, sat right at her side ready to render first aid in case of a collapse.

Even a case-hardened old sinner, such as your correspondent, must feel a little sympathy for Peaches, regardless of the merits of her case against Daddy. He is no rose-geranium any way you take him. The child-wife seems to be a victim of circumstances in many respects. She is disfigured for life, how and why, has not been made clear, but perhaps, as she says, it wouldn't have happened if she had never met Daddy, though she admits he didn't burn her.

She is marked for life spiritually, as well as physically—a tough break for a sixteen-year-old girl, however you look at it. The pity is, so far as she is concerned, that Daddy had more than two dollars. Otherwise you would never have heard his name —or her name, for that matter.

Old friend mother-in-law was with us much of the morning session in the person of Mrs. Heenan. You have seen her, my brothers, full many a time and oft. Yes.

Of about the shape and heft of Willie Meehan, the old time roly-poly of the manly art of scrambling ears. Willie was shaped like an apple. She wore a black hat and a dark blue dress, drawn a bit tightly and skittishly about her hips. She smiled at her daughter as she sat down in the witness chair.

She followed to the stand one Mrs. Catherine Mayer, a woman of middle age, with a middle-age bob, who wore eye-glasses and a black satin dress and who told of quarrels between Peaches and Daddy while in the first bloom of their honeymoon at Cold Springs. Mrs. Mayer lives with Mrs. Heenan and corroborated much of Peaches' tales with reference to the battling at Cold Springs.

Daddy gave Mother Heenan a good strong son-in-law glare as she said, "He always called me mother."

She said Peaches was born in Columbus, Ohio, and that she herself was divorced in 1918 from her husband. She asked Mr. Mack coyly, "Do I have to tell my age?"

"Certainly not."

She replied, bridling, "I am forty-three."

Mr. Epstein produced Peaches' birth certificate, which she identified and which Mr. Mack examined carefully and then objected to. The objection was not sustained.

Mrs. Heenan, too, told of Cold Springs. She said she had gone there and leased a house at Daddy's instructions with money furnished by him, because Daddy's attorney, Captain Dale, told her they wanted everything legal in case of any action by the Children's Society, which was threatening steps against her as unfit guardian of Peaches.

She said she noticed her daughter was unhappy at once, and heard Peaches and Daddy quarreling with great vim.

Mrs. Heenan said she was with Peaches and Daddy at the battles of Cold Springs, the Fairfield and the Gramatan hotels, but always at Daddy's invitation, whereupon Daddy's countenance took on a wry expression as if he had bitten into a lemon.

She said Daddy gave her daughter the name of Peaches. Others always called her Frances. Under cross-examination by Mr. Mack, she told about Daddy coming home one night with his face very red, and said he produced a bottle from his pocket and said, "Mother, I'm drunk."

It was on this occasion, she said, that he threatened to shoot

Peaches and her, but became very contrite when she threatened to call the police. Mr. Mack demanded:

"How big was that bottle? You're a nurse and familiar with ounces, how many ounces would that bottle contain?"

Mrs. Heenan replied, "About two ounces."

Mr. Mack looked startled. A two-ounce bottle is not much of a bottle, when you are talking about liquor.

He continued to press the lady for more information.

Mr. Mack, still on the subject of Daddy's condition, demanded, "Did he stagger like this?"

Then the counsel gave a very life-like stagger around his table, and Mrs. Heenan brightened. She said, "Just like that."

She said she had advised her daughter to return to Daddy and had always tried to keep peace between them, but that her daughter failed in health until after she left Daddy. Then she picked right up again.

At the afternoon session, Arthur Leduc, a reporter on the *Evening Journal*, testified briefly to having received pictures from Daddy, and to having interviewed Daddy and Peaches time and again. He said Daddy sent for him after the separation, and wanted to know how many times he had kissed Peaches and would he testify to the calculation. Leduc denied ever having kissed the blushing bride.

The attorneys on both sides filed a stipulation to defer the matter of investigating Daddy's financial status, which is involved in the squabble, until after the main issue had been settled.

Miss Tussey was the last witness of the day. She said a man named Proctor called at her apartment last Saturday evening and she refused to see him; then her landlord, one Croner, called her downstairs and introduced her to Proctor. She pointed out Proctor, sitting next to Daddy in the court room. He is of Daddy's legal squad.

Proctor gave her $5 and a subpoena, she said. Then Daddy came in, and wanted to know about those alleged nude parties, and that alleged illegal operation, as related at the beginning of this long-winded tale. Also, she said, Daddy wanted to know if Mrs. Heenan had ever belonged to a "call house," a "call house," my friends, being an institution of great iniquity, indigenous only to this great moral country.

Then Daddy and Peaches were left free to fight their way through the crowd that jammed the court room, the corridors and the street outside, though the ozone hereabouts was so nippy today that only a case of this nature could have kept the populace waiting out in the cold.

You could scarcely stir in the court room this afternoon, the crowd was so dense. At one stage the entire grand jury, on leave of absence for the moment from its arduous duty of making the rain of justice fall on the unjust, filed into the room, and stood listening with palpitating eardrums to the recitals.

Daddy got a mild cheer as he proceeded to his waiting Rolls-Royce, from which his chauffeur and footman had to clear a pile of rubbish made up of notes tossed into the car by ladies with strangely shaped heads. Peaches also got a few scattering whoops as she appeared before the public gaze.

This is a great country, my friends!

January 31, 1927

Some heavy emoting by that buxom matron of sixteen summers and 160 pounds, Mrs. Peaches Browning, was perhaps the high blood pressure point in our little sextravaganza in the Westchester County Court House today.

One James P. Mixon, black-haired, blocky-built, young man, in a blue serge suit, well shined in spots from much sitting down, came along testifying for old Daddy Browning that he had once been one of Peaches' little playmates in her flippery-flappery days before she married that great big rubber egg man.

This James P. Mixon did not get a chance to tell just how they played, but it was suggested in questions by John E. Mack, the bland, Bryanesque-looking, up-State attorney for Daddy, that brought Peaches to her feet, denouncing James P. Mixon as a liar in spades.

James P. Mixon gave his address as No. 65 Patchen Avenue, Brooklyn, no occupation stated. He said he was born in Louisiana, and nine Southern gentlemen in the court room suddenly keeled over as they thought of the possibility that his answers to Mack's interrogations might have been, "Yes, indeed."

Henry Epstein, the bashful attorney for Peaches, who seems to be growing more forward as he becomes inured to the slush, filed an objection to each question asked James P. Mixon as fast as it was asked by Mack, and Justice Seeger in each instance sustained the objection.

But meantime the questions as presented gave one and all something of a background for speculation over their morning's morning.

Peaches and her mother, who sat side by side at their counsel's table, looked somewhat startled as James P. Mixon eased his way through the journalists jammed in the jury box, and slumped down in the witness stand.

He had a black, beetling brow and rather a snarly expression. He did not state his age, but I would guess it as in the mid-twenties.

After Mack's first few questions it dawned on the assembled multitude what James P. Mixon's errand might be, and I think no one envied him his situation, though he was examined with great care by those present who might be interested in those odd specimens of human fauna that you come upon from time to time in the nooks and crevices of life.

Of course it is only fair to give James P. Mixon the benefit of the doubt and suggest that he might have answered no to Mack's questions, but so far the witnesses in the jolly little matrimonial muck-heaving between Peaches and Daddy have run to expected form.

James P. Mixon said he had met Peaches on the Strand Roof before her marriage to Daddy, and then he sat silent in the witness chair, looking somewhat uncomfortable, as Mack queried and Epstein objected.

Mack asked:

"Did you give her money to buy underwear?"

"Did you accompany her to a room in a hotel?"

"Did she take a bath and come out in the underwear and ask you how you liked her?"

"Did you and Peaches stay over night in the hotel room?"

All these, and others the witness was not permitted to answer. Justice Seeger said, "That's far enough."

"Do you think I'm going too far?" Mack asked as if surprised.

Apparently the Court did. You see we must have some delicacy somewhere in this matter, and not reach a point where we might offend good taste. I believe my readers will appreciate this restraint.

"Do you see this girl sitting there?"

Epstein asked it when he took the witness for cross-examination. Epstein's face was white with anger, and his index finger trembled violently as he aimed it at Peaches, whose blue eyes had been fixed on Mack's amiable countenance with an expression of alarm as he presented his interrogations.

Occasionally she looked at the witness with scorn. Her mother looked at him with several scorns. I suppose it is just as well for all hands that glances do not produce sudden strangulation, or James P. Mixon might have been lugged out of the court room feet foremost.

Mrs. Heenan remains the most remarkable parent I have ever clapped these old orbs on. The remarkable thing to me is that she can sit in the court room and hear all this junk about her child without having attacks of vertigo.

Anyway, James P. Mixon said yes, he did see Peaches, though his glance at her was what you might call casual. Epstein shouted, "Is she the one you are talking about?"

"Yes."

Peaches cried, her blue eyes bubbling tears: "He lies! I never saw him before in my life."

"That's the one, is it?"

Mack roared it, his voice clattering right behind Epstein's question and also taking a good point at Peaches.

"There's no question about that, is there?"

"No."

Peaches hopped to her feet and hammered her fist on the table, shouting, "I never saw him before in my life! He's perjuring himself!"

"You keep quiet!"

Epstein admonished her thus, a trifle ungallantly, so Peaches dissolved into tears and her mother wept with her.

Old Daddy seemed to enjoy this scene. He came in this morning wearing a black overcoat piped with silk, a blue suit and a very speedy tie. He always has a battery of three fat cigars jutting out of the upper outside pocket of his coat.

He had a pair of eye-glasses perched precariously on his aquiline beak, and was industriously poring over papers of one kind and another all day, but he listened with both ears wagging as Mack queried James P. Mixon.

Also Daddy smiled when Peaches went into her big scene.

Mixon said a man who said his name was Alexander came to him after Peaches' marriage and wanted to pay him to keep still about his relations with her. Mack asked Epstein, "Is Alexander one of your investigators?"

"I never employed an investigator at any time in this action."

It seems the witness married after an alleged hotel incident with Peaches, and Mack brought out from him that Mrs. Mixon gave him the well-known ozone when she heard of his terrible past in connection with Peaches.

Mrs. Mixon appeared on the stand, a slight, dark, little woman in a pink hat and black dress, and said she had seen photos of Peaches in her husband's possession and had torn up letters signed "Frances."

You must understand that no actual testimony bearing on all this innuendo contained in Mack's questions is in the records. Justice Seeger held that anything pertaining to Peaches' life before her marriage is not germane to this hearing.

Mack's idea was to prove by incidents in Peaches' past that she could not have been as mortified and chagrined as she alleges in her demand for separation from Daddy by the matters she sets up in said demand, such as being required to appear before him *au naturel*, so to speak.

Justice Seeger did permit Mixon to testify about an alleged telephone conversation with Peaches after her marriage, in which they wished plenty of happiness to each other, Mixon having meantime become wrapped up in those holy bonds of matrimony.

We had no little comedy today, and there was a genial atmosphere to the proceedings, with the Court and counsel bandying quips.

"Are you trying to establish that the lady didn't wear clothing in the dining-room?"

So inquired Justice Seeger, as Mack queried employees of the Kew Gardens Inn as to Peaches' manner of apparel in those jolly days of her honeymoon.

Then again, when Frank W. Golden, headwaiter at the inn, seemed to hesitate in answering questions by Epstein as to Daddy's liberality in tips, Justice Seeger said:

"You can tell what he gave you. We will not take 'it away from you."

I mention this to show you that we are far from acrimony as we go forward in this matter. The only ill-feeling today was developed in the crowd that stormed the court house because some of the New York newspapers have deplored the publicity given the hearing, and said that there really ought to be a censorship of everything.

I really felt sorry for the officers of the law on guard over the court room doors and feel that something should be done to insure their protection in the future.

They were viciously assaulted by infuriated women trying to shove past them to listen to the testimony and determine for themselves if it is as terrible as they hear. Hell hath no fury like a woman trying to break into a court room.

The more dangerous were mainly women past thirty and they stepped on the cops' corns and snatched buttons off the cops' jackets, and threatened to tweak the cops' noses if the cops got too gay with them.

One of the court room doors was broken down. The court room was jammed until the seams spread. Many of the women were standing on chairs to get a peek over the heads of those fortunate enough to grab seats, and Justice Seeger admonished them of danger.

"I warn you that if anybody stands on chairs it is at her own risk. You may get hurt if the chairs give way."

The street outside the court house and the corridors inside, were jammed before the morning session began. Everybody wished to get a look at Peaches and Daddy as they made their entrance. It was the biggest day in point of excitement and attendance since the hearing began.

Charlotte Mills, that drab, troubled looking little reminder of the Hall-Mills trial at Somerville, was an early arrival, and sat in the jury box. She wore a rose-colored turban, and a black coat. Charlotte is said to have been called as a witness.

There were a lot of distinguished looking citizens in the crowd, including Lady So-and-so. I have really forgotten the moniker.

Grandmotherly looking old women, stout, housewifely looking dames and skittish looking young dolls stood all morning and all afternoon on their two feet listening in.

Occasionally gusts of laughter would roll over the room, and once there was a scattering of applause as one of Daddy's witnesses was testifying.

I am told that many a dress was torn in the struggle for the doors.

I do not see how the girls were able to stand so long. Had their husbands required it of them under any other circumstances, it would be considered cruel and inhuman treatment and grounds for alimony.

The men were just as bad. They were outnumbered by the women only because the women are more adept in a struggle for a given point through long experience at bargain counters, and also because courtesy demands that the women and children be first.

Mack tried to get Peaches' original diary of incidents prior to her marriage admitted at the morning session, also some letters by which he said he expected to prove that she was a woman of the world and had once attended a game of "strip poker" before Daddy took her for better or for worse.

All this the Court ruled out.

"Strip poker," I might explain, is a little pastime with cards wherein the loser sheds garments until—well, you really cannot talk at any length about it.

Also, Mack said in his argument on the admission of the diary and letters, he expected to prove that Peaches knew more about men before her marriage than Ford knows about flivvers. At this point Peaches cried and her mother soothed her.

Miss Marion Tussey was recalled for further cross-examination by Epstein on her testimony some days ago. She is that auburn-haired, chubby young lady friend of Peaches who said Daddy had asked her to testify for him that she knew of Peaches' relations with men before her marriage, also that Mrs. Heenan had once been connected with a house that was not a nice house.

This proposition, Miss Tussey said, had been made in the presence of her landlord, one Bondy Croner, of No. 72 West Seventy-fifth Street, and Bondy disclosed himself presently as a German who might have stepped out of an old-time tintype.

He wore a high collar and a black bow tie, a long coat, and a reddish gray moustache.

Moreover, he had an accent, and was disposed to be quite discursive as he related that Miss Tussey had told him some indelicate things about Peaches and how Miss Tussey was by no means propositioned by Daddy as she claimed.

He admitted that he got $5 on two occasions from Proctor, one of Daddy's legal representatives, when he was served with a subpoena.

"Did you give either of the $5 fees to Miss Tussey?"

"No, she already had $5."

His wife, Louise Croner, a kindly looking old German woman, wearing gold-rimmed spectacles and a black dress with a lace jabot, was even more voluble than her husband as she sat with hands folded in her lap and discoursed of her knowledge of the visit of Daddy to her house to see Miss Tussey. Epstein asked, "What did he say?"

"He said good evening."

The witness uttered it simply, and the spectators laughed uproariously. After that, Mrs. Croner said, Daddy did not open his mouth.

Margaret Lou, a rather nice, neat-looking German girl, testified to hearing part of the conversation between Croner and Miss Tussey, and also disclosed Croner as a big-hearted fellow. She said he paid her $20 a month and her room and board for her labors as a maid in his household.

Leslie Fullenwider, a slight, well-groomed young fellow wearing a pince-nez with great aplomb and employing a Southern accent, testified to buying two great contributions to literature— "The Diary of Peaches," by Peaches, and "Why I Married Peaches," by the old boy himself, for a newspaper syndicate operated by Fullenwider and Lorman Wardell.

Fullenwider gave vent to many words but not much explicit information. His favorite reply was, "I'll have to leave that to someone else."

When he was asked who wrote the diary, he said, "I don't know that 'wrote' is exactly correct. John S. Garden assembled it."

Mack asked jovially, "You distinguish between wrote and rot?"

He said Daddy had visited him and wanted to know if he and Peaches had engaged in osculation, which Fullenwider said they had not.

Lorman Wardell also testified as to the activities of the syndicate in the "assembling" of Peaches' literary life work.

He took her to his home in Demarest, N. J., and to other points, after the separation, to escape the newspaper reporters, and paid her $1,000 for the diary. They got $1,000 for it from one newspaper and about thirty-five other papers used it, he said.

John S. Garden, another slight man, young, and with an intellectual expression behind his horn rims, said he compiled the diary for the syndicate. Epstein demanded:

"You are the hot writer, the red-hot man for the syndicate, are you?"

Mr. Garden denied this, blushing vigorously.

Belle Edwards, in a big raccoon coat, said she is a waitress at the Kew Gardens Inn and waited on Peaches and Daddy and that Daddy seemed to be an ever-loving husband.

He always had flowers on the table, "which was unusual be-

cause no one else had them," said Belle Edwards, handing the
other husbands of Kew Gardens a gentle jab.

Looking at Belle and looking at Peaches the casual observer
was moved to reflect on the irony of life that one should be waiting on the other. Belle was a right nifty looking young woman.

There was other testimony along this line. Golden, the headwaiter; Edward F. McDonald, manager of Kew Gardens Inn, and
Leo Ehrenreich, a resident of Kew Gardens, who had entertained
the Brownings, testified that Daddy seemed devoted to his
Peaches.

You got a fair cross-section of life in Kew Gardens from the
testimony.

Frank Dolan, a young and handsome newspaper reporter, and
obviously of many sterling personal characteristics, testified suc-
cinctly, and I might say very well, about seeing Peaches under
photographic fire, and other incidents.

Then came the afternoon session, and James P. Mixon, and his
wife, followed by Roman Androwsky, a baldish, foreign looking
young man, with an accent and mixed metaphor, who described
himself as a "sallisman." This was finally interpreted as a salesman
for the National Insurance Company.

"What do you sell, insurance?"

"Correct."

Androwsky was what you might call the big laugh of the day
as he told of hearing a conversation between Peaches and another
woman on Riverside Drive, in which Peaches was asked by the
woman as to whether she cared for Daddy. Her alleged remark
was:

"Don't be foolish. I never could love any man, but so far I've
got what I wanted and I'll have more before I'm through."

February 1, 1927

Well, folks, it was pretty sticky up here in White Plains today
in the way of testimony, as old Daddy Browning sat on the witness stand and prattled his tale of woe against the weighty young

Peaches, and they finally put the cover back on their matrimonial garbage can for a couple of weeks.

Both sides rested after Daddy had denied all, as the tabloid headline writers say, and after Peaches had also denied all once more, just for good measure, and Supreme Court Justice Seeger, who has been hearing the case, gave the attorneys two weeks in which to submit briefs in place of oral argument.

Poor Henry Epstein, the bashful barrister who is representing Peaches, was quite overcome during his cross-examination of Daddy, probably by the fumes of Daddy's testimony. Mr. Epstein sat down very suddenly during the afternoon session while Daddy was fumbling with answers to questions. Mr. Epstein's face was quite white and his hands shook.

He asked plaintively for a little air.

Judge Seeger promptly ordered a few windows opened, while bailiffs hurried water to Mr. Epstein's succor. Peaches and her Ma, Mrs. Frances Heenan, who were seated at Mr. Epstein's table, leaned forward solicitously.

Someone dashed out into the crowded main stem of White Plains, fighting his way through the packed corridors of the court house, and returned with some spirits of ammonia. Mr. Epstein inconsiderately drank the ammonia instead of sprinkling it about the premises.

A five-minute recess was given Mr. Epstein by Judge Seeger and everybody managed to revive more or less and continue listening to Daddy. The court room was packed to what you might call suffocation and the ladies present seemed to stand it better than the men. In fact, they proved themselves gluttons for punishment, as the boys say. Some removed their modish helmets that they might not miss a word that fell from Daddy's pendant lips.

At the conclusion of the hearing Judge Seeger remarked that if he ever had another case like this he would hear it in private. He gently chided the newspaper reporters for adding comment to their reports, but I hope and trust that the Court will not deem it comment if I add one little word to his statement that other cases of this kind will be heard in private. The word is "Amen."

But it was a big day for old Daddy Browning as he sat up

there on the witness stand, with his wife eyeing him, now disdainfully, and now rather wistfully, but always eyeing him. Daddy's ma-in-law also eyed him, using two eyes for the purpose. Daddy kept his own eyes, which are rather glittering eyes, on other points of the compass. He scarcely ever glanced at the wife and her parent.

He wore a blue suit and a high turn-down linen collar that seemed about to strangle him. He kept jerking his head forward to free his neck from the embrace of the collar like an old snapping-turtle popping its beezer out of its shell.

Daddy had a reddish purplish complexion, peculiar to golfers, or Scotch inhalers, though he took occasion to deny vehemently that he ever drank to any extent in the fifty-two years of his life. He said fifty-two. He looked older, what with the wattles on his jowls, and his thin white hair.

He wore a very fancy necktie, with a diamond set in gold stuck in it. An inside pocket of his coat bulged with papers. Three fat cigars peeped out of the upper outside pocket of his coat, as usual. They must be "prop" cigars, or Daddy replaces them every day.

He kept his hands folded in his lap, twiddling the fingers from time to time as he pondered some question. Occasionally he wrinkled up his forehead, and peered at the ceiling as he thought over some interrogation. When he talked, he talked so rapidly that the words fairly tumbled over one another. Once or twice, under cross-examination, he got quite excited and yelled his answers.

One occasion was when Mr. Epstein, in a most abashed manner, handed him a photograph and asked him if it was one that he had taken home to Peaches, and said to be a photograph of Marion Dockerill. Daddy recoiled as the bailiff poked the picture at him, and bawled:

"No, that's a filthy picture. I'd be ashamed to show it if I were you."

Your ever-blushing correspondent got a fleeting glimpse of the photo as it was passed from hand to hand, and he violates no confidence in stating that it was, and doubtless still is, a photographic reproduction of a lady who seems to be posing with no drapes of any consequence about her person, not even as much as the proverbial fig leaf. Epstein asked:

"But you weren't ashamed to show it to your wife?"

"Yes, I was—maybe you showed it to her. That's a filthy picture. I understand you stole it out of some place to frame me with."

This statement was ordered stricken out by the Court. Daddy fingered the picture very gingerly, but he refused to identify it as a likeness of Marion Dockerill.

As I gathered, Miss Dockerill is an exponent of some mysteriout art of science known as numerology. Daddy said she gave both him and Peaches "readings," but Peaches didn't care for hers. Then Mr. Epstein handed him what purported to be a picture of Miss Dockerill taken from a newspaper and asked Daddy to compare this with the one he shrank from and say if they were from the same person.

Daddy handled the pictures as if he feared they might bite him, and finally remarked, somewhat cryptically, "Well, in one she seems to have a hat on."

There was some disappointment among the spectators that the original photo was not handed around more freely. It was no worse than some of the testimony, at that, though it might cause more of a sensation if hung in a hotel lobby.

Daddy hemmed and hawed no little with Peaches' attorney and had Mr. Epstein quite impatient at times. Also Judge Seeger got a bit impatient with Mr. Epstein and mildly rebuked the attorney for some of his questions to Daddy. On direct examination at the hands of his own attorney, John E. Mack, Daddy answered with surprising swiftness.

It was when Mr. Epstein asked Daddy about Peaches' charges concerning his relations with Dorothy Sunshine Browning, his ten-year-old adopted daughter, that Daddy let out another yell.

"I think more of that child than I do of my life."

He bellowed that he had never even heard of some of the other things that Peaches alleges against him. Daddy has quite a resounding voice when he puts all his lung power behind it, though it was dropping to a low whisper at times during the cross-examination. He has what you might call a "Bowery" accent—saying "boid" for "bird" and "poifect" for "perfect."

His tale was mainly the sad, sad tale of what the Broadway boys term a "sap say," meaning a "sap" trying to catch up with a little youth after he has passed that old fifty-yard line. By the way, the Roaring Forties contributed a few listeners-in today. They never heard anything like this downtown.

They called him to the stand at 11:25 this morning, and Daddy, for some reason, did not move with alacrity. He got up from his chair slowly, whispered a moment to Attorney Mack, then ambled to the witness chair. He somehow seemed very, very old as he hoisted his frame to the chair. Peaches and Mrs. Heenan watched him very closely, and Peaches' face broke into a wide smile when Daddy denied that she had walked up to him when he was talking with some other girls at a dance at the McAlpin, was introduced to him and asked him to dance with her.

Daddy rather gave the impression that Peaches, then fifteen years old, pursued him hotly in those dear, dead days of some months ago, calling him up, and one thing and another. So they were married, as the movies say, and as you must know by this time.

That mysterious burning of Peaches by acid came into Daddy's discourse, but he could throw no light on it. He said the Heenans had little to eat, and their rent and radio instalments were unpaid, and that he took care of all those little matters, besides giving Peaches $300 for clothes to enter the Spence, Central or Scudder school, all quite fashionable institutions.

Instead, he said, she had gone to Earl Carroll's theatre and got a job, not as a bathtub exhibit,* but as an extra girl. This disappointed him no end, Daddy said. He told her it was no life for a girl. After the acid incident he paid Mrs. Heenan $50 per week

* An allusion to Joyce Hawley, who sprawled in a bathtub of champagne at a party staged by Earl Carroll—an incident that produced another big-head-line story in the Twenties and put Carroll (because of his forgetfulness of the details) in a Federal cooler.

to take care of Peaches, and paid a Mrs. Mayer as a night nurse. Mack asked:

"Did you call at the Heenan home until the Pizzaro incident?"

Mr. Epstein objected to that question forthwith. There has been nothing said about Mr. Pizzaro. Who was Mr. Pizzaro, anyway?

Well, it came out that Mr. Pizzaro had been hanging around the Heenans, muttering about getting evidence to put Peaches in an institution.

So Daddy figured there was only one way out. Peaches would make him a good wife. So they were married, as I have said before. Then Daddy proceeded to a categorical denial of each and every incident of the nuptial night and thereafter, alleged by Peaches, as reflecting on his character as a gentleman and scholar, and causing her mental pain and anguish.

He took her everywhere, parties, dances, theatres. He spent his dough on her for clothes and jewelry, Russian sable and ermine coats. He called her up two or three times a day. He never hurled phone books at her, never slugged her, never set off an alarm clock in her ear, never crawled around on his hands and knees in her bed chamber and said "woof, woof" (as she had testified).

He said, "I may have crawled around on my hands and knees when I was a baby, but never since."

Mack asked, "You are not in your second childhood, then?"

"I hope not."

Oh, yes, about the gander—the African honking gander, that has been going kah-donking through the hearing. It seems that they were at a lawn party one day, at the home of some folks named Reeves, and they had the gander, and Peaches thought it would be just dandy to own the gander.

So, eager to grant her slightest wish, Daddy borrowed the gander and Peaches tied a ribbon around its neck, and down to Long Beach they went to parade the honker along the boardwalk, and have it photographed. That was that, Daddy said. He never threatened to kill Peaches and her mother, and never got drunk. The sandpapering of his shoe-trees, mentioned by Peaches as one of the causes of her mental anguish, was nothing more than a little cobbling on one of Peaches' own shoes. It was tight, so he sandpapered it for her.

Incidentally, Daddy mentioned that he often wore Peaches' tennis shoes and house slippers, and that she wore his, because they fit both ways, which statement caused some of the curious in the court to try to get a peek at Peaches' feet. Mr. Epstein learned from Daddy that he wears a No. 6 shoe. He said Peaches wanted an apartment on Park Avenue with "all corner rooms," which would have been a lot of corner in any man's town, and that furthermore, she wanted six or seven rooms, because her mother wanted two dogs while Peaches wanted three.

Mack asked, "Did you have any idea that your wife or mother-in-law was going to leave you?"

"Not my wife."

"And your mother-in-law?"

"I er-ah-er—I was hoping so."

Mrs. Heenan laughed loudly.

This was about the only dig Daddy took at Mrs. Heenan, and he seemed ashamed of it, for he quickly added, "I didn't mean that—I didn't mind her staying with us."

But he said under cross-examination that he was scarcely ever alone at any time with Peaches, and that the marriage relation was never truly that of man and wife. I believe that is the polite expression among us polite people.

A lot of those mysterious little letters that Daddy has been trying to get into the record were finally produced by Mr. Mack. They were notes written to Daddy by Peaches in his office when she would be waiting for him, and they were simple little epistles. In fact they were so simple you might call 'em childish.

She wrote one poem to him in which she sang:

> I love you.
> I love you—
> You are the idle of my dreams.

That is the way she spelled it. We can give Peaches about 89 in spelling.

When Mr. Epstein brought Peaches back to the witness stand

as one of his last witnesses, she said she had written these things at Daddy's request.

Peaches denied ever having seen the fellow, James P. Mixon, whom she denounced as a liar yesterday when he claimed to be one of her former boy friends.

Also she denied the testimony of one Swint that she used baseball players' language.

Peaches wore exactly the same outfit of blue dress and hat, and sable coat that she started out with at Carmel, and her face showed signs of strain.

About the only allegation of Peaches that Daddy admitted was buying a dozen green handkerchiefs for a St. Patrick's Day ball. Peaches said he "had hundreds" in his pocket, but Daddy defied anybody to get that many 'kerchiefs in one pocket.

Mr. Epstein examined him at great length as to his living expenses, and brought out that Daddy pays about $800 a month for the famous hired Rolls-Royce and its crew of two, but the two work in his office when not escorting him.

He said he had spent between $10,000 and $12,000 on clothes and one thing and another for Peaches, but didn't expect her to go through life as Mrs. Browning at that clip. Mr. Epstein spent some time over the matter of Daddy's ownership of a pistol, and read at length from interviews and stories printed in newspapers purporting to quote Daddy. Daddy admitted some, and denied others. Epstein asked:

"When was the first time you kissed your wife?"

Daddy puffed both cheeks full of wind, stared at the ceiling and the crowd roared.

"Wife, or before she was my wife?"

Then he admitted that the first time he had committed osculation with Peaches was on a trip to Yonkers.

Oh, yes, about that Japanese princess that Peaches said Daddy told her he would buy her when she said she wanted children. Daddy said he couldn't seem to remember a thing about any Japanese princess, and as for Peaches wishing children—well.

And then the cross-examination went past the precincts of pure literature. In reply to a question if he had ever requested his wife to sit at the dinner table at Cold Springs, in his presence, quite nude, as Peaches asserted, Daddy said, "Absolutely not. It was very cold. It would have been foolish to ask her."

As a final witness, Mr. Epstein recalled Dr. George A. Blakeslee, a neurological expert, who said he had much experience with pyscho-neurosis with the Eighty-second Division during the war.

The purport of a long question was, would all the things set forth by Peaches against Daddy, including the goose, rubber eggs, sandpapering and all the rest, cause the nervous disorder to which Peaches is said to be prone. The doctor said he thought it would.

At the morning session, Mr. and Mrs. Frank J. Farney, of Evanston, Ill., testified for Daddy. They were guests at the Kew Gardens Inn when Daddy and Peaches were living there, and the couples made a jolly foursome on many occasions. It came out that Farney, who makes nursery furniture, and is of the go-getter type of mid-westerner, was the victim of Daddy's rubber egg joke.

Farney said he thought it was a riot of a joke, at that. Moreover, he took the egg home with him. Both he and Mrs. Farney, a classy looking matron, said Daddy seemed devoted to Peaches and gave her so many things "it made me feel like a piker," as Farney put it. He said there had been chatter about children to and fro on occasion, and he offered to provide Daddy and Peaches with the nursery, but Peaches said not for her, or words to that effect.

Miss Emma R. Steiner, a picturesque woman with a rakish black hat over her white hair, testified to knowing Daddy for twenty-eight years. She said she is an orchestral conductor and that her last direction was of the Metropolitan Orchestra, at which statement the customers sat up and took notice.

She had a kind word for all, including Mrs. Heenan. She said Daddy was always devoted to his mother and she thought his relations with Peaches were ideal. She made a tremendous impression. She was frank, outspoken, and no trace of rancor marked any of her statements. The folks smiled on her as she left the stand.

Miss Margaret MacDonald, who said she is a journalist and

publicist, and Mrs. Norma Drupyke, president of the Victory
Club, of 106 West Fifty-ninth Street, New York, where Daddy
gave his famous birthday party for Peaches, testified that Daddy
always seemed a kind and loving hubby to Peaches.

Then came Daddy.

As both sides rested, Epstein moved the dismissal of the first
cause of action by Daddy, which is cruelty, but Judge Seeger
said, while he thought the motion should be granted, he would
reserve decision until he heard the arguments, which the attorneys
agreed should be in written form.

Mr. Mack thanked the Court for his patience, to which Judge
Seeger replied he had enjoyed it as much as one could be expected
to enjoy such a case, rather leaving the impression that this isn't
much enjoyment after all.

He said he had held the hearing in public only for fear he
might have been misunderstood had he held it in private, what
with great wealth on one side. But he made it clear that if the
lawyers have any more cases like this that they desire heard in
public, they had better forget his address.

·   ·   ·   ·   ·

*Some days after the trial's end, the Court awarded Mrs. Brown-
ing, "Peaches," the decree of separation she sought.*

*In the meantime—on the morning after the curtain fell on the
big show at White Plains—a New York newspaper gave it a sour
review. Runyon was moved to write in the New York* American:

I have just read an editorial in one of the leading public prints
deploring the publicity that is being given our little presentation
at White Plains, the Daddy-Peaches Browning atrocity.

It is a good editorial, at that, well written, and timely, and it
appears on a page hard by one carrying advertisements of some
highly moral and uplifting plays now running on Broadway, and
dealing with such interesting topics as miscegenation, male and
female perversion, divorce, seduction, Negro honky-tonks, night
life deadfalls, larceny, assault and battery, bootlegging, burglary,

forgery, murder, and perhaps some lesser peccadilloes of this great human race.

Also there are advertisements on this page of other shows that go in largely and liberally for female nudity, preferably young, which is hung on curtains like skinned sheep on meat hooks, or disposed in picturesque posture about the theatrical premises in the name, I believe, of Art.

Our modest offense at White Plains is out-nuded ten to one by any one of these undraped casts.

The editorial inveighed against the tabloids for making much of the Daddy-Peaches outrage, though I can remember when the newspaper in which the editorial appeared was one of the loudest organs in the land when it came to playing on our social disorders. I would like to place its accounts of the Thaw trial alongside the tabloid report on Daddy and Peaches, and show you how strong it went in those days.

But I suppose a newspaper is only human, after all.

You take a fellow who has massed a ton or two of money after a humble beginning carrying a pack, or peddling peanuts, or gathering junk, and he eventually yearns for social position for himself and his family.

And if he attains it, he is usually one of the first to deplore the manifestations of the masses, and to fail to understand them.

I suppose a newspaper that has picked up a lot of circulation and prosperity in its younger days by the huffle-scuffle, whoop-tee-do methods of presenting the news that they used to call yellow journalism, finally comes upon the same yearning.

I would not be surprised to see the tabloids one day wearing journalistic high hats and deploring some new and popular form of newspaper enterprise, just as they are now high-hatted and deplored by some of their venerable reformed brethren.

But, if you ask me, I think the publicity that is being given Daddy and Peaches is a good thing.

I do not mean to say that the case itself is a good thing. On the contrary, I am as hearty a deplorer as the writer of the editorial I have been talking about when it comes to deploring the case. But as long as such cases are permitted in the courts of law they ought to get plenty of publicity, if only because it mirrors to the rest of humanity the sappiness of some of its representatives, and perhaps of the law, too, and thus may possibly act as a deterrent to other saps.

The whole trouble is with the New York law that requires, or permits, the kind of testimony that has been produced in the Daddy-Peaches case. As I understand it, Peaches wouldn't live with Daddy on a bet, and she is about as welcome now to that dizzy old beezark as a case of smallpox.

But under the law they have to go into court and give a lot of odious reasons why they no longer desire any part of each other's company.

In other States, the mere statement of desertion, or incompatibility, or any one of a dozen other causes is sufficient ground for a split-out between unhappy couples.

In New York you must have trimmings, and the result is generally unfit for publication. I do not say the New York law is wrong. I merely speak of net results.

I hear lawyers criticizing the newspapers for publicizing incidents like the Daddy-Peaches affair; but what of the legal fraternity that files proceedings of this nature as hooks for the publicity?

I believe if I had been Peaches' attorney I would have rested on the African honking gander, and had I been representing Daddy I would have closed with my cross-examination of Maw-in-law, showing that she was on deck at all times right from the bell.

Supreme Court Justice Seeger, who is presiding at the hearing, had it in mind to hold the thing in private when it first opened at Carmel. His chief thought was to protect Peaches as a minor. But his decision to hold it in public was, I think, quite sound, because, as he said, the parties to the case had never before shrunk from publicity. On the contrary, they had sought it with astonishing avidity.

I was greatly relieved by Judge Seeger's decision. My years and my spats would make it most unseemly and undignified for me to be eavesdropping at keyholes and waylaying witnesses hot off the stand in quest of news of the proceedings. Anyway, I might have gotten my second-hand information garbled up by the time I presented it to the public, and I can garble it first-hand good enough to suit any one.

You may be sure the newspapers would get the news, even if the case were held behind closed doors. And as a newspaper reader you would expect it of your favorite publication, and cavil at its lack of enterprise did it fail.

They would have gotten it, if all other sources were shut off, from Daddy and Peaches themselves, with fresh photographic postures of them after each session.

As one of my readers remarked to me the other day:

"I am astonished at the newspapers printing that awful stuff— but, say, tell me just what it was they had to leave out, will you?"

Peaches capitalized on her notoriety in vaudeville. It was esti-mated that she earned $125,000 before the vaudeville public lost interest in seeing her "in person."

Browning died in 1934. A codicil to his will said Mrs. Brown-ing had caused him "great mental distress" and "unnecessary ex-penditure of money," and declared he did not want her to get a widow's share of his estate. His will devised ninety per cent of his money to charitable institutions, and provided for payment of $14,000 a year to the other Browning protégé, Dorothy Sunshine, whom he had gone through the legal formality of adopting as a daughter.

Peaches sued for a widow's third of the estate, and evidence was presented that the Wall Street debacle of 1929 had deflated Mr. Browning's estate and ego considerably. Peaches settled her claim for $170,000, of which, of course, lawyers took their usual share.

Peaches soon acquired another husband. The marriage lasted about a year. Another marriage, and still another, followed, to swell her scrapbooks.

Twenty years after the epic trial in White Plains, Peaches was still living her life in headlines.

Early in 1947, her fourth husband, who was described in news-

*papers as a "member of a wealthy, meat-packing family of Colum-
bus, O.," asked a San Francisco court to declare his marriage with
Peaches null and void on the ground that her divorce from her
third husband had not been concluded when the fourth marriage
occurred.*

*About the same time, her father, William B. Heenan, aged 69,
applied to her publicly for financial assistance. He said he hadn't
heard from her in three years.*

*Her mother announced: "My daughter is the wisest of all the
girls who made the headlines in the Twenties. Most of them are
broke but Frances has all her money in real estate."*

THE ETERNAL BLONDE

Long Island City, New York, April 19, 1927

A chilly looking blonde with frosty eyes and one of those marble, you-bet-you-will chins, and an inert, scare-drunk fellow that you couldn't miss among any hundred men as a dead set-up for a blonde, or the shell game, or maybe a gold brick.

Mrs. Ruth Snyder and Henry Judd Gray are on trial in the huge weatherbeaten old court house of Queens County in Long Island City, just across the river from the roar of New York, for what might be called for want of a better name, The Dumbbell Murder. It was so dumb.

They are charged with the slaughter four weeks ago of Albert Snyder, art editor of the magazine, *Motor Boating*, the blonde's husband and father of her nine-year-old daughter, under circumstances that for sheer stupidity and brutality have seldom been equalled in the history of crime.

It was stupid beyond imagination, and so brutal that the thought of it probably makes many a peaceful, home-loving Long Islander of the Albert Snyder type shiver in his pajamas as he prepares for bed.

They killed Snyder as he slumbered, so they both admitted in confessions—Mrs. Snyder has since repudiated hers—first whacking him on the head with a sash weight, then giving him a few whiffs of chloroform, and finally tightened a strand of picture wire around his throat so he wouldn't revive.

This matter disposed of, they went into an adjoining room and had a few drinks of whiskey used by some Long Islanders, which is very bad, and talked things over. They thought they had committed "the perfect crime," whatever that may be. It was probably

139

the most imperfect crime on record. It was cruel, atrocious and unspeakably dumb.

They were red-hot lovers then, these two, but they are strangers now. They never exchanged a glance yesterday as they sat in the cavernous old court room while the citizenry of Long Island tramped in and out of the jury box, and the attorneys tried to get a jury of twelve men together without success.

Plumbers, clerks, electricians, merchants, bakers, butchers, barbers, painters, salesmen, machinists, delicatessen dealers, garage employes, realtors and gardeners from the cities and the hamlets of the County of Queens were in the procession that marched through the jury box answering questions as to their views on the death penalty, and their sympathies toward women, and other things.

Out of fifty men, old and young, married and single, bald and hairy, not one was found acceptable to both sides. Forty-three were excused, the State challenged one peremptorily, the attorneys for Mrs. Snyder five, and the attorneys for Gray one. Each defendant is allowed thirty peremptory challenges, the State thirty against each defendant.

At this rate they may be able to get a jury before the Long Island corn is ripe. The State is asking that Mrs. Snyder and her meek looking Lothario be given the well-known "hot seat" in Sing Sing, more generally known as the electric chair, and a lot of the talesmen interrogated today seemed to have a prejudice against that form of punishment.

Others had opinions as to the guilt or innocence that they said they couldn't possibly change. A few citizens seemed kindly disposed toward jury service, possibly because they haven't anything at hand for the next few weeks, but they got short shrift from the lawyers. The jury box was quite empty at the close of the day's work.

Mrs. Snyder, the woman who has been called a Jezebel, a lineal descendant of the Borgia outfit, and a lot of other names, came in for the morning session of court stepping along briskly in her patent-leather pumps, with little short steps.

She is not bad looking. I have seen much worse. She is thirty-three and looks just about that, though you cannot tell much about blondes. She has a good figure, slim and trim, with narrow shoulders. She is of medium height and I thought she carried her clothes off rather smartly. She wore a black dress and a black silk coat with a collar of black fur. Some of the girl reporters said it was dyed ermine; others pronounced it rabbit.

They made derogatory remarks about her hat. It was a tight-fitting thing called, I believe, a beret. Wisps of her straw-colored hair straggled out from under it. Mrs. Snyder wears her hair bobbed, the back of the bobbing rather ragged. She is of the Scandinavian type. Her parents are Norwegian and Swedish.

Her eyes are blue-green, and as chilly looking as an ice cream cone. If all that Henry Judd Gray says of her actions the night of the murder is true, her veins carry ice water. Gray says he dropped the sash weight after slugging the sleeping Snyder with it once and that Mrs. Snyder picked it up and finished the job.

Gray's mother and sister, Mrs. Margaret Gray, and Mrs. Harold Logan, took seats in the court room just behind Mrs. Snyder. At the afternoon session, Mrs. Gray, a small, determined-looking woman of middle age, hitched her chair over so she was looking right into Mrs. Snyder's face.

There was a rather grim expression in Mrs. Gray's eyes. She wore a black hat and a black coat with a fur collar, a spray of artificial flowers was pinned to the collar. Her eyelids were red as if she had been weeping.

The sister, Mrs. Logan, is plump and pleasant looking. Gray's wife has left him flat, in the midst of his troubles and gone to Norwalk, Conn., with their nine-year-old daughter. She never knew her husband was playing that Don Juan business when she thought he was out peddling corsets. That is she never knew it until the murder.

Gray, a spindly fellow in physical build, entered the court room with quick, jerky little steps behind an officer, and sat down between his attorneys, Samuel L. Miller and William L. Millard. His back was to Mrs. Snyder who sat about ten feet distant. Her eyes were on a level with the back of his narrow head.

Gray was neatly dressed in a dark suit, with a white starched collar and subdued tie. He has always been a bit to the dressy side, it is said. He wears big, horn-rimmed spectacles and his eyes have a startled expression. You couldn't find a meeker, milder looking fellow in seven states, this man who is charged with one of the most horrible crimes in history.

He occasionally conferred with his attorneys as the examination of the talesmen was going forward, but not often. He sat in one position almost the entire day, half slumped down in his chair, a melancholy looking figure for a fellow who once thought of "the perfect crime."

Mrs. Snyder and Gray have been "hollering copper" on each other lately, as the boys say. That is, they have been telling. Gray's defense goes back to old Mr. Adam, that the woman beguiled him, while Mrs. Snyder says he is a "jackal," and a lot of other things besides that, and claims that he is hiding behind her skirts.

She will claim, it is said, that while she at first entered into the conspiracy to kill her husband, she later tried to dissuade Gray from going through with it, and tried to prevent the crime. The attorneys will undoubtedly try to picture their respective clients as the victims of each other.

Mrs. Snyder didn't want to be tried with Gray, but Gray was very anxious to be tried with Mrs. Snyder. It is said that no Queens County jury ever sent a woman to death, which is what the State will ask of this jury, if it ever gets one. The relations among the attorneys for the two defendants are evidently not on the theory of "one for all and all for one." Probably the attorneys for Gray do not care what happens to Mrs. Snyder, and probably the attorneys for Mrs. Snyder feel the same way about Gray.

Edgar Hazelton, a close-trimmed dapper looking man, with a jutting chin and with a pince-nez balanced on a hawk beak, who represents Mrs. Snyder, did most of the questioning of the talesmen for the defense. His associate, Dana Wallace, is a former district attorney of Queens County, and the pair are said to be among the ablest lawyers on Long Island. It is related that they have defended eleven murder cases without a conviction going against them.

Supreme Court Justice Townsend Scudder is presiding over the court room, which has a towering ceiling with a stained glass skylight, and heavy dark oak furniture with high-backed pews for the spectators. Only no spectators were admitted today because the room was needed for the talesmen.

The court room is so huge it was difficult to hear what was going on at any distance from the bench. I believe it is the largest court room in the country. It was there that the trial scene in the picture *Manslaughter* was filmed.

In the court room on the floor below was held the trial of Mrs. Nack in the famous Guldensuppe murder thirty years ago, when the reporters used carrier pigeons to take their copy across the river to Park Row.

Microphones have been posted on the tables, and amplifiers have been rigged up on the walls, probably the first time this was ever done in a murder trial, but the apparatus wasn't working any too well today, and one hundred and twenty newspaper writers scattered around the tables listened with their hands cupped behind their ears.

Here is another record, the number of writers covering the trial. We have novelists, preachers, playwrights, fiction writers, sports writers and journalists at the press benches. Also we have nobility in the persons of the Marquis of Queensbury and Mrs. Marquis. The Marquis is a grandson of the gent whose name is attached to the rules governing the manly art of scrambling ears, but the young man wore a pair of fancy-topped shoes yesterday that surprised me. It isn't done you know, really!

The Reverend John Roach Straton was present wearing a Buster Brown necktie that was almost unclerical. A Catholic priest was on hand, but he carried no pad or pencil to deceive us. Some of the writers came attended by their secretaries, which shows you how far we have gone since the days of the carrier pigeons at the Guldensuppe trial.

There were quite a number of philosophers. I have been requested by my Broadway constituency to ascertain if possible what, if anything, philosophy suggests when a hotsy-totsy blonde with whom a guy is enamoured tells him to do thus and so. But then a philosopher probably never gets tangled up with blondes, or he wouldn't be a philosopher.

Mrs. Snyder showed signs that might have been either nervousness or just sheer impatience during the day. Her fingers constantly toyed with a string of black beads at her throat. Her entire set-up suggested mourning. She has nice white hands, but they are not so small as Gray's. His hands are quite effeminate.

In fact, the alienists who examined Gray and pronounced him quite sane say he is effeminate in many ways. Gray showed no signs of nervousness or any particular animation whatever. He just sat there. It must be a strain on a man to sit for hours knowing the eyes of a woman who is trying to get him all burned up are beating against the back of his neck and not turn around and give her at least one good hot glare.

April 27, 1927

Some say Mrs. Ruth Snyder "wept silently" in court yesterday. It may be so. I could detect no sparkle of tears against the white marble mask, but it is conceivable that even the very gods were weeping silently as a gruff voice slowly recited the blond woman's own story of the murder of her husband by herself and Henry Judd Gray.

Let no one infer she is altogether without tenderness of heart, for when they were jotting down the confession that was read in the court room in Long Island City, Peter M. Daly, an assistant district attorney, asked her:

"Mrs. Snyder, why did you kill your husband?"

He wanted to know.

"Don't put it that way," she said, according to his testimony yesterday. "It sounds so cruel."

"Well, that is what you did, isn't it?" he asked, in some surprise.

"Yes," he claims she answered, "but I don't like that term."

A not astonishing distaste, you must admit.

"Well, why did you kill him?" persisted the curious Daly.

"To get rid of him," she answered, simply, according to Daly's testimony; and indeed that seems to have been her main idea throughout, if all the evidence the State has so far developed is true.

She afterward repudiated the confession that was presented yesterday, with her attorneys trying to bring out from the State's witnesses that she was sick and confused when she told her bloody yarn five weeks ago.

The woman, in her incongruous widow's weeds sat listening intently to the reading of her original confession to the jury, possibly the most horrible tale that ever fell from human lips, the tale of a crime unutterably brutal and cold-blooded and unspeakably dumb.

Her mouth opened occasionally as if framing words, and once she said no quite distinctly, an unconscious utterance, which may have been a denial of some utterance by the lawyer or perhaps an assurance to her soul that she was not alive and awake.

This is a strange woman, this Mrs. Ruth Brown Snyder, a different woman to different men.

To the inert Henry Judd Gray, her partner in crime, sitting at the table just in front of her, as soggy looking as a dummy in his loose hanging clothes, she was a "woman of great charm," as he said in his confession which was outlined in court by a police officer yesterday.

To big, hale and hearty George P. McLaughlin, former police commissioner of New York City, who heard her original statement of the butchery, she was a "woman of great calm," as he said on the witness stand yesterday.

To the male reporters who have been following the trial she is all that, anyway, though they construe her calm as more the chill of the icy Northland, whence came her parents.

The attorneys for Mrs. Snyder, the nimble Dana Wallace and Edgar Hazelton, indicated yesterday clearly that part of their line of defense, in this devil-take-the-hindmost scramble between Ruth and Henry Judd is to be an attempted impeachment of the confession, and Gray's attorneys showed the same thought.

Samuel L. Miller, representing Gray, charged that the confession of the corset salesman was secured while he was under duress and by intimidation and threats.

Gray sat with his chin in his hands, his eyes on the floor, scarcely moving a muscle as Mrs. Snyder's confession, damning him in almost every word, was read. I have never seen him show much animation at best, but yesterday he seemed completely sunk. He occasionally conferred in whispers through his fingers with one of his attorneys, but with not the slightest show of interest.

It was Gray who slugged poor Albert Snyder with the five-pound sash weight as the art editor lay asleep in his bed, so Mrs. Snyder's confession relates, while Mrs. Snyder stood outside in the hall, seeing, by the dim light thrown into the chamber of horror by an arc in the street, the rise and fall of the paper-wrapped weight in Gray's hand.

What a scene that must have been!

Twice she heard her husband groan. Roused from an alcoholic stupor by that first thump on his head, he groaned. Then groaned again. Silence. Out came Henry Judd Gray, saying: "Well, I guess that's it."

But the confessions do not jibe here. The outline of Gray's confession, which will be read today, indicates Gray says he dropped the weight after whacking Snyder once, and that Ruth picked it up "and belabored him."

"Those were Gray's words—'belabored him,'" ex-Commissioner McLaughlin said yesterday.

District Attorney Newcombe overlooked an opportunity for the dramatic yesterday that old David Belasco, sitting back in the crowd, probably envied, in the reading of Ruth's confession. This was first identified by Peter M. Daly, the assistant mentioned above, after Ruth's attorneys had failed in a hot battle against its admission.

Newcombe stood before the jury with the typewritten sheets in one hand and talked off the words without elocutionary effort, the microphone carrying his voice out over the silent court room. The place was jammed. Women again. At the afternoon session they almost tore the buttons off the uniforms of the coppers on guard at the doors, trying to shove past them. The cops gallantly repulsed the charge.

The first paragraphs of the confession, made to Daly soon after the murder and under circumstances that the defense is attacking, were given over to a recital of Ruth's early life—born on Manhattan Island thirty-three years ago, a schoolgirl, an employee in the same magazine office with Snyder, then an artist when she married him.

The thing has been told so often before that I here go over it sketchily. Soon she was unhappy with her husband, fourteen years older than herself. He constantly belittled her. He threatened to blow out her brains. He was a good provider for herself and their nine-year-old daughter, but wouldn't take her out—so she took to stepping out, as they say. An old, old yarn—Friend Husband a non-stepper, Friend Wife full of go.

She met Henry Judd Gray, the corset salesman, in Henry's restaurant in the once-throbbing Thirties in New York, and the first thing anybody knew she and Henry were thicker than is meet and proper. She told Henry of her matrimonial woes, and Henry, himself a married man, with a young daughter, was duly sympathetic.

But let's get down to the murder.

She wrote Henry and told him how Albert Snyder had threatened her life. She wrote in a code they had rigged up for their own private use, and Henry answered, saying the only thing to do was to get rid of Albert. They had talked of ways and means, and Gray gave her the famous sash weight and went out to Queens Village one night to wipe Albert Snyder out.

They got cold feet that night and Albert lived. Then Snyder again threatened her, the confession said, and told her to get out of his house, so she wrote to Henry once more, and Henry wrote back, saying, "We will deliver the goods Saturday." That meant Saturday, March 19. They arranged all the details by correspondence.

Henry arranged his alibi in Syracuse and came to New York the night she and her husband and child were at the Fidgeons' party. She left a door unlocked so Henry could get in the room of her mother, Mrs. Josephine Brown, who was away for the night. Ruth saw him there and talked with him a moment when she came back from the party with her husband and child.

Henry had the sash weight which she had left under the pillow in Mrs. Brown's room for him. He had chloroform, some cheese-cloth and a blue cotton handkerchief. Also, she had hospitably left a quart of liquor for him of which he drank about half. She put her child to bed, then went into her husband's room and waited until he was asleep, then returned to the waiting Henry.

They talked briefly, and Henry kissed her and went into Albert Snyder's room. She stood in the hallway and saw Gray pummel the sleeping man with the sash weight as related. Then Gray tied Snyder's hands and feet, put the handkerchief, saturated with chloroform, over his face, besides stuffing his mouth and nostrils with the gauze, also soaked with chloroform. Then Henry turned Snyder over so the art editor's face would be buried in a pillow and rejoined Ruth.

Henry Judd wore rubber gloves at his sanguinary task, the confession said, and he went to the bathroom to wash his hands. He found blood on his shirt, so Ruth went into the room where the dead man lay, got one of Albert Snyder's shirts and gave it to Henry Judd. Then they went into the cellar and burned the bloody shirt and put the sash weight into a tool box after rubbing it with ashes.

Now, they returned to the sitting room, this pair, and Henry Judd suddenly thought of some picture wire he had brought along, presumably to tie Snyder's hands and feet. At least, he had two pieces, Ruth said. One he had lost, so he took the other and went into the death chamber and wrapped the wire around Albert Snyder's throat tightening it with his fingers.

Then he went around and upset the premises generally, to bear out the robbery idea, then sat and gossiped, talking of this and that until daybreak, when Henry Judd tied his sweetheart's hands and feet and left to return to Syracuse. She first went out and got a wallet out of Albert Snyder's pocket and gave it to Henry Judd. She does not know how much it contained.

After Henry's departure, she rolled out of her mother's bed, whereon he had placed her, and aroused her little daughter, telling her to get a neighbor.

Such, in substance and briefly, was the story of that night in Queens Village.

There was a supplemental statement with reference to some letters, including one from Gray, sent from Syracuse after he had departed for New York to join hands with her in the slaughter. Peter M. Daly asked her, at a time when Gray had not yet been definitely hooked with the crime, how she reconciled the postmark with her statement of the murder and she said it was part of Henry's alibi.

Thus Ruth was "hollering copper" on Henry, even before she knew Henry was "hollering copper" on her. They didn't stand hitched a minute after the showdown came.

Wallace wanted to know if Mrs. Snyder hadn't said she was confused and sick while making the statement, but Daly said no. He admitted Mrs. Snyder had a crying spell and that a physician was called in. Wallace mentioned it as a fainting spell, but Daly wouldn't concede it was such. It seemed to be agreed it was some kind of a spell, however.

Daly said she asked if she could see Gray when he got to town. He said she seemed to know that Gray was on his way to New York. The defense devoted more time to Daly than to any other witness so far, Millard of Gray's counsel joining in the cross-examination.

Gray's attorneys had objected to some questions asked by Wallace and now Mrs. Snyder's lawyers objected to Millard's questions.

This case has been presented from the beginning in rather a disordered manner, it seems to me, like one of those new-fangled plays that violate all the established rules for the theatre.

For instance, at the morning session, Millard started out cross-examining Lieutenant Dorschell, of the New York Police Department, relative to a drawing made by Gray of the hardware store in Kingston, where he bought the sash weight and the picture wire. This drawing was made at three o'clock in the morning of

Gray's arrival in New York after his ride from Syracuse, where he was arrested. Millard inquired into the physical condition of Gray at the time he made the drawing and Dorschell said he seemed to be all right.

Millard then explained to Justice Scudder that he wanted to show under what conditions the drawing was made. He said he desired to present testimony showing that the drawing came after a long examination of Gray by the police, and to that end Justice Scudder gave him permission to call and cross-examine a witness who had not appeared before.

It is certainly somewhat unusual to bring in for cross-examination by the defense a witness who would ordinarily be one of the State's most important witnesses.

The witness was Michael S. McDermott, another lieutenant of New York Police, who brought Gray from Syracuse, and who told with infinite detail of Gray's confession. He said Gray took the thing as a joke at first, maintaining his complete innocence.

McDermott said Gray seemed to find the company he was in "congenial" most of the journey, a statement that produced a light giggle in the court. He said that Gray at no time seemed to become serious until they told him they had the contents of his wastepaper basket, which included the Pullman stub.

" 'Do you know, Judd, we have the Pullman ticket you used from Syracuse to New York?' Then he said, 'Well, gentlemen, I was at the Snyder home that night.' "

McDermott said Gray voluntarily launched into a narrative of the bloody night in Queens Village. He told how Gray had subsequently given this same narrative to a stenographer and identified and initialed the various articles used in the commission of the crime.

Now the State proceeded to establish the purchase of the sash weight and picture wire by Gray in Kingston, March 4, last.

Margaret Hamilton, a buyer for a Kingston store, who knows Henry Judd, said she saw him there on that date. She is a stout lady, and wore a startlingly red hat and red scarf.

Arthur R. Bailey, a thin, gray, studious looking man, wearing glasses, a clerk in a Kingston hardware store, didn't seem to remember selling a five-pound sash weight on March 4, although he identified what you might call a bill of sale in his handwriting, taken from the records of the store. He said his store sold any number of sash weights, but he never recalled any transaction involving one sash weight. Mr. Bailey obviously didn't care about being mixed up in this trial business, anyway.

John Sanford, a young Negro, testified most briefly to getting this sash weight from the warehouse.

It seemed a lot of bother about a sash weight that has lost some of its importance since the doctors testified that the wallops with it alone did not cause Snyder's death.

Reginald Rose, youthful, black-haired, black-browed and a bit to the sheikish side, a ticket seller for the New York Central, told of selling Gray a railroad ticket to Syracuse and a Pullman seat reservation to Albany on the night of March 19 for the following day, which was the day after the murder. Gray made the return reservation immediately upon his arrival in New York the night he ran down for the killing.

Millard became a bit curious over Rose's clear recollection of this particular sale of a ticket out of the many a ticket seller makes every day and it developed that Rose even remembered how Gray was dressed. He wore a fedora hat and an overcoat.

Rose said he remembered the sale because it wasn't common-place to sell a railroad ticket to Syracuse and a seat to Albany.

Now came testimony about the party which Mr. and Mrs. Snyder and their small daughter, Lorraine, attended the night of the murder. It was at the home of Milton C. Fidgeon, and Mr. Fidgeon himself took the stand, stout, smooth of face and prosperous-looking.

There had been liquor at the party said Mr. Fidgeon. He served one drink, then someone asked if it was not time for another, so he went into the kitchen to produce the second shot.

Mrs. Snyder came to him there and said she wasn't drinking, but to give her portion to her husband. The Snyders went home about two o'clock in a pleasant frame of mind, as Mr. Fidgeon said on cross-examination by Wallace.

Right back to old Father Adam, the original, and perhaps the loudest "squawker" among mankind against women, went Henry Judd Gray in telling how and why he lent his hand to the butchery of Albert Snyder.

She—she—she—she—she—she—she—she. That was the burden of the bloody song of the little corset salesman as read out in the packed court room in Long Island City yesterday.

She—she—she—she—she—she. 'Twas an echo from across the ages and an old familiar echo, at that. It was the same old "squawk" of Brother Man whenever and wherever he is in a jam, that was first framed in the words:

"She gave me of the tree, and I did eat."

It has been put in various forms since then, as Henry Judd Gray, for one notable instance close at hand, put it in the form of eleven long typewritten pages that were read yesterday, but in any form and in any language it remains a "squawk."

"She played me pretty hard." . . . "She said, 'You're going to do it, aren't you?' " . . . "She kissed me." . . . She did this. . . . She did that. . . . Always she—she—she—she—she ran the confession of Henry Judd.

And "she"—the woman-accused, how did she take this most gruesome squawk?

Well, on the whole, better than you might expect.

You must remember it was the first time she had ever heard the confession of the man who once called her "Momsie." She probably had an inkling of it, but not its exact terms.

For a few minutes her greenish blue eyes roared with such fury that I would not have been surprised to see her leap up, grab the window sash weight that lay among the exhibits on the district attorney's table and perform the same offices on the shrinking Gray that he says she performed on her sleeping husband.

She "belabored him," Gray's confession reads, and I half expected her to belabor Gray.

Her thin lips curled to a distinct snarl at some passages in the statement. I thought of a wildcat and a female cat, at that, on a leash. Once or twice she smiled, but it was a smile of insensate rage, not amusement. She once emitted a push of breath in a loud "phew," as you have perhaps done yourself over some tall tale.

The marble mask was contorted by her emotions for a time, she often shook her head in silent denial of the astounding charges of Gray, then finally she settled back calmly, watchful, attentive, and with an expression of unutterable contempt as the story of she—she—she—she ran along.

Contempt for Henry Judd, no doubt. True, she herself squawked on Henry Judd, at about the same time Henry Judd was squawking on her, but it is a woman's inalienable right to squawk.

As for Henry Judd, I still doubt he will last it out. He reminds me of a slowly collapsing lump of tallow. He sat huddled up in his baggy clothes, his eyes on the floor, his chin in hand, while the confession was being read. He seems to be folding up inch by inch every day.

He acts as if he is only semi-conscious. If he was a fighter and came back to his corner in his present condition, they would give him smelling salts.

The man is a wreck, a strange contrast to the alert blonde at the table behind him.

The room was packed with women yesterday, well-dressed, richly-befurred women from Park Avenue, and Broadway, and others not so well dressed from Long Island City, and the small towns farther down the Island. There were giggling young schoolgirls and staid-looking matrons, and my friends, what do you think? Their sympathy is for Henry Judd Gray!

I made a point of listening to their opinions as they packed the hallways and jammed the elevators of the old court house yesterday and canvassed some of them personally, and they are all sorry for Gray. Perhaps it is his forlorn looking aspect as he sits inert, numb, never raising his head, a sad spectacle of a man who admits he took part in one of the most atrocious murders in history.

There is no sympathy for Mrs. Snyder among the women and very little among the men. They all say something drastic ought to be done to her.

How do you account for that—

But while Henry Judd's confession puts most of the blame on the woman, Mrs. Snyder's attorneys, the pugnacious Edgar Hazelton and the sharp Dana Wallace, who remind me for all the world of a brace of restless terriers with their brisk maneuvers, began making an effort yesterday that shows they intend trying to make Henry Judd the goat.

When District Attorney Newcombe stood up to read Gray's confession, a deep silence fell over the room, packed from wall to wall. Many of the spectators were standing. Mrs. Snyder leaned forward on the table in front of her, but Gray never raised his eyes from the floor, then or thereafter.

You could hear little gasps as of horror or unbelief from some of the women spectators as Newcombe read on in a cold, passionless voice, especially when the confession got down to the actual murder.

It began with the story of their meeting in Henry's restaurant about two years ago. They were introduced by Harry Folsom of New Canaan, Conn., who had picked Mrs. Snyder and another up in the restaurant, so ran the confession, rather giving the impression that the blonde was one of those women who can be "picked up." Gray said:

"She is a woman of great charm. I probably don't have to tell you that. I did like her very much, and she was good company and apparently a good pal to spend an evening with."

I looked over at Mrs. Snyder as this paragraph was read, and there was a shadow of a smile on the marble mask. The expression altered when the story began to tell an instant later of them starting intimate relations in August. Gray added:

"Prior to that she was just a woman I respected."

Perhaps I should here explain that most of this confession was made by Gray on the train when he was being brought from Syracuse to New York after the murder and later elaborated in its details by him.

Well, they got very friendly, and soon she was calling him up and writing him. "She played me pretty hard," he said. He went out to her house for luncheon, and met her mother, although he did not think the mother knew anything of their relations.

Presently Mrs. Snyder got to telling of her unhappiness with Albert. Gray told her, he says, that he himself was married and had a fine wife and was very happy at home, so there could never be anything between him and Mrs. Snyder.

She told him of several attempts she had made on Albert Snyder's life, once giving him sleeping powders, and again bichloride of mercury, but Albert kept on living.

Finally, said Gray, "She started to hound me on this plan to assist her."

The plan for killing Snyder, presumably. But the little corset salesman added quite naively, "I have always been a gentleman and I have always been on the level with everybody. I have a good many friends. If I ever have any after this I don't know."

He said he absolutely refused to listen to the charmer's sanguinary wiles at first, then "with some veiled threats and intents of love-making, she reached the point where she got me in such a whirl that I didn't know where I was at."

Clarence A. Stewart, superintendent of the safety deposit vault of the Queens-Bellaire Bank of Queens Village, testified that Mrs. Snyder rented two boxes, one under the name of Ruth M. Brown, the other under the name of Ruth M. Snyder. Stewart is a mild-looking man who kept his overcoat on while testifying. He stood up when asked to identify Mrs. Snyder and peered at her through his specs.

Edward C. Kern, cashier of the same bank, heavy-set and bland, testified to the contents of these boxes. In the box taken in the name of Ruth M. Brown was $53,000 worth of insurance policies on Albert Snyder and receipts for the payment of the premiums. In the box under the name of Ruth M. Snyder were papers mainly of a family nature relating to the affairs of Ruth and her dead husband, such as fire and burglary insurance policies, receipts and the like.

There seemed to be plenty of fire insurance on the Snyder home. There was some Roxy Theatre stock among other things and papers representing small investments by the dead art editor.

Samuel Willis, a tall, spare, elderly resident of Queens Village, told of seeing Henry Judd Gray waiting for a bus at 5:50 on the morning of March 20, hard by a police booth at Hillside Avenue and Springfield Boulevard, in Queens Village. Police Officer Smith, on duty there, was indulging in a little pistol practice at bottles and Willis said Gray remarked after the officer finished:

"I'd hate to stand in front of him and have him shoot at me."

The bailiffs had to rap for order. Cross-examined by Samuel L. Miller, the witness said his attention was attracted to Gray "by that little dimple in his chin." He said Gray took the bus with him and he saw no more of Henry Judd. This was just after Gray had left the Snyder home to hurry back to Syracuse, you understand.

April 29, 1927

There was little breathing space left in the yellowish-walled old court room when the morning session opened.

In the jam I observed many ladies and gents with dark circles around their eyes which indicated loss of sleep, or bad livers. I identified them as of the great American stage, playwrights, producers, actors, and even actresses.

They were present, as I gathered, to acquire local color for their current, or future contributions to the thespian art, and the hour was a trifle early for them to be abroad in the land. They sat yesterday writing through the proceedings and perhaps inwardly criticizing the stage setting and thinking how unrealistic the trial is as compared to their own productions.

Among the other spectators comfortably chaired, or standing on tired feet, were ladies running from a couple of inches to three yards wide. They were from all parts of Long Island, and the other boroughs of the large and thriving City of New York, the inmates of which are supposed to be so very blasé but who certainly dearly love their murder cases.

A big crowd waited in the hallways and outside the court house. Tearful females implored the obdurate cops guarding the stairs and the court room doors, to ease them through somehow.

It was a strange gathering. Solid-looking citizens found a morning to waste. They would probably have felt greatly inconvenienced had they been requested to spend the same amount of time on a mission of mercy. Several preachers and some of our best known public "pests" were scattered around the premises. What a fine commentary, my friends, on what someone has mentioned as our vaunted intelligence.

Peggy Hopkins, Countess Morner and what not, Joyce, the famous grass-widow, came again to dazzle all the beholders with the magnificence of her display. It was Peggy's second visit. Probably she didn't believe her eyes and ears on her first visit that a lady had seemed to have some difficulty in getting rid of her husband. Peggy never did, you can bet on that. She wore a suit of a distressing green and a red fox collar and arrived at the court house in a little old last year's Rolls-Royce.

Paul Mathis, a thin, dark youth, was the first witness. He remembered carting Henry Judd from the Jamaica Station to the subway on Fifty-eighth Street, March 20, the morning of the murder.

The fare was $8.55. Gray gave him a five cent tip. It is not likely Mathis will ever forget Henry Judd if the young man is like the average taxi jockey.

William L. Millard of Gray's counsel, verbally belted away at Mathis rather snappishly, trying to find out if the young man's memory of Henry Judd hadn't been encouraged by the district attorney's office. Millard has a cutting voice when he is cross-examining and is given to sharp asides. The Court has generally admonished him on several occasions.

Justice Scudder does not allow the lawyers to get far out of conversational bounds. My friend, Senator Alexander Simpson, of Hall-Mills fame, would probably feel his style was quite cramped in Justice Scudder's court.

Van Voorhees, a thin, middle-aged man, conductor of the train that carried Gray back to Syracuse from his murder errand, identified Gray. So did George Fullerton, a dusky porter.

"We concede the defendant was on the train," said Millard, closing that line of testimony.

Now came Haddon Gray, of 207 Clark Street, Syracuse, the insurance man who unwittingly helped Judd Gray with his famous alibi. Haddon and Judd had been friends twenty years, but are not related. Gray is a young man of brisk manner and appearance, of medium height, with black hair parted in the middle and slicked down. He was neatly dressed and displayed a lodge emblem on his watch chain and another on his lapel. He spoke very distinctly.

Haddon Gray said Judd had enlisted his support in Syracuse in the keeping of a date in Albany with a woman Judd referred to as "Momsie." Judd had once shown him a photo of "Momsie." Haddon Gray said he now knew her as Mrs. Snyder.

This obliging Haddon, thinking he was merely assisting an old pal in a little clandestine affair, hung a sign, "Don't Disturb," on Judd's door at the Onondaga Hotel, rumpled the bed, called the desk downstairs and left word he was ill and was not to be aroused before a certain hour, and finally mailed some letters that Judd had written. All this after Judd had left Syracuse for New York.

Judd told Haddon he was afraid his firm might check up on him, wherefore the arrangements set forth above. Haddon did not hear from Judd again until Sunday afternoon, March 20, when Judd, just back from his bloody errand to Queens Village, called him on the telephone. Haddon Gray and a friend named Harry Platt went to see Judd at the Onondaga and Judd said he had not kept the "date" in Albany as a telegram from Momsie had reached him there summoning him on to New York. Then the witness said Judd told him a startling story.

He—Judd—said he had gone to the home of Momsie while she and her husband were out and entered by a side door. He was waiting in a bedroom when he heard Momsie and her husband returning. Then he heard a great commotion and looking out through the door of the room he saw Momsie slugged by a dark man.

Henry Judd told Haddon he hid in a closet, and two men came

in and rummaged around in the closet over his head, looking for something. Then they went out and Henry Judd bolstered up his courage and looked about. He went into a bedroom and found Momsie's husband on the floor. He lifted the man onto the bed, and said in doing so he must have gotten blood on his vest and shirt as he bent over the man and listened if his heart was beating.

He showed Haddon Gray the shirt and said it was Snyder's shirt but the witness wasn't clear as to how Judd explained having it. Also Judd had a suitcase containing the suit of clothes he had worn to New York, also the bloody shirt and a briefcase, which Harry Platt took to get rid of at Judd's request. Platt took the suitcase to his office.

After relating this tale Judd went to Haddon's home and spent the evening playing with Haddon's children. Haddon came to New York after Judd's arrest, saw his old pal in jail and said:

"Judd, did you do this?"

"Yes, Haddon; I did."

Henry Judd, inert, head down as usual, never glanced up as he heard his boyhood friend testify, and Haddon Gray proved in his testimony that he was about as good a friend as a man could hope to have.

Harry Platt, an insurance adjuster of Syracuse, very bald, rather florid, and with glasses, was next. There was a touch of the old beau to Harry's appearance. He repeated the tale of slugging told him and Haddon by Judd. He said he gave the suitcase to his stenographer to be destroyed.

Mrs. Anna Boehm, of Syracuse, stenographer for Platt, a plump lady wearing glasses and obviously a bit nervous, told of receiving a package from Platt containing a suitcase. In the suitcase was a suit of clothes and a hat. She gave it to her husband. The husband, Anthony Boehm, corroborated that statement. He burned the package in a furnace.

At 12:27, Newcombe stood up and said:

"*The People Rest.*"

There was a sudden stir and the bailiffs rapped for order. All the attorneys gathered about Justice Scudder's bench in a conference with the Court.

When the State rested rather sooner than was generally expected, the attorneys for the defendants asked for time to prepare certain motions. They were given until four o'clock in the afternoon. These motions, all for dismissal on one ground or another, were probably presented more on the broad premise that they can't rule you off for trying, rather than the expectation they would be granted. Millard wanted the motions made in the absence of the jury, but Justice Scudder saw no necessity for that.

If the jurors didn't understand the motions any better than most of the laymen collected in the court room, Justice Scudder was quite right. The language was quite technical.

Now the woman and the crumpled little corset salesman, their once piping-hot passion colder than a dead man's toes, begin trying to save their respective skins from the singeing at Sing Sing, each trying to shove the other into the room with the little green door.

"What did Mrs. Snyder say about the confession of Gray's—that squawk?" I asked her attorneys yesterday.

"Well, let's see, she said he—" began Dana Wallace, the buzzing, bustling little man who sits at Mrs. Snyder's side in the court room when he isn't on his feet, which is seldom.

"She said—Well, wait now until I recall what she said," put in Edgar Hazleton, the other attorney for the woman.

They seemed at a loss for words. I suggested: "Did she say he is a rat?"

"Well I suppose it would amount to that in your language," replied Wallace. (What did he mean "my" language?) "Only she didn't use that term."

"No, no," chimed in Hazleton, "not rat."

"She said, in substance, 'and to think I once loved that—that—' Well, I think she used a word that means something like coward," Wallace concluded.

"Do you think she will keep her nerve on the stand?" I asked.

"Yes," they both answered in unison.

I am inclined to think so, too.

Whatever else she may lack, which seems to be plenty, the

woman appears to have nerve. Or maybe she hasn't any nerves. It is about the same thing.

In any event, she has never for a moment cowered like her once little pal of those loving days before the black early morning of March 20. She has been cold, calm, contemptuous, gusty, angry, but never shrinking, save perhaps in that little walk to and from the court between the recesses. She then passes before the hungry eyes of the spectators.

That seems to be her most severe ordeal. She grips her black corded-silk coat in front with both hands, and seems to hasten, her eyes straight ahead. However, we shall see about that nerve now.

April 30, 1927

We were, in a manner of speaking, in the chamber of horrors with Mrs. Ruth Brown Snyder yesterday afternoon, mentally tiptoeing along, goggle-eyed and scared, behind her, when the blond woman suddenly gulped, and began weeping.

She had taken us, just before the tears came, step by step to a bedroom in her little home in Queens Village. We were standing there, you might say, all goose-pimply with the awfulness of the situation as we watched, through the medium of the story she told on the witness stand, the butchery of her husband by Henry Judd Gray.

Maybe the ghost of the dead art editor suddenly popped out on her as she got us into that room and was showing us the picture of the little corset salesman at his bloody work while she was trying to stay his murderous hand. Anyway, the tears came, welling up into the frosty eyes of the blonde and trickling down over that marble mask of a face.

Plump Mrs. Irene Wolfe, the gray-haired matron of the Queens County jail, hurried to Mrs. Snyder's side and put her arms around the weeping woman. A few sips from a glass of water, and Mrs. Snyder was again composed sufficiently to go on with the fearful tale of the killing of her husband that she started early in the afternoon and by which she hopes to save herself from the electric chair.

She blamed it all on Gray, even as he will blame it all on her. The baggy little man sitting inertly, as always, in the chair just a few feet from her listened to the woman with only an occasional glance at her.

Yet it would be interesting to know his thoughts. This was his old Momsie. This was the woman he once thought he loved with a great consuming love—this woman who was trying to consign him to the electric juices. He seemed to stagger slightly as he walked out of the court room at the close of the session, whereas before he had tried to put a little snap into his tread.

This woman broke down twice while she was on the witness stand, once when she had us in that death chamber, with Henry Judd Gray pounding the life out of her husband, as she claims, and again when she mentioned the name of her nine-year-old daughter, Lorraine.

But in the main she was as cold and calm sitting there with a thousand people staring at her as if she were at her dinner table discoursing to some guests. She kept her hands folded in her lap. She occasionally glanced at the jury, but mostly kept her eyes on Edgar Hazleton, one of her lawyers who examined her on direct-examination.

This examination was not concluded when Court took a recess at 4:30 until Monday morning. It is the custom of Queens County courts to skip Saturday.

Mrs. Snyder wore the same black dress and black coat that has been her attire since the trial started. She made one change in hats since then, discarding a tight-fitting thing that made her chilly chin jut out like an iceberg. Someone probably told her that the hat was most unbecoming, so now she wears one with a brim that takes some of the ice out of the chin.

Her dress and coat are neither fashionable nor well cut, so I am informed by ladies who may be taken as authorities on the subject. Still, they make her look smaller than her weight of around 150 pounds would indicate. She wears black silk stockings and black pumps.

Her face was flushed a bit today, probably from excitement, but she uses no make-up. Slap a little rouge and powder on Mrs. Snyder, give her a session with a hairdresser, and put some of Peggy Joyce's clothes on her, and she would be a snappy-looking young matron.

When her name was called by her attorney, Hazelton, soon after court opened this afternoon, she stood up quickly and advanced to the witness chair with a firm step. She had been twisting her hands and biting her nails just before that, however, indicating she felt nervous, which is not surprising, in view of the eyes turned on her.

It seems a great pity that old man Hogarth isn't living to depict the crowd scene in the court room yesterday. Tad * might do it, but Tad has too much sense to risk his life and limbs in any such jams.

Some strange-looking characters almost fought for a chance to leer at the principals in the trial. Apparently respectable men and women showed the court attendants cards, letters, badges, birth certificates and automobile licenses in an effort to impress the guardians of the portals with their importance and the necessity of their getting into the court room.

Dizzy-looking dolls said to represent the social strata of Park Avenue—the upper crust, as I understand—were there, not a little proud of their heroism in getting out so early. Some were escorted by silly-looking "muggs" wearing canes and spats.

But also there were men who might be business men and women with something better to do, standing chin deep in the bloody scandal of this bloody trial and giving some offense to high heaven, it seems to me, by their very presence.

The aisles were jammed so tightly that even the smallest copy boys, carrying copy of the day as it ran red-hot from the fingers of the scribbling writers of the newspaper delegations, could scarcely wiggle through. The women outnumbered the men about three to one. They stood for hours on their tired feet, their eyes and mouths agape.

* Tad was the penname of T. A. Dorgan, satiric artist whose drawings were a popular syndicated newspaper feature in the Twenties.

Justice Scudder peered over his glasses at a jammed court room and warned the crowd that at the first disturbance he would order the premises cleared.

Then he bowed slightly to the attorneys for the defense and Hazleton arose and stepped up to the table in front of the jury box.

He is a short, serious-looking man, with a hawk nose, and a harsh voice. A pince-nez straddled his beak. He wore a gray suit, and a white starched turned-down collar and a black tie yesterday morning. The collar flew loose from its neck and moorings early in Hazleton's discourse and one end scraped his ear.

He at first stood with his hands behind him, but presently he was gesticulating with his right, waggling a prehensile index-finger most forcibly. He perspired. He stood on his tiptoes. He was so close to Henry Judd that he almost stuck the index-finger in the defendant's eye when he pointed at Judd.

Occasionally a titter ran over the crowded court room at some remark made by Hazleton, who has an idiomatic manner of expression. That's what most of the crowd came for, apparently—to laugh at something, even though it might be human misery! The bailiffs would bawl "Silence!" and glare around furiously.

The purport of Hazleton's opening was about what had been anticipated. He said he expected to show that Henry Judd Gray was the arch criminal of the whole affair, and he depicted him in the light of a crafty, designing fellow—

"Not the man you see sitting here," yelled Hazleton, pointing at the cowering Henry Judd, while the eyes of the jurors turned and followed the finger. It was quite possible to believe that the villain described by Hazleton was not the man sitting there. Henry Judd looked anything but villainous.

Hazleton spoke about an hour, then Samuel L. Miller, of Gray's counsel, stepped forward, dark, stout, well-groomed and slick-haired—a New York type of professional young man who is doing all right.

He laid a batch of manuscript on the table in front of the jury and began to read his opening, rather an unusual proceeding. He read directly into a microphone which stood on the table. Both opening addresses partook more of the nature of closing appeals. Miller had evidently given no little time and thought to his address and had dug up a lot of resounding phrases, but he was comparatively brief.

Harry Hyde, manager of the Jamaica branch of the Prudential Life Insurance Company, was the first witness called for Mrs. Snyder. He is a thin man with a Woodrow Wilson face and glasses, and he kept his new spring topcoat on as he sat in the witness chair. His testimony was what you might call vague.

Hazleton tried to show by him that Mrs. Snyder had called at his office relative to cancelling the insurance on her late husband's life, but he didn't recognize Mrs. Snyder as the woman and didn't remember much of the conversation.

He did faintly recall some woman calling at his office, however, and speaking of the Snyder policies. District Attorney Newcombe moved to strike out the testimony, but the motion was denied.

John Kaiser, Jr., another insurance man of Jamaica, a heavy-set rotund man with a moustache and horn-rimmed specs, testified on the subject of the insurance policies that are said by the State to have been reasons for the murder of Albert Snyder.

He said he recalled Mrs. Snyder coming to his offices and discussing the policies, but he couldn't recall the exact nature of the conversation.

Hazleton made a point of a clause in the policy that bore Snyder's signature, reserving the right to change the beneficiary.

Mrs. Josephine Brown, mother of Mrs. Snyder, was called.

Mrs. Brown is a woman who must be around sixty. She speaks with a very slight accent. Mrs. Brown is a Scandinavian. Her face is wrinkled and she wears gold-rimmed glasses. She was dressed in black but her black hat had a bright ornament. She gave her answers clearly and quickly.

She said her daughter had been operated on for appendicitis when she was a child and that the wound had to be reopened when she was eighteen. She lived with her daughter and son-in-law for six years and told of the visits to the Snyder home by Gray. On the third visit she told her daughter not to let Gray call again as "it didn't look right." Gray came no more.

On the occasions of his visit Mrs. Brown said Gray talked mainly about the stock market.

Newcombe examined her closely as to her knowledge of Gray's relations with her daughter. She admitted she called him Judd and had never told Albert Snyder of his visits to the Snyder home. She was away on a professional visit the night Henry Judd hid in her room on murder bent.

So many daffy women and rattle-headed men outside, eager to see whatever they might see, rushed the court house corridors at one o'clock on a rumor that Mrs. Snyder was on the stand, that the confusion took on the proportion of a riot. The halls and stairways were packed with struggling females. They pushed and shoved and pulled and hauled, and squealed and squawked. It was a sorry spectacle. The cops on duty at the court house were well nigh helpless against the onrush for a time.

Justice Scudder heard the tumult from his chambers and went out to take a look. Then he ordered the hallways cleared. In the meantime, the court room was jammed, and the spectators piled into the press section, grabbing all unoccupied seats. For half an hour the cops outside the court room would not recognize credentials of any kind until they could stem the human tide to some extent.

I doubt if there has ever been anything quite like it in connection with these trials, and I speak as a survivor of the Hall-Mills trial, and of the Browning trial, which wasn't a murder trial, except with relation to the King's English. The court room is said to be one of the largest in the country, but it could have been three times as large today and there wouldn't have been room for the crush.

A big crowd stood in the street outside all morning and afternoon, though they can see nothing there except the photographers at their sprinting exercises when a witness walks out of the court house.

When Mrs. Snyder was sworn as a witness, Justice Scudder told her in a quiet voice that she was not required to testify as the law protected her but that on the stand she is subject to the same cross-examination as any other witness.

She turned in her chair and looked the judge in the face as he talked, and bowed slightly.

Her voice is a soprano, and very clear. It came out through the amplifiers much harsher than its natural tone, of course. The microphone on the desk in front of the witness stand was in the line of vision between Mrs. Snyder and Hazleton, and she cocked her head to one side to get a clearer view of the lawyer.

She often emphasized some of her words, for instance, "We were *not* happy," when answering Hazleton's question about her married life with Albert Snyder. She never glanced at the staring crowd, though she often looked at the jury. As for the members of that solemn body, most of them watched her closely as she talked for a time, then their attention seemed to wander. Juror No. 11 never looked at her at all, but then Juror No. 11 never seems to be looking at anyone on the witness stand.

He has a faraway expression. Possibly he is wondering how business is going while he is away listening to all this murder stuff.

Mrs. Snyder's first attack of tears came early in the examination, but was very short. The second time court suspended operations for several minutes while she wept. A dead silence reigned. It is well for men to remain silent when women weep, whatever the circumstances.

I asked a lot of men how she impressed them. They said they thought she made a good witness for herself. Then I asked some of the girls, who have been none too strong for Mrs. Snyder, just as a general proposition. They, too, thought she had done very well.

You must bear in mind that this woman is talking for her life. If she is the cruel and cunning blond fury that Gray's story would cause you to believe, you would expect her to be calm. But if she is the wronged, home-loving, horror-stricken woman that her own tale would imply, her poise is most surprising.

She always referred to Albert Snyder as "my husband," and to her former paramour as "Mr. Gray"—"I tried to stop Mr. Gray from hitting my husband and he pushed me to the floor. I fainted and when I came to I pulled the blanket off. . . ."—It was here that she was overcome by tears the second time.

She pictured Gray as the aggressor in the love-making of their early meetings. She wasn't happy at home, and she accepted the advances of the little corset salesman to intimacy. She said Gray was her only love adventure.

He borrowed her money and didn't pay it back, she said. He first suggested the idea of getting rid of her husband, and mentioned poisoning to her. Wherever Gray said "she" in his confession, Mrs. Snyder said "he" in her testimony today. They have turned on each other with a vengeance, these two once-fervid lovers. There is no doubt they hate each other thoroughly.

It was difficult to tell just what effect Mrs. Snyder's tale had on the jury, of course. In fact it would be unfair to make a guess until her tale is finished. It certainly had some elements of plausibility, despite the confession she now says was obtained under duress, and despite the motive of Albert Snyder's life insurance that is advanced by the prosecution.

Mrs. Snyder's attorneys attempted to show today that she had tried to have the insurance reduced to cut down the premium, but their evidence on that point did not seem particularly strong. She insisted in her testimony that this had been the purpose.

She smiled just once with any semblance of joy, which was when Justice Scudder admitted, over the objections of the State, the bank books showing that Albert Snyder and Ruth had a joint account. It is by this account that the defense expects to show that Albert Snyder had full cognizance of his wife's payment of the premiums on the policies.

She says Gray always referred to Albert Snyder as "the governor." Once she accidentally tripped over a rubber gas tube in the house and pulled it off the jet. She went out and when she came back her husband was out of doors and said he had nearly been asphyxiated. She wrote Gray of the incident, and he wrote back:

"It was too damn bad the hose wasn't long enough to shove in his nose."

When she testified in just that language there was something in her manner and way of speaking out the word that caused a distinct stiffening among the women in the court room.

"Brazen!" some of them whispered.

This gas jet incident, by the way, was alleged by the State to have been one of the times when Mrs. Snyder tried to murder her husband.

She says Gray threatened to kill himself and her if she didn't do what he told her. She was afraid of Gray, she said, although the drooping little man in front of her didn't seem to be anything to be afraid of. She tried to break off with him, she said, and he threatened to expose her.

She said Gray sent her sleeping powders to give "the governor" on the night of the party at Fidgeons', which was Albert Snyder's last night on earth. Moreover, Gray announced in the letter accompanying the powders, according to her testimony, that he was coming down Saturday to finish "the governor."

He came down all right.

"My husband was asleep. I went to my mother's room, where I met Mr. Gray. We talked several minutes. He kissed me and I felt the rubber gloves on his hands. He was mad. He said, 'If you don't let me go through with this I'll kill us both.' He had taken my husband's revolver. I grabbed him by the hand and took him down to the living-room.

"I pleaded with him to stop when we got downstairs, then I went to the bathroom. I said to Mr. Gray, 'I'll bring your hat and coat down to you.' I heard a terrific thud. I rushed to my husband's room. I found Gray straddling my husband. I pulled the blankets down, grabbing him and then I fainted. I don't remember anything more."

That's her story and I presume she will stick to it.

May 3, 1927

For five hours and a half yesterday questions went whistling past that marble chin of Mrs. Ruth Brown Snyder's, but she kept on sticking it out defiantly from under the little brim of her black hat, like a fighter that can't be hurt.

At a pause just before recess in the old court room with the sickly yellow walls in Long Island City she reached out a steady hand, picked up a glass of water from the table in front of her, took a big swig, and looked at Charles F. Froessel, the assistant district attorney, who had been cross-examining her, as much as to say "Well, come on."

But Froessel seemed a bit fagged out, and mopped a steaming brow with a handkerchief as Justice Townsend Scudder granted a motion by one of Mrs. Snyder's attorneys for a recess until to-morrow morning.

The dialogue between Froessel and Mrs. Snyder toward the close of the day was taking on something of the aspect of a break-fast table argument between a husband and the little woman, who can't exactly explain certain matters that the old boy wants to know.

She is a magnificent liar, if she is lying. You must give her that. She stands out 'mid keen competition these days, if she is lying. And if a liar she is a game liar, one of those "that's my story and I'll stick to it" liars, which is the mark of the able liar.

And I regret to report that she seems to impress many of her listeners in the light of a wonderful liar rather than as a poor wid-owed soul falsely accused. The men were rather softening up toward the blond woman at the close yesterday in sheer admira-tion of her as a possible liar, and even the women who leer at her all day long had stopped hating her. They seemed to be com-mencing to think that she was reflecting credit to femininity just as a prodigious liar.

Even Henry Judd Gray, the baggy-looking little corset sales-man who was on trial with her for the murder, and who has been sitting inert and completely befogged since the case began, sat up yesterday as if they had suddenly puffed air into him.

He had a fresh haircut and clean linen and looked all sharpened up. He half started when she fairly shrilled "no" at Froessel when he was asking her about the life insurance on Albert Snyder. Per-haps Gray had heard her say "no" in that same voice before.

It was about the life insurance for $53,000 on Snyder's life that the assistant district attorney was most curious in his cross-examination, and about which Mrs. Ruth Brown Snyder was the least convincing. It was to double in the event of her husband's death by accident, and the State claims that Albert Snyder didn't know his wife had taken it out.

It was a very bad session for her on that particular point. Her answers were at times vague and evasive, but her voice never lost its snap. She said the only motive Gray could have had for killing her husband was to get the life insurance money, and when it was suggested to her that she was the beneficiary, she argued: "Well, he knew he would get it away from me just as he got money from me before."

"Isn't it a fact, that you and Gray planned to spend that insurance money together?" she was asked.

"No," she said quickly.

Most of her answers were sharp yesses, or noes. In fact, Froessel insisted on yes-or-no answers, though sometimes she whipped in a few additional remarks to his great annoyance.

He hectored and badgered the blonde at times until her counsel objected and the Court admonished him. Froessel, a plump-built man of medium height, in the early forties, has a harsh voice and a nagging manner in cross-examination. He wears spectacles and is smooth-shaven and persistent, and there is no doubt that Mrs. Snyder at times wished she had a sash weight handy.

She broke down once—that was when she was again leading the way into the room where her husband was butchered, and where she claimed she saw Judd Gray astraddle of Albert Snyder in the bed. She repeated the story she told on her direct-examination.

"I grabbed Judd Gray and he pushed me to the floor and I fainted. When I came to I pulled the blankets off my husband and—"

Then the tears came. There was a microphone on the witness stand, and her sniffles came out through the amplifiers quite audibly. Mrs. Irene Wolfe, the plump matron of the county jail, moved to her rescue with water, and presently Mrs. Snyder went on.

"Watch her hands," a woman advised me. "You can always tell

if a lady is nervous by her hands. If she presses them together she is under a strain. If they are relaxed, she isn't nervous."

So I watched Mrs. Snyder's hands as they lay together in her lap. They were limp, inert. Once or twice she raised one to adjust a strand of yellow hair that drifted out under the little black hat, or to apply a small handkerchief to her well-shaped nose.

Under a dim light, backgrounded by the old brown plush hangings behind the judge's bench, and seated on an elevated platform, the black-gowned figure stood out distinctly. Occasionally she fingered the black jet beads at her throat, and she always leaned forward slightly, the white chin pushed out belligerently. Her feet were still. She sometimes shook her head to emphasize a "no." Her voice, a little raspy through the "mike," has a musical quality.

Her speech is the speech of your average next door neighbor in the matter of grammar. I mean to say she is no better and no worse than millions of the rest of us. She says "ain't" but I just read a long dissertation by some learned fellow who says "ain't" will eventually be considered good grammar.

She displayed more boldness than adroitness in her denials when it was patent that she didn't care to go into details.

But she showed no disposition to hide anything about her affair with Henry Judd Gray.

May 4, 1927

That scared-rabbit looking little man, Henry Judd Gray, the corset salesman, is now engaged in what the cops would describe as "putting the finger" on Mrs. Ruth Brown Snyder, only such a short time back his ever-loving, red-hot Momsie.

He seems to be a fairly expert "finger man," so far. Perhaps his proficiency goes back to his early youth and much practice pointing the accusatory digit and saying, "Teacher, he done it."

He lugged us through many a rendezvous in many a different spot with Mrs. Snyder yesterday afternoon, while the lady, who had done a little "fingering" herself for three days, sat looking daggers at Henry Judd, and probably thinking arsenic, mercury tablets, chloroform, picture wire and sash weights.

This. was after she had come out of a spell of weeping when her little daughter, Lorraine, was on the stand. That was a spectacle, my friends—the child in the court room—to make the angels shed tears, and men hide their faces in shame, that such things can be.

Henry Judd had scarcely gotten us out of the hotels which he and Mrs. Ruth Brown Snyder infested in the days—ah, yes, and the nights—when their heat for each other was up around 102 Fahrenheit, when a recess was taken until this morning.

Everybody was weary of traipsing up and down hotel corridors and in and out of hotel rooms, but Henry Judd kept making a long story longer under the direct examination of Samuel L. Miller, the stout, sleek-looking young lawyer who is associated with William L. Millard in defending Gray.

Henry Judd hadn't gotten right down to brass tacks, which is after all the story of the butchery of Mrs. Snyder's husband, Albert, and which Henry Judd will undoubtedly blame on the blond woman who has made him out the arch-sashweighter of the bloody business.

He had gone over his own early life before he met Mrs. Snyder and was a happy little corset salesman, with a wife and child down in New Jersey. He wept when he spoke of that, but composed himself with a stiff jolt of water from the same glass that had but recently been pressed by the lips of his former sweetie.

It was a dull, dry recital, especially those numerous little excursions to hotel rooms. A trip to one hotel room might be made exciting, but when you start going through one of these modern hotels, room by room, the thing lacks zest.

Gray stepped to the stand with a quick tread, and an almost soldierly bearing, which was most surprising in view of the fact he has looked all folded-up like an old accordion since the trial started. He did not commence straightening up until Friday, when he found Mrs. Snyder nudging him toward that warm chair at Sing Sing.

He raised his right hand with great gravity as the clerk of the court administered the usual oath. He did not sit down until told to do so by Justice Townsend Scudder, and he listened gravely while Justice Scudder told him he did not have to testify unless he wished. Gray bowed to the Court.

Sitting there was a scholarly-looking young fellow, such a chap as would cause you to remark, "There's some rising young author," or maybe a college professor. He wore a dark, double-breasted suit of clothes with a white linen collar and a tie that had an almost indecorous stripe. A white handkerchief peeped out of the breast pocket of the coat.

His dark hair, slightly kinky, made a tall pompadour. His horn-rimmed spectacles have yellowish lenses, which, added to the old jail-house tan he has acquired, gave him a sickly complexion under the stand lamp by the witness stand with its three lights like a pawnbroker's sign.

His hands rested quietly in his lap, but occasionally he raised one to his probably throbbing forehead. His voice is slow and steady, and rather deep-throated. A cleft in the middle of his chin is wide and deep. The psychologists and philosophers have noted it without knowing just what to make of it. He has a strange trick of talking without moving his upper lip. Or maybe there isn't anything strange about it.

He answered Miller's questions without hestitation and with great politeness. You might say with suavity, in fact.

"I did, sir," he would say. Always the "sir." He would impress you as a well-educated, well-bred, well-mannered young chap. You can't see inside 'em, you know. He has a remarkably bad memory that will probably get him in trouble when the abrupt Froessel, of the district attorney's office, takes hold of him.

"My memory does not serve me well as to conversation," he remarked on one occasion. He did not seem to be abashed by any of the very personal questions asked him, or rather read by Miller, who has a stack of typewritten notes in front of him. He is obviously frightened, however, which is not surprising when you consider he is facing the electric chair.

He invariably referred to the blond woman, who he says got him in all this mess, as "Mrs. Snyder," his tale of their introduction in Henry's restaurant by one Harry Folsom not varying from hers. He said he did plenty of drinking when he was with her on those hotel trips, and on jaunts through the night life of New York. She told him of her domestic troubles and he said she talked of leaving her husband and putting their child in a convent. He told her, so he said, that he hated to see a home broken up, which sounded almost ironical coming from a gent with a wife and child himself.

They exchanged Christmas presents, and he bought one for her mother.

Gray's own mother cried bitterly when her son took the stand. Mrs. Snyder talked much to him on insurance, Henry Judd said, and once he had induced her to pour out some arsenic which she had in the house to poison rodents, and one thing and another, as she explained to him.

But he hadn't reached sash weights and such matters when Justice Scudder declared the recess. It was a long day in court, with much happening before the defense for Mrs. Snyder rested and the defense of Gray began with the immediate production of Henry Judd.

Out of the dark tangles of this bloody morass there stepped for a brief moment a wraith-like little figure all in black—Lorraine Snyder, the nine-year-old daughter of the blond woman and the dead art editor. She was, please God, such a fleeting little shadow that one had scarcely stopped gulping over her appearance before she was gone.

She was asked just three questions by Hazleton as she sat in the big witness chair, a wide-brimmed black hat shading her tiny face, her presence there, it seemed to me, a reproach to civilization.

Justice Scudder called the little girl to his side, and she stood looking bravely into his eyes, the saddest, the most tragic little figure, my friends, ever viewed by gods or men.

"You understand, don't you, that you have to tell the truth?" asked Justice Scudder kindly. I thought he was going to seize the child in his arms.

"Yes," she said faintly.

"Then sit right down there and listen carefully," said Justice

Scudder. "If you do not understand the question just say, 'I do not understand.' Lean back in the chair and be comfortable. The Court rules the child shall not be sworn."

So she sat down and the jurors gazed at her and everybody in the room felt like bawling. Mrs. Snyder gasped and shed tears when her child appeared—tears that probably came from her heart.

She hasn't seen Lorraine since her arrest. I doubt if Lorraine saw her mother across the big room or that the child fully comprehended where she was. Surely she could not know that all these strange-looking men gathered there were trying to kill her mother. It was a relief when Lorraine left the stand. Two minutes more and they would have been short one reporter in the press section.

"Lorraine," said Hazleton, "do you remember the morning your mother called you?"

"Yes, sir."

"Was it daylight or dark?"

"Light."

"And how long after she called you did you call the Mulhausers?"

"Right away," piped the child.

"That's all," said Hazleton.

"Not one question by the district attorney, Your Honor," said Newcombe.

"No questions," said Miller of Gray's counsel.

Thereafter while Gray was being examined, Mrs. Snyder sat with her elbows on the table, her head bowed, a picture of dejection as great as that presented by Gray for some days. The child seemed to have touched her heart, and the defiant pride with which she has faced her accusers disappeared.

Finally the head came up again and the greenish blue eyes, a bit watery, were leveled on Gray, but it soon drooped once more. The woman seemed a picture of remorse. One-tenth the thoughts she was giving to Lorraine at that moment applied three months ago would have kept her out of that court room.

Mrs. Snyder was on the stand three hours and a half yesterday.

She quit the witness chair at 2:05 at the afternoon session and walked with slow step back to her seat at her attorneys' table followed by plump Mrs. Wolfe, the jail matron.

She was "all in." She kept her head down as she passed in review before the leering eyes of the spectators. Her face was a dead, dull white. Her dearest girl friends, as Mrs. Snyder calls them, couldn't have called her pretty without being arrested for perjury. She looked very badly indeed. She had no pep left but still I defy any other woman to produce any pep after so many hours of dodging.

The conclusions of some of the more nervous listeners at the close of Mrs. Snyder's examination were that hereafter no blonde shall be permitted to purchase a window sash weight without a prescription and that all male suburbanites should cancel their life insurance forthwith and try all the doors before going to bed.

She left not one but two doors open for Henry Judd Gray, so Froessel dug out of her. I think the fact of these unlocked doors will weigh heavily against Mrs. Snyder when the jury commences tossing the evidence into the scales of consideration. That, and the insurance that "the governor" didn't know was loaded on his life. He was carrying plenty of weight along with this mortal coil, was "the governor." That was Henry Judd Gray's name for him. Imagine the gall of the little whippet who sneaked into Albert Snyder's home and had a jocular title for him!

Not much jocularity to Henry Judd Gray now as he shrinks in and out of the court room in Long Island City while the ponderous machinery of the law grinds the sausage of circumstance into links of evidence.

It is likely that the case will go to the jury by Friday. It has taken two weeks to try a mother that the citizens of Pueblo County, Colorado, could have settled in two minutes under any cottonwood tree on the banks of the Arkansas, if all the State of New York has developed is true. But the citizens of Pueblo County are forehanded and forthright gents.

Spectators were permitted to remain in the court room during the noon recess and the ladies brought their ham sandwiches and tatting right along with them to while away the hour. They gossiped jovially about the troubles of their sister, Ruth, and a lovely time was apparently had by all. Strange it is, my friends, that morbid impulses move the gals to bite and kick for a place on the premises where a sad, distorted version of life is being aired.

The reader may recall that yesterday I drew attention to the blonde's magnificence as a liar, if she were lying, and today she stepped right out and admitted her qualifications as a prevaricator. She claimed the belt, you might say, when the following tête-à-tête came off between her and Assistant District Attorney Charles F. Froessel when the cross-examination was in progress this morning. "You lied to the neighbors?" "Yes." . . . "You lied to the policemen?" "Yes." . . . "You lied to the detectives?" "Yes." . . . "You lied to Commissioner McLaughlin?" "Yes." . . . "You lied to the Assistant District Attorneys?" "Yes." . . . "You lied to your mother?" "Yes." . . . "You lied to your daughter?" "Yes." . . . "You lied to everybody that spoke to you or with you?" "Yes."

If that isn't lying it will do until some lying comes along.

Mrs. Snyder came in for the morning session looking a bit more marbley than usual. She seemed somewhat listless as Froessel began "madaming" her again. Her voice was tired. Still, nearly six hours on a witness stand is not calculated to enliven anyone.

Froessel started off in soft accents as if he wished to be a gentleman no matter how painful, possibly in view of the fact that some folks thought he was a little harsh with her Monday. By about the third question, however, he was lifting his voice at the witness. He desired brevity, yes or no, in her answers, since she had a penchant for elucidation. Froessel didn't seem to realize that a blonde loves to talk.

She sat all morning with her hands in her lap; listless, loose hands they were. The familiar black jet beads were missing from the throat in the morning, but she came back with them in the afternoon and toyed with them constantly. Nerves at last!

The greenish blue eyes looked at Froessel so coldly that once he shivered and glanced around to see whence came that draft.

The blond woman wasn't as self-possessed as she had been the day before and she got somewhat tangled up right off the reel as to what she had testified with reference to her knowledge of Gray's murderous intentions against "the governor." The poor old "governor"! There were two strikes on him any time he walked under his own rooftree.

The ice in the blonde cracked up as Froessel kept picking at her, and her voice was petulant as she answered one question with: "I tell you I don't remember what I did."

She was sore at Froessel, that was apparent. It takes a bold man to deliberately make a blonde sore, even though she be a prisoner of old John Law. Froessel yelled at her with great violence, especially when she tried to go beyond his questions, and she gave him some very disquieting glares.

"May I explain that?" she asked a couple of times.

"You may not!" he said acidly, and the greenish blue eyes sizzled.

"Just answer questions, madam, and do not attempt to explain matters," said Justice Scudder from the bench, peering down at her over his glasses.

"Well, yes or no covers so much, Judge, I can't answer," she replied sulkily.

Froessel escorted the woman back to her home in Queens Village and to that bloody early morning of March 20. He went over her story on that occasion with her, word by word. He got a bit excited at her answers and hammered the table with great violence.

"No buts—no buts!" he yelled.

"I object to the attitude of the district attorney," interposed Hazleton, and Justice Scudder chided Froessel, but requested Mrs. Snyder to be more direct in her answers.

"And when you went into the room of your mother you saw Henry Judd Gray was there again. . . . And the first thing he did was to kiss you?"

"Yes."

"And you kissed him?"

"Yes."

"Knowing, or believing, whatever you want to say, that he was there to kill your husband?"

"Yes."

Just like that.

Three gentlemen contemplating marriage to blondes hastened to the telephone booths to cancel their troth, shivering in their boots as they went.

She said that the thud she heard while she was in the bathroom was the impact of the sash weight landing on the sleeping Albert Snyder. It must have sounded like Babe Ruth hitting a home run, judging from her description, though the doctors found no fracture of the skull.

Anyway, that was when she rushed to her husband's room to find Gray on the bed astraddle of Albert Snyder, when she grabbed at Gray, when he pushed her away, and when she fainted—as she told it.

Froessel was very curious about her actions after she came out of the faint. He wanted to know if she had tried to do anything for her husband in the way of kindly ministration. Any wifely aid? Any tender care?

"No," she said, just like that. She hadn't done a thing, merely pulled back the blankets and took a quick look at him. She said she didn't see the wire around his throat or anything like that. She didn't even touch the body to see if it was cold.

Jim Conroy, another assistant district attorney, got out the suitcase that was checked at the Waldorf by Gray and which was recovered by the police after the murder.

"Whose pink pajamas are these?" asked Froessel, as Conroy, a young man, blushingly held up some filmy robes de nuit, as we say at the club.

"Mine," she said.

"Whose blue pajamas are these?" asked Froessel, and Conroy gingerly exhibited more slumber suitings.

"Gray's," she answered, grimly. No "Mr. Gray," not even "Judd Gray," today. Just Gray-like.

"Whose toilet articles are in this box?" inquired Froessel.

"Both," she said, laconically.

Hazelton objected to the district attorney "parading for the forty-ninth time adultery before this jury—we are not trying that." The spectators glared at Hazelton for interference with their just due for all the effort it cost to get into the court room.

Froessel picked up a copy of the confession she made immediately after the murder and read it line by line, asking after each line, "Is that the truth?"

He finally got tired of asking that and requested her to say "yes" or "no" at proper intervals and save his breath.

She denied most of the statements attributed to her in the confession, especially with any reference to her part in the actual slaughter of her husband. She had more lingual vigor left at the finish than he did.

May 5, 1927

Bloody apparitions rising out of his memory of that dreadful night in Queens Village probably gibbered at the window of Henry Judd Gray's soul yesterday afternoon.

His voice kept lifting, and hurrying, as he sat on the witness stand, telling his version of the murder, until finally as he reached the climax of the tale, it came pouring out of the amplifiers with a rush, hard driven by a note of terror.

You wouldn't have been much surprised to see the little corset salesman suddenly leap up and go tearing out of the crowded court room with his hair on end. The red fingers of fear were clutching his heart as he said:

"I struck him on the head, as nearly as I could see, one blow. I think I hit him another blow, I think I hit him another blow because with the first blow he raised up in bed and started to holler. I went over on the bed on top of him, and tried to get the bed-clothes over his mouth, so as to suppress his cries." A distinct thud was heard and a commotion stirred the men and women packed like sardines in one part of the court. A couple of court attendants quickly picked up the limp form of Warren Schneider,*

* Albert Snyder had modified the family name.

brother of the dead man, and carried him from the court room, beating the air with his hands and crying aloud, "Albert, Albert."

Few eyes turned to see. They were all watching the man on the witness stand, up to this moment more like a baggy dummy, popping out, through a mechanical mouth, words thrown in by the ventriloquist's voice.

"He was apparently full of fight. He got me by the necktie. I was getting the worst of it because I was being choked. I hollered, 'Momsie, Momsie, for God's sake help me.' I had dropped the sash weight. She came over and took the weight and hit him on the head, and throwing the bottle of chloroform and the handkerchief and the wire and everything onto the pillow."

Necks craned for a look at the woman who has been called "The Bloody Blonde," as she sat almost hidden from view among her attorneys and guards, and the spectators crowded in close around her on every side. The blond head, covered with a little black hat was bent low. You could not see the marble white face at that moment. It was between her hands. She was crying. Her mother, Mrs. Josephine Brown, was crying. So, too, was the mother of Henry Judd Gray, a small woman in black. She was sitting so close to Mrs. Snyder she could have reached out and snatched the black hat off the blond head.

The spectators gasped. For one brief moment, a least, Henry Judd Gray, most of the days of his life a dull, drab sort of a fellow, busied with a corset clientele, attained the proportions of a dramatic figure.

He was gulping as he turned on the high light of his tale, and frequently swigged water from the glass on the table in front of him. His attorney, Samuel L. Miller, stepped to the bench at 4:30, the usual hour of the afternoon recess, and suggested the recess to Justice Scudder.

"Oh, I can go on all night," Gray spoke up, addressing his remarks to the Court. "There are some points that I want to. clear up."

Justice Scudder nodded.

The little corset salesman started to backtrack in his story and Justice Scudder said, "You told us that a moment ago."

"Well, I'd like to go back if possible, Your Honor, because we went down into the cellar."

"Very good, but don't repeat."

"I see," said Gray, picking up the crimson trend of his story, on down to where he said, his voice now lifting even above any previous note:

"I tied her feet. I tied her hands. I told her it might be two months, it might be a year, and it might be never, before she would see me again—and I left her lying on her mother's bed, and I went out."

His voice broke. The eyes that show much white, like the eyes of a mean mule, glistened behind the yellowish glasses in the vague light of the old court room. Henry Judd Gray, but a few minutes before the stark figure of a dreadful tale of blood, was close to blubbering.

As the Court announced the recess, a babble of voices broke out in the court room, and men and women stared at one another and argued noisily.

"I say to you that if ever human lips uttered the truth, this was the time!" bawled Willard Mack, the playwright, one fist clutching a wad of paper, the other his hat, as he stared about him wild-eyed and excited. "They'll never shake that fellow!"

"The man told a good story," ruminated David Belasco, the famous dramatist and producer, who hasn't missed a day of the trial. "I thought he would. A good story, indeed—indeed—but," and he shook his gray head, "weak in spots, weak in spots."

Thus the opinions differed among the celebrities, and we had a fresh batch of them, including Olga Petrova, and Irving Berlin, and Ruth Hale, the Lucy Stoner, who would officially be Mrs. Heywood Broun if her conscience permitted. Also Frankie Farnum, the hoofer, as well as all our good old standbys like the Marquis of Queensbury.

One thing is certain, Henry Judd Gray made a far stronger impression on the side of veracity than did the lady who is popularly referred to as his paramour. At times I thought Henry Judd was undergoing all the keen pleasure of a small boy telling a swell ghost story to his playmates such was his apparent joy, but along toward the finish my flesh was creeping, like everybody else's.

At first he seemed to have a certain air of bravado, perhaps a remnant of the same curious spirit that may have sent him into the murder in the first place—the desire of a weakling fellow to show off, you might say.

But gradually it became rather apparent it seemed to me, that here was a man who had something on his chest that he greatly desired to unload. He was making public confession, perhaps by way of easement to a sorely harassed conscience.

That is, if he was indeed telling the truth, the whole truth, and nothing but the truth, so help him God. He put all the blame on the woman, to be sure.

He said she egged him on to the murder, steadily, insistently, until he found himself sprawling on top of poor Albert Snyder that night in Queens Village. He said she plied him with liquor at all times. He made himself out pretty much of an "A-No. 1" fathead right from taw, a victim of an insidious blonde, though at no time yesterday did he mention any of his feelings for her, if any.

That will perhaps come today. He babbled all their indiscretions, though it was expected he would tell even more—and worse. In fact, it was rumored during the afternoon that Gray's counsel intended asking the court to bar the ladies from the court room, a canard that had several hundred females prepared to go to law for their rights as listeners.

If anyone retains an impression that Prohibition still prevails in the land, they should read Henry Judd Gray's testimony, although they may get a vicarious snootfull before they have gone very far, if they are susceptible to suggestion.

Henry Judd was quite a rumpot to hear him tell it, especially when he was with Mrs. Snyder. He said she cared for gin, while he went in for Scotch. He inhaled all of a small bottle of whiskey left for him by Mrs. Snyder and most of a quart that he found himself in the room the night he waited in the Snyder home on murder bent.

In fact, one gathered the murder was conceived in whiskey

and executed in whiskey, as is not uncommon with many other forms of crime these days. They were in bed together in the Waldorf, and she had come in "so plastered up" that he had a lot of trouble getting her into the feathers, when she first suggested the murder to him.

It was born in that bed in the Waldorf, he said, about the third week in February of 1927. "The plan that was later carried out," as Henry Judd put it.

One way and another, Henry Judd gave Mrs. Ruth Brown Snyder quite a bad reputation with the jurors, who sat listening open-mouthed to his tale, though it must be admitted he didn't spare himself. He pictured himself more as an able two-handed drinker than as a murderer, however. He gave the palm to Mrs. Snyder in this respect.

"I had two or three drinks," or "I had four or five drinks," or "I drank plenty."

This was the tenor of the early part of his discourse, tending to show no doubt that he was generally well tanked-up when he was with Mrs. Snyder. In fact, he said he was usually in a fog. He must have been if he drank all he says, what with the quality of liquor these days.

Mrs. Snyder's favorite pastime was trying to knock her husband off, as one gathered from Henry Judd's tale. She told Gray she had tried sleeping powders, gas, auto accidents, and bichloride of mercury, but had no luck. She put it just that way to Gray, he testified—"no luck."

She gave him four mercury tablets when he had an attack of hiccoughs, so she informed Gray, and the corset salesman says he remarked, "My God, don't you know that's deadly poison?"

"I thought so, too, but it only made him vomit."

"It is a wonder it didn't kill him."

"It is a wonder," she agreed, "but it only made him vomit fifteen or sixteen times that night."

"What were the aftereffects of this?" Gray asked her, he said.

"It apparently cured the hiccoughs," she replied.

"Well, that's a hell of a way to cure hiccoughs," Gray said was his comment. There were no titters from the crowded court room. Somehow, the situation in which poor Albert Snyder moved, was commencing to dawn on the spectators. They gazed in wonder and awe at the blond woman who is all the Borgias rolled into one, if what Gray says is true.

She was despondent most of the day. The defiance with which she faced the world at first has faded. Only once or twice she sat up yesterday and glared at Gray. His recital of the ten-day trip that they took through New York State, told without the omission of any of the details, was probably shameful even to this woman who must be shameless, if what the man says is the truth.

He admitted he borrowed money from her, but he claimed he had paid it all back a little at a time, except $25, which he still owes her. Mrs. Snyder will probably always have something coming to her. The impression you got from Gray's early recital was of a most despicable little tattle-tale, but you must bear in mind the man is fighting for his life, and men stoop to anything when life is at stake.

Gray's testimony, as drawn from him by Attorney Miller, was really not much different from the story set forth in his original confession made to the police and already read into the records of this case, save in detail, until he came to the murder.

You may remember Mrs. Snyder says she was in the bathroom when she heard a thud, and looked into her husband's room to find Gray astride her husband on the bed. She said she tried to pull Gray away, that he pushed her, and that she fainted, and recalls nothing else.

It is for the twelve good men and true to say who is telling the truth. For the first week of the trial, the blond woman appeared to be the stronger character of the two, and with the little corset salesman an inert heap in his chair, she was apt to impress the casual observer.

Now the situation is just reversed. The woman seems to be completely sunk, and while I wouldn't say that Gray stands out as any Gibraltar, he at least shows some signs of life. But where she seemed defiant, he appears repentant in his attitude. He did not hate Albert Snyder—he had never met the man, he testified yesterday, though he may have seen him on one occasion with Mrs. Snyder, whereas he claims the woman often expressed to him her dislike of her husband. Gray said:

"She asked me once if I would please help her out by shooting her husband. I said absolutely no. I had never shot a man in my life, and I wasn't going to start in by murder. She asked me if I knew of any other plan, and I said absolutely no, I could not help her out, and she must see the thing through alone."

But she kept at him, he said. Blondes are persistent, as well as insidious. She kept at him. Drunk, or sober, he was always hearing the suggestion that he step out to Queens Village and slaughter Albert Snyder. You couldn't have seen the average man for heel-dust after the first crack from the lady, but Henry Judd held on.

He suggested something of Mrs. Snyder's regard for him by testifying she said she would rather have him at home at all times instead of traveling around with those corsets, though he were only a truck driver.

"I told her that was impossible, that I had a family and a home to maintain and that they must be taken care of—that I would not break up my home," Henry Judd so declared, though it was quite apparent he didn't have any qualms about breaking up Albert Snyder's home.

He often cleared his throat as he talked, probably stalling a bit for time before his answers, though in the main he answered only too readily to suit attorneys for Mrs. Snyder. Both Dana Wallace and Edgar Hazleton were on their feet several times objecting to the testimony.

Henry Judd said he didn't know much about life insurance, but testified Mrs. Snyder had shown him one of her husband's policies and wanted to know how much she would get from it in case of his death. It would appear Mrs. Snyder went to work on that murder thought with Henry Judd soon after they met in the often-mentioned Henry's restaurant.

He at first told her that she was crazy and advised her to have a doctor look at a bump on her blond head. But she kept at him. She wrote him every day and bought him silk pajamas. She even bought a Christmas present for his little daughter, who is about the same age as Lorraine. This was when there was a general exchange of presents between Henry Judd and Mrs. Snyder. She told him she enjoyed spending money on him.

The story of their ten-day trip to Kingston, Albany, Schenectady, Amsterdam, Gloversville, Booneville, Watertown and Syracuse was interesting only in its disclosures of the fact that you can get plenty of liquor in those spots. At least, Henry Judd did. He took a few drinks about everywhere they stopped, and they both got loaded in Scranton, Pa. when the trip was coming to an end.

It was when they got back from that journey that Henry Judd commenced to be more reasonable when she talked of making a murderer of him. He finally told her he would buy some chloroform for her but wouldn't help her use it. In the end he fell for it.

She had spoken about some heavy instrument, such as a hammer as a good thing to use in tapping Albert Snyder while he slept before the chloroform was applied.

"I think I suggested the window weight," remarked Gray, quietly. He bought one on a trip to Kingston, a little later, bought the chloroform, the colored handkerchief, and all else.

"I went to Albany and had a lot of drinks, and I got to thinking this thing over, and I thought how terrible it was and I—"

"One moment," bawled Hazleton, and the Court said never mind what he thought, to Gray.

He said Mrs. Snyder wrote him outlining what he should do, just as he related in the original confession, and he obeyed her instructions, he said. He didn't say why. That remains the most interesting thing that he has to tell—Why?

He told of going down to Mrs. Snyder's March 7 with the idea of disposing of the murder matter then, but Mrs. Snyder met him at the kitchen door and said the time wasn't ripe. He walked around Queens Village quite a bit before he went to the house, Gray said; the mention of his wanderings telling more of his mental trepidations than anything else could have done.

Then came the plans for the second attempt, which proved only too successful.

"My God," Mrs. Snyder said to him at a meeting before the murder, "you're certainly nervous, aren't you?"

"I certainly am. I hardly know what I am doing."

Henry Judd shed what we might accept as a sort of sidelight on the Mrs. Snyder that was before she bogged down under the strain of the past two weeks, when he testified about the letters she wrote to him when he was on the road, and the murder plot was well afloat.

She asked about his health. About his business. She mentioned little Lorraine. Then she told him to drop down by her home Saturday night and bring the things he carried, which were the murder things. She concluded:

"I hope you aren't as nervous as you were."

May 6, 1927

Mankind at last has a clue, developed by the Snyder-Gray trial, as to the approximate moment when a blonde becomes very, very dangerous.

Gentlemen, if she asks you to try out a few sleeping powders, that is the instant you are to snatch up the old chapeau and take the air.

Henry Judd Gray gave this valuable tip to his fellow citizens from the witness stand yesterday, when he was under cross-examination.

He said that not until Mrs. Ruth Brown Snyder induced him to serve as a sort of guinea pig of experimentation with sleeping powders, which she purposed using on her husband, did he realize he was completely under the spell of her magnetism that caused him to later join hands with her in the slaughter of her husband, Albert Snyder.

It was in May a year ago, that he inhaled the powders for her so she might see how they would work. He had knocked around with her quite a bit up to that time, but it seemed the old spell hadn't got down to business. After that, he said, he knew he would do anything she wanted.

He was in her power. Narrowly did I escape writing it powder. It wasn't fear, he said; no, not fear. She had never threatened him. It was more magnetism than anything else.

"And this magnetic force drew you on even without her presence and was so great it overcame all thoughts of your family —of your wife and child?"

So asked Dana Wallace, one of Mrs. Snyder's attorneys, who was cross-examining for her side. There was a note of curiosity in the lawyer's voice.

"Yes," said Henry Judd Gray, and the spectators turned from him to peer at Mrs. Snyder, the blond magnet. She looked about as magnetical as a potato yesterday. She sat crouched at her attorney's table with her black hat between her hands most of the time, though now and then she lifted her face to glare at Henry Judd.

One side of the marble mask is now red from the pressure of her hand against it as she listens to the man who claims she magnetized him into a murderer. He was surprisingly steady under Wallace's hammering at his story of the crime.

Someone remarked it may be because he is telling the truth. It is always rather difficult to rattle a man who sticks to the truth, a bright and highly original thought for the editorial writers.

Wallace is trying in his cross-examination to make it appear that Henry Judd's was the master mind of the murder, and, while Henry Judd is not dodging a lot of activity in the matter, he is harking back to the original defense of man, the same being woman. I wonder if Eve was a blonde?

Early in the cross-examination, Wallace had Henry Judd standing up in the witness chair with the sash weight that figured to such an extent in the butchery held in his hands, showing the pop-eyed jurors just how he slugged the sleeping art editor on the early morning of March 20.

Henry Judd has a sash-weight stance much like the batting form of Waner, of the Pittsburgh Pirates. He first removed his big horn-rimmed glasses at Wallace's request.

"Show us how you struck."

"I used both hands, like this."

So explained the corset salesman, lifting the sash weight, which weighs five pounds, and looks like an old-fashioned coupling pin over his right shoulder. He "cocked it," as the ball players would say, pretty well back of his right ear. He is a right-hand hitter.

The tags tied to the sash weight to identify it as evidence dangled from the heavy bar below Gray's hands. The jurors and the spectators stared at the weird presentation. Gray did not seem at all abashed or nervous. Wallace asked, "How hard did you strike?"

"Well, I could not strike very hard."

He said Mrs. Snyder had done a little practicing with the sash weight first—perhaps a bit of fungo hitting—and found that the weight was too heavy for her, and asked him to pinch hit for her when the time came.

"Did you practice with her?" demanded Wallace.

"Well—ultimately," remarked Gray.

It was a gruesomely humorous reply, though I doubt if Henry Judd intended it that way.

You may recall that he said on direct examination that after he whacked Snyder one or two blows—he is not sure of the number—he dropped the sash weight to pile on top of the struggling art editor, and that Mrs. Snyder picked up the weight and beaned her husband.

Wallace picked on Gray on that point no little and in the course of the dialogue the corset salesman uttered one tremendous truism.

"You testified you thought you hit him another blow because at the first blow he raised up in bed and started to holler," said Wallace. "Didn't you hear Dr. Neail testify here that any of the three blows that struck Snyder would by itself have rendered him unconscious?"

Gray gazed owlishly at the lawyer through his thick yellowish lenses, and said, "I was there, Mr. Wallace, and Dr. Neail wasn't."

One thing Wallace did manage to do was to make it rather

clear in his cross-examination that Gray did a lot of able, if murderous thinking, in going about the crime, especially for a man who was as soaked with booze as Gray claims he was. He had already drunk enough in his story to sink the battleship *Mississippi*.

He started out with the inevitable "I had a few drinks" with which he prefaces most of his answers, and Wallace interrupted.

"Is there any day you know of in connection with this case that you didn't take a lot of drinks?" he demanded.

"Not since I've known Mrs. Snyder," replied Gray with surprising promptness.

When closely pressed, he was almost defiant, and sometimes a trifle stubborn. Wallace kept asking him about the chloroform—whose thought was that?

"Wasn't it your idea?" Wallace asked.

"Well, let it be my idea," replied Gray.

He admitted he picked up a piece of Italian newspaper on the train en route to New York to kill Snyder and that it was after the murder he had suggested the mention of two foreigners by Mrs. Snyder, whereas in the original plan for the crime, a colored man had been in their minds as the fictitious object of suspicion.

It developed, too, from his cross-examination that the murder was finally planned in a chop suey place in Jamaica. He admitted he took the wire from his office with which Snyder's throat was bound. He said she had told him to get rope, but he didn't get the rope because "his mind was on his work" and he didn't think of it until he was leaving his office.

"Well, was Mrs. Snyder's presence or spirit around you in the atmosphere dominating and controlling you when you picked up the wire?" demanded Wallace.

"It might have been," said Gray.

"Do you believe in such things?" queried Wallace, eyeing the man carefully.

"I might," answered Gray.

It seems that Henry Judd has some sense of shame left anyway, and probably a lot of remorse. Wallace got to questioning him on his testimony that he and Mrs. Snyder occupied Lorraine Snyder's room for their intimacies whenever he went to the Snyder home.

"In spite of the fact that you had a little girl of your own, you did that?" asked Wallace.

"I'm ashamed to say I did," replied Gray.

"You forgot your own flesh and blood?"

"I'm ashamed to say I did."

Mrs. Snyder raised her head and looked at him. Then she shook her head and dropped her face in her hands again. Gray said that, with only one or two exceptions, they always used the child's room as their trysting place, if that is what you call it.

Wallace referred to the plot for the murder formulated in the chop suey joint as "the Chinese plan," and Millard asked, "Is that facetious, Your Honor?"

"The Court is quite ignorant," replied Justice Scudder, wearily. "The Court could not say. Proceed, gentlemen."

Gray said, rather surprisingly, that he was not thinking of murder when he prepared his Syracuse alibi. He didn't know why he had picked up the waste in the street in Rochester that was used to give Albert Snyder chloroform. At times he didn't remember, too.

Hazleton darted to Wallace's side at intervals and coached his partner on some questions. Gray held himself in such a collected manner that both Miller and Millard, his counsel, were grinning gleefully.

He admitted he had felt the hands of the dead man, Snyder, though later he said it might have been the foot, and "announced to the widow," as Wallace casually put it, he thought the art editor was defunct. He said Mrs. Snyder was standing at his side at the moment.

But he claimed he never saw the wire around Snyder's neck. He pressed a pistol into Snyder's hand though he couldn't exactly explain why. He denied Wallace's suggestion it was to show Snyder's fingerprints on the gun.

He admitted removing his glasses before entering the bedroom, and said the reason he took them off, he thought, was in case of anything in the way of a fight.

"So your mind was so attuned to the situation, that although you were drinking, you were preparing yourself for a combat?" asked Wallace. "Not necessarily—no," replied Gray.

That was where he was weak—on his explanation of his apparently well-planned actions leading up to them.

"And you remember that occasion very well when you struck Snyder, don't you?" asked Wallace.

"I do not remember very well now," answered Gray.

He claimed he was in a haze from the time of the murder until he had passed Albany on his way back to Syracuse, yet he admitted sweeping up the cellar to hide his footprints and arranging to have the sash weight covered with ashes to make it appear it hadn't been touched. He said he did these things "automatically."

"You mean your mind was working to protect yourself?"

"Not necessarily—no."

"Well, what did you do it for?"

"I don't know."

Court then recessed until ten o'clock this morning.

Our line-up of celebrities was fairly strong again yesterday taking the field as follows:

Marquis of Queensbury, L. F.

Dave Belasco, R. F.

Olga Petrova, 1 b.

Francine Larrimore, 2 b.

Thurston, 3 b.

Willard Mack, ss.

Clare Briggs, c. f.

Lois Meredith, c.

One-eyed Connolly, p.

Mr. Brick Terrett, one of the gentlemanly inmates of the press section, circulated a petition among his brethren that Thurston, the magician, be requested to conjure up a few additional seats from his hat for the newspaper folks.

It was a swell idea.

This remains the best show in town, if I do say so, as I shouldn't. Business couldn't be better. In fact, there is some talk of sending out a No. 2 company and 8,000,000 different blondes are being considered for the leading female role. No one has yet been picked for Henry Judd Gray's part but that will be easy. Almost any citizen will do with a little rehearsal.

May 7, 1927

The Snyder-Gray murder trial—you instinctively put the woman first in this instance—is about over, and the twelve good men and true, who have been stolidly listening to the horrible tale for two weeks will decide soon what shall be done with this precious pair, the cheaters who tried to cheat the laws of God and man and wound up trying to cheat each other.

At about three o'clock yesterday afternoon, all hands rested as they say when they have dug up all the testimony they think will do any good, or any harm, either. If the Sabbath peace and quiet of any neighborhood is offended by loud stentorian voices, that will be the lawyers warming up for a lot of hollering Monday.

Court has taken a recess until then. Dana Wallace will open in defense of Mrs. Snyder. William L. Millard will follow Wallace, in an effort to talk Gray out of the chair.

Richard S. Newcombe, the grave district attorney of Queens County, will do most of the arguing for the State of New York.

And what, think you, do the blond woman and the little corset salesman expect from the twelve good men and true?

Gray—nothing. Gray's attorneys say he now has a clean conscience, since relieving it of the details of the butchery of Albert Snyder, and he thinks the jury will believe his story of how the woman wound her insidious blond coils about his life until he couldn't help doing anything she desired.

I gather from the statement that he expects no clemency. Blessed be he who expects nothing, for mayhap he will not be disappointed. I suppose that deep down Gray is hoping for mercy.

And the blonde? You can always look for a blonde to say something unique. Mrs. Ruth Brown Snyder says, through her attorneys, Dana Wallace and Edgar Hazleton, that she doesn't see how "any red-blooded men" can believe Gray's story—that hers was the heavy hand in the hammering and chloroforming and wiring to death of her husband.

He seemed to be red-blooded himself, this Albert Snyder, whose ghostly figure has stalked in the background of this horrible screen presentation of human life and death for two weeks. Much of that red blood is still on a pillow on which his head rested when Gray first beat down upon it with the sash weight, and which was still lying on the district attorney's table along with the other horrible exhibits of the crime after Court took a recess yesterday afternoon.

Two hundred men and women gathered about the table, pushing and struggling with each other for a mere peek at the exhibits. Several hundred others had gone into the street outside to pull and haul for a view of Olga Petrova, as she stood beside her Rolls-Royce, being photographed, and of Leon Errol, the comedian, and other celebrities who honored us with their presence yesterday.

That scene in the court was one that should give the philosophers and psychologists pause. The women were far more interested in the bloody pillow than they would have been in a baby buggy. It was the last thrill left to them after Gray and Mrs. Snyder walked out of the court, the woman passing rows of the leering eyes of her sisters with her head down, but with a dangerous gleam in the greenish blue eyes.

Henry Judd started off the day with a good big jolt of water from the glass on the table in front of the witness stand. He imbibed water while he was on the stand at the same rate at which he used to drink whiskey, if he was the two-handed whiskey-wrestler that his story would indicate.

Wallace touched briefly on Gray's whiskey drinking again as he went into the corset salesman's finances. He wanted to know if Henry Judd always paid for the drinks. Henry said he did, a statement which interested all the bootleggers present. They wondered how he could do so much elbow-bending on his income.

That was about $5500 a year, out of which Gray gave his family $3500 a year. He had around $2000 left for himself. Wallace asked:

"And you visited night clubs and went to parties and did your drinking and clothed yourself on $2000 a year?"

"That is correct."

And then the philosophers and psychologists really had something to think about. Also the domestic economists then and there present.

Wallace seemed to be trying to connect Gray's purchase of some shares of stock in the corset concern for which he worked with some possible interest in the death of Albert Snyder, for financial reasons.

Q. May I ask you, with your mind in the condition it was under Mrs. Snyder's dominance, and being fully aware of your own home conditions and business affairs, what did you expect to gain by aiding and bringing about the death of Albert Snyder? What was your idea, your personal idea, of what you would gain?

A. That is what I would like to know.

Q. What's that?

A. That is what I would like to know.

Q. And without any reason for it that you know of, a man of your intelligence, you struck a man over the head with a sash weight and did the things you say you did?

A. I did.

Q. And you want to tell this jury you do not know why you did it?

A. I am telling.

Q. What did you intend to do after it was all over?

A. I didn't intend to do anything. I was through.

Henry Judd fell into a slightly philosophical strain as he proceeded. He may have been qualifying to cover the next murder case for some newspaper. Also his attitude toward Wallace became gently chiding. He remarked, "One sometimes does things under the influence of liquor that one does automatically."

It sounds quite true.

Wallace whipped many a question at Gray and then shouted, "I withdraw it" before Gray could answer. He could not keep the little corset salesman from going beyond the question at times. Henry Judd was inclined to be verbose while Wallace tried to keep him pinned down to yes and no.

"Are you answering my questions that way because in one form it involves her and in another form it involves you?"

"I am already involved."

May 9, 1927

If you are asking a medium-boiled reporter of murder trials, I couldn't condemn a woman to death no matter what she had done, and I say this with all due consideration of the future hazards to long-suffering man from sash weights that any lesser verdict than murder in the first degree in the Snyder-Gray case may produce.

It is all very well for the rest of us to say what *ought* to be done to the blond throwback to the jungle cat that they call Mrs. Ruth Brown Snyder, but when you get in the jury room and start thinking about going home to tell the neighbors that you have voted to burn a woman—even a blond woman—I imagine the situation has a different aspect. The most astonishing verdict that could be rendered in this case, of course, would be first degree for the woman and something else for the man. I doubt that result. I am inclined to think that the verdict, whatever it may be, will run against both alike—death or life imprisonment.

Henry Judd Gray said he expects to go to the chair, and adds that he is not afraid of death, an enviable frame of mind, indeed. He says that since he told his story to the world from the witness stand he has found tranquility, though his tale may have also condemned his blond partner in blood. But perhaps that's the very reason Henry Judd finds tranquility.

He sat in his cell in the county jail over in Long Island yesterday, and read from one of the epistles of John.

"Marvel not, my brethren, if the world hates you. We know that we have passed from death unto life, because we love the brethren. He that loveth not his brother abideth in death. Whosoever hateth his brother is a murderer: and ye know that no murderer hath eternal life abiding in him."

A thought for the second Sunday after Pentecost.

In another cell, the blond woman was very mad at everybody because she couldn't get a marcel for her bobbed locks, one hair of which was once stronger with Henry Judd Gray than the Atlantic Cable.

Also she desired a manicure, but the cruel authorities would not permit the selected one to attend the lady.

Thus Mrs. Snyder will have to go into court today with hangnails and just those offices that she can give her bobbed bean herself. I fear that this injustice will prove another argument of sinister persecution when the folks start declaiming against burning the lady, if such should chance to be the verdict of the jury.

However, with all her troubles about her fingernails and the marcel, Mrs. Snyder did not forget Mother's Day. She is herself a mother as you may remember, though the fact seemed to skip her mind at times when she was all agog over Henry Judd. Also she has a mother, who spent the Sabbath very quietly in that house of horror in Queens Village with Mrs. Snyder's little daughter, Lorraine.

From the old jail Mrs. Snyder sent her mother this:

> Mother's Day Greeting—I have many blessings and I want you to know how thankful I am for all that you have done for me. Love to you and kiss Lorraine for me.   RUTH

Henry Judd Gray, although calm yesterday, declined his breakfast. Moreover, he scarcely touched his lunch. Mrs. Snyder, on the other hand, is reported to have breakfasted well and was longing for some of the good Signor Roberto Minotti's spaghetti and roasted chicken at noon.

They both attended divine services at the jail in the afternoon. Mrs. Snyder seems quite calm, though at similar services last week she was all broken up. As between the two, the blonde seems to be rallying for the last round better than her former sweet daddy of the days before the murder.

Judge Scudder, the tall, courtly, dignified man, who has impressed all beholders of this proceeding as one of the ablest jurists that ever wrapped a black robe around himself, will charge the jury at some length because he must outline what consists of four different degrees of homicide. He will undoubtedly devote much time to the conspiracy charge in the indictment.

The jurors are men of what you might call average intelligence, I mean to say there are no intellectual giants in the box. They are fellows you might meet in any club or cigar store, or speakeasy. A good jury, I call it. I doubt if they will be influenced by any psychological or philosophical twists that the lawyers may attempt to offer them, if any.

May 10, 1927

Mighty short shrift was made of Mrs. Ruth Brown Snyder and Henry Judd Gray by that jury of Long Islanders—the verdict being murder in the first degree for both, the penalty death in the electric chair.

The twelve men went out at 5:20 yesterday afternoon and were back in the box ready to deliver their verdict at 6:57, an hour and thirty-seven minutes. They took off their coats as they entered the jury room, hoisted the windows for a breath of air, and took two ballots.

The first was ten to two for first degree murder, so I understand, the second was unanimous. Justice moved on the gallop against the murderers once the jury got hold of the case.

Mrs. Snyder, standing up to hear the verdict, dropped in her chair and covered her face with her hands. Henry Judd Gray, standing not far from her, held himself stiffly erect for a moment, but more like a man who had been shot and was swaying ever so slightly for a fall. Then he sat down, pulled a prayer book out of his pocket and began reading it.

He kept on reading even while the lawyers were up at Justice Scudder's bench arguing with the Court against immediate sentence. Mrs. Snyder sat with her face buried between her hands. Justice Scudder finally fixed the time of sentence for Monday morning at ten o'clock.

Gray finally put the prayer book back in his pocket and sat looking straight ahead of him, as if he had found some comforting passage in the word of the Lord. He said to his guard on his way to his cell, "I told the truth and my conscience is clear. My mother is glad I told the truth and God Almighty knows I told the truth."

"Oh, I thought they'd believe me—I thought they'd believe me," moaned Mrs. Snyder to Father Patrick Murphy when she met him in the hallway going back to the jail. But before she left the court room there was a flash of the old defiance that marked her demeanor until the late stages of the trial.

"I haven't lost my nerve. My attorneys know that I have not had a fair trial, and we will fight this verdict with every ounce of strength."

They have a curious custom in New York State of taking the prisoners before the clerk of the court after a verdict is returned and setting down their "pedigree"—age, occupation, habits and the like. John Moran, the clerk of the Queens County Court, sits in a little enclosed booth like a bank teller's cage, just in front of the judge's bench, and Mrs. Snyder was asked to step up there. Mrs. Irene Wolfe, the matron of the county jail, and a guard supported her, the man putting his arm around the blond woman as if he was afraid the black-gowned figure would crumble and fall.

The law is a harsh institution. It would have seemed more merciful to take the woman away at once to some quiet place, where she could allow the tears she was choking back with difficulty to fall as they might.

But they stood her up there and asked her a lot of questions that seemed fatuous in view of what is already known of her, and she answered in a low voice—Ruth Brown Snyder, thirty-two years old, born in New York and all that sort of thing. Married? A widow. The tears began trickling down the marble-white cheeks.

Then they finally took her out of the court room by the same path she had trod so often the last couple of weeks. She was pretty thoroughly licked at that moment, and small wonder, for she had just heard twelve men tell her she must die.

Gray stood up before Moran, still holding himself stiffly, but did not weep. In answer to one of the set questions as to whether he is temperate or otherwise he said temperate, which sounded somewhat ironical in view of Gray's testimony during the trial as to the prodigious amounts of liquor he consumed.

He, too, was finally taken away, still walking as if he had put a ramrod down the back of his coat to hold himself so. Henry Judd Gray had said he expected such a sentence, and he was not disappointed.

The pair probably knew they were gone when they received word to make ready to return to the court room in such a short time after the jury retired. Rumor had tossed the verdict pretty well around Long Island City and the court room when the announcement came that the jury was ready to report, and the verdict was a foregone conclusion.

A few hours' delay might have produced hope for one or the other of the man and woman that fate tossed together with such horrible results. It was still daylight over Long Island City, although the yellowish-walled old court room was vaguely lighted by electric lamps, which shed less illumination than any lights I ever saw.

There was a painful stage wait, and in came Mrs. Snyder and Gray, the former between two matrons, Mrs. Wolfe and another, and Gray between two guards. Attorney Edgar Hazleton came in with her. He had evidently gone out to steel her for the verdict. He knew what it was, no doubt of that. She walked in with her little quick, short steps, but her face was gray—not white-gray, a dull, sickening gray.

The man walked firmly, too, but you could see by the expression in his eyes he felt what was coming. He seemed to be holding himself together with a strong effort.

Now a stir told of the coming of Justice Scudder, a lean, stooping figure in his black robe, bobbing his head to the right and left with little short bows like an archbishop. The crowd always rises at the entrance of the judge, then sits down again in some confusion, but this time everyone seemed to adjust himself in his seat again noiselessly.

Justice Scudder peered around from under the green-shaded stand lamp on his desk with an inquiring expression, and, as the roll of the jurors was called, they answered in very low voices. Only one said "here" rather loudly, almost defiantly, it seemed.

The clerk of the court motioned the jurors to stand and then Mrs. Snyder and Henry Judd Gray were also told to rise. They stood there, Mrs. Snyder just behind Gray, leaning against the table. Gray had no support. They could not see each other.

Ten women fainted in the court room in the course of the day, such was the pulling and hauling and the general excitement of the occasion, but Mrs. Ruth Brown Snyder remained as cool as the well-known old cucumber, even when she heard herself termed enough different kinds of animals to populate the zoo.

She was mentioned as a serpent by William L. Millard. Also as a tigress. Still, Millard gave her a back-handed boost, at that, when he called her a sinister, fascinating woman. Perhaps Mrs. Snyder would have been just as well pleased if he had left off the sinister.

Cruel, calculating and cunning, he said she was. She kept her eyes closed while Millard was berating her, supporting her head on her right hand, an elbow leaned on the table. Her left hand was across her breast. Once she dabbed her eyes with a little kerchief, as if she might be mopping away a few tears.

But all that Millard said about Mrs. Snyder was just a few sweet nothings compared to what Dana Wallace said about Gray. He was "human filth," "diabolical fiend," "weak-minded," "despicable creature," "falsifier," and finally a "human anaconda," which is interesting if true, and ought to get Harry Judd a job in any side show.

The little corset salesman just stared straight ahead while Wallace was blasting him. However, he was upright and alert and heard everything Wallace said, probably figuring it sounded libelous. His mother and his sister sat near by and comforted him.

There was much talk of the Deity on all sides. Both Millard and Wallace appealed to Him, and so, too, did the district attorney, when he came to summing up for the State. Newcombe was brief, and omitted brickbats for the defendants. He did compare Mrs. Snyder with a jungle cat, possibly just to make sure that no animals had been left out.

The district attorney was in what you may call a soft spot, anyway, with the defendants at loggerheads, and each trying to push the other into the electric chair. However, from the beginning Newcombe has conducted this case with singular simplicity of method, and without any attempt at red fire.

Millard's argument for Gray was as expected, that Henry Judd was a poor fool, a dupe, and a lot of other things that mean a chump, who was beguiled by the woman.

However, he astonished the populace by advancing the theory that Mrs. Snyder slipped Henry Judd a dose of poison the night of the murder, expecting her little playmate in blood would fold up and die also after he had assisted in dispatching Snyder. The poison didn't work, Millard said.

Furthermore, Millard made the first open suggestion of abnormality in Mrs. Snyder. I heard hints that Gray's attorneys intended trying to show that the lady wasn't altogether normal, during the trial, but all that junk was kept out—by agreement, as I understand it—and only in his argument yesterday did Millard mention the abnormality.

For Mrs. Snyder, the defense was she was the victim of Henry Judd, "the human anaconda," and he was but "hiding behind the woman's skirts." This caused Lieutenant McDermott, of the Police Department, to suggest mildly to me that it was a great phrase and true, in the old days, but now a woman's skirts are nothing to hide behind if a gent wishes to be really concealed.

Both Millard and Wallace were in favor of their clients being acquitted. Millard's was something of an appeal for pity, but Wallace said, in the spirit of Mrs. Snyder's defiance throughout this trial, that she was not asking for pity, she was asking for justice.

In some ways it was a disheartening spectacle, if one happened to think how many spectators would have been attracted to

Long Island City to hear a few pleas for the Mississippi Flood sufferers. In another, it was something of a tribute to the power of good old publicity. It pays to advertise. We have been three-sheeting Henry Judd and Ruth to good purpose.

• • • • •

Ruth Brown Snyder and Henry Judd Gray were executed in the electric chair at New York's Sing Sing Prison soon after 11 P.M., on January 13, 1928. Their counsel had exhausted every legal device to gain new trials, every means of exerting pressure upon Governor Alfred E. Smith to commute the sentences of one or both to life imprisonment.

Runyon did not cover the execution.

Gray was buried in the Rosedale Cemetery near East Orange, New Jersey, and Mrs. Snyder in Woodlawn Cemetery, The Bronx, New York.

ARNOLD ROTHSTEIN'S FINAL PAYOFF

New York City, November 19, 1929

If the ghost of Arnold Rothstein was hanging around the weather-beaten old Criminal Courts Building yesterday—and Arnold always did say he'd come back after he was dead and haunt a lot of people—it took by proxy what would have been a violent shock to the enormous vanity of the dead gambler.

Many citizens, members of the so-called "blue ribbon panel," appeared before Judge Charles C. Nott, Jr., in the trial of George C. McManus,* charged with murdering Rothstein and said they didn't know Rothstein in life and didn't know anybody that did know him.

Arnold would have scarcely believed his ears. He lived in the belief he was widely known. He had spent many years establishing himself as a landmark on old Broadway. It would have hurt his pride like sixty to hear men who lived in the very neighborhood he frequented shake their heads and say they didn't know him.

A couple said they hadn't even read about him being plugged in the stomach with a bullet that early evening of November 4 a year ago, in the Park Central Hotel.

Well, such is fame in the Roaring Forties!

They had accepted two men to sit on the jury that is to hear the evidence against McManus, the first man to pass unchallenged by both sides being Mark H. Simons, a stockbroker, of No. 500 West 111th Street, and the second being Eugene A. Riker, of No. 211 West 21st Street, a traveling salesman.

* Not to be confused with George McManus, cartoonist-humorist of *Bringing Up Father* fame, no relation of George C.

206

It seemed to be a pretty fair start anyway, but just as Judge Nott was about to adjourn court at four o'clock, Mark H. Simon presented a complication. He is a dark complexioned, neatly dressed chap, in his early thirties, with black hair slicked back on his head. He hadn't read anything about the case, and seemed to be an ideal juror.

But it appears he is suffering from ulcers of the stomach, and this handicap was presented to Judge Nott late in the day. James D. C. Murray, attorney for McManus, George M. Brothers, Assistant prosecuting attorney, in charge of the case for the State, and three other assistants from District Attorney Banton's office, gathered in front of the bench while Mark H. Simon was put back in the witness chair and examined.

The upshot of the examination was his dismissal from service by Judge Nott, which left Riker, a youngish, slightly bald man, with big horn specs riding his nose, as the only occupant of the jury box. Judge Nott let the lonesome looking Riker go home for the night after instructing him not to do any gabbing about the case.

The great American pastime of jury picking took up all the time from 10:30 yesterday morning until four o'clock in the afternoon, with an hour off for chow at one o'clock. Thirty "blue ribboners," well-dressed, solid looking chaps for the most part, were examined and of this number Murray challenged a total of fourteen. Each side had thirty peremptory challenges. Attorney Brothers knocked off nine and four were excused.

George McManus, the defendant, sat behind his attorney eyeing each talesman with interest but apparently offering no suggestions. McManus was wearing a well-tailored brown suit, and was neatly groomed, as usual. His big, dark-toned face never lost its smile.

Two of his brothers, Jim and Frank, were in the court room. Frank is a big, fine-looking fellow who has a nifty tenor voice that is the boast of the Roaring Forties, though he can be induced to sing only on special occasions.

Only a very few spectators were permitted in the court, because there wasn't room in the antique hall of justice for spare chairs after the "blue ribboners" were all assembled. A squad of the Hon. Grover Whalen's best and most neatly uniformed cops are spread all around the premises, inside and out, to preserve decorum.

Edgar Wallace, the English novelist and playwright, who is said to bat out a novel or play immediately after his daily marmalade, was given the special privilege of the chair inside the railing and sat there listening to the examination of the talesmen, and doubtless marveling at the paucity of local knowledge of the citizens about a case that he heard of over in England. Mr. Wallace proved to be a fattish, baldish man, and by no means as young as he used to be.

A reflection of the average big towner's mental attitude toward gambling and gamblers was found in the answers to Attorney Murray's inevitable question as to whether the fact the defendant is a gambler and gambled on cards and the horses, would prejudice the talesmen against him. Did they consider a gambler a low character?

Well, not one did. Some admitted playing the races themselves. One mumbled something about there being a lot of gamblers in Wall Street who didn't excite his prejudice.

Attorney Murray was also concerned in ascertaining if the talesmen had read anything that District Attorney Banton had said about the defendant, and if so, had it made any impression on the talesman? It seemed not. One chap said he had read Banton's assertions all right, but figured them in the nature of a bluff.

Do you know anybody who knew Rothstein—pronounced "stine" by Mr. Brothers, and "steen" by Mr. Murray—or George McManus? Do you know anybody who knew either of them?

Do you know anybody who knows anybody connected with (*a*) the District Attorney's office? (*b*) the Police Department? Were you interested in the late political campaign? Ever live in the Park Central? Ever dine there? Know anybody connected with the management? Did you ever go to a race track?

Did you ever read anything about the case? (This in a city of over 4,000,000 newspaper readers, me hearties, and every paper carrying column after column of the Rothstein murder for months!) Did you ever hear any discussion of it? Can you? Suppose? Will you? State of mind. Reasonable doubt—

Well, by the time old John Citizen, "blue ribboner" or not, has had about twenty minutes of this he is mighty glad to get out of that place and slink home, wondering if after all it is worth while trying to do one's duty by one's city, county and state.

November 20, 1929

A client—or shall we say a patient—of the late Arnold Rothstein popped up on us in the old Criminal Courts Building in the shank o' the evening yesterday. He came within a couple of aces of being made juror No. 8, in the trial of George C. McManus, charged with the murder of the said Rothstein.

Robert G. McKay, a powerfully built, black-haired broker of No. 244 East 67th Street, a rather swanky neighborhood, was answering the do-yous and the can-yous of James D. C. Murray as amiably as you please, and as he had already passed the State's legal lights apparently in a satisfactory manner, the gents at the press tables were muttering, "Well, we gotta another at last."

Then suddenly Robert G. McKay, who looks as if he might have been a Yale or Princeton lineman of say, ten years back, and who was sitting with his big legs crossed and hugging one knee, remarked in a mild tone to Murray, "I suppose I might say I knew Arnold Rothstein—though none of you have asked me."

"Ah," said Attorney Murray with interest, just as it appeared he was through with his questioning.

"Did you ever have any business transactions with Rothstein?"

"Well, it was business on his part, and folly on mine."

"Might I have the impertinence to ask if you bet with him?"

McKay grinned wryly, and nodded. Apparently he found no relish in his recollection of the transaction with "the master mind," who lies a-mouldering in his grave while the State of New York is trying to prove that George McManus is the man who tossed a slug into his stomach in the Park Central Hotel the night of November 4, a year ago.

Attorney Murray now commenced to delve somewhat into McKay's state of mind concerning the late Rothstein. He wanted to know if it would cause the broker any feeling of embarrassment to sit on a jury that was trying a man for the killing of Rothstein, when Judge Charles C. Nott, Jr., who is presiding in the trial, remarked, "I don't think it necessary to spend any more time on this man."

The late Rothstein's customer hoisted his big frame out of the chair, and departed, a meditative expression on his face, as if he might still be considering whether he would feel any embarrassment under the circumstances.

They wangled out six jurors at the morning session of the McManus trial, which was enlivened to some extent by the appearance of quite a number of witnesses for the State in the hallways of the rusty old red brick Criminal Courts Building.

These witnesses had been instructed to show up yesterday morning with the idea that they might be called, and one of the first to arrive was "Titanic Slim," otherwise Alvin C. Thomas, the golf-playing gambling man, whose illness in Milwaukee caused a postponement of the trial a week ago.

"Titanic Slim" was attended by Sidney Stajer, a rotund young man who was one of Rothstein's closest friends, and who is beneficiary to the tune of $75,000 under the terms of the dead gambler's will. At first the cops didn't want to admit "Titanic Slim" to the portals of justice, as he didn't look like a witness, but he finally got into the building only to learn he was excused.

The photographers took great interest in the drawling-voiced, soft-mannered, high roller from the South, and Sidney Stajer scowled at them fiercely, but Sidney really means no harm by his scowls. Sidney is not a hard man and ordinarily would smile very pleasantly for the photographers, but it makes him cross to get up before noon.

The State's famous material witness, Bridget Farry, chambermaid at the Park Central, put in an appearance with Beatrice Jackson, a telephone operator at the same hotel. Bridget was positively gorgeous in an emerald-green dress and gold-heeled slippers. Also she had silver stockings and a silver band around her blond hair. She wore no hat. A hat would have concealed the band.

Bridget, who was held by the State in durance vile for quite a spell, is just a bit stoutish, but she was certainly all dressed up like Mrs. Astor's horse. She sat with Miss Jackson on a bench just outside the portals of justice and exchanged repartee with the cops, the reporters and the photographers.

Bridget is nobody's sap when it comes to talking back to folks. Finally she left the building, and was galloping lightly along to escape the photographers, when her gold-heeled slippers played her false, and she stumbled and fell.

An ambulance was summoned posthaste, as the lady seemed to be injured, but an enterprising gal reporter from a tab scooped her up into a taxicab, and departed with the witness to unknown parts. It is said Bridget's shinbone was scuffed up by the fall.

Some of the State's witnesses were quite busy at the telephone booths while in the building getting bets down on the Bowie races. It is a severe handicap to summon a man to such a remote quarter as the Criminal Courts Building along toward post time.

November 21, 1929

Twelve good men, and glum, are now hunched up in the jury box, in Judge Nott's court, and they are all ready to start in trying to find out about the murder of Arnold Rothstein.

But the hours are really tough on a lot of folks who will figure more or less prominently in the trial. Some of the boys were wondering if Judge Nott would entertain a motion to switch his hours around and start in at 4 P.M., the usual hour of adjournment, and run to 10:30 A.M., which is a gentleman's bedtime. The consensus is he wouldn't.

George Brothers, one of District Attorney Banton's assistants, who is in charge of the prosecution, will probably open the forensic fury for the State of New York this morning, explaining to the dozen morose inmates of the jury box just what the

State expects to prove against the defendant, to wit, that George McManus is the party who shot Arnold Rothstein in the stomach in the Park Central Hotel the night of November 4, a year ago.

You may not recall the circumstances, but McManus is one of four persons indicted for the crime. Another is Hyman Biller, an obscure denizen of the brightlights region of Manhattan Island, who probably wouldn't be recognized by more than two persons if he walked into any joint in town, such is his obscurity.

Then there is good old John Doe and good old Richard Roe, possibly the same Doe and Roe who have been wanted in forty-nine different spots for crimes ranging from bigamy to disorderly conduct for a hundred years past. Tough guys, old John and Richard, and always getting in jams. McManus is the only one on trial for the killing of Rothstein, probably for the reason he is the only one handy.

November 22, 1929

"Give me a deck of cards," said "Red" Martin Bowe plaintively, peering anxiously around Judge Nott's court room in the dim light of yesterday afternoon, as if silently beseeching a friendly volunteer in an emergency.

"Get me a deck of cards, and I'll show you."

You see Red Martin Bowe had suddenly come upon a dilemma in his forty-odd years of traveling up and down the earth. He had come upon a fellow citizen who didn't seem to savvy the elemental pastime of stud poker, and high spading, which Martin probably thought, if he ever gave the matter any consideration, is taught in the grammar schools of this great nation—or should be.

So he called for a deck of cards. He probably felt the question was fatuous but he was willing to do his best to enlighten this apparently very benighted fellow, Ferdinand Pecora, the chief representative of Old John Law on the premises, and to show the twelve good men, and glum, in the jury box just how that celebrated card game was conducted which the State of New York is trying to show cost Arnold Rothstein his life at the hands of George McManus.

But no deck of cards was immediately forthcoming. So Martin Bowe didn't get to give his ocular demonstration to the assembled citizens, though a man came dashing in a little later with a nice red deck, while even Judge Nott was still snorting over Martin Bowe's request.

Possibly if Mr. Pecora can show a night off later some of the boys who sat in the back room yesterday might be induced to give him a lesson or two in stud poker. Also high spading.

Martin Bowe is a big, picturesque looking chap, who is getting bald above the ears, and who speaks with slow drawl and very low. In fact all the witnesses displayed a remarkable tendency to pitch their voices low in marked contrast with their natural vocal bent under ordinary circumstances and the attorneys had to keep admonishing them to talk louder.

"Gambler," said Bowe, quietly, and without embarrassment, when asked his business. Then he went on to tell about the card game that will probably be remarked for many years as Broadway's most famous joust. It began on a Saturday night and lasted into the Sunday night following. Martin said he previously played five or six hours at a stretch, and then would lie down and take a rest. He stated:

"It started with bridge, then we got to playing stud. The game got slow, and then some wanted to sport a little so they started betting on the high spade."

"I lose," remarked Bowe calmly, when Pecora asked how he came out. McManus was in the game. Also Rothstein, "Titanic," Meyer Boston, Nate Raymond, "Sol—somebody." A chap named Joe Bernstein was present, and several others he didn't remember, though Sam Boston later testified Bernstein was "doing something and he wasn't playing." It is this Bernstein, a California young man, who "beat" Rothstein for $69,000 though Bernstein was never actually in the play. He bet from the outside.

As near as Bowe could recollect, Raymond, Rothstein, Mc-Manus and Bernstein were bettors on the high card. He heard McManus lost about $50,000. Rothstein was keeping a score on the winnings and losings. McManus paid off partly in cash and partly by check, while Rothstein was putting cash in his pocket, and would give out I.O.Us. Bowe said he heard Rothstein lost over $200,000. The redoubtable "Titanic" won between $20,000 and $25,000 from McManus. Pecora asked: "What about Meyer Boston?"

"He wins."

Under cross-examination by James D. C. Murray, Bowe said he had often known McManus to bet as much as $50,000 on one horse race and never complain if he lost. He said:

"It's an everyday occurrence with him. He always paid with a smile."

After the game, he said, Rothstein and McManus were very friendly; they often ate together at Lindy's. Rothstein won something from McManus in the game, but Bowe didn't know how much.

It was a rather big day for the defense. In his opening address to the jury, George Brothers, assistant district attorney, didn't seem to offer much motive for the possible killing of Rothstein by McManus other than the ill feeling that might have been engendered over the game in which they both lost.

That, and the fact that McManus fled after the killing, seemed his strongest points, while Attorney Murray quickly made it clear that part of the defense will be that Rothstein wasn't shot in room No. 349 at all, and that he certainly wasn't shot by George McManus.

Murray worked at length on Dr. Charles D. Norris, the city Medical Examiner, trying to bring out from the witness that the nature of the wound sustained by Rothstein and the resultant shock would have prevented Rothstein from walking down three flights of stairs, and pushing open two or three heavy doors to reach the spot in the service entrance of the hotel where he was found, especially without leaving some trace of blood.

During the examination of the doctor, the expensive clothes that Arnold Rothstein used to wear so jauntily were displayed, now crumpled and soiled. The white silk shirt was among the ghastly exhibits, but the $45 custom-made shoes that were his hobby, and the sox were missing. Dr. Norris didn't know what had become of them.

The jurors, most of them business men on their own hook, or identified in salaried capacities with business, were a study while Martin Bowe and Sam Boston were testifying, especially Bowe, for he spoke as calmly of winning and losing $50,000 as if he were discussing the price of his morning paper.

You could see the jurors bending forward, some of them cupping their hands to their ears, and eyeing the witness with amazement. That stud and high spade game had been mentioned so often in the papers that it had come to be accepted as a Broadway fable. Probably no member of the jury, for none of them indicated in their examination that they are familiar with sporting life, took any stock in the tales of high rolling of the Broadway gamblers.

But here was a man who was in the game, who had lost $5,700 of his own money, and who knew what he was talking about. It was apparent the jurors were astounded by the blasé manner of Bowe as he spoke of McManus dropping $50,000 as "an everyday occurrence," and even the voluble Sam Boston's glib mention of handling hundreds of thousands of dollars yearly in bets on sporting events impresses them.

November 28, 1929

Nothing new having developed in the life and battles of Juror No. 9, or the Man with the Little Moustache, the trial of George McManus for the murder of Arnold Rothstein proceeded with reasonable tranquility yesterday.

Just before adjournment over Thanksgiving, to permit the jurors to restore their waning vitality with turkey and stuffin', the State let it out rather quietly that it hasn't been able to trace very far the pistol which is supposed to have ended the tumultuous life of "the master mind" a year ago.

On a pleasant day in last June—the fifteenth, to be exact—it seems that one Mr. Joe Novotny was standing behind the counter in his place of business at No. 51 West Fourth Street, in the thriving settlement of St. Paul, Minnesota, when in popped a party who was to Mr. Joe Novotny quite unknown, shopping for a rod, as the boys term a smoke-pole.

Mr. Novotny sold the stranger a .38-calibre Colt, which Mr. Novotny himself had but recently acquired from the firm of Janney, Sempler & Hill, of Minneapolis, for $22.85. The factory number of the Colt was 359,946. Mr. Novotny did not inquire the shopper's name, because it seems there is no law requiring such inquisitiveness in Minnesota, and Mr. Novotny perhaps didn't wish to appear nosey.

No doubt Mr. Novotny figures the stranger was a new settler in St. Paul and desired the Colt to protect himself against the wild Indians and wolves that are said to roam the streets of the city. Anyway, that's the last Mr. Novotny saw of pistol No. 359,946, and all he knows about it, according to a stipulation presented by the State of New York to Judge Nott late yesterday afternoon, and agreed to by James D. C. Murray, attorney for George McManus, as Mr. Novotny's testimony.

It may be that some miscreant subsequently stole the gun from the settler's cabin in St. Paul or that he lent it to a pal who was going to New York, and wished to be well dressed, for the next we hear of No. 359,946 is its appearance in the vicinity of Fifty-sixth Street and Seventh Avenue, Manhattan Island, where it was picked up by one Bender, a taxi jockey, after the shooting of Arnold Rothstein. A stipulation with reference to said Bender also was submitted to Judge Nott.

The State of New York would have the jury in the trial of George McManus believe it was with this gun that Rothstein was shot in the stomach in room 349 in the Park Central Hotel, and that the gun was hurled through a window into the street after the shooting. It remains to be seen what the jury thinks about this proposition.

It is not thought it will take any stock in any theory that the gun walked from St. Paul to the corner of Fifty-sixth Street and Seventh Avenue.

If the settler who bought the gun from Mr. Novotny would step forward at this moment, he would be as welcome as the flowers in May. But those Northwestern settlers always are reticent.

It was around three o'clock in the afternoon when Mr. James McDonald, one of the assistant district attorneys, finished reading the 300 pages of testimony taken in the case to date to Mr. Edmund C. Shotwell, juror No. 2, who replaced Eugene Riker when Mr. Riker's nerves bogged down on him.

It was the consensus that Mr. Shotwell was in better physical condition than Mr. McDonald at the conclusion of the reading, although at the start it looked as if Mr. McDonald would wear his man down with ease before page No. 204.

Juror No. 9, who is Norris Smith, the man with the little moustache, whose adventures have kept this trial from sinking far down into the inside of the public prints long ere this, sat in a chair in the row behind the staunch juror No. 2, which row is slightly elevated above the first row. Juror No. 9, who is slightly built and dapperly dressed, tweaked at his little moustache with his fingers and eyed the press section with baleful orbs.

What juror No. 9 thinks of the inmates of the press section would probably be suppressed by the censors. And yet, without juror No. 9, where would this case be? It would be back next to pure reading matter—that's where.

Juror No. 9 was alleged to have been discovered by newspaper men bouncing around a Greenwich Village shushery and talking about the McManus trial, though he convinced Judge Nott that he hadn't done or said anything that might impair his status as a juror in the case. Finally it was learned juror No. 9 was shot up a bit in his apartment at No. 420 West Twentieth Street on February 29, 1928, by a young man who was first defended by James D. C. Murray, now McManus's counsel.

November 30, 1929

Draw near, friend reader, for a touch of ooh-my-goodness has finally crept into the Roaring Forties' most famous murder trial. Sc-an-dal, no less. Sh-h-h!

And where do you think we had to go to get it?

To Walnut Street, in the pleasant mountain city of Asheville, North Carolina. Folks, thar's sin in them hills!

Here we'd been going along quietly for days and days on end
with the matter of George McManus, charged with plugging Arnold Rothstein with a .38, and the testimony had been pure and
clean and nothing calculated to give Broadway a bad name, when
in come a woman from the ol' Tarheel State speaking of the
strangest didoes.

A Mrs. Marian A. Putnam, she was, who runs the Putnam grill
in Asheville, a lady of maybe forty-odd, a headliner for the State,
who testified she had heard loud voices of men, and a crash coming from the vicinity of room 349 in the Park Central Hotel the
night "the master mind," was "settled." And that later she had
seen a man wandering along the hallway on the third floor, with
his hands pressed to his abdomen and "a terrible look on his face."

Well, there seemed nothing in this narration to mar the peaceful trend of events, or to bring the blush of embarrassment for
this city to the cheek of the most loyal Broadwayer. Then James
D. C. Murray took charge of the witness and began addressing
the lady on the most tender subjects, and developing the weirdest
things. Really, you'd be surprised.

Handing the lady a registration card from the Park Central
Hotel and assuming a gruff tone of voice several octaves over the
perfunctory purr that has been the keynote of the trial to date,
Murray asked, "Who are the Mr. and Mrs. Putnam indicated by
that card as registered at the Park Central on October 28, 1928?"

"I am Mrs. Putnam."

"Who is Mr. Putnam?"

Mrs. Putnam hesitated briefly, and then replied, "A friend of
mine to whom I am engaged."

There were subdued snorts back in the court room as the spectators suddenly came up out of their dozes and turned off their
snores to contemplate the lady on the witness stand.

Mrs. Putnam wore a rather smart-looking velvet dress, with a
gray caracul coat with a dark squirrel collar, and a few diamonds
here and there about her, indicating business is okay at the Putnam grill.

But she didn't have the appearance of one who might insert a
hotsy-totsy strain into the staid proceedings. She looked more like

somebody's mother, or aunt. She described herself as a widow, and here she was admitting something that savored of social error, especially as the lady subsequently remarked that "Mr. Putnam" had occupied the same boudoir with her.

The spectators sat up to listen and mumbled we were finally getting down to business in this trial.

Murray now produced a death certificate attesting to the demise of one Putnam, who died in 1913, the attorney asking, "The Mr. Putnam who occupied the room with you wasn't the Mr. Putnam who died in 1913, was he?"

At this point Mrs. Putnam seemed deeply affected, possibly by the memory of the late Mr. P. She gulped and applied her handkerchief to her eyes, and the spectators eyed her intently, because they felt it would be a thrill if it transpired that the deceased Putnam had indeed returned to life the very night that "the master mind" was shot.

But it seems it wasn't that Mr. Putnam, and Mr. Murray awoke some very antique echoes in the old court room as he shouted, "Who was it?"

Well, Mrs. Putnam doubtless restrained by a feeling of delicacy, didn't want to tell, and Judge Nott helpfully remarked that as long as she didn't deny she was registered at the hotel, the name didn't seem important. Murray argued Mrs. Putnam's fiancé might be a material witness for the defense, so Judge Nott let him try to show it.

Finally Mrs. Putnam said the man's name was Perry. He is said to be a citizen of Asheville, and what will be said of Mr. Perry in Asheville when the news reaches the sewing circles down yonder will probably be plenty. Not content with touching on Mr. Perry to Mrs. Putnam, the attorney for the defense asked her about a Mr. Elias, and then about a Mr. Bruce, becoming right personal about Mr. Bruce.

He wanted to know if Mr. Bruce had remained with Mrs. Putnam one night in her room at another New York Hotel, but she said no. Then Murray brought in the name of a Mr. Otis B. Carr, of Hendersonville, N. C., and when Mrs. Putnam said she didn't recall the gentleman, the attorney asked, "Did you steal anything out of a store in Hendersonville?"

Mrs. Putnam said no. Moreover, in reply to questions, she said she didn't steal two dresses from a department store in Asheville and that she hadn't been arrested for disorderly conduct and fined $5. Before Murray got through with her some of the listeners half expected to hear him ask the lady if she had ever personally killed A. Rothstein.

Mrs. Putnam couldn't have made the State very happy, because she admitted under Murray's cross-examination that she had once denied in Asheville, in the presence of Mr. Mara, one of the district attorney's assistants, and County Judge McCrae, of Asheville, that she ever left her room in the Park Central the night of the murder.

She said her current story is the truth. Mr. Murray asked her if she hadn't said thus and so to newspapermen in Asheville. She replied, "I did."

A young man described as Douglas Eller, a reporter of an Asheville paper, was summoned from among the spectators in the court room and brought up to the railing, where Mrs. Putnam could see him. The lady was asked if she knew him, and she eyed him at length before admitting she may have seen him before. Mr. Eller retired, blushing slightly, as if not to be known by Mrs. Putnam argues one unknown in Asheville.

Murray became very curious about the Putnam grill in Asheville. Didn't she have curtained-off booths? She did, but her waitresses could walk in and out of them at any time, a reply that Mrs. Putnam tossed at Murray as if scorning utterly the base insinuation of his question.

Did she sell liquor? She did not. She had been shown pictures of Rothstein and McManus and Biller, but she couldn't recognize any of them. She was mighty reluctant about telling the name of a lady friend with whom she dined in her room the night of the killing, but finally admitted it was a Mrs. Herman Popper. She explained her reluctance by saying, "I don't want to get other people mixed up in this."

The most important point to the State in the trial of George McManus yesterday seemed to be the key to room 349 in the Park Central Hotel, which, according to testimony, was found in a pocket of an overcoat hanging in the room.

This overcoat bore the name of McManus on the tailor's label in the pocket.

The prosecution will, perhaps, make much of this as tending to show the occupant of the room left in a very great hurry and didn't lock the door, besides abandoning the overcoat, though Detective "Paddy" Flood said the door was locked when he went there with a house detective to investigate things.

It was Detective Flood who told of finding the key. He was relating how he entered the room and found, among other things, an overcoat with the name of George McManus on the label. He was asked, "What other objects did you find?"

"A handkerchief in the pocket of the overcoat with the initials 'G. Mc.' There were other handkerchiefs in the drawer in the bedroom and a white shirt."

"Did you find anything else in the coat?"

"A key, in the right-hand pocket, for room 349."

"A door key."

"Yes."

Aside from that, the testimony brought out that "the master mind," as the underworld sometimes called Arnold Rothstein, died "game."

Game as a pebble.

In the haunts of that strange pallid man during his life, you could have had 10 to 1, and plenty of it, that he would "holler copper," did occasion arise, with his dying gasp.

Indeed he was often heard to remark in times when he knew that sinister shadows hovered near—and these were not infrequent times in his troubled career, living as he chose to live, "If anyone gets me, they'll burn for it."

And cold, hard men, thinking they read his character, believed they knew his meaning. They felt he was just the kind when cornered by an untoward circumstance, that would squeal like a pig. It shows you how little you really know of a man.

For when the hour came, as the jury in Judge Nott's court room heard yesterday, with the dismal snow slanting past the windows of the grimy old Criminal Courts Building—when Arnold Rothstein lay crumpled up with a bullet through his intestines, knowing he was mortally hurt, and officers of the law bent over him and whispered, "Who did it?" the pale lips tightened, and Rothstein mumbled, "I won't tell and please don't ask me any more questions."

Then another "sure thing" went wrong on Broadway, where "sure things" are always going wrong—the "sure thing" that Rothstein would tell.

But as the millionaire gambler lay in the Fifty-sixth Street service entrance of the Park Central Hotel that night of November 4, 1928, with the pain of his wound biting at his vitals, and the peering eyes of the cops close to his white countenance, he reverted to type.

He was no longer the money king, with property scattered all over the Greater City, a big apartment house on fashionable Park Avenue, a Rolls-Royce and a Minerva at his beck and call, and secretaries and servants bowing to him. He was a man of the underworld. And as one of the "dice hustlers" of the dingy garage lofts, and the "mobsters" high and low he muttered, "I won't tell."

A sigh of relief escaped many a chest at those words, you can bet on that.

Detective Flood, who knew Rothstein well, was one of those who bent over the stricken man.

Patrolman William Davis, first to respond to the call of the hotel attendants, also asked Rothstein who shot him, but got no more information than Flood.

The head of the millionaire gambler was pillowed on a wadded-up burlap sack when Davis reached the scene, which was important to the State in trying to show that Rothstein was shot in the hotel, in that it had been said that Rothstein's overcoat was put under his head.

Before the session was completed, the tables in the court room were covered with exhibits of one kind and another taken by

Flood and other officers from room 349 in the Park Central.

There was a layout of glasses and a liquor bottle, and ginger ale bottles on a tray. But, alas, the liquor bottle was very empty. Also the State had the dark blue overcoat with the velvet collar that was found in a closet of room 349, said overcoat bearing a tailor's label, with George McManus's name on the label.

Likewise, handkerchiefs found in the room were produced and these handkerchiefs were elegantly monogrammed. One was inscribed "g Mc M.," another like "G. M. A." with the "G" and "A" in small letters, and the "M" big. A third was monogrammed "J. M. W." with the "J" and "W" in small letters on either side of the large "M" while the fourth bore the marking "J. M."

A white shirt with collar attached, some race tracks slips, and a window screen with a hole in it, were spread out for the jurors to see. Also the .38-calibre pistol, which one Al Bender, a taxi driver, picked up in Seventh Avenue.

This is supposed to be the pistol with which Rothstein was shot, and the screen is supposed to be the screen through which the pistol was hurled out into the street after the shooting, though the point where the pistol was picked up is quite a hurling distance from room 349.

While Flood and some other officers were in the room Hyman Biller, a cashier at the race track for McManus, and under indictment with McManus for the murder of Rothstein, came in with Frank and Tom McManus, brothers of George, and remained about twenty minutes.

It was the failure to hold Biller on this occasion that brought down much criticism on the heads of the Police Department, for Hymie was never seen in these parts again.

The lights were burning in room 349 when Flood got there. Four glasses stood on the table which is the basis of the indictment returned against McManus, and Biller, and the celebrated John Doe and Richard Roe. The State claims four men were in the room when Rothstein was summoned there by a message sent by McManus to Lindy's restaurant.*

* The State inferred Rothstein was summoned to pay the overdue IOUs given in the high spade game described by Martin Bowe.

Vincent J. Kelly, elevator operator at the Park Central, testified he was working on the service elevator the night Rothstein was shot, and saw Rothstein in the corridor, holding his hands across his stomach, and didn't see him come through the service doorway, through which he must have passed to make good the State's contention he came from upstairs.

He heard Rothstein say, "I'm shot."

Thomas Calhoun, of Corona, Long Island, thirty-two, a watchman on the Fifty-sixth Street side of the hotel at the time of the murder, saw Rothstein at 10:47 standing in front of the time office at the service entrance. Calhoun ran and got Officer Davis.

He heard Rothstein say something to the policeman about taking his money, and it was his impression that Rothstein had his overcoat over his arm and that it was put under his head as he lay on the floor, which impression was not corroborated by other testimony.

Through Calhoun, Attorney Murray tried to develop that Rothstein might have come through the swimming pool by way of Seventh Avenue. While cross-examining Calhoun, Murray suddenly remarked, testily, "I object to the mumbling to the District Attorney."

He apparently had reference to Mr. Brothers, of the State's legal display. Everybody seemed to be a bit testy yesterday, except the ever-smiling defendant, McManus, who just kept on smiling.

Calhoun heard Rothstein say, "Call my lawyer, 9410 Academy."

Thomas W. McGivney, of No. 401 West 47th Street, who was also near the service entrance, testified he had taken Rothstein's overcoat off his arm and placed it under his head. Rothstein's overcoat hasn't been seen since the shooting.

McGivney, a stout looking young man with a wide smile, and a rich brogue, gave the spectators a few snickers, but by and large it wasn't an exciting day one way or the other.

* * * * * * * *

On December 6, after a year, a month and a day of investigation and prosecution, the murder of Arnold Rothstein was rele-

gated to the limbo of unsolved mysteries. General Sessions Judge Nott refused to let the evidence against McManus go to the jury. He directed that a verdict of not guilty be delivered without allowing the jury to leave the box for deliberation.

Prosecutor Banton admitted that the State had failed to establish a case fit to go to the jury. The general supposition that Rothstein was killed for "welshing" on his losses in the big Saturday night-to-Sunday night game remained supposition.

The cases against Biller and the figurative Richard Roe and John Doe were dropped.

Ferdinand Pecora went on to bask in bigger spotlights. See the chapter in this book on Morgan the Mighty.

AL CAPONE

Chicago, October 6, 1931

A fragrant whiff of green fields and growing rutabagas and parsnips along with echoes of good old Main Street, crept into the grime-stained Federal Building here today as your Uncle Sam took up the case of Al Capone and gathered a jury in what you might call jigtime.

It is a jury made up mainly of small towners and Michael J. Ahern, chief counsel for Al Capone, frankly admitted dissatisfaction to the Court about it.

He wanted all these persons dismissed but Judge Wilkerson overruled his motion. The jury was sworn in with nine veterans of court room juries among the twelve good men and true, and tomorrow morning at ten o'clock the Government of these United States starts work on Al Capone.

The truly rural atmosphere of the proceedings today was evidenced by horny-handed tillers of the fruitful soil, small town store-keepers, mechanics and clerks, who gazed frankly interested at the burly figure of the moon-faced fellow causing all this excitement and said,

"Why, no: we ain't got no prejudice again Al Capone."

At least most of them said that in effect, as Judge Wilkerson was expediting the business of getting a jury to try Capone on charges of income tax evasion.

Your Uncle Sam says Al Capone owes him $215,000 on an income of $1,038,000 in six years.

Your Uncle Sam hints that Al Capone derived this tidy income from such illegal didoes as bootlegging, gambling and the like.

"Do you hope the government proves the defendant guilty?"

was one question asked a venireman at the request of counsel for the defense.

Apparently none cherished that hope.

"Have you any desire that the defendant be sent to jail?" was another question requested by the defense.

"Well no," was the general reply.

Al Capone sat up straight in his chair and smoothed his rumpled necktie. He felt better. The G-men—as the boys call 'em—want to put Al Capone in a Federal pokey, or jail, for anywhere from two to thirty-two years, to impress upon him the truth of the adage that honesty is the best policy.

As Al Capone sat there with the scent of the new-mown hay oozing at intervals from the jury box, he was a terrific' disappointment to the strictly seeing-Chicago tourist who felt that Al should have been vested at least in some of the panoply of his reputed office as Maharajah of the Hoods. Perhaps a cartridge belt. Some strangers felt this Chicago has been misrepresented to them.

The jury as it now stands is as follows: Louis G. Wolfersheim, Chicago; Louis P. Weidling, painter, Wilmington, Ill.; Burr Dugan, farmer, DeKalb County; A. C. Smart, painter and decorator, Libertyville; W. J. Hendricks, lubricating engineer, Cook County; George M. Larsen, wood patenter; Dalton; W. F. McCormick, receiving shop, Maywood; A. G. Maegher, country store-keeper, Prairie View; Ambrose Merchant, real estate agent, Waukegan; Arthur O. Prochno, insurance agent, Edison Park; John A. Walker, abstractor, Yorkville, and Nate C. Brown, retired hardware dealer, St. Charles.

Selection of the jury in one day is regarded as amazingly quick work, and the trial may not be as long drawn out as expected.

Capone arrived for the opening session fifteen minutes ahead of time, which is said to be a record in punctuality for him.

A big crowd was gathered on the Clark Street side of the dingy old building waiting to see him, but Al popped out of an automobile and into the building like a fox going into a hole. Not many of the curiosity-seekers got a good peek at him.

He entered the court room alone and was quickly surrounded by a crowd of reporters, male and female, who began bouncing questions about his ears. They asked him if he was worried, and he replied, logically enough, "Who wouldn't be worried?"

He was scarcely the sartorial spectacle familiar to the winter inmates of Florida, where Al's sport apparel is one of the scenes of interest. In fact, he was quietly dressed this morning, bar a hat of pearly white, emblematic no doubt, of purity.

'Twas a warmish morning and Al, being stout, is susceptible to the heat. Then, too, he was in a hot spot. His soft collar was already crumpled. He frequently mopped his forehead with a white handkerchief. His swarthy jowls had been newly shaved. His black hair now getting quite sparse was plastered back on his skull.

Judge Wilkerson himself is a fine looking man with iron-gray hair. He is smooth shaven. His eyebrows are black and strong. He wore no flowing robe, like New York judges. He was dressed in a quiet business suit of dark color and wears horn-rimmed glasses.

His voice is clear and very decided. He sits far down in his chair while listening, but when he is doing the talking he leans far forward over his desk, his shoulders hunched up.

Wilkerson made it very clear to the men in the jury box that Capone is being tried on charges of violating the income tax law and nothing else.

Capone's chief counsel, Ahern, a tall, good looking chap of perhaps middle age, who wore a gray suit and tan shoes, approached the railing in front of the bench as court opened this morning, flanked by his associate in the defense, Albert Fink, a ruddy-faced, baldish man given to easy attitudes.

Ahern's first approach was with a mild protest against the arrangement of the court room by which the thirty or more representatives of the press were crowding defense attorneys out of house and home. He was satisfied when the scribes were shoved off a bit so their hot breath would not beat against the back of Al Capone's neck.

George E. Q. Johnson, the United States district attorney in charge of prosecution, is a forensic looking man. He has a pink complexion, a rather beaming countenance and a mop of gray hair, all mussed up.

At the request of Ahern, Wilkerson asked the veniremen:

"Do any of you belong to any law enforcement organization? Counsel asks specifically about the Anti-Saloon League?"

None did, it seemed.

"Have any of you ever contributed to a law enforcement organization?"

Well, one man had once chipped in ten dollars to the Crime Commission. His confession didn't seem important to the attorneys at the moment.

None of Capone's so-called bodyguards were in evidence anywhere around the court house, I am reliably informed. Naturally, I wouldn't know 'em myself. Al goes to his citadel, the Hotel Lexington, out south, as soon as he leaves the court. It used to be a noted hostelry. The President of the U.S.A. stopped there during the World's Fair. Now it is Capone's G.H.Q.

October 8, 1931

"What do you do with your money—carry it on your person?"

An income tax examiner asked this question of Al Capone in September, 1930, when Al was seeking a settlement with your Uncle Sam and could produce no books, bank accounts or anything else in writing bearing upon his financial transactions.

And, according to a transcript of the examination, Al replied:

"Yes, I carry it on my person."

He must have had plenty of room on his person, judging from a letter his attorney at that time wrote to the Internal Revenue Bureau, for this letter, the basis of argument lasting most of the day's sessions, admitted Capone's income was nearly $300,000 in the years 1926 to 1929, inclusive.

Capone's lawyer at that time was Lawrence B. Mattingly, Washington income tax expert. In fighting the admission of the letter, one of Al's present lawyers, Albert Fink, characterized the letter as a confession by a lawyer in behalf of a client.

He argued that no lawyer has the right or authority to make a confession for a client.

Judge Wilkerson finally overruled objection to the admission of the letter, which was undoubtedly a big victory for the government. Capone seemed deeply concerned when he heard the Court's ruling.

Judge Wilkerson said he believed the weight of authority was in favor of the admissibility of the document.

The letter was read to Judge Wilkerson, but not to the jury, which was sent from the room while the lawyers argued. It was produced by Samuel Clawson, of Washington, one of the attorneys representing the government, as soon as court opened today.

The letter was written by Mattingly when he was endeavoring to adjust Al Capone's income tax troubles with the government, and traced Capone's financial rise from a modest $75 per week, prior to 1926, to an income of $26,000 in that year, $40,000 in 1927, "not to exceed $100,000" in 1928, and "not to exceed $100,000" in 1929.

The source of the income was mentioned as an organization, the nature of which was not described, in which a group of employes had a third interest, and Capone and three associates a fourth.

Mattingly wrote:

"Notwithstanding that two of the taxpayer's [Capone's] associates, insist that his income never exceeded $50,000 in any one year, I am of the opinion his taxable income for the years 1926 and 1927 might be fairly fixed at not to exceed $26,000 and $40,000 respectively, and for the years 1928 and 1929, not to exceed $100,000."

Capone listened to the letter with keen interest. He seemed in great humor, although it was what you might call a tough day for his side. The letter went on:

"The so-called bodyguards with which he [Capone] is reputed to surround himself, were not as a general rule his personal employes, but were employes of the organization who participated in its profits."

Referring to Capone's assets, the letter said:

"The furniture in the home occupied by the taxpayer while he was in Florida was acquired at a cost not to exceed $20,000. The house and grounds have been thoroughly appraised, and the appraisal has been submitted to you. There is a mortgage against the house and grounds of $30,000. His indebtedness to his associates has rarely ever been less than $75,000 since 1927. It frequently has been much more."

The letter was produced by the government attorneys on the appearance of George E. Slentz, of Washington, D. C., first witness of the day. Slentz is chief of the power-of-attorney section of the Bureau of Internal Revenue, and Attorney Clawson wanted him to identify the letter written by Mattingly.

Helen Alexander, vault clerk at a state bank in Cicero, identified a contract for a vault signed in 1927 by Al Capone and Louis De Cava. She identified Capone's signature and pointed him out in the court room, but she did not recall seeing Capone at the bank in connection with her duties.

Louis H. Wilson, connected with the Internal Revenue Collector's office here, testified to a conference with Mattingly, who said Capone owed income tax, and was willing to pay.

There was another conference at which Capone was present in person, and also C. W. Herrick, Internal Revenue agent. Everything said at the conference was duly set down by a stenographer.

Judging from the transcript of that conference, read in court today, Capone's chief answer to questions about his income was: "I would rather have my lawyer answer that."

He denied having anything to do with a dog track, never owned a race horse and never had a bank account.

After Capone left the conference Mattingly told Wilson he would get some facts together as best he could and make a return. He recommended, Wilson said, that the government get busy at once, as Capone had some money at the moment, and would pay up.

But apparently Mattingly's task was a little difficult. He reported he couldn't get definite records on Al Capone's income. Finally Mattingly produced the letter that caused the excitement today.

At the rate the trial is traveling now, it will take several weeks to conclude it. The defense attorneys are contesting every inch of legal ground. Al is getting a good run for his money, anyway.

He came and went today mid the usual excitement outside the court house, but the crowds do not seem able to pick the hole he bobs out of with any degree of success.

Chicago, October 9, 1931

The soft murmur of the blue breakers caressing old Miami shore sort o' sneaked into Judge Wilkerson's court room this afternoon, between shrill snorts of the Chicago traffic coppers' whistles outside, as witnesses from the sunny Southland connected Al Capone up with $125,500 transmitted from Chicago to Miami by wire.

Having shown to the jury in the Federal Court where all those potatoes went, your Uncle Sam was going about the business of trying to prove whence they came when Judge Wilkerson adjourned to a half day session tomorrow.

The last witness of the day, one John Fotre, a sharp-featured citizen, wearing a slightly startled expression, who is manager of the Western Union branch office in the Lexington Hotel here, was identifying a money order showing some of the money went to Capone from Sam Gusick, when Wilkerson called a halt.

The Lexington Hotel is sometimes spoken of as "the Fort," and is said to be the citadel of the Capone forces. Sam Gusick is reputed to be one of Al Capone's business managers. Fotre said he couldn't say if it was Sam Gusick in person who sent the dough per the money order in question, because he didn't know him.

Much of the money was traced to the purchase and improvement of the celebrated winter seat of the Hidalgo of the Hoods on Palm Island, in Biscayne Bay, between Miami proper and Miami Beach.

It was traced through Parker Henderson, Jr., whose testimony indicated he was in Capone's confidence to an amazing degree. He was manager of the Ponce de Leon Hotel in Miami.

It was there Capone stopped when he first went to Florida in 1928, at which time, and later, according to the testimony today, the good burghers of Miami were so perturbed by his presence they held meetings.

How Henderson came to arrive on such terms with Capone did not appear, but it was Henderson who negotiated the purchase of the home, and who handled large sums of money for Capone in improving the place.

Henderson testified to signing numerous Western Union money transfers with the name of Al Costa, turning the money over to Nick Serritela, who worked for Capone, or to Capone himself.

They were generally for sums of $1,000 or $1,500. Other transfers were in the names of Peterson and Serritela. There were over twenty different transfers, amounting in all to $45,000, of which about $15,000 was transmitted to Henderson personally to be spent in improving the Palm Island property.

The rest was for Capone.

These transfers refer only to the telegraph office in Miami. Later witnesses added $30,300 as having gone through the Western Union branch in Miami Beach.

Capone listened with great interest as the witness testified.

Henderson narrated the detail of the purchase of the Palm Island property, which was made in his name. Later he transferred the property to Mrs. May Capone, Al's wife.

Henderson came to Chicago, May, 1928, and saw Capone and got money to pay off the men working on the improvements.

He said Al invited him to stay at the Metropole Hotel, then the Capone G.H.Q., and while there he saw such celebrities as Ralph Capone, Jack Gusick, Charley Fuschetti, Jack McGurn, a party called "Mops" and others.

This was after Capone was living on Palm Island. The money came in batches of from anywhere from $600 to $5,000. Some of the transfers were to Albert Capone, a brother, but the witnesses said Alphonse Capone signed for many of them.

Vernon Hawthorn, a Miami attorney, told of a meeting at which Capone and a number of officials of Miami and Dade County, Florida, were present. It was in 1928; Capone had just appeared in Florida and the good citizens of Dade wanted to find out what the celebrated visitor intended in their startled midst. Al said he was there to rest.

The witness said Capone told him he was in the cleaning and

pressing business in Chicago. Finally, the witness said, Al admitted his business was gambling and that he was interested in a Cicero dog track. Furthermore, that he had bought a home in Miami.

The question was asked him at that meeting, "What do you do?" and according to the transcript read this morning, Capone said, "I am a gambler. I bet on horses."

"Are you also a bootlegger?"

"No, I never was a bootlegger in my life."

He said the Palm Island home was in his wife's name. He denied he had received any sums of money from Charles Fuschetti under the name of Costa.

Morrisey Smith, day clerk and cashier at the Metropole Hotel, Chicago, where Capone used to have his headquarters in a suite of five rooms, was examined by Attorney Grossman, who asked, "Who paid for this suite of five rooms?"

"Mr. Capone."

He did not know how much. Grossman handed him the cash sheets of the hotel and Smith picked out a payment of $1,500 for rooms in 1927. No period of time was stated. He was registered as Mr. Ross. The witness testified to numerous other payments, always in cash.

Counsel for the defense could not see what this was all about and spoke to the Court about it. The judge replied, "I presume it's to show he had money. If you pay out something you must have something coming in."

A party for Al's friends who came to the Dempsey-Tunney fight was listed. It cost $1,633. Al gave "small gratuities" to the hotel help now and then, Smith's idea of a "small" gratuity was something surprising. He explained, "He would give five dollars or something like that." Fred S. Avery was manager of the Hotel Metropole when Capone was there. He went to see Capone on one occasion and asked him about a little money and Capone personally paid him the next day. His bills ran around $1,200 to $1,500 a week. Avery said the Dempsey-Tunney entertainment ran two nights.

The life of Riley that Al Capone is supposed to live on Palm Island was reflected in testimony brought out by your Uncle Sam before Judge Wilkerson and the jury in the Federal Court this morning.

The butcher, the baker, and the landscape maker from Miami were among the witnesses, not to mention the real estate man, the dock builder, the telephone agent, and the chap who supplied the drapes for 93 Palm Island.

It came out that quite a batch of meat was gnawed up in Al's home in the course of several seasons—a matter of $6,500 worth. Also plenty of bread, and cake, and macaroni was consumed.

The telephoning was terrific. Someone must have been on Al's phone almost constantly. In the course of four Florida seasons there was gabbing, mainly at long distance, to the tune of over $8,000 not counting wrong numbers, but your Uncle Sam contented himself with standing on $4,097.05 in two years in his effort to prove Al must have had plenty of income because he spent plenty.

Your Uncle Sam argues that if a man spends a raft of money he must necessarily have a raft of money to spend, a theory that sounds logical enough unless your Uncle Sam is including horse players.

We had a slight diversion after Wilkerson adjourned court until Monday, with another warning to the jurors not to permit anyone to communicate with them.

The diversion consisted of the seizing of the mysterious Phillip D'Andrea, Capone's bodyguard who has been sitting behind Al since this trial started, by a United States deputy marshal, and the alleged discovery on his person of a .38-calibre John Roscoe, or pistol.

D'Andrea was ordered by Judge Wilkerson to stand trial for carrying a revolver in the court room, and was taken to jail.

D'Andrea is a short, stout bespectacled individual, who dresses well, and looks like a prosperous professional man.

He has been described as a friend of Capone's and Al seemed

much perturbed by his seizure. He waited around while D'Andrea was in the marshal's office, with Capone's attorneys, Ahern and Fink, trying to get him out of his trouble.

Al said he didn't know D'Andrea carried a gun, and didn't believe he did.

The twelve men, most of them small towners, and of occupations that would argue a modest scale of living, listened intently to testimony that indicated Al's comparatively elaborate existence, although the reputed magnificence of Al's Palm Island estate dwindled somewhat in the imagination of the urban listeners when expenditures for improvements were related.

These expenditures were not unusually heavy. In fact, Al was depicted in some of the testimony as a householder with a repugnance for being "gypped" in small details.

This morning Capone had on fresh scenery in the form of a dark-colored double-breasted suit of greenish hue, white linen, a green tie and black shoes. He had gone back to his famous white hat.

The attendance at the session today was positively disappointing. Fewer than a dozen persons sat in the seats assigned to spectators when court opened. Can it be that Chicago is losing interest in Al Capone?

William Froelich, of government counsel, read a list of money transfers to the jury showing the transfer of a total of $77,500 to Capone in Florida.

W. C. Harris, office manager of the Southern Bell Telephone Company at Miami, was the first witness. He identified a contract for phone service between the company and Al Capone at 93 Palm Island.

Harris identified company bills for service to the Capone residence amounting to $955.55 in 1928 and $3,141.50 in 1929, a total of $4,097.05, mostly for long distance calls.

Richard Plummer, of Miami, testified to supplying the draperies for Capone's home in 1928 at a cost of $1,000. He said Capone paid him in cash.

George F. Geizer, night clerk at Capone's old G.H.Q., the

Metropole Hotel, Chicago, testified to receiving payments in cash to the amount of $2,088.25 from Capone for hotel bills on August 4, 1921.

Louis Karlinch, of Miami, testified he sold meat to Capone to the amount of $6,500 over a period of three years, nearly always getting his money in cash. The bills amounted to around $200 a week. Albert Fink, attorney for Capone, asked, "Do you think Al ate all the meat himself?"

"No. One man couldn't eat it all."

H. F. Ryder, of Miami, built a dock for Capone on Palm Island and worked around the place generally. Ryder, a small, dark-haired fellow, was inclined to be quite chatty about things. He spoke of seeing Capone with a roll of bills that would "choke an ox."

Fink wanted to know how big an ox. He also asked the witness if it couldn't have been a "Western roll," which the attorney explained is a roll of $1 bills with a big bill on top. Ryder said it might have been.

Ryder testified he still has $125 coming to him from Capone for work, but said he wasn't worried about that. He said he expected to get it when he ran into Capone. In fact, Ryder had a boost for Al.

When Ahern asked his opinion of Capone he answered, "A mighty fine man."

Curt Koenitzer, a chunky, red-faced builder and contractor in Miami, testified to building a garage and bathhouse on the Palm Island property. He was paid by one of Capone's brothers.

A swarthy, dapper chap with black hair and a black moustache was expected to turn out at least a duke, but is Al Capone's baker in Miami. His name is Milton Goldstron.

He delivered bakery supplies to Capone's house in 1929, 1930 and 1931 to a total of $1,130 and was paid by Frank Newton, caretaker of the Capone premises.

F. A. Whitehead, hardware merchant, testified to the building of iron gates for the Capone estate.

H. J. Etheritz, who is connected with Burdine's department

store in Miami, testified to purchases by Capone of drapes amounting to $800.

Joseph A. Brower, landscape gardener, testified to doing some work on the Capone estate. He was paid $2,100 in checks signed by Jack Gusick. He said Capone described Gusick as his financial secretary.

Frank Gallatt, of Miami, said he was hired in 1929 to put up some buildings on Palm Island. Capone himself did the hiring, he said. Also Capone had paid him personally between $10,000 and $11,000 in cash.

October 12, 1931

A gleaming diamond belt buckle, one of a batch of thirty purchased by Al Capone at $277 apiece, or $8,310 for the lot, was flashed before the astonished eyes of the jury today.

Al bought these buckles for his friends. One of the buckles is said to have been worn by Alfred (Jake) Lingle, Chicago underworld reporter, who was assassinated in June of last year, for which crime Leo V. Brothers is now doing a stretch in the penitentiary.

The jurors peered at the buckle with interest. Each buckle is said to have been engraved with the initials of the recipient, but markings on the buckle displayed today were not revealed, a fact that is doubtless causing someone to heave big sighs of relief.

Judge Wilkerson seemed to think the exhibition of the buckle to the jurors might be with the idea of giving them a line on the quality of the gewgaw, and he remarked, "The quality of the goods makes no difference. It is immaterial whether the defendant got value received or not as long as he spent the money."

In other words, Al may have been "gypped," but that doesn't enter into the case.

Besides diamond buckles, Al passed suits of custom-made clothes around among his friends at $135 per copy, though not so many of these. He also had shirts made at from $22 to $30 apiece, with the monograms $1 each. His ties cost $4 each and handkerchiefs $2.75 apiece. He bought them by the "bunch."

We got right down to Al's skin today.

We found out Al wears silk union-suits at $12 a smash, and athletic "shorts" at $5 a clip. A Mr. J. Banken, of Marshall Field's and who evidently has an abiding artistic interest in his business, told us about that.

Albert Fink, Capone's attorney, who is a fellow you wouldn't think gave much thought to underwear, or other gents furnishings, perked up and interrogated Banken about those union-suits, especially after Banken had described them as a fine silk, "like a lady's glove." Fink leaning forward asked, "Warm?"

"No, not warm. Just a nice suit of underwear."

"How much are they now?"

"Ten dollars."

"Aha," said the attorney, reflectively, "they've gone down?"

"Yes, two dollars," replied Banken, and it looked for a moment as if he had a sale.

The testimony revealed Al as rather a busy and shrewd shopper. While he is usually pictured as a ruthless gang chieftain, he was today presented as a domesticated sort of a chap going around buying furniture, and silverware, and rugs, and knickknacks of one kind and another for his household.

He was shown buying linoleum for the kitchen, and superintending the interior decoration of his home on Palm Island, and personally attending to other details the average citizen is glad to turn over to friend wife.

Moreover Al appears to have been somewhat conservative in big household purchases, considering the amount of plunder he is supposed to have handled.

He spread out more when buying for his own personal adornment in the way of clothing, and neckties, and night shirts.

Oscar De Feo, of Marshall Field's, recalled making over twenty suits for Al and a few topcoats, along with suits for four or five of Al's friends at a total cost of around $3,600.

Samuel J. Steinberg, jeweler, who told of the diamond buckles, also said Al stepped into the store one day and bought twenty-two beaded bags at $22.50 apiece.

During the morning session we furnished Al's Palm Beach home from top to bottom, besides sending some furnishings out to a Prairie Avenue address, where his mother lives.

From Henry E. Keller, an elderly man from Miami, we had a clue to Al Capone's start in life.

Keller was dock foreman for Al on the Palm Island place, at a salary of $550 per month, and one day, when having lunch with Al, Al asked him where he was born. Keller replied, "In the old Tenth Ward, in New York."

"Is that so," said Al, according to the witness, "why, I came from New York. I got my start as a bartender on Long Island "

Al often grinned at the testimony, especially when we got down to his underwear.

October 13, 1931

Your Uncle Sam chucked a sort of Chicago pineapple of surprise under Alphonse Capone's lawyers this afternoon by suddenly announcing these United States of America rested its case against its most conspicuous income tax dodger of the hour.

"What?" ejaculated Mr. Michael J. Ahearn, the urbane Irishman, who has been leading the defense.

"Huh," exclaimed Mr. Albert Fink, his bluff and gruff associate.

Then their chairs rattled in chorus as they pushed them aside to step up to Judge Wilkerson's bench in the Federal Court.

Even Al Capone sensed something unusual and leaned forward to listen to the attorneys, his round features set in seriousness, a plump hand rigid before him.

Messrs. Ahern and Fink admitted their astonishment. You gathered they felt your Uncle Sam had sneaked up on them very suddenly from under cover of a day of dry proceedings all along the line of trying to connect Al Capone up with the gambling profits of the Cicero joints.

These profits, the government asserts, amounted to $177,500 in 1927 and $24,800 in 1928, a total for the two years of $202,300.

The startled attorneys argued desperately for the next half hour for a little delay to get their line of defense consolidated, and bring witnesses from New York and other points. But all their conversation did them no good.

It was 2:20 P.M. when the government lawyers concluded with the direct examination of a handwriting expert named Herbert Walters, only witness of the afternoon, who testified certain endorsements on a cashier's check bought with the profits of a Cicero gambling house were in the handwriting of Al Capone.

Indications are the defense will be comparatively brief. Capone's reputed huge gambling losses may be one line. That some of Al's lavish expenditures was on borrowed money may be another.

The government had a short, square-jibbed chap named Bobby Barton walking in and out of the court room every few minutes for identification by different witnesses as the man who handled a large sum of money for Jack Gusick, but Barton was never called to the stand.

The testimony throughout the trial has depicted Gusick as the money man of the Capone combination. He received the money, and apparently cut it up, too, and one witness testified Gusick told him on no occasion to give anyone else any of the money gathered in at Cicero, "not even Al."

Among the things presented by the government which the Capone attorneys say they never heard of before the case opened and against which they have had no time to prepare was the letter from Capone's income tax expert, Lawrence Mattingly, to C. W. Herrick, local revenue collector, offering to compromise Al's indebtedness to the government.

Fred Ries, the man whose testimony is said to have convicted Jack Gusick and Ralph Capone of income tax violations, was today's principal witness.

Ries was the cashier of the Radio and Subway gambling houses in Cicero in 1927 and had charge of all the finances. He identified a cashier's check for $2,500 made payable to J. C. Dunbar, which he cashed and turned over to Bobby Barton. Ries said he was J. C. Dunbar.

He said that as cashier he bought cashier's checks with the profits of the establishment, which he gave to Bobby Barton, who in turn gave them to Jack Gusick. He said he bought over $150,-

ooo worth of checks in 1927. By profits he meant any surplus over the bankroll of $10,000.

There was a long discussion by the attorneys and the Court when Grossman offered the cashier's checks in evidence and Ahern objected.

The jury was sent from the room and Grossman questioned the witness further to show the Court he was going to connect Al up with the checks. Finally Judge Wilkerson decided to admit the checks.

Johnny Torrio, predecessor of Capone as Chicago's gang lord, and now living on Long Island, was not called upon to testify, although he was subpoenaed. The contempt case against Phil D'Andrea, Al's bodyguard, who has been in the coop since Saturday morning when he was grabbed with a pistol on his pudgy person, was postponed until Friday.

October 14, 1931

Your correspondent cheerfully yields the palm he has borne with such distinction for lo these many years as the world's worst horse player to Mr. Alphonse Capone.

Yes sir, and ma'am, Al wins in a common gallop, if we are to believe the testimony brought up in his support today.

Up to closing time this afternoon Al had lost upwards of $217,000 of all that wrong money that your Uncle Sam has been trying to show went into the Capone pockets from gambling operations in Cicero, and what-not, and the end is not yet.

A string of bookmakers testified to clipping Al for his potatoes on the races. He was a high player, betting from $1,000 to $5,000 on a race, according to the testimony, and he must have picked out more lizards, beetles, armadillos, crocodiles, anteaters, polecats, penguins and polar bears than your correspondent on one of his best days.

Al never seemed to win. At least every bookmaker that went to the post today, testified to knocking him in for anywhere from $15,000 to $25,000. There were several other bookies in the paddock outside the court room when court adjourned.

Apparently Al didn't believe all horse players must die broke. He was belting away at 'em through 1924 down to 1927.

At the rate the bookies are going now, Al will not have any more of that $266,000 income that your Uncle Sam charges to him by the time court is over tomorrow.

Milton Held, a betting commissioner, testified Al lost between $8,000 and $10,000 at the Hawthorne track in 1924 and about $12,000 in the fall of 1925.

Oscar Gutter, a dark-complexioned little man with a low voice who also described himself as a betting commissioner, said Capone lost about $60,000 in 1927 on bets he handled.

Both Held and Gutter admitted on cross-examination that they had been summoned within the past few days to Capone's headquarters at the Lexington Hotel, where they conferred with Al and his lawyers.

Held said Capone would bet anywhere from $200 to $500 on a horse. Gutter told of bets from $1,000 to $3,000. Once Al bet $6,000 on a nag. He always paid off his losings in cash, either personally or through a "secretary."

The bookmakers say when they paid Capone off on rare occasions when he won they sent checks in the name of "Andy Doyle."

Then came a burly, fat-faced, black-haired chap who described himself as Peter Penovich, Jr. His name has often entered into the case as one of the partners and managers of a Cicero gambling house.

He said he had been subpoenaed by the government. Had appeared before the Federal Grand Jury and had been at the Federal Court House nearly every day for months. He was never called as a witness in this case by your Uncle Sam.

Penovich said he originally had twenty-five per cent of the Cicero place and later his "bit" was cut down to five per cent. Ralph Capone had told him he was to be chopped.

He said Ralph Capone had told him Frankie Pope was the boss of the place.

Ralph Capone is Al's older brother, and stands convicted of income tax violations along with Jack Gusick.

George Leidermann testified he was a café owner and is now a bookmaker. He said he had a book in 1924 with three other partners and that he often booked to Capone. Al would bet from $500 to $1,000 and would sometimes be betting on two or three horses to a race. Sometimes he would make as many as twenty bets a day. He figured Al lost $14,000 or $15,000 with him in 1924. In 1925 he beat Al for $10,000.

Leidermann admitted he now is running a gambling house under the direction of George "Bugs" Moran, seven of whose followers were massacred St. Valentine's Day in 1929.

Sam Rothschild, who said he was in the cigar business, with bookmaking on the side, said Capone had made perhaps ten bets with his books. These bets were all up in the thousands. He didn't recall Capone ever won.

A bald-headed chap named Samuel Gitelson testified he recorded bets for his brother, Ike, a bookmaker, and that Al had lost about $25,000 to the book.

Edward G. Robinson, the movie actor who has given movie characterizations that some believe are Al Capone to the life, was present in the court room peering at Al.

October 16, 1931

That Al Capone is the victim of a wicked plot, conceived in Washington and partly hatched in Miami, was the substance of an utterance by Michael J. Ahern, as he addressed those twelve tired good men and true in Judge Wilkerson's court this afternoon.*

Ahern was making the closing address on behalf of Al, whose trial on a charge of beating your Uncle Sam out of his income

---

* It became a legend that agents of the United States Treasury Department began looking into Capone's income tax record after President Hoover walked through a hotel lobby in Miami Beach, unnoticed, while Capone was being pleasantly mobbed by hero-worshippers. The implication was that the President, piqued, ordered the G-men into action. The truth appears to be that Chicago business men, despairing of Capone's arrogant depredations being checkmated by local police and prosecutors, besought intervention by Federal authorities.

tax is nearing a close, and ought to be handed over to the jury about noon tomorrow.

Ahern went clear back to the Punic wars and the time of Cato, the censor, whose cry was "Carthage must be destroyed," and said there are a lot of Catos around nowadays, especially around Washington, whose cry is "Capone must be destroyed."

Several years ago when Al first lit in Miami he was summoned before what Mr. Ahern spoke of as a "Spanish Inquisition" of officials and citizens of Miami, and interrogated closely as to his purpose there.

A stenographer took down the testimony at that time, during which Al is said to have admitted he was a gambler, and all this was introduced into the present case.

Ahern insinuated the inquiry was prompted from Washington just before an election and gave it as an idea the thing was the beginning of a plot to undo Al Capone.

Quite a gale of oratory zipped around the corridors of the old Federal Building before the day was done, what with Ahern's remarks, a lengthy outburst by his associate, Albert Fink, and a long lingual drive by Samuel G. Clawson, of your Uncle Sam's team of lawyers.

What Ahern and Fink said, when you boiled it down to a nubbin, was that your Uncle Sam hasn't proved all those things said about Al Capone in the indictments, and that he is entitled to his liberty forthwith.

What Clawson said, reduced to a mere hatful, is that Al had a lot of income and didn't pay tax on said income, and therefore ought to be put in the cooler.

Ahern who began the closing defense argument at 2:30, said the government had attempted to prove its case by circumstantial evidence. He declared the government was seeking on meager evidence to convict the defendant because his name is Al Capone, "a sort of a mythical Robin Hood."

It was his opinion Ahern said, that the government might better have diverted the money it has spent proving Al's profligacy to establish free soup kitchens.

Those twelve good men and true have gone into a big huddle on Al Capone.

Judge Wilkerson of the Federal Court handed the now famous case over to them with a batch of instructions, which struck the listeners as very fair to Al, at 2:41 this afternoon.

Your Uncle Sam claims Al owes him $215,000 tax on an income of over $1,000,000 derived from illegalities such as Cicero gambling, and one thing and another, in the years 1924 to 1929 inclusive, and wants to clap him in the Leavenworth Penitentiary for anywhere from one to thirty-two years.

Al's claim is that Uncle Sam didn't prove the income alleged, although of course, he entered a plea of guilty last July to the very charges for which he has just been tried, under an arrangement with representatives of your Uncle Sam by which he was to take a jolt of two years and a half in prison.

It was Judge Wilkerson's declaration on hearing of this agreement, "You can't bargain with the Federal Court," that brought on the long trial. It closed with the solemn marching out of the twelve good men and true this afternoon.

Capone was certainly all sharpened up this morning. He has been gradually returning to his old sartorial glory the last few days, and he fairly bloomed today.

He wore a grass-green pinchback suit, reminiscent of Florida. He had on heliotrope socks and tan shoes. Al has meticulously refrained from jewelry during the trial, save for a thin, diamond-studded platinum watch chain.

The judge is rather a thick-set man, of medium height, with a thick shock of iron-gray hair. He told the jury:

"You are the sole judges of the facts of the case. The jury has nothing to do with the question of punishment. That rests with the Court.

"This is a criminal case and I shall give you some general rules applicable to criminal cases. The indictment is not to be considered evidence of the guilt. The defendant is presumed to be innocent until proven guilty beyond a reasonable doubt. He is entitled to the benefit of that presumption."

Judge Wilkerson explained the meaning of a reasonable doubt. If the jurors had a reasonable doubt it was their duty to acquit the defendant. If they believed the evidence proved him guilty beyond a reasonable doubt they should return a verdict accordingly.

In order to convict on circumstantial evidence the jury must be satisfied that the circumstances alleged are true.

Wilkerson told the jury to take up each count and return an opinion on each. He said it was not necessary for the government to show the exact amount of income alleged. The Court explained at length the meaning of income under the law. He quoted the provisions of the income tax law at length.

He said the jury might consider the evidence of the way the defendant had lived and the evidence of the money transmitted to him in determining if Capone had a taxable net income. He added:

"The expenditure of money alone isn't sufficient evidence of taxable income; the possession of money alone isn't sufficient evidence of taxable income. But the expenditure and possession of money may be considered in arriving at a conclusion as to whether the income existed.

"The charges of willful attempt to evade the tax couldn't be sustained unless there were some facts to show the attempt. The jury must first be convinced that the taxable net income of $5,000 existed. The mere failure to file an income tax return doesn't of itself prove an attempt to evade the tax but such failure must be considered with its relations to other actions."

The statement of a duly authorized agent may be considered against a principal, said Judge Wilkerson, dealing with the famous Mattingly letter to the revenue collector admitting Al had had an income of $266,000 for the years charged.

If the jury found that the statement of Mattingly were within the authority of the defendant, he continued, it might be considered in determining the guilt or innocence of the defendant.

If they felt Mattingly had exceeded the scope of his authorization, then they should disregard the letter, he said.

On the subject of the corpus delicti or body of the crime, the court said that might be established by the circumstantial evidence. It is not incumbent on a defendant to testify in his own behalf, the judge said.

"This case will determine whether any man is above the law."

So said George E. Q. Johnson, United States attorney, in the final argument on behalf of your Uncle Sam this morning.

"Gentlemen, the United States Government has no more important laws to enforce than the revenue laws. Thousands upon thousands of persons go to work daily and all of them who earn more than $1,500 a year must pay income tax.

"If the time ever comes when it has to go out and force the collection of taxes, the Army and the Navy will disband, courts will be swept aside, civilization will revert to the jungle days when every man was for himself."

Pointing at Capone, Johnson demanded:

"Who is he, this man? Is he a mythical modern Robin Hood, as defense counsel has described him?

"The Robin Hood of history robbed the rich to give to the poor. Did Capone buy thousands of dollars worth of diamond belt buckles for the unemployed? Did the $6,500 worth of meat go to the unemployed? No, his purchases went to his mansion on Palm Island. Did he buy $27 shirts for the men who sleep under Wacker Drive? No, not he."

Johnson traced the early history of Capone, starting with the time when the defendant was a bartender at Coney Island. Then he said he was next heard of at Jim Colosimo's restaurant in Chicago. All the time, he said, the defendant was becoming more affluent. Johnson went on:

"Then we come to 1924, when this gambling establishment in Cicero was shown to have a profit of $300,000."

"Even if we take the defense statement that he had only an eight per cent share, his profits would have been $24,000. Let me remind you that the record shows profits of $215,000 in 1925.

"Then we come to 1926.

"Pete Penovich had a little gambling place of his own, which he gave up because of Capone's mob. In the parlance of the gentry, he was 'muscled' out. His successor, Mondi, was also muscled out, and after this there was no competition in the gambling business in Cicero."

Johnson drew attention to testimony, by Fred Ries, former associate manager of a Cicero gambling resort. Ries, he said, admitted that after taking out running expenses he bought cashier checks for Bobby Barton. Johnson went on:

"And Bobby Barton bought money orders transmitting $77,000 to Capone in Florida. Defense counsel was strangely silent about this. Even the master mind who plans the perfect crime—and this was intended to be the perfect tax crime—slips sometimes.

"Capone went to Florida, where he had occasion to spend a lot of money on his home in Palm Island. Again the master mind who attempted the perfect crime slipped when he gave his financial secretary, Jack Gusick, checks to pay his bills."

He scoffed at the testimony of defense witnesses that Capone lost $327,000 betting on the horses. He referred to them as "so shifty they couldn't look you in the eye."

Johnson reminded the jurors the defense lawyers had talked to them for four hours, but made no reference to the money orders sent from Capone's headquarters in the Lexington Hotel in Chicago to Capone in Florida.

He declared the records showed $77,000 was sent and received between Chicago and Florida.

Johnson warned the jury to remember the men and women who pay a tax on incomes over $1,500 a year. He contrasted them with Capone, whom he flayed for evading taxes during "this time of national deficit."

.   .   .   .

If members of the jury were fearful of what might happen to them in consequence of their upholding the law against the law-

less and ruthless Capone, their verdict did not indicate it. They found Capone guilty on five charges. He was sentenced to eleven years imprisonment.

Reliable reporters said Capone had expected his political satraps to fix it for him to get off with a lighter sentence; they said he felt double-crossed. He actually served seven and a half years, in Federal prisons at Atlanta, Georgia; Alcatraz Island, California; and Lewisburg, Pennsylvania, which is considered the convicts' "country club." The "Big Guy" showed he had influence behind prison bars, and any punishment he suffered under man-made law was not rigorous. The punishment arranged by some other power was.

When he left Lewisburg, considerately protected by official secrecy, in November, 1939, it was to go to Johns Hopkins Hospital in Baltimore to be treated by an eminent syphilologist. He was not cured. The man who was the overlord of vice in Chicago suffered all his last years from the disease he had facilitated wholesale in its ravages upon others. Fittingly, it left him racked in body and—his doctors said—reduced to the mind of a child. Except for two or three brief intervals, he wasted the rest of his life within the walls of the home on Palm Island, at Miami Beach, that was among his ill-gotten gains.

It was asserted, by persons who claimed to know his affairs and doings, that he no longer had any say-so in gangdom in Chicago. The Federal Government, after having supposedly gone over his haunts with a divining rod, decided he couldn't dig up more than $30,000 and accepted that amount in 1942 as settlement for its claim for some $200,000 in unpaid income taxes.

Capone continued to live on in luxury, guarded like a tycoon, another five years and must have had means of support that weren't visible. In 1946, James M. Regan, Sr., elderly director of a horse-racing wire news service in Chicago, made a 98-page statement to police in which, among other things, he detailed how gangsters identified with Capone's career were endeavoring to seize control of Chicago's racetrack gambling rackets. A few weeks later Regan died of lead-poisoning—administered with a gun on a busy Chicago street in broad daylight, just as such things happened in the "old" days. A little later, it was intimated that a syndicate of Capone mobsters had cleaned up a sweet $3,000,000 in the sugar black market.

Whatever part Capone played in the machinations of Chicago's underworld definitely ended January 25, 1947. "I don't want to die in the street," he once said. He didn't. He died in bed, his boots off, of a complication of syphilis, pneumonia and apoplexy. There were some to grieve his death—he was surrounded at the end by his mother, Therese; his father, Ermio; a sister, Mrs. Mafalda Mariote; two brothers, Ralph and Matthew; his wife, May; a son; and, of course, his bodyguards. He was forty-eight years and eight days old.

The man in whose outlaw empire an estimated 250' gangsters died violently between 1925 and 1930 alone, went for a last ride longer than most he had arranged. His body was carried in a hearse from Miami Beach to Chicago to rest, at last, in Mount Olivet Cemetery. Even in death, there was no Capone co-operation with society; the physician who tended him in his last days was refused permission to make an autopsy in the interest of science.

MORGAN THE MIGHTY

Washington, May 23, 1933

Morgan, the mighty, is on the spot!

We wait, anxiously, for the earth to rock.

Nothing happens, except a slight tremor of excitement, as the world gets up on tiptoe to look and listen.

It turns out to be an income tax inquiry, something like Al Capone's or any of the other boys.

Morgan, the mighty, one of the richest men on the face of the globe, pays no income tax in 1931 or 1932. He does not remember about 1930.

His twenty partners in the J. Pierpont Morgan firm, many of them supposed to be very wealthy, pay an aggregated income tax of $48,000 in 1930, and none whatever in 1931 and 1932. That's all of them, understand. Losses, you know, losses, losses, losses.

Morgan, the mighty, appears as he sits at a table with some of our noted Senators in a room foggy with cigar and cigarette smoke, not the fabled giant of world financial history, not the titan who juggles nations like Bill Fields juggles cigar boxes, but a benign old gentleman somewhat harassed by questions popped at him by a person with a jutting jaw and a horribly legal mind, named Ferdinand Pecora.

A nice old gentleman who is trying to make answer to these questions with all the patience that he might exercise in telling a small child just how high is up. A kind old gentleman who seems slightly bewildered at times by the insatiate curiosity of this Pecora person, and whose memory wabbles occasionally, as the memories of old gentlemen will do.

Surely, surely, this is not the Great Morgan who has been pictured as a pirate of the financial high seas, and at whose slightest frown the biggest moguls of the money marts shake and shiver in their boots!

Why, you say, he would make a lovely Santa Claus, with his build and all, if he had white whiskers.

But it is none the less Morgan—Morgan, the Mighty—son of Morgan, the Magnificent, to whom the old gentleman refers with fond intonation in his voice several times during the day.

Master of wealth, and even human destiny. Overlord of commercial realms, and far-flung financial kingdoms—this is undeniably Morgan undergoing a prying into his affairs as a private banker that may yet produce the earthquake we have been anticipating.

This is Morgan, the mighty, being examined by a busy, keen-eyed New York lawyer, and a bunch of eagerly listening country bankers, and merchants, and small business and professional men, representatives of 120,000,000 people.

Slowly, painstakingly, and with a wealth of detail—his lawyers and his business associates banked behind him—he answers Mr. Pecora's questions, telling how his concern has deposits of over $300,000,000, and how it functions in all its personnel and capacity, until Pecora gets down to income tax questions.

Then he does not remember. He knows nothing whatever about income tax matters connected with his firm. But before the Senate committee adjourns to go into executive session, Morgan, the mighty, makes a request that his income tax expert be examined that no suspicion or wrong impression may be left from Pecora's questions and his own answers as to these matters.

So the expert appears, and there is in Pecora's questions to him, over and beyond the questions dealing with the individual returns of Morgan, the mighty, and his partners, the inference that a loss of over $21,000,000 was written into a Morgan House return by the expedient of taking in a new partner.

At times during Morgan's examination you rather feel sorry for him. It is warm. He perspires. He mops his face frequently with a large handkerchief. Toward late afternoon he looks tired. You say to yourself, "That jutty-jawed fellow oughta let this old gentleman be. He's got him plumb worn out."

Possibly Senator Carter Glass, of Virginia, has this humane

feeling. He endeavors to spare Morgan some of the Pecoran in-
sistence in asking again and again about income tax matters. It is
amazing how curious Pecora is about income tax, but Morgan
can give him no help. He says, "I don't know."

Senator Glass says he himself does not know much about his
income tax matters, leaving them to experts, and he sees no use
in hectoring Morgan.

This develops into a slight spat between Senator Glass and
Senator Couzens, of Michigan, who says he resents some one
witness being treated any differently from another in the august
presence of the committee that is digging into the banking affairs
of the community.

Pecora handles Morgan about the same as he would handle a
witness in the case of the People of the State of New York
versus Robert Roe.

He seems cold, implacable. Even when Morgan smiles at him
with great geniality Pecora does not smile back, though one good
smile always deserves another.

The session ends with the feeling among those who listen that
Pecora is trying to clean all the windows in the great House of
Morgan so he can get a good peek inside.

When the investigation began this morning we were in a big
high-ceilinged room on the third floor of the great white Senate
Office Building, where the noble Senators have their offices. The
ceiling of the room is tinted a nice baby-blue. There are models
of sailing ships on the shelves just under the ceiling at either end
of the room.

The walls are of white marble. Three great glass chandeliers
that must have cost a pretty penny hang from the ceiling. This
is the official hearing room of the Senate Banking and Currency
Committee.

The long corridor leading to the doors of the committee room
is crowded with men and women unable to gain admittance
but waiting there for a peek at the great Morgan. They struggle
at the doors, arguing with the door tenders. They are struggling
long after the hearing starts. They struggle so audibly that members of the committee complain they cannot hear a word. Street-

cars grinding along in the street outside the open windows add to the din.

In a front row sits young Junius Morgan, a fine-looking chap, with all the striking Morgan characteristics in his features. Beside him sits Martin Egan, publicity man of the Morgan forces, and once a famous war correspondent.

Now here comes J. Pierpont Morgan himself through a rear door. He is preceded by his attorney, John W. Davis, Democratic candidate for the Presidency in 1924, a gray, immaculate-looking man. There is great confusion as Morgan advances through the crowd of spectators. It is said he arrived in Washington with a stout bodyguard. This is not in evidence today.

He is a powerful looking man, easily six feet tall, with much meat on his huge frame. He weighs well over 200 pounds. He is sixty-six years old, but looks older. His face is ruddy, his features heavy. He has a big, predatory looking nose.

He is dressed in a dark blue suit with a faint pin stripe. His shirt is starched white linen.

His tie is black with white fingers. A huge Oriental pearl adorns the tie. He wears a heavy, old-fashioned watch chain of gold across his vest, the middle hooked in a buttonhole by a crossbar. A green-stone crest ring is on the little finger of his left hand. A pair of eye-glasses dangle by a cord alongside his watch chain.

He is a well-kept, well-groomed looking man. His head is bald and shiny. He has a huge, bristly moustache now quite white. His eyebrows are black and bushy. He looks like a most benign old gentleman as he enters the court room, carrying a battered Panama hat in one hand, and smiling gently on all the world, but later on you see the lightning behind the brows, and sense the thunder in the voice.

He is surrounded by his partners and aides as he enters. There is Thomas W. Lamont, George Whitney, and other members of the Morgan firm, very rich men, all. Mr. Morgan takes a chair at one end of the room, and the photographers surround him with a temerity they have never before displayed. He poses for them with astounding amiability, his huge hands resting on his knees. He even conjures up a placid beam for the camera men.

Not in the memory of man has a Morgan submitted so tamely to a public photographing. Mr. Morgan gazed about with apparent interest. Indeed, he seemed to be getting something of a kick out of the proceedings, now that he was well into this untoward experience. He posed over and over again for the photographers until somebody in authority came along and said, "That'll do, boys."

He chatted easily with those around him. Then he was asked to take a seat at the committee table, right in the center on one side with Costigan of Colorado to his left and Bulkley of Ohio to his right. He says something to Bulkley as he sits down, and smiles broadly.

Now Pecora enters, swarthy, brisk, and smiling, with a pack of nimble young assistants at his back. Two boys enter lugging a big black trunk between them. This is some of Pecora's evidence. It certainly looks ominous. Pecora wears a suit of "pepper-and-salt" design, and white linen. He has curly iron-gray hair and a jutting jaw and is very clean looking and business like.

Senator Fletcher, of Florida, in a morning coat with black braid, an elderly man of slow movement and speech, opens the proceedings by calling the committee to order. A number of Senators who are members of the State Banking and Currency Committee but not members of the subcommittee come in and take chairs at the table, including the tall, stately looking McAdoo of California, his lean neck surrounded by his characteristic white linen collar that would choke the average man. Senator Fletcher asks of Pecora, "Who is your first witness?"

Mr. Pecora, without rising from his chair, replies briefly, "J. P. Morgan."

And the examination is under way.

Pecora does not rise from his chair as he interrogates Morgan. His voice is very calm as he goes through a long preamble of questioning which is designed to establish who Mr. Morgan is. As if everybody didn't know.

Well, it seems that he is senior partner of the firm of J. P. Morgan & Co., of Wall Street, with twenty partners in the

New York concern, and that they do a private banking business up in so many millions it makes your head swim to think of them. The Morgan deposits alone are $340,000,000.

As Morgan concludes he leans back in his chair and looks placidly at the committee as much as to say, "There, now boys, I have cleared everything up for you."

Pecora does not look at Morgan while questioning him, but Morgan looks at Pecora in answering and frequently smiles. Perhaps he feels it might be well to conciliate this gentleman until he finds out what is up his sleeve.

When he finally learns this, Morgan ceases to smile. The angry blood comes into his face. The veins in his neck thicken. He is biting his back teeth together so hard the muscles of his neck twitch.

When Pecora finally gets down to the matter nearest and dearest his investigatorial heart, the income tax, Morgan seems to get very nervous. He hauls a white handkerchief out of his breast pocket and mops his face.

An income tax return covering the two days, January 1 and January 2, 1930, inclusive, which return is separate unto itself, is the subject of much inquiry by Pecora. Says Morgan uneasily, "I don't know anything about income tax returns."

Pecora asks, "Do you know that deductions for losses of $21,071,862 are claimed in the returns for those two days?"

Morgan replies, "I don't know."

Then Morgan says he thinks that in view of the fact that the various income tax matters Pecora asked about had been left unexplained and might be wrongly construed, he thinks Mr. Leonard Keyes, his general manager and income tax expert, ought to be heard.

Keyes says he prepares all the returns for J. P. Morgan & Co. and all the individual partners, and in 1930 the aggregate amount paid by the twenty partners was $48,000. In 1931 it was nothing, and ditto 1932.

He says the two returns for 1930 were due to a change in the Morgan partners. S. Parker Gilbert was admitted January 2, 1931, and although no business was transacted on January 1, a holiday, the return showed profits of nearly $2,225,000 for only one day, in brokers' commissions and the like. But it was this two-day return that shows a loss of over $21,000,000.

May 24, 1933

There sit the great J. Pierpont Morgan, proud overlord of the financial world, and his faithful henchmen, all damp with perspiration—the great Morgan who admits he pays Great Britain income taxes in the same years he pays nothing to his own United States.

And there the swarthy Ferdinand Pecora, son of Italian immigrant parents, patiently beats his way through a weird jungle of high finance until the twisting trails around him are alive with all manner of strange things in the form of disclosures that will astound this nation.

Somewhere, close at hand, the dark-browed Pecora believes, lies the lair of the most powerful influences on the public and commercial life of the United States that have existed in all its history, but as he presses on you will read (and perhaps weep), as he shows today how scores of distinguished citizens were "preferred clients" of the House of Morgan.

How they were "given the opportunity" of buying at $20 per share a stock that was sold on the market at all the way from $34 to $50. They were given this "opportunity" before the stock was handed out to the public. They were "on the inside," so to speak, perhaps because in each case it was the same as with William Woodin, to whom a member of the firm of J. P. Morgan & Co. wrote coyly:

"We just want you to know that we are thinking of you."

You will read how Norman H. Davis got a loan, amount unknown, but still unpaid, from the House of Morgan.

You will read, also, how the House of Morgan distributed its deposits of millions over a wide area of banks and trust companies in New York, Boston, Pittsburgh, Philadelphia and Chicago, so that its influence was necessarily woven into the very fabric of the banking system of the country.

Morgan himself sits nearly all day in the witness chair, with a big fat book of typewritten pages in his pudgy hands. It contains records of his firm. When he is asked a question by Pecora he thumbs the pages somewhat helplessly, as if saying to himself, "Now what in Sam Hill is all this I've got here, anyway?"

Then he generally turns and gets a line on the matter in question from those behind him, usually George Whitney. The great Morgan frankly admits he does not know a whole lot about the details of his business, just as he is in the dark on his income tax matters—except those relating to Great Britain.

Only once in the long history of the House of Morgan has there ever been a public statement of its policy and procedures, he says, in the course of his examination. This was made by "father." Morgan never says "my father." Just "father." You can see that this old gentleman, who somehow doesn't look so benign as he did yesterday in the light of the day's revelations, adores the memory of his distinguished sire.

"You refer to the time some twenty years ago when he testified at a public inquiry?" asks Pecora.

"The only time," replies Morgan softly.

He perhaps wishes it still remains the only time there have been disclosures bearing upon the Morgan firm.

It is George Whitney, one of the younger Morgan partners, who is finally pushed forward to bear the brunt of the more startling revelations of the day, when Morgan says he thinks Whitney will know more about the matter of the financing of the Alleghany Corporation * by the Morgan company than anyone else.

It is this corporation in which the eminent gentlemen, including Colonel Charles A. Lindbergh, were the favored of the Morgans in the matter of buying stock.

Whitney is said to be called "Icicle" Whitney in Wall Street, because of his cold, dispassionate demeanor, though Pecora has

* This was formed around the minority, but controlling, stock interests held by the Van Sweringen brothers, Cleveland real estate promoters, in the Nickel Plate, Chesapeake & Ohio, and other railway properties. Alleghany Corporation subsequently came into control of Robert R. Young, another Wall Street stock-operator.

the ice thawing and running all over the premises when he finally gets to examining Whitney about his income tax return, which shows that he netted a nice profit himself on Alleghany.

Whitney is in his early forties, tall, slim, good-looking, pince-nezed, well-groomed and faintly supercilious in his attitude toward Pecora. By the way, Pecora is Italian for "lamb," I am told. This is no lamb, however, this round-headed scion of sunny It'. This is a lion of the law.

He has a curious way of sitting silent in his chair when the members of the committee start asking questions and engaging in windy debates. Pecora lets them exhaust themselves, then goes on quietly with his witness, as if never interrupted.

He asks seemingly irrelevant questions for a time, then, suddenly bang! Out pops a shot that makes you realize he has been aiming at this target all along.

Whitney gets into the proceedings in the morning and becomes spokesman for the Morgan clan when it is expected that next to Morgan himself this role will be filled by Thomas W. Lamont, one of the older members of the crowd, who is present. Whitney rises voluntarily at the morning session to explain something a member of the committee wishes to know, while Morgan is still on the stand, and then he remains standing half an hour while Pecora questions him.

Whitney seems slightly contemptuous in tone as he answers Pecora when he is asked at the morning session if it is not a fact that after paying $11,000,000 in income taxes in 1929 the combined Morgan partners paid an aggregate of only $48,000 the following year, and nothing whatever the next three years.

"So I heard here yesterday," said Whitney.

Pecora thereupon becomes a trifle sharper with the witness than he has been with any other, especially in the afternoon, when Whitney will not positively identify a photostatic copy of his income tax return, saying he prefers to inspect his own record.

"The trouble with these chaps is they have the Bourbon mind," comments Pecora on Whitney's reluctance afterward. "They cannot see that their attitude of wanting to conceal everything serves no purpose."

While Whitney is reluctantly narrating the details of the Alleghany deals and identifying lists bearing the names of our foremost citizens, Morgan sits just behind him, listening intently. It would be interesting to know the thoughts of the old financier at this time when a great democracy has him in hand and is divesting him of so many sacred secrets.

But for all we know, perhaps Morgan privately relishes the pillorying of some of the lads on the list, especially those who still owe him.

May 25, 1933

Mr. Morgan laughs until his stout sides shake today, a jovial old King of Koin, as he listens to disclosures concerning the dealings with his own firm of very, very big shots in the political world—Republican and Democratic.

His demeanor confirms a suspicion that Mr. Morgan now keenly enjoys the predicament in which these recipients of his favors find themselves. Or some of them, at any rate.

He has had his own moments of perspiration before the Senate subcommittee that is investigating his affairs, so perhaps he says to himself, "Well, let the rest of them sweat with me."

Or perhaps some of the boys didn't do right by Mr. Morgan somewhere along the line. Perhaps all of those favors apparently so freely bestowed by Mr. Morgan did not come from his heart.

In any event, Mr. Morgan laughs. And laughs.

Once he just barely suppressed a haw-haw, that, if proportionate to Mr. Morgan's size, must shake the Corinthian pillars in the huge caucus room of the Senate Office Building to which the hearing is shifted today. The effort leaves him red-faced and almost apoplectic.

He sputters trying to choke down another outburst. Mr. Morgan probably hasn't so thoroughly enjoyed himself since the last time he took a swing at a photographer's camera, and connected.

A photostatic copy of a letter from John J. Raskob, then chairman of the Democratic National Committee, acknowledging a stock-purchasing courtesy from the House of Morgan (2,000 shares of Alleghany Corporation) is produced and it has one line that seems to give Mr. Morgan a terrific "belt," as the boys say.

Especially as it is declaimed in the ringing tones of Mr. Ferdinand Pecora, who is conducting the investigation for the Senate committee. Mr. Pecora seems to like the line himself.

It runs like this:

"I sincerely hope the future holds an opportunity for me to reciprocate."

He laughs again when Mr. Pecora asks questions as to the identity of Mr. Joseph Nutt, of Cleveland, another gentleman invited to partake of the crumbs from the rich man's board, and is still laughing when it is disclosed that Mr. Nutt is treasurer of the Republican National Committee.

Finally everybody commences laughing with Mr. Morgan. Perhaps it is his idea to leave 'em laughing when he says good-bye, anyway.

Besides the names of Mr. Raskob and Mr. Nutt, we hear from the same list of favored subscribers to Alleghany stock, the names of Mr. Cornelius Bliss, former treasurer of the Republican campaign committee and Charles D. Hilles, New York Republican leader.

Well, it appears that the only party that has a right to kick about Mr. Morgan's beneficence is the Socialist.

On another list of persons let in on the ground floor, so to speak, in the matter of purchasing Standard Brands, another House of Morgan project, is the name of the late Calvin Coolidge.

Mr. Coolidge was given the opportunity of buying 3,000 shares in July, 1929. He left the Presidency in March of the same year.

The name of United States Senator William Gibbs McAdoo also appears on this list. Senator McAdoo reads a statement to the committee immediately upon convening this morning in which he sets forth that his dealings with the House of Morgan were ten years after his resignation as Secretary of the Treasury, and four years before he became Senator, and that they wound up with a net loss of some $3,000 to him.

Mr. Morgan, who appears vestless today in tribute to the

local weather, begins laughing almost at the same moment that Mr. McAdoo relates his loss.

John J. Raskob is also on this Standard Brands list. Likewise William H. Woodin, Secretary of the Treasury, Bernard Baruch, Norman H. Davis, our celebrated ambassador-at-large; Charles A. Lindbergh, General John J. Pershing, R. B. Mellon, brother of the former Secretary of the Treasury, and others.

The Lindbergh account is explained by Mr. Whitney with the statement that the House of Morgan generally advises the Colonel about his investments. In answer to a question from Mr. Pecora, Mr. Whitney says he thinks Calvin Coolidge's name must have been suggested by Thomas Cochran, a Morgan partner, though he isn't sure.

These persons it appears, were all invited by the House of Morgan to buy the stock. Mrs. S. Parker Gilbert, wife of the former agent-general of reparations, is mentioned as an invitee.

Before the session goes into recess over the luncheon hour, Mr. Morgan asks permission to make a statement. He takes the witness chair, and unfurls a crumpled bit of paper that he has evidently had wadded up in his big fist for some time.

He reads this statement aloud. It is about the income tax he paid to England in the years that he did not pay income tax to his Uncle Sammy.

He gazes at Mr. Pecora to see if that gentleman wishes to ask him any questions, and Mr. Pecora shakes his head. Says Mr. Morgan, gratefully, with an extra wide beam, "Thank you, Mr. Attorney, I am very much obliged."

Says Mr. Pecora, "Er-ah, wait a minute, please. If the English system were in vogue here you would be required to pay much more income tax to this country than you do to England?"

Says Mr. Morgan, agreeably, "Oh, yes, but not nearly so much as I paid in 1928 and 1929."

Some of the Senators gather about his bulky figure as the session recesses. Mr. Morgan chats with them a moment and then exits laughingly.

Mr. Will Rogers, the cowpuncher-humorist, another of the world's rich men, arrives for the session to see if Mr. Morgan needs any assistance. The only difference between Mr. Rogers and Mr. Morgan financially is perhaps $8.35. Complains Mr. Rogers, "They are always annoying us rich guys."

The examination of Mr. George Whitney takes up most of the morning. Mr. Morgan sits behind him, one hand on Mr. Whitney's chair. Mr. Whitney reads a long, printed statement.

Mr. Pecora inquires, "Who prepared this statement?"

"Why—"

Demands Mr. Pecora when he finds the preparation is a matter of some doubt, "Well, whose phraseology is it?"

At this point Mr. Will Rogers, who has listened intently to the reading, leans over to this correspondent. He whispers, "I think it's Bugs Baer's."

Nothing is going to happen to Mr. Morgan. Indeed local bookmakers are commencing to offer plenty of 2 to 1 that Mr. Morgan winds up out-laughing the subcommittee, despite the efforts of some to laugh with him.

You must not think that because he pays no income taxes to this country that Mr. Morgan has no income at all. I mean you must not start shedding any tears of sympathy for him on that score. He manages to scrape enough together every year to carry on the yacht *Corsair* and the house at Glen Cove, and the one in Lunnon.

And anyway, perhaps Mr. Morgan fears that if he came forward voluntarily and offered to contribute to the support of Uncle Sam, when he doesn't have to, it might increase the mortality rate in this country through heart disease.

But I must suggest it to Mr. Morgan.

It will give him something to keep on laughing about.

May 26, 1933

Blazing mad is Mr. Ferdinand Pecora!

You can hang your hat on his jutting chin as he sticks it out far beyond normal today, and lets fly a verbal blast at a group of United States Senators that almost knocks them out of their chairs.

Irked by petty criticism of his methods in showing how the great House of Morgan manipulates, and perhaps by a disposition that became very evident today on the part of some of the Senators to lend a kindly cloak of secrecy to old Mr. Morgan's business, Mr. Ferdinand Pecora cuts lose with fiery tongue.

And as he concludes a roar of applause sweeps the huge caucus room of the Senate Office Building, in which the examination of the Morgan goings on is being held, and smothers an intended answer to the infuriated Mr. Pecora from his chief heckler, the aged Senator Carter Glass, of Virginia.

The applause, rising with amazing suddenness and continuing some time, spatters over old Mr. Morgan himself, in person, and in the flesh, as he sits among his personal entourage smoking a huge cigar.

It startles the Senators. Some of those who have been only luke-warm in their enthusiasm toward Mr. Pecora's efforts to spade up all the financial skeletons in the House of Morgan that he can locate, begin running to the cover of declarations of confidence in Mr. Pecora.

He has just let them know, in effect, that he does not care a tinker's cuss about them, and the resultant applause gives the Senators a faint sniff of the public attitude toward this investigation. The Senators know that a mere roomful of applause may possibly be elaborated into fearful thunder as it goes out over the land.

The moral of all this is: never get an Italian mad.

Mr. Pecora arrives for the session looking quite moody. He has been in attendance on an executive session of the committee which decides that it isn't going to permit Mr. Pecora to make public certain matters that he considers positively vital to this investigation into the House of Morgan.

It is plain that he is seething inwardly as he takes his seat and calls for his first witness, Mr. George H. Howard, a New York lawyer, who is president of the United Corporation and the New York United Corporation.

These are light and power concerns. Mr. Pecora's intention is to show that the House of Morgan made colossal sums through stock operations in United. He is proceeding slowly with Mr. Howard, a somewhat hesitant witness, when old Senator Glass, who has been something of an obstructionist throughout the inquiry, starts growling.

He wants to know where the inquiry is leading. He wants to know why Mr. Pecora is asking all these questions. He asks the witness himself if the United Corporation has ever violated any Federal statute in its business dealing; Mr. Howard very promptly says no.

Mr. Pecora his face pale, his teeth gritted, sits silent while the old Virginian talks. He has often had to endure Senator Glass' interruptions and objections. The Senator is given to little witticisms and irrelevancies that sound strange in an inquiry of this nature.

Senator Kean, of New Jersey, a placid-looking man with a large gray moustache, asks Mr. Howard if it isn't customary for railroads and other corporations to do thus and so with their stocks and securities. You may hear of Senator Kean again before the inquiry is over. Other Senators gabble somewhat aimlessly. Says Mr. Pecora, suddenly, "All right! I'll tell you what it's all about!"

He picks up and reads the Senate resolution directing this inquiry, the terms of which are so sweeping that they give the Senate committee power to do just about anything it desires, and adds that he is proceeding under this resolution.

Now Senator Couzens, of Michigan, a ruddy, strong-featured citizen who has been the bulwark of the Pecoran efforts throughout, rises to his feet and says, "I ask the chair to rule whether the examination is proceeding under the terms of that resolution?"

Old Senator Fletcher, of Florida, another staunch supporter of Mr. Pecora and the inquiry, says it does. Senator Couzens says, "I now ask if that is a complete answer to the gentleman from Virginia?"

Senator Glass starts roaring. He says he does not consider it a complete answer.

He says no one informed the subcommittee as to what Mr. Pecora expected to bring out. He even goes so far as to say that he does not recall seeing anything in the minutes of the subcommittee authorizing Mr. Pecora to conduct the examination.

At this, Mr. Pecora flares out, "I did not solicit this assignment; it was offered to me; I accepted, and I have done the best I can do to fulfill it. I have worked day and night at it. But it would be impossible for me, in New York, to call up the committee every time I thought I had a lead and ask instructions how to proceed. If the committee thinks it is any pleasure to do all this work, it is mistaken, and if it thinks that the compensation of $255 per month that I receive is any incentive, it is also badly mistaken."

There is in his tone and manner the inference that if they do not like what he is doing he will withdraw, although later on Mr. Pecora takes pains to deny for the record a statement appearing in print that he would resign unless the committee does as he desires about admitting certain evidence.

Senator Glass starts to reply but you cannot hear him for the applause. It is difficult to hear Senator Glass at any time, as he throws his words out of one corner of his mouth. The Senators try to ignore the applause. When it dies away, Mr. Pecora then states the purpose of his examination of Mr. Howard. Senator Glass wants to know why all this wasn't brought forward before, and he insists he is still not satisfied with the method of procedure.

He also complains about the publicity some of the executive sessions have received, and says he doesn't care about the House of Morgan, or any other house but that he is not going to see any injustice done it. Then Senator Glass closes with a self-eulogy to the effect that he is the only man who has done anything about the banking laws, anyway.

Mr. Morgan appears today in a gray suit with a single-breasted three-button coat. The old boy has an excellent tailor. His clothes fit him well despite a large "bay window." His linen is purest white, and starched. His shoes are low tans.

As he sits down the photographers close in around him and Mr. Morgan submits to his daily ordeal with a grace that continues to amaze the boys.

"Smile now," one of them orders, and the great financier beams. "That's great!" he remarks as the camera men let fly with a raft of flash bulbs. "Shoot a lot of them. I own stock in the General Electric."

Young Junius Morgan is asked by one of the photographers to pose with his father and he immediately takes a chair alongside his distinguished sire and they smile together.

Young Junius is tall, good looking, neatly groomed. He has black hair, slightly gray.

Young Junius displays great curiosity about the flash bulbs and a photographer explains them to him in detail, with the elder Morgan also listening intently.

The old gentleman even goes so far as to chat pleasantly with a newspaperman. Let this newspaperman try to get in at 23 Wall next week and see what happens to him.

The observers are somewhat surprised to see that these very rich people are rather human after all. If the inquiry continues much longer it will wind up with everybody being just like this with the Morgan crowd.

Senator Fletcher lauds Mr. Pecora at length, and says that the attorney often consulted with him as chairman of the subcommittee, and that he is proud of Mr. Pecora, and that he deems him thorough and efficient. Senator Barkley, of Kentucky, also put in a boost for the now somewhat surprised Pecora, and added it is too bad he isn't getting more money. Indeed, the session winds up as a general plug for Mr. Pecora, though he remains somewhat moody looking when the committee recesses until next Wednesday.

May 26, 1933

I presume you really might call the inquiry into the petty affairs of Mr. J. Pierpont Morgan, "The Revenge of the Photo Grabbers."

For years, it has been Mr. M.'s favorite pastime to play ring-around-a-rosy with the Photo Grabbers, most faithful, and conscientious, and hardest working of all the newspaper tribes. Why, I once knew a Photo Grabber—but never mind.

In playing with Mr. M. the Photo Grabbers were always "It."

He loved to chase them, and tag them. If he could get a camera away from one of the Photo Grabbers and tag his man with the lens box, the game was a big success for Mr. M. Of all our public characters, only Mr. Gene Tunney came close to Mr. M. as an adept chaser of Photo Grabbers.

And of course, at best, Mr. Tunney was only an amateur. He never had Mr. M.'s wind, or depth. Especially depth. This is evidenced by the fact that Mr. Tunney has abandoned the pastime altogether. He is a retired Photo Grabber chaser.

Now, for the first time in his long career, at the game, Mr. M. is "It."

When he enters the august presence of the Senate committee which is delving (as we say) into his goings on, the Photo Grabbers swarm all over him and take his picture with impunity, and also with all kinds of cameras.

The first day of the inquiry, when Mr. M. looked up and found himself surrounded by lenses, he seemed somewhat startled, and I thought he was going to pick a few of the boys up and start throwing 'em about. But I suppose he reflected on the danger of hitting a United States Senator with a Photo Grabber, which would be high treason beyond a doubt, and so dismissed the idea.

Instead, he gathered a great big broad smile together, and spread it over his countenance, and beamed at the Photo Grabbers with such cordiality that several of them seized their mills and retreated some distance.

They felt that a smile on Mr. M.'s face, especially in the presence of Photo Grabbers, augured no good to them. But I am inclined to give Mr. M. the benefit of the doubt and suggest that he smiled merely because he wished to look beautiful in the pictures.

Day in and day out, since then, the Photo Grabbers have been blasting away at Mr. M.'s rugged features, and never once has he rebuffed them. Flashlights, stills, movies—they were all one to him.

Occasionally one of his aides tried to shoo the Photo Grabbers away, but Mr. M never requested it. He even went so far as to chat with Photo Grabbers while they were taking his picture, although I am bound to say that some of the Photo Grabbers considered this an unwarranted liberty on Mr. M.'s part.

He was docile, tranquil, and wholly peaceable. So much so, in fact, that one of the Photo Grabbers privately confided to me that he thinks the old boy is going back. He didn't say back where. Not back to the Senate committee's room after this inquiry, if he can help it, you can bet on that.

Today there were only a few Photo Grabbers present in the inquiry room. Satiated with pictures of Mr. M., most of the boys had gone on to fresher subjects. They've got enough pictures of him now to last them for years to come.

I thought Mr. M. glanced around with real regret for the missing ones. He had on a new pair of tan shoes, too. I fear Mr. M. has succumbed at last to an old complaint among our public characters. It is known as Camera-itis.

That's the trouble with the Photo Grabbers centering their attention on one character for several days at a stretch. It makes the subject utterly lens-conscious. Thus when the Photo Grabbers suddenly let him alone, he develops a yennion for them. I mean he wants to see them around.

I suppose the next time Mr. M. comes back from a trip abroad and looks around and sees no Photo Grabbers waiting for him on the dock, he will be right peeved about it. Still, he will be peeved if they are there, so it's all even.

May 31, 1933

It is getting so you are practically nobody unless you are on the kind Mr. Morgan's preferred list.

Only don't call it "preferred" list. The House of Morgan does not care for the term.

"It gags," says Mr. George Whitney, "the icicle," handsome, debonnaire—a movie director's idea in the flesh of a big Wall Streeter, which Mr. Whitney certainly is.

Mr. Whitney means that the term "preferred list" gags him and, doubtless, his associates in the House of Morgan. Nobody bothers to tell Mr. Whitney how the "preferred list" itself is gagging a large number of American citizens.

And yet it is conceivable that in the years to come, when some scion of an old American family is claiming proud heritage, and is asked, "Did your folks come over on the *Mayflower?*" they will haughtily reply, "No, but you will find our name on Mr. J. Pierpont Morgan's list."

Let us see, now, how the "list" that may determine future bluebloodedness in America shapes up at this time. We have so far:

Four or five candidates for President of the United States of America.

A Justice of the Supreme Court of the United States.

A Secretary of the Treasury of the United States of America.

Two Senators of the United States of America.

An Ambassador-at-large of the United States of America.

One parcel of small-time judges.

One job lot consisting of a chairman and treasurers of political parties.

One large batch of millionaires.

Another large batch of ex-millionaires.

One lot of bush-league political bosses, bank directors, business men and lawyers.

One large barrel of parties not yet sorted and identified.

Even one of our celebrated war correspondents and radio broadcasters almost gets on the list this morning.

Senator Reynolds, of North Carolina, perusing a string of names longer than a hack driver's dream, finds the monicker "F. Gibbons" staring him in the face, and inquires, "Does this mean Floyd Gibbons?"

Nineteen necks along the press bench crack audibly as the boys lean forward, breathless, and I may say, somewhat envious, to catch the reply.

Mr. Whitney looks blank, then confers with some of his assistants behind him before he answers, "I think it's one of our clerks."

The press bench falls back indignant. The list remains palpably discriminatory against newspapermen.

Old Senator Carter Glass, of Virginia, whose waspish buzzing about the ears of Mr. Pecora, and whose declamation that he will not stand by and see any injustice done the House of Morgan, featured the inquiry last week, waves a large portfolio of telegrams and letters at the committee today.

He says some of these are missives calling him a no-gooder in various terms, and threatening his life, while others are big boosts for him as an American patriot, and a Southern gentleman, suh.

Senator Glass' threat to read these contributions strikes terror to every heart, for much of the morning session has already been given over to senatorial digressions, with Mr. Pecora sitting idly by unable to ask a question for half an hour, hand running, but it comes out that Senator Glass does not mean at once.

He puts in much of the noon recess being photographed alongside his portfolio of knocks and boosts, and his gray felt hat sitting jack-deuce on his head, as the faro bank players would say. Presently along comes Mr. Pecora, and the two pose together with big smiles on their faces, though the spectators are offering 8 to 5 that neither means a single wrinkle of their smiles.

Mr. Pecora keeps burrowing into the transactions of the House of Morgan, throwing behind him as he delves, plenty of financial dirt. He begins with Mr. George H. Howard, president of the United Corporation as a witness, but presently Mr. Whitney steps up voluntarily to answer some questions that Mr. Howard seems dubious about, and Mr. Pecora always welcomes Mr. Whitney.

Mr. Pecora realizes that Mr. Whitney is one man who knows more about the House of Morgan than all the rest put together, so every time Mr. Whitney bobs up, Mr. Pecora says, "Why, sit right down, Mr. Whitney."

Then Mr. Whitney sits down and they keep him sitting. However, it must be said for Mr. Whitney, that he doesn't just sit. He also thinks; Mr. Whitney is no dumbbell. He is extremely intelligent, suave and sure of his ground.

Not far behind him sits old Mr. Morgan, gazing at the witness in admiration and probably wondering how Mr. Whitney can remember so many details of the Morgan business when Mr. Morgan himself can remember so few.

June 1, 1933

Our little inquisition into the doings of Mr. J. Pierpont Morgan opens today with sideshow features.

A female midget about knee high to a grasshopper, from the Ringling Circus now playing in Washington, is brought into the Senate caucus room and Mr. Morgan obligingly holds the wee lady on his knee while the photographers get busy and the spectators giggle.

It looks like a ventriloquist act.

I mean you half expect to hear the small figure on Mr. J. Pierpont Morgan's knee, pipe, "Now, Uncle John, tell me the story of the Bad Old Bear."

And Mr. Morgan to reply, "I don't know any story about a bear, Melissy, but I'll tell you one about the Great Big Bull."

Mr. Morgan seems to enjoy the experience for a spell, and handles the midget as gently as if she were a costly doll. Indeed, the midget isn't much bigger than a doll such as Santa Claus might bring any good little gal at Noel. And by the way, Santa Claus also gets into the inquiry today when Senator Bob Reynolds, of No'th Ca'lina, finally hits upon a name for those famous lists heretofore designated, to the distress of the House of Morgan, as "preferred."

Senator Bob speaks of them as "Santa Claus lists."

It seems a happy compromise.

It is just as well Senator Carter Glass is not present to see the performance with the midget. It might tend to confirm the aged Virginian's contention that the investigation is mainly a circus.

In fact, it is only just the other day while supplying some of the clowning that the Senator is remarking that all we need to make the thing complete is peanuts and red lemonade. Of course, he didn't think of midgets.

But the philosopher may see something else in this picture of Mr. Morgan, sitting there with a benign expression on his face, and a midget on his knee. The philosopher may see the midget as occupying toward Mr. Morgan the same relative position now occupied by the proletariat of these United States of America.

That is to say, we are all more or less on Mr. Morgan's financial knee.

There is this difference between us and the midget, however: Mr. Morgan occasionally bends us over his financial knee, south side uppermost.

While the midget is roosting on Mr. Morgan's knee, a scout reports the sinister figure of Mr. Dexter Fellowes, the Ringling press-agent, lurking in the corridors. He is afraid to enter in person and sends the midget in with a proxy.

The proxy finally overdoes himself and shifts the midget to Mr. Morgan's other knee, and crushes into the picture himself, at which Mr. Morgan looks irked, and mutters, as if to say, "Just for that you've all got to get off."

But he puts the midget down on the floor tenderly enough, and turns to beam at his immediate following, the members of which are utterly aghast at the proceeding. No one can think up out of his experience in Wall Street a precedent for a great financier posing with a midget on his knee.

The members of the Senate committee are not in the room when this incident takes place. They hear of it later and are greatly annoyed, possibly because there are no midgets left to pose on their knees. The sergeants-at-arms are instructed to guard against similar invasions of Mr. Morgan's privacy. Some of the committee fear that Mr. Fellowes may return with an elephant and try to put him on Mr. Morgan's knee.

The photographers are barred from the caucus room, after enjoying a long field day, although they are scarcely to blame for littering up the place with midgets.

Senator Fletcher, of Florida, chairman of the committee, denounces the incident with some vociferousness, as he calls the session to order and asks the newspapers not to print the pictures.

The crowd applauds Senator Fletcher's statement that he considers the midgeting of Mr. Morgan an outrage. The first thing we know, we will all commence to feel sorry for poor Mr.

Morgan, and forget the bewildering financial sleight-of-hand that Mr. Ferdinand Pecora is exposing in the manner of the tobacco ads.

Mr. Morgan does not appear to take the business of the midget seriously. Perhaps he thinks he may have brought the midget in himself in one of his pockets by accident.

A man never knows when he may find a midget on his person.

Anyway, as soon as we are relieved of the sinister presence of Mr. Leif and his midget we feel greatly relieved and the inquiry proceeds.

The opening of the morning session is long delayed. This because of the rule adopted by the skittish members of the committee that Mr. Ferdinand Pecora must reveal to them in advance what he expects to bring out during the inquiry. It is old Senator Glass' idea, but some of the others fell in with surprising alacrity.

The senatorial committee has the inquiry slowed down to a walk and seems to love the pace. At the beginning Mr. Pecora was going through the mass of evidence like water through a tin horn. He was bringing out the high spots one after the other with bewildering rapidity.

Now the members of the senatorial committee spend much time mumbling. The mumbles leave Mr. Pecora sitting silent at the head of a long table at which the Senators are assembled. He gets in a question just now and then. But Mr. Pecora remains sweetly patient with the gentlemen. After all, it is their inquiry and Mr. Pecora is getting the terrific sum of $255 per month for sitting around.

Mr. George Whitney is again on the stand most of the day. Mr. Whitney is our only sex appeal in this inquiry. The ladies enjoy gazing at Mr. Whitney. In fact we hear that if it wasn't for Mr. Whitney, the female attendance at the inquiry would fall to low ebb. As it is, the ladies continue to occupy the best seats.

Mr. Whitney today wears a dark blue sack suit with a starched white linen collar against a colored shirt. A crest ring and a wrist watch are his only jewelry. His iron-gray hair is combed to a gloss. His nose glasses are delicately balanced on his patrician beezer.

Toward the close of the morning session Mr. Whitney seems to grow somewhat Wall Streetish toward Mr. Pecora who is cheerfully trying to show how the House of Morgan lends millions of dollars without collateral and far beyond the limits permitted a public bank.

Mr. Whitney refers to a matter of $30,000,000 as "a relatively small amount." I am inclined to think that it is this supercilious, not to say blasé attitude toward money on Mr. Whitney's part that impresses the ladies. They can see what a handy thing around the house a man must be who considers $30,000,000 "a relatively small amount."

Mr. Morgan seems to start slightly, as Mr. Whitney speaks of the thirty million in this offhand way and to gaze keenly at Mr. Whitney. You know Mr. Morgan got his start by carefully saving all his thirty millions, and perhaps it alarms him to hear a young man speak so casually of them.

The inquiry drags on toward six o'clock reminding many of the spectators that it is supper time in Washington. Dinner time to you swells, perhaps, but supper time in Washington. The folks began going home. All Senators except Senator Fletcher, the chairman, and Alva Adams, of Colorado, had departed.

Senator Adams is a banker in Pueblo, Colorado. He is sticking to the inquiry in the hope that he may learn some new ideas for Pueblo. I doubt if Senator Adams will ever persuade the Puebloans to Mr. Whitney's idea that $30,000,000 is a "relatively small amount of money."

If the attendance keeps falling off we may have to take this show on the road.

June 2, 1933

If Mr. J. Pierpont Morgan should fall into a barrel of onion soup—may the fates forfend!—the chances are he would come up with a rose in his hand. At least you gather this impression from the testimony today in the Senate inquiry into the private financial life of Mr. Morgan.

In one of the darkest hours of the long, long night of Wall

Street, Mr. Morgan—or rather one of Mr. Morgan's bright young blades—joined with other financiers in an attempt to prop the market, at that moment aslant, like the Leaning Tower of Pisa.

They bought a job lot of those checks that seemed to be most afflicted with what the deep sea divers call the "bends," and wound up making over $1,000,000 for the rescue mission. Which brings us to the thought that to him who hath shall be given. Also a stitch in time saves nine. Likewise you can't keep a squirrel on the ground.

Mr. George Whitney, that cool, calm, suave, impeccably arrayed gentleman who comes out the most limelighted of all the members of the House of Morgan, tells the story today. Give Mr. Whitney a question, and a few quotations, and he is one of the finest financial raconteurs in the world. I spoke yesterday of Mr. Whitney being our only sex appeal in this inquiry. I said the ladies enjoyed gazing at him. A committee of ladies waits on me this morning to inform me that I am all wrong in my impression that Mr. Whitney is entirely responsible for the feminine attendance at the inquiry. They say:

"We really like Mr. Morgan better than anyone else. Mr. Whitney is very nice, but his answers to Mr. Pecora's questions indicate that he may be a man very handy with excuses when he comes home. Anyway, he can undoubtedly out-talk any woman. Mr. Morgan is our candidate."

Well anyway, Mr. Whitney gives a thrilling word picture of that black hour in Wall Street in 1929, when you couldn't find another drying towel on the rack, and when in fact, to use Mr. Whitney's own language, all was chaos. Or do you remember it yourself?

In this hour, a little group of intrepid souls gathered in Mr. Morgan's office and said to each other, "Well, boys, what will we do?"

Mr. Whitney recalls the names of the members of this devoted band: his brother, Dick Whitney,* now president of the New

* Not long afterward he had to resign the post. He was prosecuted for defalcations in the accounts of customers of his brokerage house, and forced to serve a term in prison.

York Stock Exchange, the Messrs. Potter Williams, Mitchell and George F. Baker, Jr., all representing big financial institutions.

"Well, boys, what will we do?"

So they do it.

They pool their resources, and buy up Alleghany, Allied Chemical, American Can, Anaconda, F. & O., American Telephone, Columbia Gas, Bethlehem Steel and others. ("Vas you dere, Sharlie?") The liquidation some months later finds them winner, off of $37,000,000 worth of buying, to the tune of $1,067,000.

Your correspondent, grown calloused to anything short of $90,000,000, whispers disdainfully to the brilliant young Mr. Julius Berens, financial editor of the New York *American*, "It doesn't sound like much profit."

Mr. Berens pauses in his voluminous note-making and whispers back, "You may sneeze at it, but it makes a big noise to me."

History does not record that the errand of mercy embarked on by these philanthropists put the market back on an even keel, although it is only fair to say it had its beneficial effects at the time.

Mr. Morgan, who enters the inquiry room rather cautiously this morning, perhaps fearful that some miscreant may be lurking about to slip a midget into his pocket, listens to Mr. Whitney's recitation quite enthralled.

Indeed, Mr. Whitney, in his many hours on the witness stand, must have been a liberal education to Mr. Morgan, especially in the matter of the affairs of the House of Morgan, which Mr. Morgan frankly confessed early in the inquiry are somewhat of a mystery to him.

He hasn't muffed a word uttered by Mr. Whitney, and he has been watching Mr. Whitney with an approving gaze, and many head-noddings, as if saying to himself, "I think I'll have to raise this young man's salary."

Mr. Ferdinand Pecora, who says Mr. Whitney is about as clever a witness as he ever tackled, concludes his examination of the gentleman shortly before noon today, and is starting in on young Mr. Thomas Stillwell Lamont, son of old Thomas W.

Lamont, of the Morgan firm, when the Morgan attorney, John W. Davis, once a candidate for President of these United States, ups with objections.

Finally the inquiry adjourns until Monday morning when it will be resumed with young Lamont on the stand. Mr. Pecora expects to get through with the House of Morgan by Tuesday. He will then start taking up other more or less celebrated houses of Wall Street.

The one touch of tone, or class, needed to make our inquiry the high-tonedest affair from top to bottom on record, is provided this morning by Senator Bob Reynolds, of North Carolina, who works in a couple of real kings.

Senator Bob, a husky, ruddy-faced gentleman, who omits all "r's" from his conversation, is the chap who tagged the Morgan favor rolls as "Santa Claus" lists.

He opens the inquiry this morning with a series of questions directed at Mr. Whitney. He wants to know a few names on the foreign lists of the House of Morgan.

Senator Bob has a large voice. You can imagine him singing "Carolina Sunshine" most effectively.

Senator Bob asks Mr. Whitney if he has ever heard that a member of royalty was asked to subscribe to the Morgan units at the inside figure. Mr. Whitney looks somewhat perplexed. The crowd in the inquiry room leans forward expectantly.

Senator Bob becomes specific. He wants to know if Mr. Whitney has ever heard that King Albert of Belgium was ever offered the privilege that so far seems to have been allotted only to members of our best families.

Mr. Whitney replied, "I not only never heard of it, but I am sure it isn't true."

Then Senator Bob asks him about members of the French Government, and King George of England, and members of King George's family.

Mr. Whitney insists, "I am sure that it not true."

Then Senator Bob says, "Now there is another chap I want to ask you about, I can't pronounce his name. Sometimes I call him

Moose-oo-leeny, and sometimes Muss-a-lon-ey. Well, anyway, whatever it is, did he ever participate in these units?"

Mr. Whitney thinks not, but he says he will supply the committee with copies of the foreign lists of the House of Morgan.

Mr. Pecora bows politely and with respect to Mr. Whitney as he excuses him from the stand, and Mr. Whitney bows in return. They have the measure of each other's steel, these two gentlemen, one the scion of Italian immigrant parents, the other of a proud old American family.

•   •   •   •   •

The investigation by a subcommittee of the United States Senate Committee on Banking and Currency, into the House of Morgan and other private banking enterprises, was followed by the establishment in 1934 of a Security and Exchange Commission having powers to regulate stock exchanges and the issue and sale of securities. The Senate committee's special counsel, Ferdinand Percora, was appointed by President Franklin D. Roosevelt to be one of the original members of the commission.

Less than a year later, in January, 1935, Mr. Pecora resigned from the SEC to become a justice of the Supreme Court of the State of New York.

Mr. Morgan was not done with Washington investigating committees. In the same room in which he testified in 1933, he appeared again in 1936, to answer questions of a Senate committee, headed by Gerald P. Nye, that was investigating the roles munitions manufacturers play in international relations. Nye, a diehard isolationist, espoused the theory that the bankers' loans and credits to Great Britain and France exercised a direct influence on the attitude of the Wilson Administration toward the two sets of belligerents in Europe in 1914-16—that they were what made the U.S. turn against German kultur. Mr. Morgan admitted without evidence of same that his firm had established the $3,000,000,000 in credits for supplies from this country that enabled Great Britain and France to stave off a German victory until the United States entered the war in 1917.

Mr. Morgan lived to see and help finance Lend-Lease to Great Britain, France and Russia under parallel circumstances beginning in 1940. He died March 13, 1943, in Boca Grande, Florida, aged seventy-five.

It turned out that Runyon's wisecrack, in one of the foregoing stories, that the only difference between Will Rogers and Morgan was $8.35, was wiser than Runyon probably realized. The Morgan estate, when Federal and State death imposts and debts had been paid, turned out to have a net worth of $4,047,791—not a great deal more than the estate of the thrifty actor. (Senator James Couzens, most outspoken critic of Morgan in the investigation committee, left an estate rated bigger than Morgan's. It had been his practice to have a substantial part of his wealth, made in Ford Motor Company, in tax-free government bonds.) The preceding master of the House of Morgan, J. P. the First, who lived and thrived in a less investigated and regulated era, had left an estate of $69,000,000.

POSTSCRIPT

Sports writing was popularly regarded as Runyon's metier. Besides the trials covered in this book and many others, Runyon, as indicated in the foreword, reported wars, revolutions, a Eucharistic Congress, political conventions, transatlantic flights, kidnapings; he composed memorable verse that passed into national folklore; he wrote short stories; he collaborated on a Broadway play, and he was the producer of several movies. Yet it was probably as sports writer that he was best known. For that reason, it may have seemed incongruous to some readers, and non-readers also, of the sports pages, that Runyon was regularly assigned to "coverage" of murder trials—reportage that usually did not interfere with continuance of his daily sports column.

Perhaps in explanation, these asides on murder trials appeared in his sports column at various times:

A big murder trial possesses some of the elements of a sporting event.

I find the same popular interest in a murder trial that I find in any city on the eve of a big football game, or pugilistic encounter, or baseball series. There is the same conversational speculation on the probable result, only more of it.

There is even some betting on the aforesaid probable result.

Before a big horse race, or football game, or baseball series, the newspaper writers and fans sit around of an evening and argue the matter with some heat. At a trial, the newspaper men—and women—do the arguing, but without the heat. They lack partisanship in the premises. That is furnished by the murder trial fans.

Perhaps you did not know there are murder trial fans. They are mainly persons who have no direct interest in the affair. They are drawn by their curiosity.

Some come from long distances, but do not marvel over this. Persons have been known to travel half way across the continent to see a basketball game.

I am not one of those who criticize the curiosity of the gals who storm the doors of the court room, as we say in the newspaper stories of a trial. If I did not have a pass that entitled me to a chair at the press table, I would probably try an end run myself.

If I had not seen them, I know I would have been consumed with curiosity to peer at Mrs. Snyder and Judd Gray just to see what manner of mortals could carry out such a crime. It is only a slight variation of the same curiosity that makes me eager to see a new fistic sensation, or a great baseball player.

It strikes me that the court room, with a murder trial in issue, develops a competitive spirit, if I may call it such, more tense and bitter than is ever produced on any field of sport. Of course, this is not surprising when you consider that as a rule human *life* is at stake.

The trial is a sort of game, the players on the one side the attorneys for the defense, and on the other the attorneys for the State. The defendant figures in it mainly as the prize. The instrument of play is the law—it is the ball, so to speak. Or perhaps I might call it the puck, for it is in the manner of hockey more than any other sport that it is jockeyed carefully back and forth by the players.

And the players must be men well schooled in their play, men of long experience and considerable knowledge of what they are doing. They must be crafty men, quick of thought and action, and often they are very expensive men.

There are about as many newspaper men at a big murder trial as ever covered a heavyweight championship fight or a world's series—perhaps four hundred of them, counting the telegraph operators.

They discuss the form displayed by counsel for one side or the other during the day's session of court, just as the boxing writers chatter about the form displayed by the principals in a big match after the day's training.

They discuss the different witnesses as they appear to them, just as the boys go over the members of a football line and backfield, or over the horses carded to start in the Kentucky Derby.

And the thrills are just as numerous as in any sporting event I ever saw, with something new popping up at every turn, something in the form of what you might call a new play by the State or the defense. Often it starts off as involved as a hidden-ball maneuver and it takes you a little time to figure it out before the play gets in the clear.

The game of murder trial is played according to very strict rules, with stern umpires called judges to prevent any deviation from these rules.

Someone is killed, perhaps in a peculiarly cold-blooded manner. You might think that the idea would be to get the guilty into court as speedily as possible to hear the details of the crime briefly related, and to at once impose the penalty of the law.

But this is not the way the game of murder trial is played, especially if it is played under the rules of circumstantial evidence, which are very intricate rules. Under these rules everything must be done just so. The game must be played by what strikes the layman, like myself, as roundabout and unnecessary and tedious methods.

If the defendant has money enough to engage an imposing team of players, or attorneys, the game becomes more complicated than ever, for high-priced players in the game of murder trial know all the rules from A to Izzard. They can see a play by the other side coming up a long way off and take steps to circumvent it.

And for some reason the feeling on both sides often becomes very bitter. I sometimes wonder if the players feel toward each other the bitterness that they not infrequently express in court, or do they hob-nob all friendly together, like Brown's cows, as baseball players fraternize after a game in which they have attempted to spike each other. I suppose they do.

And yet they are supposed to be engaged in a sort of common

cause, which is to determine the guilt or innocence of the defendants. I believe they are presumed to be innocent until they are proven guilty.

A player of the game of murder trial for the State represents the people. His function, as I understand it, is to endeavor to convict any person who has transgressed the law to the end that justice may be done and the majesty of the law upheld. It is inconceivable that he would wish to convict an innocent person.

But it has been my observation that the player or attorney for the State is quick to take any advantage of the rules of the game of murder trial that puts his side in front, and equally quick to forestall any moves by the other side. I presume the player for the State is generally firmly convinced beforehand by his study of the evidence that he is playing for the life of a guilty person, hence his enthusiasm in his cause.

Or perhaps I should call it zeal. I doubt that any State's attorney is ever enthusiastic over contributing to the taking of human life. He but does his duty. His remuneration financially is rarely that of the players on the other side, who might naturally be expected to show plenty of zeal on defense.

It is a strange game, this game of murder trial, as played under the rules of circumstantial evidence. I suppose if a defendant is really innocent he has all the worst of it for a time, yet, paradoxically enough, if he is guilty he has all the best of it.

It nearly always is the case in a murder trial that the personality of the victim of the crime remains very shadowy and vague. From what I heard in the Snyder-Gray trial, I never got a right good picture of Albert Snyder except that he was a fellow who liked to putter around with motor boats.